ÆTERNITAS

A. F. T. BOWEN

ISBN 97-0-557-21134-0

PROLOGUE

Yanshan Mountains
Hebei Province, China
1971

The morning mists lay heavily in the valleys between the steep slopes, glowing eerily as the sun rose over the peaks. Wraithlike shreds of fog swirled and eddied as breezes arose from the warming land. The fantastic shapes of limestone outcroppings thrust their way through the haze, transforming into jade vases and heavenly tortoises, filling the canyons between the mountains.

A lone figure made its way through the scraggly undergrowth, occasionally slipping on the moist earth as he struggled up the mountainside. The path he followed was rarely used and was not cleared like the many animal trails scattered over the area. He was a young man, wearing the rough clothes of a peasant and carrying nothing with him but a small cloth sack around his waist.

He paused at an outcropping and looked back the way he had come, his eyes searching for the little farm he had started out from before dawn that morning. But he could see nothing through the fog. The only sounds were his own labored breathing and an occasional rustle in the bushes as some small animal searched for its breakfast.

Many men had gone into this section of the mountains before Kian Sheng and few had returned. But the lure of ancient treasure was hard for any poor farmer to resist. His family barely survived on the meager earnings their small farm brought to them. Still, Kian was proud that he did own his farm, the land passed down through generations along with the stories of the treasure. The legends varied depending upon who was telling them, but they all agreed that it was the most precious treasure in the history of mankind, to be valued as life itself.

All of these thoughts ran through Kian's mind as he hiked up the steep mountain pass. He was looking for a particular marker, an outcropping of rock said to look like two dragons intertwined in battle. *Or mating, according to Grandfather*, he chuckled to himself.

Gnarled branches of the scrubby trees snagged on his clothing and roots poked out between rocks like the desiccated fingers of his ancestors reaching up from their tombs to hinder his way. The heavy fog made it hard to discern anything beyond a few feet, so he was nearly on top of the formation when he finally saw it.

It does look somewhat like two dragons if you don't stare at it for too long, he thought.

He found the path beside the rock formation and pushed his way through a tangle of branches. After only a few paces he came to an abrupt halt, feeling his courage waver as he saw the next part of his journey. A narrow path snaked its way along a cliff face ahead of him, barely wide enough for him to creep along sideways. For a moment he considered turning back, but decided he must continue since he had come this far. Kian's father called this tendency stubbornness, but his grandfather told him he was just strong-willed.

He kept his back to the rock face of the cliff as he worked his way around a curve and did his best not to look down other than to glance ahead to make sure that the ledge had not crumbled away.

His heart pounded as his foot slipped once and he thought his fate would be the same as his uncle's, who had disappeared on the mountain years ago. He instinctively pressed his body closer to the rock and found a stony protrusion on which to steady himself. Kian regained his footing and continued on his way.

His uncle was not the first member of his family to have vanished in the search for the treasure. There had been many others in the long branches of his family tree who had never returned from their quests. His ancestors had lived in the shadow of the mountains since the time of the unifier and first emperor, Qin Shi Huang. Family legend said that one member of the Sheng clan helped to build the magnificent tomb in which the emperor was said to have been laid to rest over two thousand years ago. But family legends were seldom true as Kian had been told by his father too many times. He did anything he could to quell his son's adventuresome spirit, even going so far as to send him to college in Beijing to get him away from the lure of the mountains. Poor grades and lack of money ended his father's hope that Kian would escape the same fate as his family's previous adventurers.

It seemed as though he had been edging along the cliff for hours, but it was only a few minutes until his leading hand came upon an opening in the rock. He quickly scooted around the corner and into the safety of a small cave.

He pulled a wad of tinder out of the sack at his waist and lit it with a few sparks from his flint. It quickly flared up and illuminated the cave, revealing that it was merely the antechamber to another, larger cavern. Kian moved forward, untying his torch from the side of his bag.

He nearly dropped the torch in astonishment as its light revealed the enormity of the cavern. The stalactites overhead were larger around at the base than Kian's grain shed. They reached nearly to the floor in some areas, being met by stalagmites from the floor to form columns reminiscent of the great palaces of ancient emperors.

Kian tore his eyes away from the natural wonder surrounding him and pulled out his map to get his bearings. It was old and tattered, like most of his belongings. His great-grandfather had copied it from an even older version that was itself a copy. No one knew how many copies had been made or if the original still survived somewhere. Kian just hoped his version was accurate.

He studied the features pictured on the map and attempted to match them to his surroundings. The flickering light of his torch twisted shadows around the ancient formations, making it difficult to define their true shapes. He continued deeper into the cavern as he did so and soon found himself along a path that appeared on the old parchment. Searching for the next marker on the map, he looked up just in time to stop himself from walking directly into a deep pit.

Kian gasped and stepped back. The pit wasn't shown on the map at all.

Lifting his torch higher, he could see the far edge of the chasm about fifteen feet away. *There's no way I can jump that far*, he thought and looked to either side to see if there was a way around it. To the left, the pit hugged the wall with no possible way of getting past it, but to the right was a small shelf of rock protruding every three feet or so. Each shelf was nearly two feet across, so there was plenty of room for him to step onto it. He would have to be very careful, but he should be able to make it across.

He normally would not take such dangerous risks as these, but the last season's crops were poor and he feared his family would go hungry before the end of winter. If he could find the treasure, he would be able to buy food for a thousand winters. His father had argued with him about his decision to seek the treasure, calling him a reckless fool. His grandfather merely looked him in the eye and, finding something that seemed to satisfy him, he nodded and closed his eyes.

Holding his breath, Kian stepped gingerly onto the first outcropping. It seemed sturdy enough so he dared to put his full weight upon it. It held. He moved to the next projection with no problem, and the next. He relaxed a little bit as he was now halfway across and felt more confident that he would succeed. Two more steps and a hop onto the other side and he would be safely across the pit. He decided to take them quickly to get it over with.

Take a deep breath and then three quick steps, he commanded himself. *One, two, three*!

He took a moment to congratulate himself on getting so far so quickly. Then he turned around and saw his next obstacle.

His shoulders sagged as he perceived another pit ahead. Once again it was not shown on his copy of the map. This chasm was much larger than the one he had just gotten around. It was more than fifty feet to the other side, and ran from one wall of the cavern to the other. How in the world was he going to get past this one? There were no convenient protrusions along either side to help him across this vast gulf.

Kian studied the walls to see if perhaps there was some kind of handholds. He searched for ten minutes and saw nothing. In frustration, he knelt down to spill the light of his torch into the abyss and discovered it was a mere ten feet to the bottom of it. He could easily let himself drop to the bottom and then climb up the other side.

But what was that glint of white he just saw out of the corner of his eye? He leaned further over the edge to get a better look. It took a moment for Kian to make out the shape in the dim light of his torch. A human skull was lying next to a jumble of rocks, a few more bones protruded here and there amongst them. As much as it disturbed him by signifying the danger in his quest, it also encouraged him that he was on the right track.

I'll just have to be more careful than he was, Kian told himself as he prepared to lower his feet over the edge.

He held onto his torch in one hand as he dangled over the rim by the other and then let go. He stumbled as his feet landed on uneven ground and he fell backwards onto a particularly sharp rock.

After rising to his feet and feeling for any major damage to the injured portion of his anatomy, he picked up his torch from where it had fallen. The area immediately surrounding him was relatively smooth except for the very spot on which he had landed. There was an indentation about the size of two men and nearly a foot deep. What struck him about this area was the regularity of the edges. It was exactly rectangular in shape, the outline perfectly straight. He bent down to examine it more closely, scraping away some of the rocks and debris beneath him.

As his knee hit the bare rock he had uncovered, there was a soft click and then a grinding noise began. He felt the ground tremble beneath him and stood quickly, confused and frightened. The vibrations continued and he feared it was an earthquake that would trap him in the cave like the unfortunate person whose skeletal remains he saw only a few feet away.

A few feet away, Kian thought quickly. *Perhaps he ran and that is what doomed him. I will stand my ground and not shrink from my destiny.*

It took all of his courage to stay when the rumbling grew stronger and the ground before him began to open. The quaking became so intense that he began to lose his balance, the edge of the chasm opening before him was inches away.

Before he knew what happened, he was pitched into the blackness. His scream ended abruptly as he hit the floor below. Every bone in his body felt as if it had been struck by a hammer and all of the breath had been knocked out of him. He forced his mind to stop racing and pushed the fear away. *I am still alive*, he told himself, *and I will get out of here*. He opened his eyes and saw that his torch continued to burn.

But what shone in that light he could not comprehend. Shiny surfaces and polished metal that sparkled in the torchlight reminded him of the restrooms at the university he had attended in Beijing. Any further comparisons never had the opportunity to form in his mind as he was crushed by the door that had fallen off its tracks when it had opened to let him in.

1

Genetics Lab
Thompson State University
Clark, New Jersey

"Bugs," Dr. Emily Forester stated, "as we affectionately call our subjects, are everywhere. But we'll be working specifically with 'cave bugs', the microbacteria found in the harsh environments of the subterranean world."

The small group of new students standing around the lab table listened attentively to the introduction to their project.

"The bugs we have here in the lab have been initially harvested from caves around the world, and, after much trial and error in reproducing their natural habitats, we've managed to grow colonies of many of them. The first thing you'll be learning is the proper care and feeding of the colonies, just like they were your pets."

Several of the students smiled or chuckled.

"The whole point of this research is, as you know, finding new treatments for cancer and other diseases. The enzymes that some of these bugs produce, as a natural defense against other microbes encroaching on their territory, have been found to be deadly to many common viruses and cancerous cells."

She escorted the group to the next room in the lab. The complex of machines and equipment, some looking much like a brewery's vats, left very little room for the students to stand. Some of the taller students found themselves ducking under large steel pipes that ran from one vat to another. And the myriad gauges and indicator lights made the room seem more like a nuclear reactor control room than a genetics lab.

"This is where we grow our colonies, as well as extract samples for testing. The tests themselves are run in the next room," she ushered them inside, "where we have access to the second largest mainframe on the east coast to store and analyze the genetic data."

The students seemed to Emily to be suitably impressed. She certainly hoped so. It had taken two years of almost constant badgering by her and the other scientists in the lab to convince the university that it would be in their best interests to invest in a better computer system.

"My current project involves one of the most toxic enzymes found to date, from a bug that was discovered in Yellowstone National Park. So far the enzyme has killed breast cancer cells, lung cancer cells and colon cancer cells in our initial phase of testing. Our current trials involve leukemia."

"Excuse me, Dr. Forester," one of the students spoke up.

"Yes, Mr. Murray, was it?"

"Yes," he smiled, "Is it possible that one enzyme can kill all types of cancer?"

"Very possible," Emily answered. "The key to killing a cancer cell lies in the enzyme complex known as telomerase which stabilizes the length of telomeres, the repeats at the end of every chromosome that protect them from destabilizing during replication. As a person ages, the telomeres shorten leading to the death of the cell when it can no longer reproduce. The exceptions to this life span occur only in germline, or reproductive cells or the stem cells of renewal tissues such as bone marrow and the basal cells of the skin. And somehow, cancerous cells find a way to keep telomerase production in action when the cell should have killed itself due to the accumulated mutations that made it cancerous in the first place."

She walked over to a computer console and punched up a 3-D diagram illustrating her point.

"Now, previous experiments have shown that the telomere length of cancer cells is generally much shorter than that of the germline and stem cells, so we can stop the production of telomerase in cancer cells without totally destroying the telomeres in germline cells."

But privately Emily still worried that this new chemical would be too strong even for them. However, it still did not dampen her enthusiasm for her work. Every day the chances seemed greater that this would be a breakthrough treatment for millions of people suffering from various forms of cancer.

She had kept this feeling, as well as her new ideas, to herself. Her colleagues tended to be traditionalists and preferred an atmosphere of quiet dignity in the lab rather than overt excitement.

A small bell dinged somewhere in the lab.

"Okay, that's all for now," Emily dismissed the students. "Remember to be here thirty minutes early next time so you can be fitted for your protective gear," she called after them as they filed out of the room.

Once they had all left, she turned off the timer signifying that her tests were complete. She took a deep breath and headed over to the computer at her desk on the other side of the room, passing the neatly ordered shelves of reference books and documentation of previous experiments she kept close at hand. The rest of her work area was just as organized and spotless. She found it easier to concentrate when everything around her was neat and tidy.

She was trying not to get her hopes up as she pulled up the results on the computer, yet felt herself holding her breath as she began to examine the data. Each time she ran another test the outcome had been the same. All cancerous cells ceased to reproduce and were easily dispatched with a small dose of radiation. Too much success made her more wary of positive results. Her business was one filled with failure and a triumph such as this was unheard of, but she had been careful to follow procedure to the letter to assure that no contamination was present in her specimens.

And Emily was harder on herself than most of her colleagues. She was also harder on her lab assistants, which had earned her the nickname "Dr. Slow". She took more time to complete each test and rejected the results if there was the slightest trace of contamination. Emily looked at every detail of the results. Focusing only on the effect of the chemicals on cancer cells was not in her method. Trying to look at the big picture, searching for unexpected effects, was what took up hours of her time.

Whether she had acquired this habit from her father, who had been as obsessive about his classic car collection, or if she had picked it up from her professors' lecturing was anybody's guess. But Emily felt it was important enough to double-check everything she did when it came to altering human cells. There had only been a few reported cases of deaths from various experimental genetic treatments, but she didn't want a single one attributed to her lack of foresight and research.

It was well after seven o'clock when she printed out the results and got herself a cup of coffee from the lounge before returning to her desk to continue reviewing the data. Scanning the lines of information and looking through microscopes was hard on her eyes, and after ten years of research she was forced to wear glasses. This did nothing at all to hide her luminous amber colored eyes from the admiring men around the campus. Her long legs, glistening honey brown hair and soft, feminine curves didn't hurt either. She sometimes found it amusing, and other times found it annoying, how many professors and students secretly ogled her as she walked by.

But she could care less what they thought of her looks. It was what she did in the lab that was important to her. If her research resulted in a cure for cancer, she would be recognized around the world as the foremost scientist in her field. Winning a Nobel Prize wasn't at the top of her list, but it would open a lot of doors for funding new research.

Not even winning the Nobel Prize would get me a grant in this godforsaken place, she thought ruefully and began to go over the data collected by the computer.

Two hours later, she had finished her preliminary report and was beginning to feel the strain of working fifteen hours straight. The results were nearly the same as in previous tests, but this time the computer's projections of the effectiveness of the microbial chemical were somewhat disconcerting. It almost seemed too strong for the job at hand, like using a shotgun to kill a fly. She verified that she had used the same amount as in previous experiments and was at a loss as to why this time should be different. After another half an hour she decided she was too tired to figure out the reason for the intensity of the reaction, locked up the lab and called it a night.

As she trod wearily down the hall, she passed a couple of night janitors heading into work. She gave them a nod and tired smile as they went by.

"Working late, Doctor?" one of them asked.

Emily was surprised that they spoke to her. And she was more than a little concerned by the tone of the man's voice. It had too much of a lascivious quality to it for normal conversation.

"Um, yes. I was. Good night." She made her way down the hall, trying not to walk any faster than she normally would.

Just as on any campus in the country, it wasn't always safe for a lone female to be walking around after dark. Emily felt for the mace in her purse and mentally ran through the taekwando moves she had learned as a teenager.

She had made it to the parking lot and was putting the key in the door of her car, a midnight blue 1969 Lotus Élan S4 Coupe her father had given her for graduation, when she was startled by a voice behind her.

"Emily!"

She turned to see her least favorite person approaching across the lot.

"Emily!" Dr. Robert Chisek called out again as he strode toward her. He was a part-time professor of Archaeology, but his full-time position was as the Staff Director, which made him feel that he knew everyone personally, and therefore called everyone by their first names.

He purposefully put a spring into his step to offset the obvious signs that he was deep into mid-life. The receding hairline, the expanding waistline and multiplying wrinkles clearly showed his age.

"Working late again?" he asked her.

She turned to him resignedly, "Hello, Bob. I'm just leaving." Emily did not feel like having to politely turn down another offer of going for coffee.

If he asks me again I'm going to scream, she gritted her teeth. *That or I'll run over him.* She opened her car door, smiling unconsciously at the thought of flattening him beneath her tires. She didn't really hate him, but his pathetic attempts to hit on her were getting on her nerves.

"Then I guess you wouldn't want to go for some coffee," he said hopefully.

"No, I just want to get home and get some sleep," Emily yawned, opening her door and sliding into her car.

"Okay then, I'll take a rain check on the coffee," Chisek smiled as brightly as his sour face would allow. "You really shouldn't work so late, Emily."

"Sometimes I just lose track of the time," she explained and started her car. "And why don't you take some of your own advice?" she smirked and pulled the door shut before he could say anything else.

Revving up the engine of her little roadster gave some vent to her annoyance. Her father had lovingly restored every one of the 1600 cubic centimeters of twin cam engine, and Emily relished every minute behind the wheel.

As she pulled away she wondered if Chisek would ever stop trying to ask her out for coffee. She decided he probably wouldn't. He'd been at it ever since he found out the she and Sam had formerly been an item.

She forced herself to stop thinking about Sam. The only thing good she had ever gotten out of that relationship was the inspiration for her research from the frequent caving expeditions on which Sam would drag her along. Anything else that happened five years ago was a mistake and she had moved on. End of story. As long as she kept telling herself that she was fine. It also helped that, even though they worked at the same university, they were on opposite sides of the campus and rarely ran into one another. When they did, the civilized coolness Emily feigned kept their conversations short.

Emily often thought that if they got together and talked about what had happened they might be able to be friends again. But she knew the hope that you can be friends after a love affair is over is rarely fulfilled and theirs didn't exactly end on a happy note. She remembered their last argument.

"Sam, your cavalier way of dealing with colleagues isn't making you any friends, you know."

She stood in the center of their perpetually messy dining room/office, her arms crossed and brow furrowed.

"Any idiot can have friends, Em. I'm trying to make an impact on modern anthropology."

"You're making an impact alright. But it's also hurting my chances of a decent career."

"You're over-exaggerating."

"No, I'm not, Sam. People are thinking I must be as crazy as you to live with you."

"Crazy? Who said I'm crazy?"

"Only half the faculty. You're making too many enemies and I can't take the chance that it will hurt my career as well."

"So what are you saying?"

"It's over. I'm moving out."

Sam had stood in shocked silence for a moment and then went ballistic.

"Don't move on my account! I'll go!"

He stormed through their apartment grabbing his things and throwing them into whatever box or suitcase he could find.

He was carrying the last box out the door to his car when he turned to Emily.

"You know, Em. You'll be a great scientist someday. You're already good at sacrificing everything for some obscure principle."

She thought she had seen the last of Sam Hunt. He didn't say where he was going, and at that point she really didn't care. She moved out of that apartment a few weeks later when she was offered a position in the Molecular Biology department at Thompson State. Two years later she was startled to find Sam at one of the staff social events. That was also when Chisek had started bothering her. He knew she and Sam had been in a relationship in the past, and he loved doing anything to annoy Sam, who was his academic rival in the Archeology and Anthropology department. Though Emily seriously doubted if Chisek's pursuit of her bothered Sam at all.

He probably thinks it's funny, she thought angrily and then mentally kicked herself for thinking about Sam again.

She arrived at her condo after a thirty minute drive and pulled the car into the garage. It was more expensive to buy a condo with a built in garage underneath, but it certainly made her feel safer when she came home from work at odd hours.

There were two messages on the answering machine when she got inside. She already knew that one would be her mother. Her mother called almost every day to check on her. It made her feel like a college freshman even though she was thirty-four and had been on her own for fifteen years. But Emily knew it was really because her mother was lonely. Her father had passed away from a heart attack the year after she received her doctorate and her mother had no one living with her at the Forester family ranch since then. She'd call her back after she had slept a few hours.

The next message was yet another offer from MorGen Corporation, a huge international pharmaceuticals company. She had told them before that she wasn't interested. The idea of people making money from genetic research that should be public property made her blood boil. She made enough money at the university to live comfortably and she didn't care to line the pockets of a multi-billionaire. Many of her coworkers thought she was crazy for refusing the job offers, but she knew she wouldn't be happy knowing the benefits of her work were being withheld from those who couldn't afford to pay for it.

She also knew her mother felt she lacked ambition because she stayed at the university when she could be making three times as much working for MorGen or some other large corporation. Maybe she did lack ambition, but she was happy where she was and her finances were just fine.

Looking around at the designer furnishings she had purchased over the years reinforced the feeling that she was doing well. The sleek leather sofa and chairs, mahogany dining room suite, hand loomed rugs, and original artwork on the walls reflected her elegant tastes, while the slate-floored kitchen opening onto a mini greenhouse with a rock garden and waterfall encompassed her love of the outdoors.

She had no problem affording such luxuries since she rarely spent money on other diversions such as eating out or going to social events. Another thing her mother lectured her about. But she hated going to bars, restaurants or other locations peopled with uneducated bores. She'd rather spend time at home working on her latest decorating project or out in the mountains climbing rocks. These were the only two things she did that had nothing to do with work, her only forms of relaxation. But as a result she had a beautiful home she felt proud of, and a great physique with which she was pleased. Except for when it drew the attention of men like Chisek.

She headed up the wrought iron spiral staircase to the second floor loft, kicking off her shoes as she reached the top and letting her toes sink into the plush carpet of the bedroom. It would be wonderful to fall into bed and sleep undisturbed for eight hours, but she was sure that wouldn't happen. Every time she fell asleep, she was either awakened by the phone, or a strange nightmare she couldn't remember once her eyes were open. She'd been having trouble sleeping for the last month or so. Her doctor told her it was from stress, her mother told her it was because she needed a man around the house, other women at the lab told her it was because she needed a man in her bed. Whatever the reason, she had lately resorted to taking sleeping pills to get some decent rest. She would usually wake up after a few hours, but at least she got some sleep.

She slipped out of her jacket and tossed it on the velvet upholstered wing chair in the corner, following that with the rest of her clothes. She longed to take a hot bath in her whirlpool tub in the adjoining bathroom, but she was too tired even for that. So, she just grabbed the old t-shirt she slept in, threw it on and climbed into the four-poster featherbed. She looked over at the bottle of pills on her nightstand, wondering if she should take some. She decided she was so exhausted that she could fall asleep without them.

But before she could shut off the bedside lamp, the phone rang. She ignored it and turned out the light anyway. The phone kept ringing as she settled into the warmth of the down comforter, and then the answering machine kicked in.

"Emily, I know you're there and you're probably not asleep yet," Donna Washington, another scientist at the lab, sounded almost frantic as she spoke. "Pick up the phone, this is important!"

Emily reached for the phone in the darkness, "It had better be," she warned Donna.

"Someone broke into the labs right after you left," Donna reported.

"What?! Was anything taken?" Emily sat straight up in bed.

"We can't tell yet, but they trashed the place pretty good."

Emily was shocked into silence for a moment.

"Em? You still there?" Donna asked.

"Yes. I'll be right there." Emily hung up the phone and climbed out of bed, throwing on her clothes as she stumbled across the room in the dark.

Hardly believing it could be true, she wondered who would break into the lab and destroy her work. Even a rival scientist wouldn't go that far. But who else could have gotten into the building so quickly after she left? The thought that someone at the university could be behind it made her very uneasy.

There was nothing left. Her computer was smashed into small pieces, her samples had been destroyed, the records of her last three years' work had been burned in the trash can, and all of her backup disks were missing. That latter item being what Emily worried about the most.

She had always kept those locked in a small safe hidden behind the desk, but somehow the thief knew exactly where to look. And the safe hadn't been tampered with that she could see, so they must have had the combination. No one in the lab could know it. Most people she worked with didn't even know she had a safe. She'd put it in the previous year after an old friend at another university had their work stolen.

But what was the most baffling was the large hand painted with red spray paint on the door of her office. It covered the entire door and in the center of the hand was a glaring eye. The police told her it was the symbol of a fanatical religious group that called themselves "The Hand of God" that they had been watching for several years. The investigating officer was puzzled as to why they had left behind a calling card. Previous incidents could never be tied to them due to lack of evidence.

She told the police what was missing and what was destroyed and a little about what she was researching. They had left after telling her the usual "We'll do everything we can."

Now she sat in what was left of her office and looked at the chaos surrounding her. All of the work she had done over the last two years was lost. It would take months to duplicate the work, and that was only if she could get the time on the equipment she needed. If she had to go on a waiting list, it would be another two years until she got back to this point.

She groaned aloud and laid her head down on her desk.

"Don't worry, Emily. We'll find out who did this and see that you get your work back," Chisek stood in the doorway trying to act sympathetic. He wasn't very good at it.

"And how are you going to do that?" she demanded. "Are you psychic by chance?"

"Now, Emily. There's no need to be sarcastic. I happen to have a few connections that may be able to help us out."

"Connections? With whom?" Emily asked suspiciously.

"Higher-ups at some other universities. They could tell me if someone suddenly had a breakthrough in a line of research like yours."

Obviously Chisek didn't believe religious protesters had caused the damage any more than Emily did.

"That could be helpful," Emily admitted. "*If* this was done by another scientist. And I find that hard to believe. Why would they trash the samples, too? If it were me, I'd take them. It would be that much less work to do."

"Who else could it be? If it was someone in one of those wacko religious groups that say you're playing god, they wouldn't have stolen the disks would they?"

"Maybe if they wanted to see what we were up to besides stopping us," Emily ventured.

"And why would they single out your lab?" Chisek asked smugly.

"I have no idea," her tone left no room for argument.

"Well, if you'll just give me a report on what your recent project was, I can start calling my friends for help."

Chisek threw his request out so casually, Emily almost told him.

"Why don't you let me know who to call and I'll take care of it myself," she smiled at him. She never trusted him before, and she wasn't about to start now. She just had a feeling he was up to something.

"Uh, I suppose I could do that," he stammered. "I'll get you their names and numbers tomorrow."

He left so quickly that Emily barely had time to thank him before he was out of sight. It made her think he had no connections at all and was just attempting to get on her good side again.

She took another look around the depressing scene in her office and decided she might as well start cleaning it up. She started with her desk and cleared away the debris that was once her computer. She hoped she'd be able to get a new one before the end of the week, but red tape usually held up any special requests. Maybe Chisek would be able to hurry it up for her if she was nice to him. The thought of kissing up to that moron made her feel worse than she already did.

As she dumped that last piece of her keyboard into the trash, she noticed something odd. She didn't keep many personal items in her lab like some of her other co-workers, but she did have one memento from her college days that she usually kept on the shelf above her desk. It was a sketch of her dream lab. A place she designed herself that had everything she wanted to do her work. It had been done one rainy weekend when she and Sam had been daydreaming about their futures. At one point in time, their future was supposed to be together.

Emily growled at herself for thinking of Sam yet again.

But the distraction was only momentary as she picked up the frame that had held the sketch. What was so peculiar about it was not that it was damaged or destroyed, but that it was untouched and perfectly centered on the shelf when everything else was broken or had been shoved onto the floor. But the sketch itself was missing.

2

Yanshan Mountains
Hebei Province, China
Present Day

Samuel Clemens Hunt was not a happy man. And try as he might, he could find no humor in the situation as his namesake would have. He stood on the edge of the excavations in the pouring rain watching the trenches fill with water. Worse yet, the embankment to the south of the site had turned into a slow moving mass of thick mud that threatened to refill the cave that had taken years to excavate. He wiped away the water dripping into his pale blue eyes. His normally unruly brown hair was slicked flat against his head. Sam ignored the fact that he was soaked through and continued looking for ways to prevent this expedition from being a total disaster.

Some people would say it already was. From the time they had arrived in Beijing a month ago it had been one delay after another. First, customs held their surveying equipment for inspection. The officer in charge had said they were making sure that no terrorists had sabotaged it. Sam hardly believed that.

Luckily, their Chinese partners had pulled a few strings and gotten their equipment released after only a few days. But by then, their arranged transportation had given up on them and left them without the means to reach their dig site. They were left stranded in Pingyu, still over fifty miles from the dig site.

Once again they relied on their Chinese colleagues to find a solution. They found transport for the team of Americans and their gear the next day, though a dilapidated old Red Army surplus truck certainly wasn't what Sam had expected. He wasn't about to complain under the circumstances.

After they had finally reached their destination in the Yanshan Mountains, they discovered an elderly farmer had decided that their neatly divided survey zone would be an ideal corral for his three goats, farming space being at a premium in the rocky landscape. Zhen Li, the anthropologist from the Institute of Vertebrate Paleontology and Paleoanthropology in Beijing who had worked on previous excavations at the site, had a few words with the farmer who then graciously took his livestock elsewhere.

They had finally begun making some progress on the excavation which was located in and around the cave when the weather turned on them. It had now been raining for two days straight even though the rainy season shouldn't have started for another six weeks. And it wasn't just a gentle shower, but coming down in buckets nonstop.

Sam gave up looking for a way to save the site. The protective tarps they had put down when the rain began had already floated away, and mudslides covered half of the area. The cave itself was half flooded and the banks of the nearby creek had disappeared under water that threatened to eventually reach their campsite if the rain didn't end soon.

He shook his head in disgust and turned to go back to the relative dryness of his tent.

The first thing he did upon entering his tent was to turn on the small propane heater. It wasn't really cold outside, but being drenched from head to foot made it seem that way.

He turned on his laptop computer that sat on the short collapsible table next to his cot while he stripped out of his wet clothes. Reaching for a towel, he caught a glimpse of himself in the shaving mirror hanging above the cot.

Don't I look pathetic, he sneered at himself. He could see the expression of hopelessness and frustration in his eyes. He didn't want to be on this excavation in the first place.

He pulled off his soaked shirt. *At least going to the gym is paying off*, he thought, noticing the new definition of his biceps. He had started working out partially as a way to relieve stress, but also because he noticed at the age of thirty-eight he wasn't as fit as he used to be. Long days sitting in a chair at the museum doing paperwork hadn't helped either.

It wasn't just the excavation that was making him feel so cynical, though. His whole life had been on a downslide for the last few years. Even though he had gotten a "promotion" to curator of the paleoanthropology department of the university's museum, he knew it was just a way to keep him out of the classroom where he caused the most damage. At least that was according to Dr. Robert Chisek, who didn't think Sam's method of teaching was proper. Or sane for that matter. He used the same textbooks that were common in anthropology classes across the country, but Sam often used them to demonstrate what not to do. And worse yet, he used them to point out errors in evolutionary theory.

Many people thought he was a closet creationist when they first met him. When you accentuate how little we know about the evolution of mankind or even the mechanism of evolution itself, people tend to think you're either a creationist or ufologist. But Sam just liked to make it plain to his students that they shouldn't limit their thinking just because something doesn't fit into currently accepted theories. The hominid family tree has changed drastically in the last fifty years, becoming more of shrub, and things will keep changing with each new discovery.

But Sam felt part of Chisek's attitude probably stemmed from the fact that students stood in line for hours to sign up for Sam's classes, only to be turned away, while Chisek's classes were never filled. Whatever the reason, it was Chisek who had seen to it that he was promoted and sent on fruitless expeditions like this one.

"There's been a report of probable hominid fossils in the caves there," Chisek had assured him.

"You know as well as I do, that in the last five years that site has only turned up animal fossils."

"Sam, the site is barely a hundred miles away from Zhoukoudian. Who's to say there weren't Homo erectus there as well?"

Sam already knew how close the home of Peking Man was to the caves that Chisek was trying to sell him on, but he was sure Chisek wouldn't send him on a trip that may actually yield a new find.

"But it really makes no difference if there is or not," Chisek continued. "The university has already funded half of the expedition and has a team in place doing the initial survey."

And here he was, supervising several grad students in a futile attempt to make the excavations worthwhile. Sam silently ordered himself to knock off the finger pointing. It was more his own fault than Chisek's that his life was a mess.

He finished putting on a warm, dry hunter green fleece pullover with the khaki pants he had just donned before sitting down to write his email reports on their progress.

Reaching for his glasses, he nearly fell off of his campstool when Zhen Li bellowed from outside the tent.

"Dr. Hunt!"

Sam zipped the flap open and let Dr. Li inside. He also was dripping wet and more than a little dirty.

"Where have you been?" Sam asked him, "You look like you were mud wrestling."

Zhen's black hair was plastered to his skull and smears of mud were evident all over his clothing, but his deep brown eyes gleamed with excitement.

"I was exploring and found a cave nearby on higher ground," Zhen explained, "The farmer whom we met when we arrived told me about it. The entrance is almost completely blocked but I could just fit through. I think it may be a part of the same cave system.

"Any signs of habitation?" Sam asked eagerly.

"It looked like there were soot marks along one wall."

"Is the entrance within the excavation permit zone?" Sam held his breath.

"Yes, well within it."

"This is a lucky break," Sam was thrilled. "The site here will take weeks to clean up, but now we can just forget about this mess and work in the cave you found."

He could not believe that something was finally going right for the team. He felt sorry for the other team members who were younger and less experienced than he was. Sam was used to the hardships and disappointments of working in the field. And this trip was turning out to be one of the worst.

But now they had an opportunity to salvage what time they had left and possibly make some contribution to the university's museum archives.

"Let everyone else know that we'll be working in the new cave starting tomorrow morning," Sam instructed Zhen, "Then meet me back here and we'll go start the survey."

Zhen smiled knowingly, "I am anxious to get started as well," and he left the tent to talk to the other anthropologists and students.

Turning back to his computer, Sam sat down to make his daily report. Instead of a report of their progress, it had lately become more of a report on how much of the university's money they were wasting. Everyday he checked his email, waiting to see the notice that they were to return to the States and abandon the site for the season. Part of him actually wanted that, at least before Zhen had discovered the new entrance.

Sam felt even more at ease in caves than he did in the classroom. He had spent countless hours exploring the caves near his boyhood home in Virginia. Sometimes his whole family went on a trip to one of the commercial caves like Luray, where tour groups plodded through well-lit and smooth passageways to the accompaniment of a tour guide's bland description of the wondrous rock formations.

At least that's how Sam saw it. He preferred the challenge of wild caves where he had to squeeze through small holes and climb over piles of rubble. He usually went with his older brother to ease his mother's mind, but there were times when he would take a risk and sneak off alone to experience the magic and mystery of underground worlds. He never went too far into the caves when he went on a solitary excursion, and he stuck to familiar passages, but he was always punished for his recklessness when he returned. Over the years he had never really outgrown the recklessness, but he did mature enough to follow basic safety techniques.

He cursed at himself for letting his optimism waver. He had been wasting too much time on self-pity ever since he was reassigned to the museum. So what if he couldn't directly affect the students with his teaching? They all came to the museum sooner or later. What did it matter if he presented his material there or in the classroom?

Feeling somewhat better about his situation, he sent off his update including their plans to move the excavations into the cave. It seemed for a moment that he had lost his satellite connection and prepared to resend his message. But before he could do so, he received a confirmation that his email was delivered.

That was the third time he had experienced problems with his computer since they arrived in China and it made him wonder just what the customs officials had done to it.

It had taken an entire day to clear away the brush and debris outside the cave entrance enough to allow them to move their equipment inside. Sam was surprised by the size of the cave and that it hadn't been used for storage or livestock pens by the farmer who had shown it to them. When he asked Zhen about it all he could say was that a local superstition kept most people away from this particular ravine. Luckily the ledge overhanging the entrance and the steep slope leading away from it had kept the rain away as well.

Two days later, the excavations in the cave were going smoothly and they had found several areas of interest in their preliminary survey. The soot marks along the wall had directed them to the hearth directly underneath it and two of the students were carefully excavating the charcoal. In a spot only a few feet away another team was uncovering the top layer of what could be a food preparation area judging from the small pieces of fossilized animal bone. It was enough evidence to give him hope that it was an ancient site.

Sam stood at the mouth of the cave with the rain pouring down behind him, happy that superstition preserved this site. He took a moment to look around at the general layout. It was large in comparison to other caves in the area. It was nearly one hundred yards deep and the ceiling was high enough for anyone under seven feet tall to stand up straight. The width varied from five to fifteen yards and they had come across some small openings that may lead to other passages. Sam was eager to explore them, but he wanted to map the main chamber and finish the preliminary ground survey before moving on.

The halogen lamps they had placed at various points within the cave lit up the entire scene as if it were a sunny afternoon outdoors. Their solar powered generator had gone dead after so many rainy days but the gas powered one sat just outside the entrance and its hum blended with the drizzle of the rain. Zhen had supervised the students in laying the grid on the cave floor that would help them to position all of their finds accurately. They had plotted the entrance location with their GPS system, but once inside the cave, they had to rely upon more basic methods since the signal from their portable unit couldn't penetrate the solid rock of the mountain to reach the satellites.

"Sam," Zhen called over to him from the back of the cavern where he stood with two of the students, "Come take a look at this."

Sam went over to the small alcove-like depression in the side of the cave where they were crouched on the ground.

"What is it?" he asked.

"Stephie noticed this odd shape to the floor and discovered that," Zhen explained pointing to a fragment showing on the floor of the cave. "It's the first we've seen on the surface."

"Interesting," Sam smiled and turned to Stephie, "What do you think it is?"

She bent down to get a closer look, brushing a stray lock of auburn hair behind her ear, "Could be a femur, but it's hard to tell if it's hominid without excavating further."

Sam looked to the other student for his opinion, "Gregg?"

Gregg crouched next to Stephie and looked over the top of his glasses.

"I'd have to agree, it's too early to tell," he nodded and pushed his glasses back into position.

Sam smiled, pleased that they weren't jumping to conclusions about the find until they had the whole picture.

"Go ahead and get started on this area. Zhen and I are going to look around some of these side passages."

Zhen looked at Sam dubiously, but followed him anyway. Once they were on the other side of the cavern from the students, Zhen spoke up.

"I don't think we should explore any further without additional equipment."

"Come on, Zhen." Sam chided him, "Most of these are probably just crevasses that don't go anywhere anyway."

"Well if they do go further, let's only go back a few hundred feet." Zhen suggested. "These caves can be treacherous."

"Been talking to the locals?" Sam chuckled, "I've heard some of the stories."

"They may be true," Zhen protested, "Most legends have some basis in fact."

"I'll agree with you on that, but I think tales of shiny monsters that eat people are more likely rooted in modern history than ancient," Sam commented.

"Probably, but we should still be careful. I don't have as much experience exploring caves as you do."

"Zhen, we're not entering the underworld here, it's just a little cave."

"I know some Mayans who would disagree with you," he joked nervously. He looked at the floor and shifted his weight from one foot to the other. "Actually, I'm a little claustrophobic."

Sam almost laughed at Zhen's admission but caught himself before he hurt his feelings. Instead he placed a hand on Zhen's shoulder.

"Why did you go looking for more caves then?"

"They didn't seem so small from the outside. And I had to find something to do. Our site was ruined from the rain."

Now Sam did laugh. "Okay, so the anthropologist in you overruled your fear. Then look at it this way-- the main cavern was most likely a communal living area, but the side passages may lead to some sort of religious or ritual area."

"But there's been no evidence to suggest that Homo erectus practiced any sort of religion," Zhen argued.

"Not yet anyway." Sam smiled, knowing Zhen felt the same way he did about pushing the limits of accepted theories.

Zhen's face lit up with the thought of new discoveries.

"I'll take the lead and we'll have plenty of light," Sam reassured him, "We're not going far. And we'll map as we go in case we find anything."

Sam was pleased he had the foresight to bring along some of his caving gear. He knew there were dozens of caves in the area that no one had ever mapped and had hoped to explore them during his downtime. One of the best pieces of equipment he had with him was the laser rangefinder which would allow them to measure precisely the distance and angles of the passages from the main cave. They put on their helmets and headlamps and put some ropes and other gear in their backpacks.

Sam chose to start at the tunnel that was closest to the cave entrance first, after marking the entrance with a triangular orange flag to let everyone know which way they had gone. The opening was only about two feet across, so Sam had to turn sideways to get his broad shoulders through without scraping off any skin. Zhen was built smaller, but still had to adjust his position a little to move comfortably.

They had only gone about thirty feet when Sam came to a wall.

"Dead end, Zhen," Sam told him and they headed back to the main cave with Zhen walking a little faster than Sam.

Once they were back out in the central room, Sam turned to Zhen, "That wasn't so bad was it?"

"Just let me pick the next one, "Zhen said with an uneasy look.

"Alright," Sam agreed with a laugh.

Zhen chose a passageway with an opening nearly six feet wide and that ran almost twenty feet above into a depression in the ceiling.

Sam stepped forward into the opening. He felt a slight breeze brush across his face.

"I think this way might have an exit to the outside," he told Zhen, "I feel a draft."

"That's reassuring," Zhen commented as he followed him inside, "It would be nice to have another way out if there's a cave-in."

"There won't be a cave-in."

"But there are also flash floods. Men have drowned in caves like this before."

"It's dry as a bone in here," Sam noted as they continued along.

"But not for long," Zhen stopped in his tracks. "I hear rushing water up ahead."

"It's probably just an underground stream," Sam assured him.

"Sounds more like a river."

As they came around a corner the sound became louder and the air felt more humid.

"Maybe it is a river," Sam agreed. "That would make this cave a good spot for a large population. We could be busy here for years."

"I don't know whether I should be happy about that or not," Zhen groaned.

"We should get our distance measure here before we go on," Sam advised and rummaged in his pack for the rangefinder.

As they moved through the cave, occasionally climbing over rubble and ducking under stalactites, Sam stopped now and then to take a reading of the distances and angles while Zhen took notes on the geological features.

It was only a few hundred feet down a gradual slope until they reached the chamber where the river cut through. It was almost cathedral-like in its size and splendor. Stalactites over thirty feet in length hung from the roof of the cavern. As breathtaking as that was, they were even more impressed as the light from their headlamps caused row upon row of delicate gypsum flowers to glow with an inner fire. The rare crystal formations were superior to any that Sam had seen in his younger days of cave exploring. The whole place was larger than any cave he had ever been in before, and he had spent most of his childhood exploring every one he could find.

Sam shook himself out of his daydream and took a more scientific look at the area. The chamber was so wide, his headlamp couldn't penetrate the darkness all the way to the other side. But he could make out enough to see that the river was at least twenty feet wide and had a very strong current. The area directly in front of them was worn smooth as if countless ancient feet had come that way before them.

"What now?" Zhen yelled over the noise of the river that echoed through the cavern.

"Let's look around a little more then head back," Sam replied in a shout.

He could tell Zhen was relieved to learn they wouldn't be there much longer. Sam was a little uneasy about the place himself. There wasn't anything obviously dangerous about the cavern, but he had learned to trust his caving instincts long ago.

They moved off to the right, past the gypsum flowers, and found another passageway. Sam shone his light down the corridor and could only tell that it sloped downwards at a steep angle and then apparently dropped off abruptly. He decided they should probably continue to follow the main path for now. As they walked on, the sound of the river receded and they came to another open area like the one surrounding the entry into the chamber, but this one was curiously circular in design. They both noticed this, but Zhen spoke up first.

"It looks like this area was cleared for some purpose," he observed.

"This place is incredible," Sam marveled, "I think we're going to need a few more people next season or we're going to be excavating in here the rest of our lives."

"You'll be doing it without me," Zhen informed him.

"Maybe if you work here longer, you'll overcome your claustrophobia," Sam suggested with a grin.

"I'd prefer a less stressful way."

"Well if you can hold out for a few more minutes, I'd like to look around this spot a little more closely," Sam said and hunkered down to get a better look.

The floor was even and smooth in the circle, and appeared to be tightly packed. There was no sign of the debris usually associated with a living area. This made Sam believe it had to be of more recent construction than the Homo erectus site in the main cave. Maybe even modern.

This was a conservative view compared to how he would have looked at the site when he was an undergrad. He would have declared it to be evidence that Homo erectus performed religious rituals until someone could prove otherwise.

"Zhen," Sam turned to him, "look around and see if there are any signs of recent use in the area. This might be someone's weekend retreat."

Sam recalled the times he'd been in small caves near his home and would find beer bottles, newspapers or fast food wrappers. Though it would be highly unlikely to find anything like that in this cave, there might be some kind of refuse to indicate how recently the clearing had been used.

"Sam, come here," Zhen rose from where he had been squatting behind a stalagmite ten feet away. He was holding a sack that was definitely modern, but not very new.

Sam joined Zhen and they examined the bag. It was a roughly woven wool with a canvas strap that had broken and been mended countless times.

"This has been here for a few decades," Sam commented as he examined it. "Is there anything in it?"

Zhen looked inside. "Something," he reached in and pulled out what appeared to be a wallet of some kind. He opened it and a few weathered pieces of paper fell out.

Sam bent to retrieve them. "Looks like a map," he said as he tried to fit the pieces together. "Someone was exploring the cave long before us."

He could feel Zhen looking over his shoulder at the map, then heard his sharp intake of breath.

"What is it?" Sam asked "Do you recognize it?" he finished laying the pieces together on the floor of the cave.

"Tuan Sheng, the farmer who lives nearby, he showed me a map like this one."

"Are you sure? Did he say where he got it?"

"He said it was the map to the underworld. His son disappeared looking for a treasure hidden somewhere in these caves."

Sam looked at the map more closely. It depicted a cave system that seemed to have some similar features to the one they were in now. The map was old and some parts of it were worn away or missing completely, but it had been drawn with much attention to detail and ornamentation. A figure in one section of the map was one Sam had seen before. The half human, half dragon form of the goddess Nu Gua, creator of mankind, was painted at the cave's entrance.

"Does he have a copy or the original of this one?" Sam wondered aloud.

"He said the original was thousands of years old and in a museum somewhere and his great-grandfather had made a copy a long time ago in his own search for the treasure."

"Then this is probably a copy of who knows how many other copies. It's probably full of inaccuracies," Sam was disappointed. Not because he was interested in any treasure, but because it would have helped them to make their own map of the caves for the excavation.

"Keep looking around," he directed Zhen, putting the bag in his own knapsack, "this is interesting, but not really what I'm looking for."

"What are you looking for?" Zhen asked as he resumed his search.

"Some clue as to why this area was cleared."

"Maybe it was a campsite for the treasure hunters."

"Possibly, but I think it's been prepared a little too thoroughly for a campsite. Not unless they were perfectionists and had to have an absolutely level floor," Sam had laid flat on his stomach and was looking across the clearing. He reached in his backpack and pulled out some reflectors.

"Here, put these in random spots around the area. I want to see how close it is to being perfectly level," he said and handed them to Zhen.

Zhen placed the reflectors all over the surface of the clearing while Sam anchored the rangefinder on a mini tripod.

Sam was preparing to take the first measurement when he felt a vibration from the surrounding rocks different from that of the river's tumultuous progress through the cavern. It was a feeling he knew well from his years of cave exploring.

"Zhen, get away from the wall!"

As Zhen turned back to Sam, a ten foot section of the wall behind him began to crumble. He sprinted across the room towards Sam, his tanned skin growing several shades paler.

Almost as suddenly as it had began, the small rockslide ended.

"Are you okay?" Sam asked Zhen.

Zhen nodded even as he stood there shaking, his eyes wide and his breath coming in short gasps.

"It's over now," Sam reassured him. "We'll head back in a minute, as soon as I pack up the gear."

Sam turned to the rangefinder and took it off its tripod. Clouds of dust still hung in the air around him, but were soon fanned away by the breeze created by the river's current. As he gathered up the last of the reflectors, something he saw out if the corner of his eye startled him.

He dropped the reflector and stood up facing the wall. His head lamp reflected off of a highly polished surface, carefully incised with symbols the likes of which he had never seen before. Circles, spirals and various combinations of lines and scythe-like curves were arranged in perfectly straight vertical lines.

"Sam?" Zhen spoke haltingly from across the room. "What is it? What's wrong?"

Not getting an answer from Sam, Zhen followed the direction of his gaze and found himself speechless as well.

Finally, Sam found his voice.

"Is this some form of local writing?" he asked Zhen.

"Not that I've ever seen. But then I'm not familiar with every type. There are hundreds counting the ancient styles."

"This would have to be the oldest one," Sam reached slowly toward the carved rock as if he were afraid to damage its surface. "A curtain of flowstone this thick would have taken at least 40,000 years to form."

Sam couldn't believe his fingertips. The wall felt as smooth as the polished granite countertops in his kitchen. He couldn't imagine how long it would have taken someone to buff the surface to its slick texture without modern power tools. Not to mention carving the designs on it so precisely. It looked as though most of it was intact, but the bottom edge was ragged as if a portion had broken off at some point.

"Let's get some shots of this before there are any more tremors," Sam suggested as he dug his digital camera out of his backpack.

"Good idea," Zhen agreed. "And if there are any more tremors, you can get a good picture of my backside while I'm running away."

3

MorGen Laboratories, Inc.
Harrisburg, Pennsylvania

The corporate offices of MorGen Laboratories were an extension of the chief executive officer's dual personality. The grounds were landscaped like a park, grass as green and smooth as a golf course, with trees and flowering shrubs surrounding small pools and benches. Inside the offices, the plush carpet that quieted all footsteps, the soft lighting and dark wood paneling all gave the impression of wealth and security. But behind the area open to the public was a very different world. The laboratories themselves were starkly white and cold in contrast. All stainless steel, shiny glass and the blinking lights of various computers and pieces of machinery.

And the man who was the very center of the MorGen universe was in his office near the public portion of the building. He glanced over the paneled walls at all of the degrees hanging in their gilded frames. All of the titles he could use, but he knew he didn't need a title to command respect. It wasn't his stature, he was of only average height, or his physical strength which was failing as he grew older, but a quiet power that shone mostly through his cement-gray eyes.

Louis Morgan sat behind his walnut desk and smiled. His smile was not a pleasant one born of happiness, but one stemming from his vast store of anger. It gave one a chill to see the self-satisfied grin reflected in those cold eyes. He was pleased that his plan was going so smoothly and that he had gained more than he had anticipated. The two men sitting across the desk from him waited patiently for their employer to speak.

Dr. Elliot Burdette sat awkwardly, his small stature making him appear almost dwarflike in the large wing chair. He was Morgan's chief scientist; though to look at him you would think he was merely someone's assistant. He was barely thirty years old and looked like a teenager.

The gentleman sitting next to Burdette showed every one of his years in the worn lines of his face. Though to call Harold Lundgren a gentleman would be stretching it a bit. Lundgren had been in the "security" business since he was a teenager living in New York. He had met Morgan when he was looking for new clients, and was impressed with Morgan's bravado even though he barely came up to Lundgren's chin. After the ensuing fight, they became inseparable.

Even after Morgan got married and had a family, he still kept in touch with Harold. But it wasn't until after he had lost both his brother and son to leukemia that Morgan had called in Harold to help him build his empire. Lundgren's job as chief of security officially meant the safeguarding of all company patents and protection of the employees. Unofficially, he was the intimidator who convinced the best scientists in the world that they couldn't refuse to work for MorGen. And if that didn't work, they simply resorted to a "hostile takeover" of the subjects work. In previous decades, that had meant physical coercion but in the computer age, Harry had become a first-rate hacker and could easily overcome any facility's safeguards.

"First of all," Morgan began, "let me thank you, Harry, for bringing this latest research to my attention," he smiled at his own joke.

"My pleasure," Lundgren intoned.

"And, Elliott, what have you found so far?" Morgan turned to the young scientist.

"What I've seen so far looks promising," he replied enthusiastically. "The applications aren't developed yet, but with the technologies we have available here, it should be no problem to take care of that."

"Excellent!" Morgan sat back in his chair and smoothed his short black hair. His hair was starting to show more gray at his temples, but he felt it made him appear more authoritative and so left it alone.

"Gentlemen," he began once again, "things have been progressing nicely and I feel we may have our vector ready for testing before the end of the month."

"But-" Burdette started to interrupt.

"I know, Elliot. We'll go ahead with the microbial research, but I'm sure we'll work the kinks out of the viral vector soon. You may go back to the lab now. I need you to supervise the changes the construction crews are making." Morgan dismissed him in a tone that ended all discussion of the matter.

Burdette rose from his seat in a kind of daze from being dismissed so unceremoniously and exited the office.

"So what's next, boss?" Lundgren asked.

"Harry, you know I don't like it when you call me that."

"Sorry, Louis. I forget sometimes." Lundgren placed emphasis on each word as he spoke.

Morgan looked him a moment before laughing, "Oh! I guess I was a little short with Elliot." His inadvertent joke made him laugh more.

After regaining his composure he explained himself, "I'm just excited about our progress, Harry. It's making me a little single-minded these days."

"I understand," Lundgren nodded.

"We've come so far in the last few months thanks to our contacts in the world's top universities."

"You never cease to amaze me, Louis," Lundgren shook his head.

Morgan smiled, "You know I've got friends everywhere. When you're in the business of saving lives, everyone wants to be your friend. Think of how many people have been cured of their illnesses by the drugs we've developed and produced!" Morgan nearly leapt out of his chair in his enthusiasm, "Millions! Millions of people have had suffering erased from their lives because we worked harder to come up with better medicines."

"And every one of those people have family and friends who are also grateful to MorGen," Lundgren volunteered.

"Harry, you took the words right out of my mouth," Morgan grinned, "And now, we're going to finally make that breakthrough in cancer treatment that the whole world has been waiting for," he sat back down and spoke clearly and quietly, "It's going to happen, Harry. It's going to happen soon."

Lundgren smiled in return, "Yes, it is. And if you'll excuse me, Louis, I have a few things to attend to that will help us reach our goals even faster."

He rose from his seat and exited the room. Once in the hall with the door to Morgan's office closed behind him, his smile turned to a look of disgust. *Only a few more weeks*, he told himself.

"It looks similar to the early forms of the pictographs," Zhen noted as he inspected the writing more closely. "But there are so few remaining examples of it that I couldn't say for sure."

"Do you know of any others like this in China?" Sam asked of Zhen.

"Not that I've ever heard of. But this inscription was hidden under layers of stone, so perhaps it's the first to be discovered," he suggested.

Sam took a few more shots of the entire inscription to be sure he had it all photographed. They'd already been away from the students for nearly four hours, and he felt they should get back soon, but not before he did a little more investigating.

"I want you to go into Beijing tomorrow to get some large sheets of paper and some charcoal so we can get a good rubbing of this also," Sam instructed Zhen. "Right now, I want to explore this area some more."

"Why don't we wait until tomorrow," Zhen proposed anxiously.

"I'm just going to look around for an hour or so and then we'll go back," Sam began searching the pile of rocks that had fallen from the ceiling.

"Alright, but if I feel another tremor you'll see me heading for the exit."

"Dr. Hunt!" a voice echoed through the cavern causing Zhen to jump. One of the students had followed their markers to find them.

"Over here," Sam called to him.

Gregg Avery was the student's team leader and the closest to getting his master's degree. This would be the last expedition he went on as a student. He was a great admirer of Sam's work and, despite the claims of others that Sam was a little far out in left field, he hoped to continue working with him professionally.

"Why did you come down here alone? You know better than to explore without a partner." Sam reprimanded Gregg as he caught his breath.

"Sorry," Gregg apologized, " no one else would come and I think you'll want to see this right away."

"What is it?"

"It's a complete skeleton! Or a least it looks like it's all there."

"What?" Sam couldn't believe what he was hearing, "Is it a modern burial?"

Even as he asked he had a feeling it wasn't.

"Not in the last hundred thousand years anyway," Gregg replied.

"But is it Homo erectus?"

"We're having a little disagreement about that," he adjusted his wire rimmed glasses nervously.

"What's the problem? Either it is or it isn't."

"Well, from what we can see of the skull so far it looks almost exactly like the fragments we found at Atapuerca."

Sam knew Gregg would be the best person to make that judgment since he had done his fieldwork last year in Spain and had spent hours examining the skulls found there.

"So you think it may be a Homo antecessor?" Sam could hear the doubt in his own voice, but secretly hoped it was true.

"The brow ridges are double-arched, which is the same as Homo erectus from this region, but the cheekbones look more like Homo sapiens. We haven't uncovered enough of the jaw yet to check that, but-"

"Okay, Gregg. You don't have to give me a complete dissertation. I just wanted your opinion."

He looked even more nervous than before, but managed to find his voice "No other fossils of Homo antecessor have been found this far east, but the skeleton bears a closer resemblance to that than any other known species."

"And?"

Sam could tell there was something else Gregg wanted to add and waited for him to continue.

"And we found an artifact with the remains," he vaguely explained.

Sam thought his heart had stopped when Gregg dropped that bombshell.

"Care to be more specific?" he asked.

"I wish I could, but I'm not sure what it is," Gregg admitted. "It's embedded in the rock under the left hand."

"Can you describe it at all?" Zhen could no longer contain his excitement either.

Gregg failed to reply because he had just noticed the inscribed wall behind them.

"Whoa," he gasped.

Sam laughed, "That's what I thought, too."

"What is it?" Gregg wondered aloud.

"We don't know yet. We were just going to do a little exploring when you got here. But let's get back to what you found," Sam guided him.

"Oh, yeah. We can't see a whole lot of it, but it's shiny."

"Shiny? Like metal?"

"It doesn't look like metal, maybe polished stone."

"But possibly something ornamental?"

"That's what we were thinking."

"Enough talk, let's go," Sam wasted no time heading back to the excavations.

He had been waiting for some kind of career-making discovery since he had turned over his first spade full of dirt in his college days. Who didn't? But if it were true, he would have to handle the release of information very carefully. Although he hadn't made any shocking public announcements about his beliefs in a long time, he wasn't fool enough to think people had forgotten. He would be one hundred percent sure before he published any paper claiming Homo antecessor had been discovered in China.

But Sam put these thoughts on the back burner as they returned to the dig site. He would wait and see what they had found before worrying about any consequences.

The other students were clustered around the fossilized remains, one of them still cleaning away some dirt.

"So what do we have?" Sam asked to no one in particular.

"Look for yourself, Dr. Hunt," said the student who had been working on the excavation as he stood and stepped back.

Right away he saw what was causing the confusion among the students. Even with the only a profile of the skull visible he could see the disparate features. It appeared almost as if someone has taken two skulls and fit pieces together to form one.

"Heather," he motioned to one of the quieter students standing at the back of the group, "Describe the nasal cavity for me. But don't think of it in comparison with known specimens. Just call it as you see it."

She knelt in the clay next to Sam and took out a magnifying glass from the tool belt around her waist. Morphology was her strong point and Sam knew she could also be very objective when needed.

"The maxillary sinuses are typical of archaic Homo sapiens," she spoke quietly, her eyes scanning the details of the skull.

"That's hardly likely on an *erectus* skull," with sarcasm aplenty, the young man who had been clearing debris when Sam arrived spoke up. "It's impossible."

"Oh?" Sam looked up at him and raised an eyebrow. "And on what do you base that conclusion, Cameron?"

"Homo antecessor has only been found in Europe. They had a very limited range."

"Were you there putting tracking devices on them?" Sam joked but his point was serious.

There were a couple of muffled snickers and several smiles as Cameron tried to regain his composure.

"Of course not, it's just that-"

"That you're not keeping an open mind. You can't eliminate a possibility just because it doesn't fit into the accepted framework. Who's to say there weren't hundreds of species of Homo at one time? There are several species of most animals in existence today except us. Our ancestors were probably just as diverse locally as other species are now."

"Go on, Heather," Sam encouraged her.

She continued looking over the skeleton, her brow furrowed in puzzlement. "I'm not sure what it is. There are similarities to several known species, but it's like someone took bits and pieces and glued them together."

"What do you mean?"

"I don't know what I mean," she sat back on her heels and continued to stare at the remains.

"Next you'll be saying it's the 'missing link'," Cameron chortled.

Sam scowled Cameron into silence and then focused his attention on the object lying under the left hand of the skeleton.

It was a disk shaped object about five inches in diameter with a hole in the center. Sam wasn't sure what it was made of, but it looked like metal with a dark green iridescent finish, almost like the inside of an oyster shell.

Which is probably all it is, he thought, trying to keep his excitement under control.

But as he leaned over for a better look, he saw it at such an angle that it seemed there was some kind of pattern just beneath the surface.

"Bring the lights in closer," he ordered without looking up. He could hardly stand waiting the few minutes it took the students to reposition the spotlights.

He picked up a brush lying nearby and carefully removed some more debris. There were three finger bones lying on top of the artifact and he dared not move them. Their placement could help to date the object.

"Did anyone take photos yet? And get some readings with the rangefinder to position this on the grid," Sam instructed. Even with the mounting anticipation, he was still following procedure to the letter. Mostly because he didn't want anyone to have the excuse that the excavation wasn't done properly to shoot down the validity of his work.

He cleared away the last of the soil covering that section of the find, and discovered that the skeleton and artifact were partially imbedded in cemented flowstone.

Sam nearly gave a big rebel yell when he realized what it meant. The fossils and the artifact could be much older than anyone would expect. Since this was a higher and drier portion of the cave it would take as much as 200,000 years for a sheet of flowstone like this to form and then harden under the loose clay. He thanked whatever Chinese gods had embedded the skeleton in the flowstone because it had kept it relatively intact. Sam's hand were nearly shaking, but he kept his composure enough to take the digital camera being handed to him and take a few shots as he tried to figure out what the artifact could be.

It took him a few moments to realize that Zhen was talking to him.

"It looks something like a *bi*."

"What?" Sam replied, not looking away from the object.

"I said it looks like a *bi*. A jade disk found in ancient Chinese burials. It's believed to be a part of death and afterlife rituals."

"If it is, this has to be the earliest appearance of it in archaeological records."

"Do you want to keep working or wait until tomorrow?" he was asking.

"We'll need to remove this whole section in a plaster jacket I think. It's embedded in a harder matrix beneath the clay so we'll wait until tomorrow," Sam replied, not taking his eyes off of the artifact. "Go ahead and gather up your tools. We'll discuss everything at dinner."

He heard the sounds of students collecting their gear and discussing the find as he continued to marvel at the object. Even if it was only a polished jade disk, it would be the oldest ever found. But something told Sam it wasn't jade or any other kind of stone.

And the fossil remains were a whole other enigma. Why had no one ever found this type of remains in East Asia before? How old would they turn out to be and how could they be so similar to those found in Spain? He wouldn't let himself even entertain the notion of this being any kind of "missing link". He didn't have that kind of luck.

We'll know for sure once we get it back to the Institute, he told himself and finally got up to join the others. He took a tarp out of their supplies and covered the area. Being in the higher cave entrance had protected the site relatively well over the millennia, but with all the rain there could be a rockslide or water leakage. And Sam definitely did not want the remains to be damaged.

After getting back to camp, he immediately went to his tent to send a report to the university on the day's work. He also sent an email to a colleague and old friend in Greece who specialized in unique artifacts.

George Baltazidis was something of a mentor to Sam when he was a student. When Sam was only a freshman, he was already known for his outspoken manner and the legendary arguments he would get into with his professors. George was the only professor who never got angry with Sam. In fact, he would often congratulate Sam on thinking outside of accepted theories.

"That's what makes a great scientist," he would say. "Any moron can just agree with what someone else says, but it takes real strength of character to stand up for what you believe." Then he would break into a mischievous grin, "Even if it *is* wrong."

It was that way of handling an unruly student that made Sam respect his teacher, and they soon became friends.

In the following years, they worked on many digs together and Sam learned that George had a few unconventional theories of his own. For instance, since George had grown up in the Greek Isles and was always surrounded by the remnants of that ancient civilization, one would suppose that he would have a classical perspective on man's history. But he had instead gotten bored with the antiquities of his homeland and looked elsewhere for more obscure cultures. Any artifact another archeologist would put aside as unknown, George would take up and try to explain. Most of the time he didn't come up with any explanation at all, but occasionally he discovered something that changed accepted theory on an ancient civilization.

George was also well known as an expert in ancient languages and Sam hoped he would recognize the characters in the inscription.

He quickly typed up a note to the museum's executive director, letting him know that they had mapped the new site and had begun excavations. He didn't bother to mention anything about the strange object they had found or the inscription on the inner cave wall because it would just be ignored anyway. Then he sent a message to George with a detailed description of the artifact along with a photo from the digital camera. He hoped George would be near his computer that night, because he couldn't wait for him to see his message. And Sam couldn't wait to hear what George thought of it.

As soon as he had finished going over the day's work with the students and stuck around long enough to eat some stew while answering questions about the dig between bites, Sam rushed back to his tent to see if George had read his email yet.

It had only been an hour since he had sent the message, but Sam knew George would be sitting down to his usual seven course mid-day meal and he always checked his email then.

Sam booted up the computer and got ready for bed while his messages downloaded. Catching his reflection in the mirror, he noticed a big difference from a few days ago. Gone was the dejected look and it had been replaced with a new optimism. It took a few years off of his appearance, he noted with some satisfaction.

He turned to his laptop and saw that he had two new messages. Both were from George.

The first one read: *Interesting find, Sam. Are you sure some of your students aren't playing a trick on you? You know how these college kids can be. I remember the time you took an old carriage wheel and planted it near one of my Mayan sites! You almost had me believing it! They're probably watching your every move, laughing at you behind your back. I would be, too! So just be careful that you don't do something you'll regret later. George*

Sam didn't get it. None of it sounded like something George would say. And what did he mean by carriage wheels at Mayan sites? Sam had never pulled a prank like that, and George had never worked on a Mayan site. Was the man going senile?

He went ahead and read the second email.

I just remembered I have reservations at our favorite restaurant next week. I'll be there on Tuesday. If you can make it, you can tell me if it was for real or not. You really should be there, and bring some pictures of your new friend! George

Now Sam was really confused. They didn't have a favorite restaurant and he wasn't sure what pictures of a new friend George meant him to bring. Neither email made any sense to Sam. He started to get worried that George really was losing his mind. He was only in his late fifties, but maybe spending too much time in the sun over the years had done something to him.

Sam reread both messages, trying to understand what George was saying. Then he realized he was taking the meanings too literally. George was trying to warn him about something without coming right out and saying it. That's why he threw in the false statement about wheels and Mayan sites, to get Sam to realize there was more to his message than met the eye. *They're probably watching your every move...* someone was most likely monitoring all of his transmissions.

His first thought was that the Chinese government would be the likely spies. But George would hardly warn him about that. The government there always spied on any Americans who came inside their borders. Sam knew that Zhen was required to report everything that happened at the excavation to his superiors who in turn reported everything to the government. So it must be someone else George was worried about.

Now the part about their favorite restaurant he did not understand at all. Whenever he stayed with George they usually ate in because his wife was probably the best cook on the island. The only place they had ever gone to more than once was a little place called Manisi's, mostly because of the well-stocked bar.

Once he thought of the name Manisi, Sam realized what George was getting at. He had told Sam the last time they spoke that he was going to be helping out at the Dmanisi site in the Republic of Georgia this month. That had to be it.

If George was going to be at Dmanisi the following week and expected him to leave his work to meet him there, Sam figured he must have something tremendously important to say.

He assumed that the "friend", whose pictures George wanted him to bring, was the fossil remains. Sam was thankful he had brought along his digital camera as well as extra memory cards for it. He would need a lot of photos. Or George may have just finally gone around the bend. In any case, Sam started to make arrangements to fly to Georgia and hoped that whoever was watching him didn't get too interested in his travel plans. He deliberately didn't use his computer to buy his plane tickets, but decided to wait until he reached the airport to purchase them. The Republic of Georgia wasn't exactly the hottest destination for Chinese tourists so he shouldn't have any problem getting a seat.

He logged off the computer and laid down on his cot to just let his mind wander over the day's events. Out of the corner of his eye, he saw his backpack lying next to the desk where he had tossed it earlier. In the excitement of the unusual discovery, he had forgotten about the old sack Zhen had found.

He sat up and pulled the backpack towards him, wanting to take a closer look at the map. He removed the wallet from the sack and was about to lay it aside, when he noticed something else inside it.

Sam reached in and was amazed to find himself holding what looked like the same material as the disk embedded with the fossils. It wasn't a full disk, but about one-third of the circle. Even having it in his hand didn't help him figure out what it could be. On the surface it resembled a compact disk but it was heavier, like it was made of metal or stone.

He turned the fragment over and over in his hands, examining it from every angle. As often as he had lectured students on keeping an open mind when finding artifacts that don't fit with accepted theory, he found himself wanting to dismiss it as site contamination. But that was almost as impossible as the artifact itself.

4

Emily had finished packing up what was left of her belongings in her office and was heading home to throw together a couple of suitcases. After the theft of all of her work a week ago, she had no idea what she would do. Then she had another call from MorGen and this time she said yes. She wasn't going to stay with them permanently, but agreed to a trial period to see if she would be comfortable working there. The only stipulation MorGen had was that any work she did while using their labs would be under their direct control. She didn't like it, but she figured she could always leave before she made any major breakthroughs and finish her work back at the university. It would be a good arrangement for the time being because she couldn't get access to the school's equipment for several months to start her experiments over.

So here she was doing something she never thought she would do. She tried to rationalize it by telling herself it would only be for a little while and she'd find some way to retain the rights to her work. But she couldn't keep her conscience bound and gagged forever, so she decided she would only stay for three months, just enough time to recreate her initial test runs.

Feeling somewhat better about her decision, she pulled into her garage and parked her car. Then she noticed the door into her house was open. She didn't recall leaving it open when she had left, but she hadn't exactly been thinking clearly the last few days. She came to the decision that she had probably left it open, but she still entered the house warily. After her lab had been broken into by persons unknown, her sense of being watched had only grown worse.

She slowly pushed the door open further and peeked into the foyer. Nothing seemed to be amiss, so she stepped into the room and turned on the overhead light. There was nothing there except the small table that she usually threw her keys on when she came home, and the security system control pad that she had forgotten to activate when she left for the lab.

Standing quietly for a moment to listen for any suspicious noises, she heard nothing. She shrugged and convinced herself that she had left the door open, even though a feeling of uneasiness still hung over her.

She headed towards the kitchen to fix something to eat before she started packing. On her way there she decided she also needed to do a little cleaning before she left as well. There were little bits of mulch from the outside flowerbeds tracked into the hallway, though she didn't remember walking around that side of the building in weeks.

It must have been the maintenance man, she thought, he always makes a mess when he fixes something. She knew she hadn't called for anything to be repaired, but tried to convince herself that was what had happened anyway.

Her feelings of apprehension subsided as she walked through the rest of the house and found nothing out of the ordinary. By the time she was finished making dinner she felt foolish for thinking someone had broken in.

But she still took some precautions that night before going to bed, making sure the security system was turned on downstairs and the small handgun in her nightstand was loaded.

"Is the lab finished yet?" Morgan asked Elliot Burdette as he entered the office.

"Yes. They just finished installing the final pieces of equipment last night," Burdette answered, "It's amazing how quickly they did it. I must say it is the most impressive laboratory I have ever seen."

"Isn't it though?" Morgan smiled dreamily, "She designed it perfectly."

"Who designed it?" Burdette inquired.

"The newest member of your team, Dr. Emily Forester."

"Dr. Forester of Thompson State?"

"The same."

"I can't believe she would come here," Burdette said incredulously. "Everyone knows how much she hates corporations making profits from medical advancements."

The smile abruptly disappeared from Morgan's face. "I know," he rose from his seat. "But I guess the opportunity to work at a state of the art facility overcame her dislike of corporate America," he put his arm around Burdette's shoulders, "And how could she resist working with one of the most renowned microbiologists in the world?"

Burdette responded to this compliment by turning red and smiling at the floor, as Morgan knew he would.

"Now why don't you show me the new lab," he suggested before Burdette got any more embarrassed.

It was easy for Morgan to play the father figure to Elliot since he was a father. *Was.* If Joshua had lived, he would be graduating from college that year. And then he would have taken a position at his father's side, running the company. But leukemia had ended Joshua's life fifteen years ago, and left Louis and his wife to deal with the pain of losing their only child. They were recovering from the grief when Joshua's uncle, Louis' brother, was diagnosed with the disease as well and died a year later. Morgan became more and more isolated in his wretchedness and spent days at a time locked in the labs at the research facility where he worked. His wife eventually packed up and moved back to her hometown, unable to cope with the extent of his mourning.

"I can't believe how quickly the company has grown," Morgan reminisced. "It seems like yesterday when I quit my job working for someone else and started my own laboratories. I worked by myself for some months until I got my first federal grant and hired an assistant."

"And a year later you got your first medical patent," Burdette chimed in, grinning with pride like Morgan was his own father.

"After that, I had so many offers from pharmaceutical companies I couldn't keep up with the orders."

And now he was the CEO of a multi-billion dollar worldwide corporation and about to make the breakthrough that every scientist on the planet dreamed of making. A cure for cancer. Not just a cure, but the total eradication of the disease from the human genome.

"Here we are," Elliot announced as they stepped off of the elevator. "We'll go through after we get changed into our suits in the locker room," he gestured to the large area to their right where rows of lockers held jumpsuits made to keep any contaminates from touching the skin of the wearer. There were specially designed goggles and boots hanging along one wall, and surgical caps and gloves in dispensers next to them.

Morgan slipped his jumpsuit on over his clothes while he looked across the hall at the lab entrance. They had already gone through one set of sealed doors to reach the locker room, and would go through another to enter the lab, keeping any cross-contamination with the outside to minimum. They went further than the federal requirements for Biosafety Level 3 which were required when working with agents that could cause fatal disease by inhalation. Because MorGen sometimes used those materials in a way not specifically sanctioned by the government, those sorts of things were taken into account by the lab's engineers when they made the designs.

They entered the existing lab first and saw some of the scientists already at work. One of them was transferring samples from a biosafety cabinet to the storage unit after examining them for any signs of progress. The vials of clear liquid looked much more harmless than they actually were. Each contained enough contagious disease to cause an epidemic of immense proportions. But they were safely contained in the proscribed manner and a chain reaction of accidents only seen in a slapstick movie would allow their release into the general population.

"This is the most efficiently designed laboratory I've ever seen. And the safest as well. Dr. Forester must be a very cautious scientist." Elliot pointed out.

"A good quality, I suppose," Morgan reluctantly agreed, "But there is something to be said for throwing caution to the wind."

Elliot's expression, though he tried to appear indifferent, showed how uneasy he was with that idea.

Morgan was aware that lately Elliot had been uncomfortable with continuing with research that wasn't strictly condoned by the scientific community. So, the addition of a scientist who was exploring other methods, as well as being an attractive woman, would help to calm Elliot's fears and keep his genius happily working for MorGen.

The new lab had much of the same equipment as Emily's lab at Thompson State, but in larger quantities and newer models. The room was quiet except for the sounds of their footsteps, but would be filled with the whirr of machinery when it was in operation. The florescent lights were tinted to soften the glare from the tons of polished metal, with strategically placed spotlights over the work stations.

Burdette pointed out the various pieces of equipment and how they were used. Morgan didn't really care. He was just glad to see Burdette was excited about his work again.

"I still can't believe how quickly the lab was put together," Burdette marveled.

"It's amazing how a little extra money in the right places can get a job done," Morgan replied dryly.

At the rear of the room, a glass walled office housed the main computer terminal and Emily's desk. As Burdette led Morgan into the office, the phone rang. Morgan was amused when the noise made Burdette jump.

"Hello," Morgan answered. "Yes, Harry...Good job....You can show me later...Thanks again, bye."

He turned back to Burdette, "Well, thank you for the tour, Elliot. I have to be getting back to my paperwork before it gets completely out of hand." He glanced around the lab again. "I envy you, Elliot. I wish I could go back to puttering around in the lab and not have to run the operation."

"You're welcome to come visit us any time to 'putter around', Dr. Morgan."

Morgan chuckled. Burdette was so easy to manipulate it almost bored him to do it.

5

The wall beneath the inscription was unbelievably smooth. Sam found it hard to believe it could have been made without the use of modern tools. He taped another piece of tracing paper to the wall and reached for his charcoal stick to make a rubbing of the final section.

Sam was alone in the cave, but he and Zhen were linked by the low-frequency induction phone, often used by cave rescue teams, that he had cobbled together from instructions he had found on the internet. The base phone had wires sunk into the ground on metal tent pegs, while Sam's unit made use of electrical fence tape. The signal was able to travel through almost a mile of cave - most of the time. Zhen was supervising the students as they prepared the plaster jacket over the skeleton and artifact while Sam recorded all the information possible about the inscription. He checked in with Zhen every half hour to let him know of his progress.

"How's it coming, Zhen?" Sam pressed the call button on his radio.

"We're just about ready to cut it free of the matrix," Zhen voice came through with only a hint of static.

"Good work. I'm about done with the last section. When I'm finished with that, I'm going to survey the area a little more."

"Any sign of other artifacts yet?"

"Nothing yet, but I'll keep you posted." Sam turned off his radio to conserve the batteries.

He continued his work with the steady rumble of the river in the background. It was soothing and Sam found himself feeling more relaxed than he had in years. It was this sense of peace that often drew him into exploring new caves. His sometimes hectic life as the youngest son of a large family made him seek out the calm, cool interior of the mountains. Over time, he learned to enjoy the challenges of overcoming his fears and ventured deeper and deeper into the caves. He'd been in tight spots more than a few times, and had a few close calls with bottomless pits, but where he was now excited him more than any place he had been before.

The last tracing was finished and he carefully rolled up the sheet of paper, placing it inside the plastic tube with the others. He still had no idea what the symbols might turn out to be, but he knew that they were going to be the subject of much debate in the coming months.

He was about to begin a preliminary survey of the area immediately surrounding the wall, hoping to find some clue as to how the surface was made so smooth, when a subtle change in the roar of the river caught his attention.

Sam listened carefully, thinking perhaps he was just imagining it. But the rumbling continued unabated and he turned back to his survey.

A moment later it became very apparent that he had not been imagining things when the river ceased to make any noise at all.

He ran into the next chamber and was startled to find his headlamp illuminating only a trickle of water running through the bottom of the riverbed. He pointed his light toward the wall where the water made its entrance and could see no sign of the raging current that had been there only moments before.

It made no sense. Even if the rain had stopped, which it hadn't, it would take days for the water level to subside.

He looked at the opening in the wall again. Before it had been filled entirely with the water rushing through, but now he could see it was a hole about ten feet in diameter and roughly oval in shape. He found himself looking for a way to climb down into the riverbed before he had evaluated the risk involved.

Deciding he had better wait at least five minutes to see if the river resumed its flow, he took a moment to call Zhen.

"Zhen, you won't believe this."

"What is it?" Zhen's voice crackled over the speaker.

"The river is gone."

"What?"

"That big river running through the chamber next to the one with the inscription. It's gone."

"What do you mean by 'gone'?"

"It stopped flowing all of a sudden. There's just a trickle left in the bottom."

"I don't like the sound of that. You'd better come back here. Are you done with the tracings?"

"Yes, I'm done. But I want to check this out before I come back."

"I don't think that's a good idea."

"I won't take long. I'm just going to walk up the riverbed a little ways into the next chamber."

"But what if it starts flowing again?"

"I'll get wet," he grabbed his headlamp and backpack, "I'll check back in five minutes."

"But-"

Sam shut off the radio and headed back to the opening.

The walls were still dripping wet and his lamp made the flecks of crystal in them glitter like diamonds. He shined his light upwards and was taken aback when he found the ceiling was lost in the darkness. Apparently there had only been a few feet of rock separating this cavern from the next but the small opening between them had been blocked by the river.

The room had a very high ceiling, but was only about fifteen feet wide. As far as Sam could see it went on for another fifty feet before there was another opening, this one smaller than the last.

It seemed to him he could hear the distant murmur of the river. A thought which made him more than a little nervous. But as he listened, it didn't seem to be getting any louder as if the sound were approaching. It was just a steady distant rumbling.

He walked along the riverbed until he reached the next opening. His light revealed a smaller tunnel, this one only five feet in height so Sam had to walk bent over. Luckily it was nearly as long as it was short and Sam found the noise of the river becoming louder.

He straightened up as he came out of the tunnel and found the reason for the sudden disappearance of the river.

At the far end of the chamber he had just entered, a section of the floor had given way and the water plunged noisily into a waterfall, ending up somewhere deeper in the cave.

It's probably washing out the rest of our previous excavation, he thought ruefully, but thankful they weren't still working the old site.

Scanning the rest of the cavern as he went, Sam turned to head back to his current excavation. But he was stopped short by the inscription on the wall next to him.

It wasn't as large as the one in the other cavern, but it was unmistakably of the same design.

But what really took his breath away was the door next to the inscription. It wasn't a crude stone or wooden doorway. It appeared to be made of steel or some similar metal, but showed no signs of rust or pitting. A jumble of rock lay at its base indicating it was recently uncovered, possibly by the same tremors that revealed the inscription in the other chamber.

He looked at it in a daze, not even being able to begin to fathom how it got there. Who made it? How did they get it here? When did they put it here? He was asking himself so many questions at once he found it difficult to focus his attention.

He noticed the lack of rust.

It can't be very old then. Sam felt a pang of disappointment.

Maybe it was an abandoned mine.

Or maybe I'm about to walk in on a Chinese department of defense installation, he chuckled silently.

He could see no way to open the door, no handle or knob, and began to feel around the edges of the door for some way to open it.

Sam realized his five minutes were up and he should check in with Zhen again, but he couldn't bring himself the leave just yet. Zhen would come down and check on him if it didn't get back soon and then he'd have someone to help him figure out how the hell to open the door.

Okay, this door doesn't have a handle, so it obviously has a different mechanism for opening. He tried to think the problem through logically and deduce what technique was needed to open the door.

He reached out and felt the surface of the door. It was cold, like most metal surfaces are, especially in a cave where the constant temperature was fifty-five degrees Fahrenheit. The surface was perfectly smooth and coated with a thin layer of dust.

The whole thing was set six inches back into the rock and there were no gaps around the edges. Examining toward the edges of the door, he noticed three small depressions in an otherwise smooth surface. Each was the size of a fingertip. Sam brushed his fingers over them and was astonished as he heard the grinding of gears and the door began to slide open.

There was a cool breeze emanating from beyond the door. Sam almost thought he could smell the freshness of the meadows below the mountains. He couldn't see anything through the doorway except the beam of his headlamp. There were no surfaces straight ahead for the light to reveal so he took a step forward and through the opening.

And he was startled when sound of his footfall echoed with a metallic reverberation. He glanced downward and was momentarily blinded by the light of his halogen lamp reflecting off of a polished floor.

The whole place was covered with reflective surfaces. He turned down his light to save his eyes and get a better look at his surroundings.

The floor was tiled in what appeared to be an enameled metal, each section nearly ten feet square and tightly joined together. His attention was drawn to a dark area on the floor across the room. He approached it cautiously, not knowing what to expect after finding a place like this hidden deep within a cave.

As he neared the object, he could see it was a large slab of stone. And once he was only two feet away from it, he could make out the shape of a desiccated human arm protruding from underneath.

Sam's first thought was that it might be the owner of the bag they had found earlier, but remembered that many people had supposedly disappeared in the area. They wouldn't know for sure until the slab was removed and the body examined.

He looked up at the ceiling to the large hole the approximate size of the piece that had crushed the unfortunate explorer. The rest of the ceiling was covered in more of the glistening metal.

Sam decided now might be a good time to get back to his phone and contact Zhen. He turned to leave just as he heard the door begin closing behind him. He attempted to run back through the door before it closed, but he was too far away.

As he stood there with his heart pounding, he realized how he was beginning to panic before he had any reason to do so.

If there's a way to open it on the outside, there should be a way to open it from in here.

But there wasn't. He spent fifteen minutes going over every inch of the door frame and found nothing resembling the other opening mechanism. He figured Zhen must be on his way down to look for him by now, but didn't stop looking for another way out.

He returned to the spot where the rock slab had fallen and looked up at the hole in the ceiling again. It was a good five feet over his head to reach the lip of the opening. He hated to step on the slab, possibly crushing the remains underneath, but that would put him a couple of feet closer to escaping.

Sam rummaged through his backpack for the length of rope he always carried with him as he tried to figure out how he could secure it on the other side of the opening. His thoughts were interrupted by a scraping noise that seemed to have come from the other side of the now sealed door.

"Zhen!" he started toward the door, "Is that-"

A tremendous blast knocked Sam back to the other side of the room and the wall in front of him began to collapse upon itself. The entire cave began to shudder and quake, large pieces of rock and metal falling from the ceiling.

He struggled to clear his head and stand up. The whole room could collapse at any moment and he needed to get out fast. He ran back over to the hole in the ceiling and jumped on top of the slab. He picked up the rope from where he had dropped it before the blast and tied it to the straps of his backpack.

Throwing his pack through the opening he prayed that it would snag on something sturdy enough to hold his weight. He pulled on the rope and the backpack came sliding back down through the hole along with a cloud of dust and debris.

The tremors in the cave were slowly subsiding when a second explosion sent Sam tumbling to the ground once again. He felt a sharp blow on his left shoulder as a rock the size of a basketball crashed into him, narrowly missing his skull. He tried to lift his arm and the pain that shot through his shoulder was agonizing. He knew he wouldn't be able to pull himself up a rope and the cave was in imminent danger of collapsing completely.

He stared blankly above him willing himself to think clearly.

Then his brain registered that his eyes were seeing an even larger hole than was previously there. More of the ceiling had disintegrated and piles of rock were scattered around him on the floor. He quickly clambered on top of the largest pile and reached for the rim of the hole.

Sam could just reach it with his right hand and pulled himself up a few inches before slipping back to the ground. He would have to jump for it and try to use his injured arm or he wouldn't make it at all.

He took a deep breath and clenched his teeth as he prepared to spring off of the rock pile. His feet left the mound at the same instant a third explosion tore through the cavern. He managed to get his arms and the top part of his torso over the lip of the opening and struggled to swing his legs up before the ground gave way beneath him.

Just as he kicked his legs up and rolled out of the cavern below, the area surrounding the hole began to collapse. He stood and quickly ran away from the unstable area and found himself looking at another ten foot climb up a sheer rock face to get out of the circular pit he now found himself in.

His arm was throbbing painfully as he frantically looked for some kind of handhold. He found a small niche he could get his hand into and began climbing as quickly as he could.

Moments later, he lay panting on the edge of the pit as the rumbling below subsided. He rolled onto his right side and peered into the pit. It was now just a jumbled mass of rock, with no sign of the room that had been there only a few minutes ago.

"Sam!" he heard Zhen's voice echoing through the cavern.

"Over here!" Sam called weakly.

Soon Zhen and Gregg appeared, running into the cavern.

"What happened?" Zhen asked. "We couldn't reach you on the phone and when we felt the tremors we thought we had better come look for you."

"I found something, but I'll tell everyone about it later," Sam coughed and spat dust. "Let's just get back to camp."

Collapsing onto the bed, Emily groaned. Morgan was a creep and a slave driver. But at least he put her up in a nice hotel. The bed was a king size and there was a whirlpool tub in the bathroom. And there was even a mini-bar and refrigerator built in under the television set. The décor was a little gaudy to her eyes. She preferred simple, classic design to the ornate, gilded look, but she wasn't about to complain. She luxuriated in the feel of the soft bed under her and didn't want to get up. But she was as hungry as she was tired and wanted to get a call into room service before the kitchen closed.

She placed her order and decided to do a little work while she waited. Her laptop was still in her suitcase, as was everything else. She didn't have time to unpack anything since Morgan's security director, Mr. Lundgren, came to pick her up at the airport and had only stopped long enough to let her drop off her luggage and check in at the hotel.

Then it was non-stop brainwashing all day long about how MorGen was the place to be. After a morning tour and an excruciating interview with Morgan himself, Emily thought she'd be able to escape to a quiet lunch by herself, but was instead forced to go to an expensive restaurant with the lab director, Dr. Burdette.

He reminded her of a boy in her high school science class who had a crush on her. And it was becoming obvious that Elliot, as he insisted she call him, was interested in things other than her work. She was certain he wouldn't have enough nerve to do anything about it though. The only reason she had lunch with him was because Morgan had insisted they get to know each other.

Tomorrow will be better, she thought, I can just get to work and not have to socialize with those corporate goons.

She had been very impressed with their facility though. They had everything she needed for her work and more. All of the equipment was brand new and top of the line and her assigned work station was perfectly designed. The more she thought about it, the more it seemed like the lab that she had designed all of those years ago as her "dream lab". She supposed someone would come up with that design sooner or later since it was functional and efficient, but she couldn't believe she was actually getting to work in it.

She was figuring out just how long it should take her to complete her work when room service arrived with her food. She took it over to the desk where she had set her computer and took a bite of salad as she retrieved her email.

The only messages she had were from her mother and Robert Chisek, the last two people from whom she'd want to hear. She groaned and read the note from Chisek first in case it had anything to do with the investigation into who had burglarized her office.

Hello, Emily! Just seeing how you're settling in at your new job. I hope you don't like it too much because I'd hate for you to leave us permanently.

Emily hit delete before she read the rest of it and moved on to the message from her mother.

Five minutes later, she was still waiting for her computer to download the email. Her mother tended to be wordy, but Emily couldn't figure out why it was taking so long to open the message. She was just about to chalk it up to an overloaded server when the message finally came up.

The first few lines were the usual "why haven't you called" and "is everything okay". But after that the rest of the message was a garbled mess of symbols and numbers. She shrugged and deleted it, figuring her mother still hadn't gotten the hang of the internet.

She finished her salad and dumped the container into the trash before heading to the bathroom to brush her teeth.

As she brushed, her mind wandered the way it did when she was totally exhausted, flitting from one idea to the next, randomly connecting things that she wouldn't normally associate with one another.

She choked on her mouthful toothpaste when she had the terrifying notion that someone from MorGen had broken into her lab.

Spitting and gasping, she rinsed out her mouth. She tried to figure out where she had gotten the idea, but the impression was a fleeting one and she was too tired to concentrate on it.

Besides, it was a little outlandish to think they would go through all of that trouble just to get her here. She knew she was doing what many considered to be groundbreaking work, but she hardly thought she was significant enough to go through the effort and possible danger of ransacking her lab.

Then she remembered something else. They may not have stolen her work, but there was that comment Burdette had made about Morgan's "loose" interpretations of federal guidelines. What exactly was it he was trying to tell her? She tried to recall the entire conversation.

Emily had been near to falling asleep in her eggplant parmesan listening to Burdette's praise of Morgan's pharmaceutical empire. She asked him the question without really expecting an answer.

"Does the man ever do anything wrong?" she remarked acidly.

Burdette looked at his plate and seemed to be thinking over his answer. "Yes. There are maybe a *few* things he could do better."

"Such as?"

"Well, he stretches the limit of what's allowable sometimes."

"I don't understand."

"He's been doing this for so long, he feels some of the guidelines shouldn't apply to him."

"You mean he breaks a few rules now and then?"

"Nothing major. He just doesn't see why certain avenues of research should be restricted because other people don't know what to do with it."

"I see where this is going."

She had felt a little tingle of fear, almost like a premonition, but pushed it aside. No matter what they were doing in the other labs, it had nothing to do with her. She was still sticking to her plan of doing her basic test and then leaving.

"I hope it doesn't make you too uncomfortable," Burdette apologized.

"Why should I care? It's not my company."

Burdette smiled shyly and turned red, "I hope you'll decide to stay, though."

It was all she could do to keep from rolling her eyes.

The whole conversation was odd. If he was so devoted to his employer, why should he tell her about what he was doing wrong? Was he that enamored with her? Whatever the reason, it made her somewhat uneasy and she resolved to keep as much to herself as possible at work. She didn't want to become involved in anything illegal.

Finally she climbed into bed and, despite her fears, fell asleep the moment her head hit the pillow.

6

Dmanisi Excavations
Republic of Georgia

Sam arrived at the excavations right as they were closing the site for the day. It was only two o' clock in the afternoon, but the dark clouds to the west portended the coming storm. Did it have to rain everywhere he went? The crumbling remains of the medieval fortress built three hundred feet above the excavations on a rocky bluff and surrounded by mountains only added to the forbidding atmosphere. It made him wish he was at George's seaside villa in Greece.

The previous night after tending to his badly bruised shoulder, Sam had explained to the rest of the team what he had found in the cave. They found it hard to believe to say the least. He decided not to tell them about the explosions because it would serve no purpose other than frightening them. But he could tell that none of them believed it was an accident.

Sam had suspicions of his own. After receiving the odd messages from George, he had been on his guard for any unusual occurrences. Whoever had set the explosives must have been trying to conceal the hidden metal chamber. And they obviously didn't care if someone was killed in the process.

That's why Sam had quickly decided to cancel the remainder of the excavations. The official message he sent to the university explained the incident as a natural cave-in and that he felt it was dangerous to continue work in that area since the excessive rainfall had certainly undermined the stability of the caves. He knew there would be no inquiry since cutting their expedition short would save the university a good deal of money. And they had already removed the fossils found in the main cave along with the strange disk which Sam now had in his backpack.

Sam didn't know if he was being paranoid or not, but he left early that morning without even telling Zhen where he was going. He had instructed everyone to start packing and left a note saying he had gone ahead to arrange their transportation. They would all be safely home in less than forty-eight hours. As to taking the disk out of the country, Sam felt guilty about deceiving the airport officials, but he felt that it was more important to get the artifact to George as quickly as possible than to follow the proper procedures which could take months. And the disk had fit neatly inside the jewel case of one of his Aerosmith CDs.

Now that Sam had safely arrived in Georgia, he hoped he had guessed right about George's message. He leaned against the truck he had rented in Tbilisi and waited.

He was soon proved correct when George's stocky form emerged from under blue tarp that had been stretched over one of the many pits around the site. He looked the same as the last time Sam had seen him at his home in Greece. His Mediterranean blue eyes still shone with the enthusiasm of a much younger man, but his graying hair and beard indicated his decades of experience. His waist had expanded a little as well, no doubt due to his wife's fine cooking, but on a frame as large as his, it was hardly noticeable.

"Sam!" he called over to him as a massive grin broke out on his face. "What are you doing here? I thought you were in New Jersey."

Sam couldn't reply as the air was being crushed out of lungs by the bear hug George was laying on him despite the sling on his left arm.

"How long has it been? Three years?" George asked.

Sam coughed, "Something like that." He leaned closer to George, "What the hell is going on?" he whispered.

"I'll tell you in a minute," George whispered back, then raised his voice, "Let me show you what we're working on."

He led Sam over to a more secluded area of the site, where no diggers were hanging around.

"Okay," Sam began, "can we stop with the cloak and dagger business?"

"Sorry about all that, but it was necessary. I'm glad you were able to figure out my message," George paused and looked around, running his fingers through his curly salt and pepper hair. "Did you bring it with you?"

"In my backpack."

"Any pictures of your friend?"

"Lots. And some sketches, too." Sam felt more than a little silly using code words.

"Let's go some place more private and I'll tell you what's going on."

"There's no one here. What's more private?" Sam asked as he followed George up a steep path into what was left of the fortress above the dig.

Sam couldn't wait to hear what was making George so jumpy. He was acting like there was a spy around every corner. Sam himself was a little nervous, but he felt that nearly being crushed to death under tons of rock in a deliberate bombing was reason enough to be uneasy.

Once they were inside a small room that must have once been part of an immense structure, George began to elaborate.

"There have been other finds similar to yours in various locations. All of them have been dated between eight or nine hundred thousand years old and they were all kept under lock and key in museum basements. Only a handful of people know about them, and most don't believe they've been accurately dated."

"But you do," Sam added.

"And I'm not the only one. There is someone else who has been secretly studying the artifacts. I found that out by accident when I went to reexamine one of them and discovered it was 'on loan' to a research facility. And one by one, all of them started disappearing."

"That's not all that's disappearing," Sam quickly explained what happened in the caves the night before.

"Incredible! I was going to ask how you got your arm in a sling, but I thought maybe you had been patting yourself on the back too hard," George always poked fun at Sam's formerly egotistical nature.

Sam pretended to ignore the comment, "You're sure they didn't just misplace the artifacts?"

George frowned, "I had them double-check. They have *disappeared.* The museums have tried to get them back and the persons who took them out don't exist anymore."

Sam's curiosity was piqued. "What exactly did they look like?"

"The description you gave me of what you found is as good as any to describe the rest."

"You're serious? Where were the other ones found?" Sam was getting more and more excited.

"Kenya, Ecuador, Alaska, Russia, Antarctica, Australia, Mexico-"

"Whoa! Just how many of these things have been found?"

"Yours will make it twenty-one."

"And they've all been dated the same?"

"Yes."

"But no one believed it so they were stuck in storage as unexplained which is how you found them."

"Exactly. None of them knew what the others had found because no one had bothered to publish a paper on a single anomalous artifact. The only person who ever did was Von Daniken and no one ever took him seriously because of his obsession with aliens."

"What did he find?"

"A cache of large stone disks with tiny symbols etched in them in a circular pattern. Kind of like an old vinyl record. I think they were actually reproductions of ones someone had seen or else they had the actual disks sealed inside the stone. Unfortunately, no one bothered to take an x-ray of them before they disappeared."

Sam took in a deep breath as he tried to digest all of the information George had just given him. He reflected a moment and asked the crucial question, "So what do you think they are?"

"Why don't I tell you after I have a look at your pictures and the disk? Let's go back to my hotel and have some dinner."

"But it's not even four o'clock yet."

"My stomach can't tell time," George grinned unabashedly as they headed for the rental truck.

"So why did I have to come here to this godforsaken place instead of taking it to your private lab? I'd much rather be spending my time on the beach and eating your wife's cooking."

"Yes," George laughed, "Anna was disappointed that you wouldn't be coming as well. But I couldn't take any chances. Too many people know me there and word would spread that you came to visit."

"I see," Sam remarked as he started the truck and pulled back out onto the dirt road that had led him to the site. "And nobody here would think anything of it?"

"Nobody who knows you, anyway," George replied

The table in George's hotel room was already covered in papers from his research when Sam added his to the pile. George was busy calling an enormous order to room service while Sam spread out the charcoal rubbings of the inscriptions over the bed.

"Oh my!" George nearly fell over himself moving in to get a closer look.

"What?! What is it? Do you recognize it?"

"A lot of it is new to me," George spoke hesitatingly as his eyes rapidly scanned the sheets, "These abstract symbols and shapes," he pointed at the first part of the rubbing. "But the last column I've seen before. It has some aspects of the earlier Chinese pictographs."

"How do you mean?"

George gave him a reprimanding look, "You still haven't learned your ancient languages, have you?"

Sam shrugged, "You're the one who passed me without taking the final exam."

"A decision I regret every day," he groaned melodramatically.

"Get on with it already. What's so different about these?"

"The earliest known forms of Chinese writing are more like actual pictures of the object they represent. Barely a step removed from primitive cave drawings. But over the millennia, they become more and more simplified with fewer strokes. An abstract or shorthand of the original picture. What's so unusual about this writing is that the characters are complex like the ancient ones, but they don't really look like a picture of anything."

Sam studied the rubbings more intently, one character at a time. "Well, this one reminds me of something," he pointed to a ladder-like spiral design surrounded by a double circle.

"You're right. That looks like a section of DNA." The lines in George's brows grew deeper as he studied the picture. "And these concentric circles with the dots between them remind me of something, but I can't place them."

"Nothing else looks familiar," Sam noted.

"Take a look at this," George pointed to the bottom right corner of the rubbing.

Sam leaned in and looked more closely at the spot George was indicating, "It looks like some kind of imperfection in the rock."

"When the rest of it was so smooth? Take a closer look."

George handed him a thin plastic magnifier.

"It's a circle with some kind of scaly texture to it. Is that a snake head?"

"It's placed almost like a signature would be on a document."

"But what does it mean?"

"It doesn't remind you of anything?"

"I think I've seen it before, but I can't remember the details," Sam was slightly embarrassed he couldn't remember since George was his professor on this subject at the university.

George sighed and shook his head, "Ouroboros."

"Oro-what?"

"The mythical snake that eats it own tail, representing the unending cycle of life. It was first depicted in Egypt in about 1600 BC."

"Oh, *that* Ouroboros!"

"It was also the symbol of the Roman goddess Ǽternitas, the personification of eternity." George waited for the next inevitable question.

"So what's it doing inscribed on a cave wall in China?"

"I wish I knew. Now," George rubbed his hands together in anticipation, "let's see that disk."

As Sam dug through his backpack, there was a knock on the door and a voice announcing their room service had arrived.

George wheeled over a cart full of covered trays and parked it next to the table. But before he could get too involved in the food, he saw the disk that Sam was holding and started sputtering.

"What is it this time?"

"I can't believe it's intact!"

It took a moment for Sam to understand what he was so excited about.

"You mean the others weren't intact?"

"No! They were just pieces, "George spluttered, "Some of them big pieces, but still just pieces!"

"I do have another piece," Sam handed him the intact disk while he searched for the other piece he had found.

George carefully took it from Sam's hand and held it under the table lamp. It shimmered under the light and they could see the faint lines running around the entire disk. It was about three inches in diameter and had a small hole in the center only an eighth of an inch wide.

Sam found the other piece and gave that to George as well.

"Yes, this is what's usually been found," he commented.

"Now will you please tell me what it is?" Sam pleaded.

"What do you think it is?" George smiled, sliding back into his teaching persona. "And forget about where it was found."

"It looks like some kind of data storage device, like a CD."

"And that's probably what it is," George announced.

"Wait a minute. How could a cd get imbedded in flowstone underneath 400,000 year-old fossils?"

"Maybe someone dropped it there."

"That long ago?"

"Actually, I think the disk is older than that," George explained nonchalantly.

"This is too much, George," Sam shook his head. "Just who exactly do you think dropped it?"

"Maybe your friend here," he gestured to the photos of the fossilized remains that Sam had spread out on the table. "But he's definitely not who made it."

Sam didn't know what to think of the story George was telling him.

"I'm not really sure who did," he continued, "But they were obviously a technologically advanced race."

"Don't even tell me you think it was aliens," Sam warned him.

"You can't rule out anything until you have proof that it's impossible or at least highly improbable," he reminded Sam. "I haven't reached any conclusions yet except for the fact that these artifacts are nearly one million years old."

Sam tried to comprehend the enormity of what George was telling him. He didn't want to question George's interpretation of the artifact's age, but he found it hard to believe anything that had obviously been created by intelligent life could be found on this planet that long ago.

"Okay, so it's older than Homo sapiens," Sam acquiesced, "And we really don't know who made it," he struggled with an idea. "But maybe we could figure out its function."

"I'm pretty sure it is some kind of data storage unit. What we need to figure out is how to access it."

Sam was startled by this idea. "Access it? Do you mean you think it really is a CD?"

"Of course. I've been working on that particular problem since I first pieced together what a complete disk would have looked like," George continued, "I made some modifications to my DVD player at home in the hopes that an intact disk would eventually be found. Anna was a little upset when she went to watch a movie and I had it in pieces all over the kitchen table," he chuckled. "But I think it's about the right size for this disk now."

"I know you're pretty good with your electronic gadgets, George, but do you really think that will work? I mean, that's supposing this thing actually is some kind electronic technology and not just a decorative artifact." Sam recalled some of the devices George had around his office to make things more efficient. He trashed his filing cabinet and never kept anything on paper again after he bought his first scanner, and now he didn't go anywhere without his laptop.

"There's only one way to find out."

"Then we'll go to your villa on Patmos?" Sam asked hopefully, looking forward to stretching out on the veranda overlooking the Aegean Sea and sipping on a martini.

"Soon enough," George smiled. "But first I want to stop by a site near Izmir and see if we can find a room like you described there as well."

"Another cave?" Sam's daydream of lounging on the beach dissolved as his interest was piqued.

"Yes. Some writing and a partial disk was found there as well."

"Why didn't you say so as soon as I told you about what I found?"

"Because as soon as you told me what had happened to it, I realized it may already have been destroyed."

Sam's enthusiasm was extinguished as the probability of George's prediction being correct set in. "Well, let's get finished up here and go find out. It might still be intact since no one has discovered any hidden rooms there yet."

"As far as we know."

Sipildagi (Mt. Sipylus)
Near Izmir, Turkey

Sam could not believe he was thousands of miles away in Turkey, because the inscription in front of him looked exactly the same as the one he had stumbled upon in China. They had arrived in Izmir early that morning after staying up half the night discussing the possible function of the disks. The city was just beginning to awaken when they drove in from Konya at five A.M. George was impatient to get to the site he had described to Sam the night before since he learned what had happened in the caves in China.

The palm-lined streets, bright lights and hotels were a drastic change from the rocky crags and olive groves just outside the city. George drove them straight down to the harbor where fishing boats preparing to cast off were moored next to the rows of charter boats, waiting for the day's first passengers heading to the Greek Isles. George booked passage for them for later that day before they grabbed some breakfast at a Turkish version of a greasy spoon diner. It was only an hour long drive and a thirty minute hike to reach the cave entrance.

"It hasn't been destroyed," George breathed a sigh of relief.

Or he could have been out of breath from the hike, Sam wasn't sure.

"When was this found?" Sam asked as he traced the characters with his fingertips, noting the similarities between this writing and the section George had pointed out to him in the inscription he had found in China. And there was also the minute image of the Ouroboros.

"The caves were found two years ago but the writing wasn't discovered until last month. I took photos and tracings that I have at home now. We're still trying to figure out how it was missed. Some people have theorized that the caves themselves are ritual maze like those found in Crete used by the bull cults. Others think it was a storage complex for the Crusaders." George explained as he continued walking.

"And what do you think?"

"There's no evidence to support either theory. The only artifacts found here were found outside the caves, not inside. This place is perfectly clean. No pots, no bones, no tools."

"Something else doesn't seem right here," Sam noted as they walked. "There should be irregularities in the surface, evidence of natural forces. Other caves in the area have an abundance of speleothems. But it's perfectly smooth. Like it was sanded down or something."

"It may have been waterproofed somehow. I don't know of any Romans or Crusaders who used sandblasters."

The floor began to slope slightly beneath Sam's feet and dampness in the air made his denim shirt feel clammy against his skin.

The musty smell of stagnant water and stale air assaulted his nostrils. That could only mean there was no fresh air getting in.

"When's the last time you were in here?" Sam asked.

"Oh, about two weeks ago. No one's been doing any work here for awhile. After they mapped the tunnel system and realized there were no artifacts, there was really no reason to come back. I just wanted you to see it so you can compare it to the site in China."

"Did it have ventilation when you were here before?"

"Of course. There are several ventilation shafts leading out of the main room that you're about to see."

"Then why does it smell like this?"

George sniffed the air. "It does seem a little stuffy in here," he shrugged.

"How much further until we reach the main chamber?"

"That's it up ahead," he gestured to the shadowy opening twenty yards ahead of them.

Sam picked up his pace, but he already knew what he'd see. He'd learned at an early age to detect a "dead" cave, one with no fresh outside air getting into it. He would have died in one when he was eleven if one of his brothers hadn't secretly followed him. After that, he was always alert for the telltale signs of a poor air supply.

A moment later they stood inside the large cavern that George had referred to as the main room. The ceiling had collapsed into a massive heap of boulders, and no sign of the ventilation shafts could be seen.

"If you start feeling dizzy, we'll head back. But there should be enough air from the main entrance to let us look around for a few minutes." Sam headed directly for the pile of rubble in the center of the room.

"I knew I should have kept guards posted," George muttered.

"I don't think it would have done any good. They would have just been bribed or ended up dead," Sam knelt to examine a boulder. "This was definitely not a natural occurrence." He held up a mangled piece of detonator fuse.

"But there was nothing here."

"Maybe you just didn't know where to look. There must have been something here to take the trouble of sneaking in and blasting the place."

"If there was, I never saw it."

"Where did you find the partial disk?"

"Just outside the door. It was found with a few potsherds and jewelry."

"Someone dropped it there?" Sam smiled wryly as he echoed George's words.

"Probably. I used to think they had found it here in the tunnels, but I never found any more like it."

"Maybe there was another door like the one I found, but concealed in some way."

"But hundreds of people went through here for months and never found anything."

"They were just looking for *anything.* I think somebody knew exactly what they were looking for this time." Sam was frustrated at the devastation caused to the site by their unknown adversaries and kicked at a pile of rock.

"Well there's nothing we can do here now. Let's head to town and get some lunch before we catch our boat," George suggested.

"I swear all you ever think about it is your next meal, George. I-" A flash of silver had caught Sam's eye amid the rubble he had knocked loose. His heart pounded as he bent to look more closely at the object.

"What is it, Sam?" George came up behind him.
Sam turned to him with a satisfied grin on his face and pointed at the item he had found, "They missed something."

"It's wedged between these two rocks," George hunkered down to help him shift a small boulder.

With a little grunting and sweating, they managed to shove the rock off of the object Sam had seen. It looked similar to a metal cigarette case, about five inches square with one end open. There were markings along the edges and a something that looked like an abstract representation of a snake eating its own tail in the center.

George took it from Sam to get a closer look. "Hmm. Let me see the disk."

Sam took his disk out of his backpack and handed it to George who immediately fit it into the opening of the case. It slid inside with a small click and the open end sealed itself.

"Well, I guess it is," Sam commented. "I just hope we can get it back open."

"I'll figure it out when the time comes," George was turning the case over and examining it closely. "This metal must be incredibly strong. Maybe titanium or a composite of some kind."

“It looks similar to the metal that lined the room I discovered,” Sam noted.

“This is getting more interesting all the time. But we’d better get going before we miss our boat.”

“Or we pass out from lack of oxygen. I’m starting to get a little lightheaded.”

“I thought it was just the excitement,” George grinned as they headed for the exit.

7

Emily found the quietness of the lab somewhat eerie. So few people seemed to be working there. At the university there were almost too many people for the size of the facilities. There were two other people in the lab with her that afternoon. A man in his late fifties who was preparing gel plates for some aspect of Elliot's work, and a younger woman who was assisting him. Neither of them had done more than nod in her direction when she had entered the lab.

Even Elliot seemed to be leaving her alone, which made her uneasy for some reason. After stopping by first thing in the morning to make sure she had everything she needed, he disappeared into a room down the hall and didn't come out all morning.

Right before she left for lunch, she knocked on the door to let him know where she was going, and was somewhat annoyed that he didn't bother to answer.

She banged on the door a little louder and, not hearing anything from the other side, she tried the handle. It was locked and there was no passkey slot to open it. But there was a security camera mounted directly over the door that might have been connected to a monitor in Elliot's office or in security, or both. Maybe he saw her and just didn't want to be disturbed, though it seemed unlikely that he would be so rude as to not acknowledge her presence in some way.

Then again, maybe he had left earlier and she just hadn't seen him, Emily went ahead to lunch and decided not to worry about it.

When she returned from lunch, she saw Elliot leaving the lab.

"Elliot," she called to him before he got around the corner.

"Oh, hi Emily," he replied with a shy lopsided grin.

"I tried knocking on your door to let you know when I was going to lunch, but I guess you didn't hear me."

There was a blank look on his face for a moment as if he didn't know what she was talking about.

"Sorry," he finally answered, "Sometimes I get so wrapped up in my work that I wouldn't hear a bomb go off."

"Is there some way I can get in touch with you if I need something? A phone extension, maybe?"

"No, there's no phone in my lab."

Emily waited a moment for him to go on, but he just stood there looking like he forgot what he was doing.

"So, is there some other way I could contact you?" Emily could not believe how empty-headed Elliot seemed for a supposed genius.

"Um, not really. But I'll be out every now and then and any other of the researchers could help you."

"Okay, thanks," she replied and he darted off before she could say anything else.

That is a very strange little man, she thought as she watched him go through the security doors and leave the lab. He seemed like his mind was on another planet. And she thought it was odd that he wouldn't have a phone in his private lab. How could anyone reach him if something important came up?

She shrugged it off and forced all thoughts not having to do with the task at hand out of her mind and focused on getting as many samples prepared as possible. That morning she had isolated the section of DNA that she wanted to target and prepped the segments to be cloned.

By the time Emily returned to the lab she had a million copies to work with in her research. The process itself, known as polymerase chain reaction, or PCR for short, had been made possible by the discovery of a gene in heat-loving thermophilic bacteria that could help the DNA withstand the high temperatures needed to replicate it.

She hoped to complete the first round of her tests before the end of the week, though she felt she might be pushing things a bit. But she was impatient to get back to the point she had reached before her work at the university was stolen or destroyed. She had been so close to finding a cure that was both safe and highly effective and that could be easily adapted for the treatment of various diseases.

She was starting to set up the first step in her initial test when Elliot returned to the lab. He first went over to his assistant and took the gel plates he had prepared to receive samples. Emily expected him to go to one of the biosafety cabinets and begin working on loading the plates with the DNA samples.

But to her surprise he disappeared back into his office, taking the gel plates with him. She assumed he must have more equipment in his private lab than she thought. And that made her wonder just what he was working on that required such secrecy.

Once again she reminded herself that it was not her concern. She was there to finish her research and that was all. It didn't matter what Elliot was working on. She wasn't in competition with anyone at MorGen, they could do whatever they wanted and she didn't care.

She kept repeating versions of those statements in her head as she continued working, but she couldn't shake the feeling that more was going on in the labs than met the eye. Elliot was certainly acting strangely and she didn't trust Morgan or his dubious sidekick Lundgren.

"Is everything alright, Dr. Forrester?" Lundgren's voice startled her.

"What?" she spun around on her chair to find him leaning against a nearby doorway, arms crossed.

"You looked distraught."

"Oh, I'm fine. I was just concentrating, that's all." She quickly went back to her work.

"I'm glad to see you can stay so focused on your work. There are so many distractions around here," he smiled in an unnerving manner. "It's best to keep to your own business, I think."

"Yes," Emily agreed, sensing his double meaning, "I tend to have a one-track mind when I'm working."

"Good," he nodded and left the room.

If Lundgren was going to keep popping up like that unannounced, Emily thought her nerves would be shot before the end of the week. The man seemed to be everywhere, watching her every move. It made her worry that she wouldn't be able to keep her progress a secret as she had planned.

So far, her entire experience at MorGen had felt like an episode of the *Twilight Zone*. She expected Rod Serling to walk into the room at any moment and make a doomsday pronouncement about working in the lab.

Alright, Emily, she chided herself, *you're letting your imagination run away with you. Take a break and get some fresh air.*

Once she was outside in the warm light of day, she felt the tension ease out of her. She sat on one of the benches in the employee smoking area and took in the beauty of the afternoon. Birds singing in the trees, butterflies hovering over the flowerbeds, fluffy white clouds drifting by overhead. It almost made her forget she was in an industrial park.

Ten minutes later she felt rejuvenated and ready to get back to work. She stood and walked back towards the building.

"Excellent."

Lundgren's voice made her jump once again. Only this time he wasn't speaking to her. He didn't seem to know she was even there, sitting as he was on a bench on the other side of a large tree.

"When the train has reached its new destination, remove the package and have it sent directly to headquarters."

Emily didn't know what to make of that odd statement. She stood still and continued listening.

"It's your job to make sure they understand. And if they decide to have him arrested, that's all the better for us," he paused to listen to the person on the other end of the line. "I don't care what method you use. Just get it."

Emily quickly moved behind another tree so Lundgren wouldn't see her as he left. She didn't know what the conversation was about, but the tone of his voice made it clear it was something covert, and she knew he wouldn't be happy if he found her eavesdropping.

Once Lundgren was safely back in the building, she returned to the bench, filled with foreboding once again.

Chora, Patmos Island
Dodecanese Islands, Greece

The whitewashed walls of George's sixteenth century family mansion gleamed in the early morning sun and the terracotta tiles on the verandah were cool under Sam's feet as he stood admiring the view of the harbor. The strong coffee that George's wife Anna had brewed for him was invigorating after a good night's sleep in an overstuffed featherbed.

The scent of the bougainvilleas growing in the yard was carried on a light breeze and Sam could almost forget about the strange and sometimes dangerous events of the last few days. Almost, but not quite. As soon as they had arrived at George's house the night before, they had begun work on the artifacts.

"It may work like a puzzle box," George said, examining the markings on the sides of the metal case. "This symbol looks like this one on the opposite side," he ran his fingers over the two symbols.

There was a soft click and the case opened. George pulled out the disk and set it on the table.

Sam looked at him with a small amount of disgust that he had figured it out so easily.

"I'd really love to know what kind of material this is," George continued, looking over the case again. "To stand up to a shock like it did- it's incredible. And this design on the top matches the symbol on the inscription."

George put the case back on the table and looked at Sam intently. "How well do you remember your world mythology?"

"Some. But I don't think I could pass one of your exams on the subject."

"Serpents and dragons figure strongly in almost every culture's myths. They can be grouped into several categories."

Sam took a seat and poured himself another cup of coffee, knowing he was in for one of George's lectures.

"The first group is the water serpents. The Christian Leviathan, Jormungander of Norse myth, Tiamat, the Assyro-Babylonian mother goddess and Vasuki, the Hindu earthquake snake that churned the sea of creation. And the Dinka myth of Eastern Sudan, Abuk the first woman whose symbol was a snake. They were all there at the beginning. Then we have the snakes who stole immortality from mankind. The serpent of Eden, the very similar tale of Torongi and Edgi from Siberia has its snake as well. And, of course, Gilgamesh had the plant of immortality stolen from him by yet another serpent. Finally we have the medical snakes. The caduceus of Hermes, Moses' brass serpent and Australia has the great evil snake, Mindi, who sends disease as well as Taipan, who gave the gift of blood to man and is a great healer."

"Where does your own Lernaean Hydra fit into all of this?" Sam asked, hoping to get him off the subject.

"That would be the regeneration serpent. There are several other myths in that category, including Ouroboros which represents the never ending cycle of death and rebirth."

"Okay, okay! I get the idea. Mankind has always had a thing about snakes," Sam suddenly remembered something and dashed back inside to retrieve his backpack.

"I didn't get to tell you *why* mankind has always had a thing about snakes," George called after him.

Sam returned a moment later carrying the fragments of the map they had found in the cave.

"Look at this," he handed it to George.

"Ah! Nu Gua. Another creation myth. She molded men out of the yellow clay, and growing tired of making one at a time, ran a rope through some mud and shook off more men, thus making the upper and lower classes of China."

"So why would she be on a treasure map?"

"You found this in the cave?"

"Yes. A local farmer said his family had been searching for the treasure for generations. The original map is supposedly over a thousand years old and in a museum somewhere."

"I would be surprised if it still was," George asserted and handed the map back to Sam.

"What makes you say that?"

"Any clue to the location of these disks has disappeared or been destroyed."

"You think that's what the treasure was?"

"What else could it be? As I was saying before, mankind has always had a thing for snakes for a reason. And it's not the reason usually tossed about in psychology books," George paused and leaned forward in his chair, "Have you ever heard of the phrase 'genetic memory'?"

"Sure. Some people have theorized that common experiences of a species are incorporated into its genetic code causing a tendency to respond in a certain way to a certain stimuli."

"Exactly. I believe the snakes found in mythology stem from a genetic memory, but what does the snake actually represent? In almost all of the myths we have a few certain themes; creation, death, healing, immortality, regeneration--"

"All of them have to do with health basically."

"And what does the shape of the snake suggest to you? It's especially noticeable in the symbol of the caduceus."

"You've got to be kidding. You think ancient man knew about DNA and genetics?" Sam thought George had finally come up with a theory wilder than any of his own.

"I think *someone* ancient did. I believe they experimented with genetic engineering with disastrous results."

For once in his life, Sam Hunt was speechless.

They continued to argue over George's theory and stayed up half of the night tinkering with George's redesigned DVD player even though Sam was pretty sure it wouldn't work. First, they couldn't get the disk to sit properly in the tray. Then they kept getting various error messages telling them the disk was unreadable. They finally called it a night and decided to tackle the problem again in the morning.

While George was devouring his third helping of eggs at breakfast, he suggested they go see a friend of his who was even more of a techno geek than himself.

"He doesn't do anything illegal," George had said, "Well, at least that anyone knows about. But he's a pro."

"I really don't know if we should bring anyone else into this. It doesn't seem to be the safest project to be working on," Sam voiced his concerns.

"We'll just tell him that it's a disk a colleague sent to you from some new type of computer and that he didn't realize you didn't have a way to play it."

"Wouldn't he know if there was a new type of computer?"

"Probably, but he won't question us. He loves a challenge and won't care where the disk came from."

Sam wasn't completely comfortable with the idea, but it seemed to be their only option.

His thoughts were interrupted by Anna's arrival on the terrace. She was carrying a cordless phone in her hand.

"It's your colleague in China," she smiled at Sam, her warm brown eyes framed by lines of thousands of previous smiles.

"Thank you," he took the phone from her. "This is Sam.

"Sam, it's Zhen. We have a problem."

Sam's pulse quickened, "Not another cave-in?"

"No. It's the fossils. They're missing."

"Missing? Were they loaded onto the train?"

"Yes. But they didn't arrive at the Institute."

"Have they notified the police?"

"Yes. They've been interrogating people at every station between here and Beijing. But someone at the Institute seems to think we never put them on the train."

Sam thought he detected a suspicious note in Zhen's voice. "But you helped me load it into the truck and drove with me to the station."

"I told them that, but they didn't seem satisfied."

Zhen wouldn't come right out and say it, but Sam could tell he thought he had done something with the fossils.

"Look, there's something going on that I'm still looking into. But there have been discoveries made similar to ours that have disappeared or been destroyed as well."

There was a minute of silence at the other end of the line. Finally Zhen spoke. "I thought there may have been," he sounded relieved.

"Keep me posted on what's going on there."

"You do the same."

George wandered out onto the patio as Sam hung up the phone.

He noticed the look of consternation on Sam's face immediately.

"What happened?"

"The fossils are missing. The Institute seems to think I took them."

Sam related his conversation with Zhen.

"And what about the disk?"

"He didn't mention it. I'm sure he knows I've got it, though. I guess he thinks I took it to preserve the integrity of the site," Sam forced out that last phrase. He knew of colleagues who had removed certain objects from excavations that didn't match the supposed date of the site. It was unethical and unscholarly and it made Sam want to personally strangle anyone who did it.

They left the villa about fifteen minutes later and headed up the hillside on foot. Sam was about to ask George where they were going when he turned and headed towards the Monastery of St. John.

"Don't tell me your friend is a monk," Sam said jokingly.

"Oh, he's not anymore," George replied with a straight face, "He decided he'd rather get married and have a large family. But he still helps out down here every week, transferring a lot of their old documents into a database and computerizing their catalog."

"Wasn't the monastery built on the ruins of an ancient temple of Artemis?"

"Yes, unfortunately. And archeological methods were not very thorough in the eleventh century," George fumed. "Every time a new conqueror comes along, they always feel the need-"

"-to make everyone forget what came before them," Sam smiled as he finished the sentence he must have heard George say at least a hundred times in his classes over the years. It was one of his biggest complaints that so much history has been destroyed due to man's ego.

"I know I say it too often, but every time we disturb a site I can't help but think about what is being lost. We know so much more than the archeologists of a hundred years ago, but in another hundred the science will be even more advanced."

"It may be sooner than that. We already use a lot of remote sensing techniques. Maybe in a few years we'll be able to see everything that's buried under our feet without turning over one spade full of dirt."

"And with the extensive computerized catalogues most universities have now, we'll soon be out of a job," George joked.

The outer walls of the monastery were added to the structure later to protect it from invading pirates and made the place look more like a fortress from the outside. But once they came through the main gates, Sam was impressed with the elegant Byzantine construction. Arched doorways and elaborate stonework filled the courtyard. Large planters containing native Greek plants were dotted about the area, giving some life to the cold stone.

George said a few words to a monk who was seated near the gate, and they were led through one of the many arches to yet another courtyard, this one with a small chapel that looked as though it had been added on recently.

Upon entering the room, it turned out not to be a chapel at all, but a computer room attached to the existing library. Sam couldn't see anyone, but he could hear the clacking of a keyboard in use. They walked around a shelf full of glass encased manuscripts and came to a desk from which the noise was emanating.

A man in his late twenties sat at the keyboard and was transcribing from a sheet of parchment. He typed for a couple of more minutes before looking up. It was hard to believe he had ever been a monk. He looked more like a model with sun-bleached hair and chiseled features that had no doubt won the heart of his wife with ease.

"George! What brings you to the library today? Another bit of obscure research for one of your farfetched ideas?" the man teased.

"Indeed I have, Peter. But first let me introduce my friend and colleague, Sam Hunt," George presented him. "Sam, this is Peter Korais."

Sam shook hands with his new acquaintance, "George tells me you can help us with a little problem we've got."

"What sort of problem?" Peter asked eagerly.

"Well, we've got a disk that we can't get to operate on our regular system," Sam explained.

"It's from a new system Sam's university is trying out and he doesn't have the equipment with him to access it."

Peter looked at George with a raised eyebrow, but didn't say anything. "Do you have the disk with you?"

"Right here," George handed it to him.

Peter examined the disk for a moment then looked at George with wide eyes, "I've never seen one like this before. Is it a new HVD?"

"HVD?"

"Holographic Versatile Disc. It can hold thousands of times more information than a standard DVD," he looked at Sam suspiciously, "These aren't going to be available to the public until 2016. How did your university get it already?"

"They're helping with the research," Sam lied.

Peter obviously didn't believe him, but went along with the explanation. "It may take awhile to access the files. I don't have an HVD player handy at the moment," he turned the disk over in his hands. "This reminds me of something I read about recently."

"Oh?" George pretended he was mildly interested.

"One of the eleventh century manuscripts mentions an object that was found on the site when the monastery was under construction. It was probably just a mirror of some kind, but I thought it was odd that they wouldn't just call it that instead of describing it as a strange object."

"Would a copy of that manuscript be close at hand?" Sam asked.

"Sure," Peter hit a few keys and pulled up the catalog. "I just entered that one last week. There it is." He slid his chair back so George and Sam could get a better look at the screen.

A scan of the document appeared. The writing was faded but legible, some of it almost running off the sides of the paper where it had crumbled with age.

"My ancient Greek isn't as good as it used to be," Sam admitted, "Help me out here, George."

"It says 'Among the ruins of the heathen place of worship was found a strange object. It was small, the size of child's hand, round and flat like unleavened bread. It reflected the light of the sun like the surface of a still pool and could not be broken with the repeated blows of a mallet.'"

"Does it mention what they did with it?"

George scanned down the page, "Just that they cleared away all the junk they found and threw it with the rest of the construction debris."

"Then it could still be around somewhere. We'd just have to locate their garbage dump," Sam was intrigued by the idea of finding another disk, but knew their chances of actually locating it were slim.

"Sam, *please*. What makes you think I don't know where an archeological site is on my own island?" George looked offended.

Peter looked at the disk in his hand again, then back to his two visitors, "George, do you care to tell me what's really going on?"

"You wouldn't believe it. But if it ends up leading to a scientific breakthrough, you'll get full credit for the help you've given us," George assured him.

"It's not that I don't trust you, George. But I do have a family to take care of and it's hard to do that while you're in prison."

"Have I ever asked you to do anything illegal?" George put on his best innocent face

Peter frowned. "Alright. I'll see what I can do. There's been some digging outside the castle walls recently. I don't know if that has anything to do with the dump, but you could check with the monastery's historian. He talked to the men who were excavating there. I think he's in the library right now. I'll call you if I have any luck with the disk."

"Thanks, Peter," George clapped him on the shoulder and he and Sam headed for the library.

"This is unbelievable," Sam lowered his voice as they entered the library.

"Not really. I already knew there were over twenty in existence. So why not twenty thousand? That room you found may have contained that many alone."

George stopped a passing monk and asked where he could find the historian. They were directed to a table in the corner where an elderly monk with a white beard sat writing, surrounded by stacks of books.

"Excuse me, brother," George spoke in Greek to the monk.

He looked up at them in surprise.

"I'm sorry to disturb your work," George apologized.

"I do not mind. I tend to get lost in my books and forget that it is also a monk's duty to help his fellow man."

"You are most gracious, brother."

"Did you have a question on the history of our beautiful monastery, or one about St. John the Theologue?"

"Actually, I just wanted to ask you about the men who were digging outside the walls recently."

"There have been several asking about the ruins in the last few months."

Sam saw the concerned look on George's face and wondered what was going on. Sam took a few years of Spanish in high school, but languages were never his forte.

"Did any of them want to know where the dump was?"

"One man did. He said he was with the National Museum and they needed to secure the area because tourists were removing artifacts."

"Excuse me a moment while I speak to my colleague."

George turned and whispered to Sam. "I think they've already been here."

"Who? Your mysterious global conspiracy?"

"This is serious, Sam. The monk said a man from the National Museum needed to know where the dump was so he could secure it from looters. I'm on the field staff of the museum as a consultant and I didn't hear anything about it. If they were concerned, they would have called *me*."

"That is not good," the monk said in English.

"I should have known you speak English, brother," George apologized. "You are a learned man."

"That's quite alright," he brushed it aside, "But if that man was not with the museum, he was on our grounds illegally. I didn't ask for identification because his request did not interfere with the monastery at all. I am sorry if this has caused any problems."

"Hopefully it was just a regular antiquities dealer," Sam said to George and then turned to the monk. "Can you describe any of the men?"

"The workers doing the digging were local men, but the man in charge was European. German, maybe? I'm not very good with accents. He was as tall as you and was about my age. He wore his hair as long as a woman's."

George thanked the monk and he and Sam left the monastery. They walked around the outside wall to a large olive grove which they continued through until they reached an open area that was roped off and marked with stakes. A few trenches had been dug and piles of unsifted soil were all around the area.

"Those weren't here before," George noted with anger in his voice.

"We'd better see what damage has been done."

George climbed down into one of the pits and punctuated each of his findings with a curse. "This is abominable! If I find that long-haired German bastard, I'm going to kill him!"

"How bad is it?" Sam asked from where he was crouched next to one of the mounds of soil.

"It looks like they used ordinary shovels and just hacked their way through it. They were definitely looking for something specific."

"How would they know where to look?"

"Maybe they have some way to detect the disks that we don't know about."

"Or maybe it was just a dealer who isn't very skilled in excavation techniques."

George stood so his head and shoulders were just above the edge of the trench. "Why won't you accept the fact that something a little out of the ordinary is going on here. It was no accident that the fossils went missing and that cave collapse was not a natural occurrence."

"Okay, the disks are unusual to say the least. And someone does seem to be trying to keep them away from the public eye. But it's just hard to comprehend why someone would go to those lengths."

"You're right about that. We don't know why they're doing this yet, but we do know it's very important to them. Important enough to nearly kill you."

Sam couldn't argue with that.

"We'll have to assume they found what they were looking for. It would take years to excavate this site. That and the fact that we don't have the budget for it is why the museum hasn't bothered with it."

"Maybe they'll change their mind once you tell them about this."

"They just might."

Sam leaned over the edge of the pit to help George out. He almost had him over the rim when the ground beneath George's feet gave way.

He tumbled back down the slope, arms flailing. He hit the bottom of the trench and landed on his rear end.

It was only a few feet, so Sam wasn't going to ask him if he was okay. But the look on George's face made Sam wonder if he hadn't landed on an ancient spearhead.

"George?"

"Wow," George whispered.

Sam immediately jumped into the trench to see what was wrong.

Still sitting in the dirt, George pointed silently to the bank in front of him.

A ragged edged opening in the side of the trench had been uncovered by George's fall. It was about three feet in height and almost the same in width. It was obvious by the placement of stones around the base of the aperture that someone had attempted to conceal it. Sam figured George had stepped in just the right place for his weight to cause a collapse of the pile of rock.

"Interesting," Sam commented, "It looks like those stones were placed there recently."

"There must still be something here if they bothered to hide it," George's growing excitement was apparent in his voice.

"It's probably just a natural cave. There are plenty on the island."

George gave Sam a reproachful glare. "There's only one way to find out," he said and clambered through the hole on all fours before Sam could stop him.

As much as Sam enjoyed exploring caves, he was getting a little tired of constantly being in them. It seemed to him as though he hadn't spent one whole day in the last month without climbing around in the dark.

"You don't even have a flashlight," Sam called after him.

But Sam quickly saw he was wrong when George's face was illuminated by a small lamp.

"They apparently left in quite a hurry," George noted as he turned the flame on the gas lamp higher. "There are some tools here as well."

He pointed towards a pile of excavation gear on the floor next to him.

"Alright, then. Let's go," Sam acceded and followed George deeper into the cave.

They crawled for ten more yards down a slight incline and then the tunnel opened out into a larger room where they could easily stand up straight.

"We're on the same side of the mountain as the Cave of the Apocalypse. And I think we're heading in that general direction."

"You mean the cave where St. John had his vision?"

"Yes. That back entrance was probably open in his time. The castle construction most likely buried it."

"And it might have been recorded somewhere in the monastery records."

The room narrowed at the far end to become a tunnel again and began to slope sharply, so they had to lean backward to retain their balance. The corridor made a turn to the right and Sam bumped into George as he came to a sudden stop.

It was another chamber, about thirty feet square. Everything about it looked like a natural cave except for the perfectly smooth floor. And to Sam's dismay, there appeared to be an abandoned excavation in one corner.

"This reminds me of a spot back in the cave in China," Sam noted.

"Hmmm," George murmured, deep in thought.

His eyes roamed over every surface in the room, searching for something. Sam knew George had more experience with the island's history and legends, so he waited patiently for him to come to some conclusion about where they were.

"I wonder what this room was used for," George said finally.

Sam was somewhat disappointed with that remark.

"Let's look around for any signs of a recent visit," he suggested and began walking around the room, holding the lamp over his head.

Sam followed him since he had no light of his own and couldn't see more than ten feet beyond George.

There didn't seem to be anything else of interest, and Sam was about to tell George that when he saw a slight irregularity in the floor.

"Give me the lamp," he made it more of a demand than he meant to in his excitement.

"What is it?" George knelt down beside him as he began to examine the spot.

"There's a depression in the floor right here."

George looked at it from a different angle, "It looks like someone was digging here.

He reached out and brushed some of the loose stone away.

"It's about the size of a man if he were curled in a fetal position."

"A burial then?" Sam suggested.

"Probably. But we'll never know now. Damn them!"

George continued to sift through the rubble as Sam continued to look around the room for any more signs of excavation.

In the silence of the chamber, there were voices.

George looked up, wide-eyed and motioned Sam over.

At first, Sam couldn't tell from which direction the voices were coming. The wall next to them had a small crack in it that went from ceiling to floor. He looked carefully, his eyes trying to follow his ears. Finally, he saw three smaller cracks in the floor, where a small amount of light was leaking through.

They both strained to make out the words, but several feet of rock muted the voices.

"What in the world…" Sam whispered.

George motioned to him to keep quiet and then stepped away from the wall gesturing to him to follow.

Once they were on the far side of the room, George spoke in a whisper so low, Sam could hardly hear him.

"It's the Cave of the Apocalypse."

Sam didn't know much about Christian theology, but he did know the history of the cave. St. John was said to have heard the voice of Jesus through an opening in the ceiling of the cave. Now he understood why George wanted him to be quiet.

Sam gave George a questioning glance and George nodded in return.

They went back over to take a closer look, this time silently.

Besides the cracks in the corner, there were circular indentations carved at regular intervals on the floor, each about one inch deep. And the walls of the chamber were as smooth as the floor they now crouched upon for a closer look.

Sam couldn't recall seeing Greek architecture like this in his college textbooks. Since he had only a master's degree in archeology and hadn't done any fieldwork of that kind for years, he would wait for George's verdict once they left the cave. But Sam didn't think ancient Greeks or even the later Byzantine rulers of the island had built the structure.

After George was ready to go, he nodded to Sam and they made their way back to the cave entrance. It was more difficult climbing back up the incline and they slipped often, the exertion making them short of breath. But that wasn't what was keeping them silent as they made their way back to daylight.

They emerged from the cave into the trench. Both of them were covered in dirt and sweat.

Sam waited a moment for George to catch his breath.

"Well, what is it?" Sam asked finally.

"I don't know."

"Do you have a theory?"

Sam knew George would.

"Yes. It might have been a storage facility for more disks."

"What makes you say that?"

"I found this wedged into one of the cracks," he held up an unmistakable shiny fragment of a disk. "But it was cleaned out pretty well if this is all that was left. There may even have been a device for playing them."

Sam stared at George as the possible implications of that idea sunk in. He shook his head.

"What I don't get is why these disks would be stored in such inaccessible locations around the world. Are they top secret? Are they dangerous?"

"We won't know that until we can play the disk we've found."

After their disheartening discovery in the cave they had returned to Peter's workroom to see what he could make of the disk.

"This is going to take awhile," he announced as they entered the room.

"How long?" George asked as he sat heavily on the nearest available chair.

"If I put aside everything else I'm working on and concentrate on this alone, I might be able to pull it off in a month."

Sam and George stared, astonished, at one another.

"That's all?" Sam asked incredulously.

"Well, it could be longer if I have to build a drive from scratch to accommodate it. It's an unusual material, isn't it?" He held the disk up to the light.

George found his voice, "Now if we can just decipher the inscriptions that fast."

"What inscriptions?" Peter asked.

George quickly filled him in on the strange symbols they had found.

"So basically you have no idea what they are?" Peter got to the point.

"Not right now, but give me a few years and I might figure it out."

"This might be a good opportunity to test out a new program I've written. I designed it to analyze and translate unknown languages."

"That would be invaluable to scholars," George noted.

"You gave me the idea for it, George."

"How did I do that?"

"One of your many lectures on the necessity of further funding for Proto-Elamite language studies."

George's brow creased as he attempted to recall the conversation, "I must've been drinking."

Peter chuckled, "I think we both were. But that's what gave me the idea. I have it finished, but I need to run a couple of tests on it yet."

"Can you show me how to use it tomorrow night?"

"Only if Anna's cooking dinner," Peter joked.

"Alright," Sam pulled his thoughts together, "We're not really sure what any of this is, but we have a few ideas anyway. I can examine the anthropological evidence, you'll be working on the disk, and George can work on translating the inscriptions."

"And I think we should have someone look at those symbols that we thought looked like DNA or chemical structures," George suggested.

"Do you know anyone?"

"One name springs to mind," George smiled.

At first, Sam balked at the idea of contacting Emily Forester. But George convinced him that she was the best choice. Their relationship had ended years ago and they were different people now. Maybe they could at least be friends. And Emily *was* one of the most respected scientists in her field.

All of George's arguments won Sam over and he agreed to contact her to ask for her help after they returned to George's for dinner. He would fly back to the university the following day and arrange to meet with her to share the information he had copied from the caves.

Sam and George stopped by Peter's house to see if he had made any progress before making their way downtown to have a few drinks. Partly in celebration of their discovery and partly because Sam had a hard time composing his email to Emily. Anytime he thought about her too much, he ended up with an empty bottle of liquor in his hand.

Peter's wife answered the door. She was a petite woman, barely over five feet tall, with golden blonde hair and brown eyes that lit up as she greeted George.

"George!" She attempted to put her small arms around George's bulky midsection. "You never visit often enough! The boys have been wondering where their Uncle George has been."

"I'm sorry, Eleni. You know how Anna hates to let me out of the house," George laughed and kissed Eleni's forehead.

"Yes, I do," she stepped back and shook a finger at him, "She's afraid of the trouble you'll get into!"

"Eleni, this is my friend Sam," George introduced him at last.

Sam had been patiently waiting while George and Eleni exchanged their pleasantries and hated to admit to himself that he just wanted to say "hello" and "goodbye" and get to a bar. But he pushed aside his unreasonable frustration and greeted her warmly. He knew his feelings were only because of his agitated state of mind.

Eleni led them into the study, where Peter was looking over the disk once again, and then returned to the kitchen.

"I just started trying to evaluate the properties of the disk. It really is amazing," he turned quickly toward a candle that was burning on a nearby table and held the disk in the flame.

"Peter! Don't-" George darted across the room, but came to an abrupt stop as Peter held the disk up for him to examine.

George touched it gingerly and looked up in surprise, "It's not even warm!"

"But yet it seems to absorb light," Peter held the disk under the desk lamp for a moment then pulled the cord, leaving them in near darkness.

The disk glowed faintly, a greenish cast to the light, which faded in a few seconds.

Peter switched the light back on.

"This leads me to believe it may be a real holographic storage device," he announced casually.

The corners of George's mouth slowly spread into a broad grin, "This just gets better and better."

"I'll keep working on it and give you an update tomorrow when I bring you the translation program," he turned to Sam. "Eleni thinks you're really a spy and you stole the disk from a terrorist organization."

"How did she get that idea?"

"She works for the Greek Embassy in Izmir and reads too many espionage thrillers," he laughed. "She thinks everyone is a spy."

"That assumption may not be too far from the truth," George said seriously. "Don't talk to anyone else about the disk, not even Eleni. The less she knows the better."

"Is it really that important?"

"It could be the most important discovery modern man has ever made."

"Alright, George," Sam interrupted. "That's enough drama for one evening and I'm dying of thirst."

George looked like he was about to lecture Sam on the importance of not taking things so lightly, but the irritated expression on Sam's face made him reconsider.

Climbing back up the hill from the harbor was hard enough when you were sober, but in the state that Sam and George were in after several hours in Manisi's cocktail lounge it was taking them twice as long as normal. They were staggering home well after midnight in a steady drizzle of rain, accompanied by George singing a Greek folk song in a key not yet invented. They reached the street George's villa was on, and turned up the side alley.

They had only made it a few feet when George collapsed onto the ground. Sam thought for a moment that his friend had finally succumbed to one too many shots of sambuca, until he saw the shadowy form behind him raising a club to strike him down as well.

Though his reflexes were slowed by the alcohol, Sam still managed to get out of the way in time to avoid the first blow. He wasn't so lucky the next time, when their assailant hit him squarely in his sore shoulder.

Sam dropped to his knees, blinded by the pain. Luckily, George chose that moment to regain consciousness and reached out and grabbed the ankles of their unknown attacker. He went down, but not for long. He quickly regained his footing and kicked George in the stomach before he could rise. George grunted and curled up in a ball, writhing in pain.

Gritting his teeth against the throbbing in his arm, Sam stepped behind the man and attempted to wrestle the club from his hands. He had nearly wrenched it free when their attacker grasped Sam's arm and flipped him over his shoulder, landing him flat on his back. Sam gasped for air after having all of the wind knocked out of him.

George made another attempt to rise and received a fist directly to his jaw, once again knocking him out. The man hastily searched through George's pockets while Sam rolled to his feet and then lunged at the shadowy figure.

They rolled across the cobblestone street, each trying to get a firm grip on the other's throat. They came to rest in a gushing downspout, where the assailant proceeded to shove Sam's head under it and squeeze the life out of him.

He sputtered as the water filled his mouth and nose, and it took the last ounce of his strength to reach up and gouge a finger into the man's eye.

The satisfying sound of a painful grunt and the removal of hands from around his throat, told Sam his fingers had found their target. He struggled to rise, coughing and leaning against the side of the building while his adversary was doubled over in pain, hands covering his eyes.

Anger took over at that point and Sam took the opportunity to aim his fist at the man's head, connecting with a sharp crack and sending him to the ground in a heap.

"George," Sam called weakly. "George, are you okay?" He staggered over to his side.

George was still out cold so Sam crawled across the alley to him and lightly slapped his face a few times.

"George!"

Finally, he showed some signs of life and mumbled something.

"What?" Sam asked.

"Anna, the house…"

"Oh, shit!" Sam realized the house may have been ransacked as well, and Anna may have been hurt.

"Come on! Get up!" Sam urged George and he struggled to his feet.

They quickly stumbled off in the direction of the house, leaving their unknown attacker lying in the rain soaked street.

They made it to the house a few minutes later and were alarmed at what they saw.

The glass doors off of the verandah were smashed to pieces and the interior of the house looked as though an army of six year-olds had been left there unsupervised for a week.

"Anna!" George called as he searched frantically around the house.

Sam helped him to look, but there was no sign of her.

George sat at the large oak kitchen table with his head in his hands. He was in physical pain from his injuries, but that didn't compare to the pain he felt from the possibility of his wife being harmed because his actions.

"We don't know that she was hurt," Sam tried to relieve some of George's worries.

George remained silent.

"She may not have been here at all."

"I wasn't," Anna said from the doorway, her hands on her hips, "though it looks like I should have been. What kind of party were you two having while I was gone?"

George stood up, his eyes wide in astonishment and relief.

"I go to my sister's for a few hours and what happens?" she continued. "You and Sam throw a party for half the island."

"Anna," George rushed to her side and embraced her.

"Don't try to weasel out of this, George," she laughed as he showered her delicate features with kisses.

"We just got back a few minutes ago, Anna," Sam informed her.

Her smile changed to a look of confusion as she absorbed what Sam was saying.

"Then what...." she began. "You mean we've been robbed?"

"Yes, but thank God you're safe!" George was still holding on to her like she might be a figment of his imagination and would disappear if he let go.

"What did they take?" Anna extricated herself from her husband's arms, her deep brown eyes flashing with anger. "Did you see anyone leaving the house? I'll—"

"You'll sit down and have a cup of coffee while we sort this out," Sam guided her to the table.

Only after they were seated in the brightly lit kitchen did she take notice of the bumps and abrasions covering various portions of Sam and George's faces.

"You've been in a fight!"

"Calm down, we're okay," George reassured her.

"Let me get the first aid kit, anyway. And *I'll* make the coffee," she insisted.

Anna rarely got the opportunity to make use of her nursing skills since she left the Peace Corps after she met George. She had spent several years in South Africa, tending to the daily illnesses of the more remote tribes. Chance brought her into George's life when she happened to be nearby on a day he had fallen into an ancient Zulu well and broken his ankle.

Since there would be no easy way to transport him out of the mountains, George stayed with the family that Anna was living with that month. Over the weeks, they spent hours talking about their hopes and dreams and plans for the future. By the time George's ankle had healed, he proposed to her and they were married in Athens a few months later.

After she had put some ice on George's jaw, patched up their cuts and given them both some painkillers, they explained to her what had happened.

"You'd better call Peter and Eleni to make sure everything is okay there," Anna suggested.

"Good lord! I hadn't even thought of that!" George jumped out of his chair and grabbed the phone.

After George apologized for waking him up, Peter told him everything was fine and he had the disk right by him on the nightstand.

The next morning, Sam bid George and Anna farewell.

"Be careful, Sam," George warned him. "They'll probably think you still have the disk and follow you."

"You be careful, too. And let me know the minute you make any progress on the symbols."

"Say hello to Emily for me," George smiled.

Sam had nearly forgotten about his message to her. He didn't know if he wanted to bring her into something that was apparently going to be dangerous. Even though they had parted on bad terms, he still cared about her and wouldn't want her to come to any harm.

Those thoughts found their way into his dreams as he slept on his flight from Athens to London. And on his connecting flight to Newark he couldn't sleep at all as he tried to imagine the extent of the operations necessary to accomplish all that their unseen foes had done.

9

Emily was exhausted by the time she returned to the hotel, but she was still excited enough about the progress she had made that day and the prospects for the future of her research that she knew she wouldn't get to sleep for a few hours. So she decided to unwind by ordering a pizza and a bottle of wine from room service while watching a little television.

She had a television at her house, but she rarely turned it on. Reading was normally what she would do to relax in the evenings, but she had neglected to pack any books and hadn't visited the hotel gift shop to buy any yet.

After locating the remote control and flipping through about a hundred channels, she finally settled on a public television station that was showing an episode of Antiques Roadshow. At least she could get some ideas on what to look for on her next trip to the flea markets.

Her pizza arrived in the middle of an older woman nearly hyperventilating after finding out her grandma's vase was worth ten thousand dollars. She tipped the delivery boy and carried her guilty pleasures over to the table, setting the bottle of wine down next to her computer.

That reminded her that she should probably check her email, so after pouring a glass of wine she accessed her account.

Scrolling down the page, she was surprised to see an email from Sam Hunt.

Her heart stuttered as she clicked open the message. She hated that a part of her was excited that he was contacting her, but her more sensible side was wondering what the hell he wanted. She knew there was only one way to find out and clicked it open.

I didn't know how to reach you other than email. They told me at the university that you were going on leave for a few months to do research elsewhere. I'm hoping you get this message quickly. This is going to sound strange, but it's very important, believe me. George and I need some help on a little project we're working on. I was going to attach the info to this email, but it's incompatible. You have to see it in person. Please let me know how to contact you and I will meet you wherever is convenient for you.

Sam

Emily continued to stare at the screen after she had finished reading. It certainly wasn't anything she would have expected from Sam. She thought if he ever contacted her again, it would be either to apologize for his behavior all those years ago or to ask her out again. Or both. But this was odd. The last she knew, he was spending the season in China supervising a training excavation with some students. Not that she kept tabs on him or anything, someone just happened to mention it to her in passing.

She was very curious as to what this 'little project' was. She remembered George Baltazidis as the only one of Sam's teachers that actually liked him. Probably because George was also someone who challenged the establishment. But somehow George did it without offending people. Now Emily wondered what the two of them were up to.

What the hell, she decided, *maybe a professional meeting will make it easier to talk.* She typed a quick reply with the hotel name and her room number and sent it off.

Three slices of pizza later, she had finished her work and settled into bed for the night. Her last thought before falling asleep was whether Sam was making up his need for her help just to see her again.

"An interesting development," Morgan grinned broadly as he leaned back in his chair.

Harry Lundgren sat across from him typing into his laptop.

"When I tapped into her system, I was just making sure she wasn't going to keep any information from us on her research. This was very unexpected," he explained.

"Any idea who this person is?"

"Dr. Samuel Hunt. He's a museum curator at the university where Ms. Forrester was working."

"And why would he be asking for her help?"

"Maybe he has a specimen he wants analyzed."

Morgan mulled it over for a moment, "I suppose that's possible, they've gotten mitochondrial DNA out of sixty-thousand year-old bones before. But I'd rather not take any chances. I don't want any information leaking out of this facility."

That was one of Morgan' biggest concerns. He ran the MorGen labs almost like a maximum security prison. No employees could contact anyone on the outside without him knowing about it first. There were no visitors allowed beyond the front desk without advance permission and a full security screening.

He jealously guarded all of the secrets that had made MorGen the leading pharmaceuticals manufacturer in the United States and anyone caught discussing confidential company information with outsiders was immediately terminated. No former employees had ever been literally "terminated", but sometimes Lundgren meted out some form of punishment that Morgan felt was necessary under the circumstances.

"I'll find out where they're meeting," Lundgren volunteered.

"Good. I want a recording of the whole conversation. And I want you to show me how to access her computer from here. I'd like to be able to keep an eye on her myself."

"Of course. It's very simple. A little chip I installed in her computer the first day she was here does all the work. It can access and transmit all of the information on her hard drive. When she's online, it automatically downloads and sends her mail to our system. All you have to do is go into the security files and open the one named 'OpForester'. All of the work she's done here as well as everything she does on her personal computer will be there."

"Harry, you're amazing. Is there anything you can't do with a computer?"

"Well, I haven't figured out how to get it to cook my dinner yet, but I'm working on it."

Sliding her keycard through the electronic lock of the lab entrance, Emily stifled a yawn. She hadn't slept well, despite falling asleep so quickly the night before. She didn't know whether to blame it on too much pizza and wine or Sam's email. In any case, she certainly needed some coffee.

As if he had anticipated her needs, Elliott appeared carrying two mugs of coffee.

"Oh! Hi, Emily!" he greeted her. "You're here early."

"Am I?" she glanced at her watch noting that it was six a.m.

"Most of us don't come in until eight."

"How long have you been here?"

"All night," he admitted, "I end up staying here most nights. I just sleep on the sofa in my office."

Emily groaned inwardly, knowing that she would be spending a lot of time with Elliott if she worked her usual shifts.

"I was just going to see Mr. Morgan," he gestured with the two coffee mugs. "There's more coffee in the lunchroom, freshly brewed," he gave her his best friendly smile and headed out the door.

She made her way to the lunchroom and poured herself a cup of steaming hot black coffee. Just the aroma made her feel more awake. She sat at one of the long tables while she sipped her coffee and thought about the work she would be doing that day.

It would be impossible to keep her work completely secret, but she could be somewhat misleading about what she was planning. The first week or two she would be preparing her samples and they would have no idea what she would be using them for. She could easily tell them anything and they would believe her.

She finished off her first cup of coffee and went for a second.

"Ms. Forester?"

Emily turned to see Lundgren, enter the cafeteria.

His presence always made her uneasy. He was menacing in appearance, but always polite in manner. It just plain gave her the willies to be in the same room with him. After hearing his phone conversation the other day, she wondered if he wasn't involved with a criminal organization in some way.

"Yes, Mr. Lundgren?"

"Mr. Morgan would like to see you in his office for a meeting before you get started this morning."

"I'll be right there," she replied pleasantly. But inside she was fearful that Lundgren had told Morgan he was suspicious of her behavior.

After Lundgren had left the room she let out a small growl of frustration and finished pouring her second cup of coffee. Then she headed reluctantly to Morgan' office.

Even if it had nothing to do with Lundgren, she felt like Morgan was constantly demanding updates on her work. He thought she was some kind of miracle worker who could complete a two years' worth of work in a few days.

If he keeps interrupting me for meetings, I'll never get done, she grumbled silently to herself before putting on a fake smile to walk into his office.

"Good morning, Emily," he greeted her with a smile that looked like it had just been peeled off of a snake.

"Good morning, Dr. Morgan."

"Please, call me Louis. We're not formal around here."

His phony camaraderie made Emily half nauseous.

"Okay, Louis," she forced herself to be pleasant. *If he wants informal, he'll get it.* "What's up?" she asked nonchalantly and flopped into a chair opposite him. Emily was pleased to see his startled reaction to her behavior. He obviously didn't expect her to be so relaxed.

"Oh, I just wanted to see how you were settling in. Do you have everything you need?"

"I think so. Your equipment is much more advanced than what I'm used to working with."

She could see the compliment pleased him.

"Wonderful. Then it shouldn't take you nearly as long to complete your tests as it did before."

There was a definite change in his demeanor. His forced affability had given way to a quiet ferocity. Despite her attempt to remain composed, Emily was taken aback.

"I'm sure it will be much easier. But you never know what problems you might run into," she tried maintain her casual manner, but it came off sounding like she was giving excuses in advance.

"Well, just let me know if you do have any problems, and I'll see that they're taken care of immediately."

"Thank you, Louis."

"This is a very crucial stage in your research and I want everything to go smoothly for you. I've got high hopes for your success."

"I'll try not to let you down," she forced herself to say words she didn't really mean.

"And I also want you to let me know if anyone is keeping you from your work as well. Now and then people get a little too friendly while they're on the clock and keep dedicated workers like you from getting their jobs done."

He was starting to sound like her father lecturing her on not letting boys get in the way of her school work. She wasn't quite sure what he meant by that but assured him she'd let him know.

"Well then, I've kept you from your work long enough, Emily. Have a good day."

She left his office somewhat confused as to the purpose of the meeting and more than a little intimidated. Then she realized *that* was the reason for the meeting. He wanted to be sure she understood he was the boss and there would be no room for mistakes on her part.

It gave her an uneasy feeling to be working for someone as malevolent as Morgan, but it also made her angry that he thought he could intimidate her.

She returned to her work with a renewed energy and determination to outmaneuver Morgan and complete her research without him gaining one penny from it.

Sam's plane arrived on schedule in the early morning hours before the sun rose and he quickly found a cab to take him home. He was exhausted and just wanted to crawl into his own bed and forget about the last three weeks. But he knew he wouldn't get any more sleep at home than he did on the plane. Too many thoughts and concerns raced through his head for him to get any real rest.

The cab dropped him off at the front door of his small Cape Cod style home in a quiet neighborhood near the Middlesex Reservoir. The house wasn't as new as some in the area, but it was well built and comfortable. He had initially just rented the house, not knowing how long he'd stay at the university, but he bought it after only one year because he had grown to like it so much.

Sam unlocked the front door and dropped his luggage in the hallway, not worrying about unpacking since he hoped to leave as soon as possible to meet Emily. He walked down the hall, past the oak staircase that led to his bedroom and the master bath, and on into the kitchen to fix himself some coffee.

As he leaned against the counter, waiting for the coffeemaker to finish brewing, he ran the events of the last few days through his mind looking for any indication of who might be behind the attacks and the attempted theft of the disk.

His first thought was that a private collector might want the disks for their rarity, but he abandoned that line of reasoning because he had never known a collector to engage in such brutal tactics.

And then the old historian at the monastery had said the man who visited him was German or something close to it. A picture sprung to Sam's mind of a new Hitler, obsessed with tracking down ancient artifacts of power, and a chill ran down his spine.

A cup of hot coffee later and Sam had exhausted all possibilities. He didn't think any of them were anywhere near the truth of the matter and came to the decision that he wouldn't worry about who was trying to suppress the evidence, but he would just focus on unraveling the mystery of the disks.

One other decision he had made was to carry some protection.

He went to the safe in his office and removed the Glock 23 .40 caliber that he kept there. It was a gift to him from his father for receiving his doctorate. It was partially for a joke that his father had presented it to him. He often said Sam was always shooting his mouth off about everything. But it was also because his father was a retired Army colonel and had always wished that Sam had followed in his footsteps like his older brothers had.

Sam remembered the last time he had spoken with Tom, his brother who was closest to him in age, like it was yesterday. But it was over fifteen years since he had last seen him, right before his brother left for Kosovo to assist in the conflict there. He came home seven months later in a casket, a victim of one of the many landmines in the area where he was stationed.

His father had never really gotten over it. He acted like he was fine, proudly recalling his war stories and mentioning how he had lost his brave son in combat. But Sam knew every time he visited his father that he wished it was Tom walking in through the front door and not Sam.

He located a spare box of ammunition in the hall closet and loaded the two clips. Stuffing the rest of the box in a small duffle bag along with his holster and earplugs, he set out for the firing range at the university to brush up on his skills.

It was also one way he released some stress after a bad day at work. Though there hadn't been nearly as many of those since he had moved out from under Chisek's direct supervision. Just the rare occasions when his path would cross Emily's and he started feeling regrets over his past mistakes.

Thinking about her again reminded him that he needed to leave a message for her at her hotel and make a couple of other quick calls which he did before he headed out the door.

It only took the first two ten round clips for Sam to feel comfortable with handling the gun again. He continued shooting for another half an hour though, to get back to the accuracy he had perfected over the years of going to shooting tournaments with his father and brothers.

They were always trying to convince him he was a natural and would be an excellent army sharpshooter. Sam realized he did have a knack for hitting the center of the target, but he was more interested in winning medals to impress girls at school than using his skills to climb through the ranks of the military.

His confidence returned by the time he had emptied the entire box, not only in his shooting ability, but his confidence that he could take on whatever was thrown at him next.

As he left the firing range, he did feel a lack of confidence in one area. He wasn't sure how he'd handle actually sitting down and talking to Emily for the first time since they'd broken up. He silently cursed George for talking him into asking her for help.

He drove to the university next to see how much paperwork had piled up on his desk since he'd been gone. As he pulled into the museum parking lot, he thought he saw Chisek entering the building.

Not now, Sam sighed in frustration. He didn't have time to listen to Chisek gloat about his expedition being cut short.

He parked his car on the far end of the lot and made his way to the side door closest to his office, hoping to avoid Chisek on his way there. Edging his way around the corner of a display case full of early primate fossils, he looked down the adjoining hallway to his office door.

Chisek was standing there talking to Sam's secretary. Sam couldn't make out what they were saying, but his secretary was standing in the doorway with her arms crossed, shaking her head.

Good old Sophie, Sam smiled to himself, always by the book.

Sam was enjoying watching Sophie in action. Usually he was in his office while the grandmother of ten fended off annoying coworkers and fielded phone calls from overenthusiastic amateur anthropologists who swear they've found the missing link. And she would never let anyone interrupt his work if they didn't have an appointment.

And Chisek was one person that was never able to get an appointment. Since Sam had begun working in the museum, there was really no reason for Chisek to visit him on official business. They were under separate branches of the administration now and that somewhat made up for how much Sam missed teaching on a daily basis.

Chisek turned and started down the hall in Sam's direction. Sam quickly slid behind the display case, knowing he was being silly, but not caring.

Once Chisek was a safe distance away, Sam continued on to his office. Sophie was back at her desk in the reception area.

"Hi, Sam," she looked up from her work, smiling brightly at him, "How-- " A look of concern descended over her face as she took in Sam's various injuries. "Goodness, Sam! I knew there had been an accident of some kind at the dig, but they didn't say you were hit by a truck."

Sam laughed, "It's not as bad as it looks, Sophie. I'd be feeling worse if Chisek had been waiting for me here."

"Oh, it was no trouble getting rid of that cretin. I enjoy aggravating him," the look of concern was replaced with a devilish grin one rarely saw on a woman of sixty.

"Sophie, you're priceless," Sam leaned over the desk and kissed her on the forehead. "Now, what's been going on while I was away?"

"Dr. Kreiger left a message concerning the annual Anthro Society's dinner, Dr. Greevy from the Smithsonian needs you to call her back about your request for the loan of a fossil collection, and Dr. Prince called from Harvard and wanted to know when you would be returning his golf clubs. And you have some mail on your desk that I wasn't sure how to answer."

"Thanks, Sophie," He headed towards his office door. "What did Chisek want anyway?"

"He said something about being concerned about your well-being. He wasn't making much sense, as usual."

Sam grunted his agreement and went through the door into his office.

The room was its usual mess with files piled on top of the filing cabinet instead of in it, books stacked on the floor, and cases of fossils that had yet to be classified shoved in the corner. There was some dust here and there and the single overhead light did little to expel the gloomy feel of the space. Only his desk was clean except for the stack of envelopes neatly placed in the center.

He sorted through the pile looking at return addresses. Most of them were from colleagues, but on the bottom of the pile was a brown envelope with no addresses at all, return or sender. Sam felt it and it seemed as thought there was nothing inside. It was sealed and had no identifying marks on it whatsoever. He opened the envelope carefully, so as not to damage anything that might be inside.

He spread it open and saw that there was a single slip of paper, similar to an index card, lying inside the envelope. There was also a photograph of what looked like the interior of a cave. Sam looked at it closely and determined it wasn't any of the caves he had visited in the last several days.

The writing on the note card startled him. It was the same type as found in the caves and on the disk.

Weird didn't even begin to describe what Sam thought of it. He ran through the list of people who knew about the disk that he was aware of. George wouldn't have sent this to him at his office in the museum without telling him about it. And he didn't think Peter would have been able to send him any more information that quickly.

Maybe it was the German who had been excavating at the monastery or the man who had attacked them in the alley, which could have been the same person for all he knew. But why would they send him more information when they had tried to steal the disk?

There were too many "maybes" floating around for Sam's pleasure. He went back out to Sophie's desk carrying the envelope.

"Sophie, did this come in the mail with the rest of the letters?"

He showed her the envelope.

"I don't recognize it. I'm pretty sure all of the letters I put on your desk were in white envelopes."

Sam was getting a little worried, thinking someone may have broken into his office. He wondered if he should call George and let him know about the note.

Whoever had sent it, he was sure he would probably hear from them again and decided to email it to George later. He tucked the rest of the mail under his arm and bid Sophie farewell.

He had a date in Harrisburg, Pennsylvania that he definitely didn't want to miss.

The sun was setting over the trees behind George's house when he finally saw Peter walking up the path from the monastery.

"It's about time!" George called to him.

"I got away as soon as I could," Peter explained as he mounted the steps from the side garden. "The monks may look harmless on the outside, but they're merciless slave drivers," he joked.

"Did you bring the program you were telling me about?"

"I've got it right here," he waved a disk in front of George's face.

George reached for it but Peter quickly pulled it away.

"Not until I have one of your special cocktails in my hand," he reminded him.

George smiled and walked over to the table set out on the verandah. It was loaded with fruits, bread and cheese with two glasses sitting next to a frosty pitcher full of a peach colored liquid.

He poured a glass for each of them and they toasted to one another's health.

"Ahhh. Delicious!" Peter complimented George's brew.

"Thank you. It's my personal cure for whatever ails you."

"It must work, your bruises are fading," Peter noted.

"Yes, and I hope to not receive any new ones. Though I might give you a few if you don't let me see this how wonderful program works."

Peter took another sip of his drink, "Do you have your laptop handy?"

"Right here," George lifted it off of the seat next to him and cleared a spot on the table for it. "Any progress on the disk yet?"

"I ran a few more tests and I'm sure it's holographic storage. I ordered some new equipment that should help me access it."

George's face brightened, "A laser?"

"A small one, among other things." Peter raised his hand to cut George off before he started to speak. "And no, I don't need any help putting it together. I heard about what happened when you were experimenting with your own a few years ago."

"He burned a hole through my new oven and nearly caught the neighbors house on fire," Anna laughed as she brought out another tray of food to replace the one George had already emptied.

George tried to look innocent, "It wasn't that bad."

"Okay," Peter set his drink down and loaded the disk into the computer. "Basically what this program does is to compare the symbol placement to the structure of all known languages, looking for any similarities. That's basically what you're doing only the computer can do it much faster."

"But can it make assumptions based on how closely related they are?"

"It takes into consideration the exact percentage of similar arrangements to make its decisions. And within the text itself it examines the number and placement of repeated symbols and the individual differences between each symbol."

"Wow. And you wrote this yourself?"

"I got a little inspiration from a friend now and then," Peter smiled and pointed upwards.

"And how quickly can we get some results?"

"It depends on how complex and unique the language is. For example, if it seems to be structured along the lines of a language currently in use, we could have part of the translation done by tomorrow. But if it has nothing in common with modern dialects, it could be months. Either way, a human brain has to guide the program. Computers don't have intuition to help them make decisions."

"Well, let's get started!"

They stayed up until the early hours of the morning, entering information into the program from the inscriptions. They were finally ready to begin the first run through at about three A.M.

"You can take it from here, George," Peter stretched and yawned. "I've got to get home to my wife before she makes me sleep outside with the dog."

"Okay, goodnight," George replied without looking up from the computer. He was already engrossed in watching the comparisons the program was making with the first of many written languages.

It constantly amazed him just how much could be done with this incredible technology. When he was a boy, it was rare for a family to have a television set or even a radio on the island, which had only recently gotten widespread electric service. But his parents had been lucky enough in business to afford these modern luxuries and George grew up in a house with all the latest gadgets. He was one of the first people on the island to own a microwave oven, a VCR, or a personal computer. Now everyone knew him as the man whose entire villa was rigged up with every electronic device available to the public, and even some that weren't that he got through his academic contacts or made himself.

The amount of information they had from the two inscriptions gave the program a lot to work with, but George knew that if they had more, it would go even faster. He had previously had extraordinary luck in tracking down several of the discs.

The first partial disk had been recovered in Peru, and was found by a friend of his at the University of Cuzco on a dig just outside the city. After being taken back to the museum there, it was properly cataloged and stored for later examination. One phone call had George promptly packing up his things to fly to Peru, much to the exasperation of Anna.

He was amazed when told where it had been found, in a cave that had been ritually sealed and hadn't been opened since before the Spanish conquistadors arrived. He examined the disk and was puzzled as to its origins, which was what made him start looking for other disks.

After a few months, he was surprised to find ten more, and they kept turning up.

But when he contacted his colleague in Peru again to tell him about his discovery, he was shocked to learn that the disk had been loaned out and never returned. The description given by the assistant curator of the man who had taken the disk was so vague as to be completely useless. He said the man's university ID seemed to be genuine and he had a signed form from the curator giving him permission to remove the disk for research. George had done a little digging into the background of the person who had supposedly "borrowed" the disk and came up with nothing but counterfeit credentials.

And as he discovered all of the disks disappearing at every museum and university around the world, he knew there was one person or group behind it all. The one connecting clue was the fake name used to sign out all of the disks.

The only museum he hadn't yet checked with was in Philadelphia, Pennsylvania. They had made the most recent find before Sam's and, assuming the disk had been stolen like the rest, it would have happened relatively recently and the incident would be fresh in the minds of those connected with it.

George tore himself away from the progress of the linguistics program with that thought and called Sam.

Sam was cruising west along the Pennsylvania Turnpike just past the exit for Lancaster at about six in the evening when his cell phone rang. He picked up the phone as he pulled over into a rest stop.

"Hi Sam, it's George."

"Isn't it past your bedtime over there?"

"When isn't it? Listen, I never got a chance to ask about the disk they have at the University of Pennsylvania's museum. Could you stop by there on your way to see Emily?"

"Too late. I already went past it. But I'll stop on my way back."

"Great. Get as much of a description as you can of the person that took the disk."

"I thought you said you hadn't talked to them about it? How do you know the disk was taken?"

"Why wouldn't it be? All the rest are gone. Why would they leave any behind?"

"Alright, alright! I'll go see what happened to it. Anything in particular I should watch for?" Sam asked while digging in his pocket for change for the soda machine.

"They were all signed out under the name Dr. A. Adama," George told him.

"Dr. A. Adama? That's an odd name," Sam commented.

"It's obviously an alias. And he usually has realistic looking counterfeit ID for whatever university he's visiting."

"Any description?"

"None that are any help," George replied, "He must have a very forgettable face."

"I'll look into it tomorrow morning."

"Tomorrow morning? Planning on staying in Harrisburg tonight?"

Sam could almost see the sly grin on George's face that would have accompanied the tone of his last comment.

"No, George. I'll probably stay at a friend's house in Philly."

"Now why would you do that? I'm sure Emily would like you to stay."

"That's quite enough, George," he retrieved his soda and turned to exit the building. "I'll call you tomorrow and let you know what I find out."

10

Lunchtime was a welcome reprieve from the sterile atmosphere of the lab. Emily did enjoy working in that kind of environment, but a sunny afternoon in spring made everything seem right with the world. But her reasons for eating her lunch outside that day weren't solely because of the weather. She needed to check her messages and her cell phone couldn't get a signal inside the building. She could have used a phone inside, but her concerns about Morgan and his need to control her made her decide to be more cautious.

She spread out her lunch on the bench beside her while she dialed up her voice mail at the hotel.

"Hi, Em, it's Sam" his message began, "I'm glad you got back to me. I'll be in Harrisburg by eight o'clock tonight. I called the hotel restaurant and made reservations for eight-thirty. I'll see you then."

Emily was surprised that Sam had arranged a meeting place for them already. He used to be so disorganized when she knew him in college. People usually do change as the years go by, but she thought living life by the seat of his pants was a character trait that Sam would never give up. Of course, the whole idea of a secret meeting about some strange project that he was working on was just like him.

She finished her lunch and headed back inside to continue preparing samples for her next series of tests, unaware that Lundgren had been taking that time to learn her voicemail access code. It was the last piece of her life that he hadn't yet intruded into. Simply by using a high-powered telescope from his office window and watching what numbers she punched in, he gained access to the message Sam had left.

Harry called Morgan to let him know.

"I'll make a reservation for eight-thirty as well and show up a little late. That way I can see where they're seated and request a good spot."

"Don't miss a word of it, Harry. I just know she's up to something. Dr. Hunt could be a go-between for the university. If they want to keep tabs on Emily's work while she's using MorGen's labs, they'll soon find out what a mistake they've made. I'll see to it their funding is pulled."

"I'll get everything on tape for you."

"Thank you, Harry. And enjoy your dinner. I hear that restaurant does a great Chicken Kiev," Morgan recommended.

"The Chicken Kiev is our specialty," the waiter responded to Emily's question.

"Then that's what I'll have," she said.

"Me, too," Sam added.

They sat at a booth on the lower level of the restaurant, surrounded by potted plants and distressed leather. The candle on the table added a romantic ambiance and the soft jazz music in the background emphasized the mood.

"Nice place," Sam noted, looking around.

"It's okay."

They sat in awkward silence for a moment. Sam continued admiring the décor while Emily toyed with her napkin and surreptitiously looked Sam over.

She noted the fading scrapes and bruises on his face, and the way he held his left arm close to his body. She wondered how he had hurt himself, but decided against asking. He'd tell her if he wanted to.

"So what's the big project you're working on?" Emily started the conversation.

Sam looked at her and smiled in his typical rakish manner, "It's kind of hard to explain the whole thing, but I have a favor I'd like to ask of you."

"And that is?" she always hated drawing information out of Sam. It was one of the things that made her break up with him years ago. He would talk a blue streak if their friends were around, but as soon as he was alone with her he'd hardly say more than three words unless they were arguing about something.

"I came across some information during an excavation in China and George had seen something similar in his work. We wondered if you could take a look at it for us and tell us if it makes any sense to you."

"So it has to do with genetics?"

"We think so."

"Do you have a sample for me to analyze or something? I always wanted the opportunity of extracting DNA from ancient bones," Emily actually felt herself growing interested in what Sam was doing for once in her life. She didn't know whether it was because she wanted to be interested in him, or because she was now settled in her career and could pay attention to someone else's.

"No, but I scanned the inscriptions onto a disk for you," he pulled it out of his briefcase.

"Inscriptions?" As interested as she was, she was also getting impatient with Sam's hesitating manner.

"Like I said, it's kind of hard to explain--"

Sam stopped in mid-sentence as the waiter arrived with their salads and dinner rolls. He looked around the room again and thanked the waiter as he left.

Emily was getting suspicious of Sam's behavior. He was acting like he was afraid of being spied on or that he was waiting for someone.

"What's going on, Sam? Tell me the truth or I'm not helping," she leaned back in her seat and crossed her arms over her chest like a child refusing to eat her vegetables.

"Okay. Just listen carefully and don't interrupt me with any questions until I'm done. And don't jump to the conclusion that I've finally gone insane either."

He proceeded to relate to her everything that had happened since he found the strange disk in China. Emily could tell he was leaving some things out, she always knew when he was lying, but she just sat quietly and listened to his story.

Sitting at a table about twenty feet away on the next level, was Harry Lundgren. He had arrived five minutes after Sam and had watched where the waiter took him to meet with Emily. Harry then requested a table far enough away that Emily wouldn't notice him but in a direct line so he could make use of the directional microphone he had brought along to listen in on their conversation.

It was cleverly concealed in his umbrella and the digital recorder he carried hooked directly into it. Had the evening spring shower not popped up, he would have used the cane he had also made with a built in microphone, and affected a slight limp.

With the umbrella resting on the seat next to him, the microphone pointed in the direction of Sam and Emily's table, he listened to their conversation on the stereo headphones. To all the other diners in the restaurant, he looked like a businessman enjoying a salad while he listened to some music.

Emily was trying as hard as she could to hold back judgment on what Sam was saying. But it was too farfetched. He might as well have said aliens landed and gave him the disk.

She could tell Sam knew what she was thinking. She made no attempt to hide the expression of disbelief on her face.

"And Peter is trying to access the disk," he concluded his narrative. He noted Emily's expression, "I told you it sounded strange."

"Strange isn't the word for it."

"But will you look at the inscription for me?"

"I suppose so. It can't hurt."

"But it could, Emily. I'm not making this up. We were attacked in Greece and I was nearly blown up in China."

"The explosion could have been an accident, and that could have just been a run-of-the-mill mugging."

"Tell that to George. He was beaten worse than I was."

Emily didn't know what to think. "Okay, I'll look at it, but I'm not promising anything. And if this is some kind of joke, I'll definitely never speak to you again."

"It's no joke, Em. And thank you for taking the time to see me," Sam smiled.

"It was no trouble," she replied. "It was nice to see you again."

"I have to admit, I thought you'd tell me to get lost."

"I considered it," she laughed.

She found herself not wanting their meal to be over, but was consoled by the fact that she would see him again as they worked on discovering the meaning of the strange writing.

"I'll look these over tonight and I'll let you know if I think I can do anything with them .I'll email you as soon as I know," Emily stood and picked up her purse.

"I'll be staying in Philadelphia tonight. I wanted to look at some files at the University of Pennsylvania tomorrow and see if I can track down some more information on the disks. One of them was in their possession until they all disappeared."

"Well, good luck. I'll contact you soon," Emily didn't know whether to hug him or just shake hands, so she went with the safer of the two options. She could tell he was disappointed and that made her feel a little smug.

But as she left the restaurant, the smugness faded and a strange feeling she had thought she had left behind years ago started to return.

After Sam had paid the bill and left, Lundgren gathered up his things and made his exit as well, having successfully recorded their conversation without their knowledge.

He smiled to himself as he drove away from the hotel. Things were going even better than if he had planned them himself.

By the next day Emily had barely looked at the information on the disk because Morgan had been giving her extra work since the morning after her meeting with Sam.

After dinner that night, she had gotten ready for bed and then popped the disk into her computer. When she first opened the file, she thought she had accidentally pulled up one of her test papers from the university. The symbols were so similar to the diagrams of amino acids and DNA structures that she immediately understood why Sam had wanted her to look at it. But he had to be joking when he said they came from a cave in China.

She stifled a yawn and decided to look at the file again the following day after work.

But after she completed her usual day's work, Morgan had more for her to do. He wanted a more detailed analysis of her testing methods, so she was forced to stay until well past eleven that night working with Elliot. Once she got back to the hotel, all she wanted to do was go to bed, but she was too intrigued by what she had seen that afternoon and instead stayed up one more hour to work on it.

The first row of symbols seemed to be very basic designs of circles and dots.

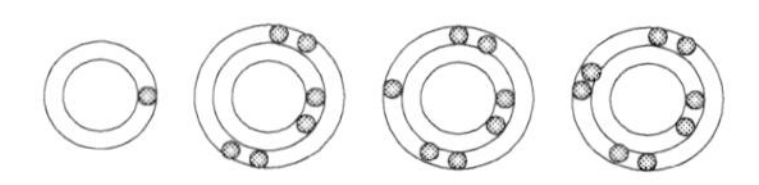

They could mean almost anything, but she felt there was something familiar about the group of symbols. She stared sleepily at them a moment longer before she had it. They looked just like atomic diagrams for hydrogen, carbon, nitrogen and oxygen, the basic elements of organic compounds. That made sense considering the next series of drawings resembled the structures of the amino acids that made up DNA, the double helix itself being the last image in the first column. She started to get the feeling she was looking at a genetics primer. The next column looked like a picture of all the human chromosomes neatly lined up in their pairs. The final column had nothing recognizable in it at all. Emily guessed it might be Arabic or some form of Chinese, but she wasn't exactly a linguistics expert.

But she did recognize the very last design in the inscription and it had kept her from a good night's sleep.

Now she couldn't stop thinking about what she had discovered and was distracted all day wondering where the inscriptions came from. She had considered calling Sam last night, but it was nearly three in the morning and she assumed he'd be asleep. She also wanted to look into it a little more before she told him about it.

And it didn't escape Morgan's attention that Emily was distracted by something. And he knew what that something was.

Harry had come to him the morning after her meeting with Sam Hunt and gave him the recording of their conversation. Then, later that day, Harry had shown him the information from the file that Emily had loaded into her computer. She had loaded it onto her hard drive for easy access which made it that much easier for Lundgren to find it.

"I think we need to see all of this," Morgan said. "There may be something of importance here."

"Or it could be a lesson plan for the university," Harry suggested.

Morgan sighed and looked at him with annoyance in his eyes, "Just get it, Harry."

Sam had been working in the University of Pennsylvania's Museum of Archeology and Anthropology since early morning following his meeting with Emily, going through their records of the disk fragments they once held. Upon arriving at the museum, he went to the archives office to see if anyone could tell him about the missing disks.

The archives office was on the lower floor and Sam remembered it from previous visits as a cluttered room filled with filing cabinets and an old man behind a desk with a logbook for signing in and out of the archives.

When he finally reached the room, he found a man behind a desk, but he wasn't old and he wasn't holding a big book. He was busily typing away on a computer and didn't look up as Sam entered.

Sam looked around the room, noticing the filing cabinets no longer filled the walls. The room was sparsely furnished and quite clean and brightly lit. The man at the computer continued to type, and as he walked closer, Sam could see he was transferring files from paper to disk.

Sam cleared his throat, "Excuse me, are you the archives registrar?"

The man looked up, startled, "I might be, what do you want?"

This was hardly the behavior Sam expected. "I just wanted to ask you about some artifacts that disappeared recently."

"Are you a cop?" the man eyed him suspiciously.

"No, an anthropologist. Sam Hunt with Thompson State University," Sam put out his hand as he introduced himself.

"Thompson State? I graduated from there!" The man stood up and shook Sam's hand, smiling now. "You're a professor there, right?"

"Was. Now I'm the curator of the paleoanthropology wing at the museum."

"I tried to get into one of your classes three times, but I could never get out of bed early enough to get there in time. It was like trying to get tickets for a Phish concert!"

Sam smiled at being compared to a rock band. He missed the excitement of the students as they filed in for the first day of class. It was almost like being on stage.

"You've done well for yourself since graduation," Sam noted. "You must have had some good references to get this position."

"Not really, but my minor was in computers. They've been transferring all the archive records onto disks and needed someone who knew his way around a mainframe."

"It seems like everyone is transferring paper documents into computers these days."

"It's so much easier to access them. Just a couple of buttons instead of digging through filing cabinets," the young man said with obvious pride. "What can I do for you today Dr. Hunt?"

"Well, like I said, I'm looking for information on some artifacts that have apparently been loaned out and never returned."

"I think I remember something about that," he sat at his computer again and typed in a few commands. "Was it just recently?"

"A few months ago at the most."

"And what was taken?"

"It was four unidentified fragments of a shiny material similar to mica or mother-of-pearl."

"When were they found?"

"1989."

"Got it! They were signed out by a Dr. A. Adama of Yale University about two months ago. The museum attempted to contact him after four weeks and Yale said they'd never heard of the guy."

"Who was here when he signed in?"

"I know it wasn't me so it must have been poor Dr. Hazlett."

"Poor Dr. Hazlett?" Sam didn't like the sound of that.

"Yeah. He was the old guy that had been the registrar here in the days before computers. He was helping me find everything so I could enter it into the system. He had a heart attack two weeks ago and died."

"I remember him," Sam found it hard to believe Dr. Hazlett would have had a heart attack. As he recalled him, Hazlett was a health nut and went for walks everyday and never ate fatty foods. He would have been almost seventy when he died, but he was as fit as a forty year old.

"It's been hard to finish this without him hanging over my shoulder, making sure I didn't miss one word in the transfer."

"Is there anymore information on the artifacts?"

"Yeah, you can use that terminal over there to access the original registry when they were cataloged," he pointed at a computer on a nearby desk.

"Thanks. I'm sorry to hear about Dr. Hazlett. He was always a great help around here."

Sam sat down at the computer and got to work. He didn't have too much trouble finding what he needed, and after a few minutes he had located the files recording the finding of the fragments. Back in 1989, their excavation team had discovered three small pieces of a disk beneath an Acheulian ax, a teardrop-shaped tool used by Homo erectus. The archeologists didn't know what to make of it. Some of them thought it was mother of pearl; others thought it was some kind of polished mica. But none of them went out on a limb to say that it was actually a manmade object, contemporary with, or even pre-dating, the ax.

Next he found a photo of the pieces laid out with the axe with their catalogue numbers written on tiny squares of paper next to them. He was surprised to see a photo still remained when the objects themselves had disappeared. But then again, the poor quality of the film made any kind of identification from the photo nearly impossible. Sam noted the numbers to see if he could at least locate the axe or other items from that area of the dig. It was a slim chance that there would be any clues, but it was worth a shot.

If it weren't for the fact that Sam was a museum curator, he wouldn't have been allowed to look for the artifacts himself, but a current intern would find them and bring them to an examining table.

As he wandered through the rows of tall shelves, filled with drawers of fossils, potsherds and ancient tools looking for the axe, he thought about the last few emails he and George had traded.

George was making some progress on the basic structure of the strange glyphs, but he thought it was going to take a while even with the new program and the additional inscription Sam had sent to him.

And Sam reported that Emily was going to help them and she would get back to him in a few days. Meanwhile, he would see what he could find out at the University of Pennsylvania.

He rounded the corner of the row that should have the axe and related objects and was startled to see someone else standing there with the drawer pulled out, examining the axe.

Their back was to Sam and in the dim light he wasn't sure who it was at first.

"Hello," Sam ventured a greeting.

The person turned and Sam was more than surprised to see his former department head, Dr. Robert Chisek standing there with a smirk on his face.

"Hello there, Sam," he returned the greeting, but in a not very friendly manner. "What brings you here?"

"Apparently the same thing that you came for."

"What a coincidence," his expression made it clear it was not chance that had brought them together in that place.

"Yes, it is," Sam's mind was racing, trying to figure out if Chisek was trying to one-up him again professionally and had somehow found out about the disks, or if something more sinister was going on.

"I was just wondering where you had gotten to," Chisek began, "You should have been back at our museum yesterday."

"I had to make a little side trip to compare notes on something," Sam explained vaguely.

"Ah. Something rare?" Chisek was fishing for clues.

"Not really, quite a few have been found in a lot of different places. I was just trying to be as accurate as possible in my report. I know how important that is for the image of the university."

Sam was using one of Chisek's favorite phrases. He was always concerned with impressing his peers at other universities with the painstaking attention paid to every detail of their collections. Even though Chisek's role at the museum was minimal, he was more directly in charge of the professors than the curators, he liked to take some credit for how prominent the museum had become in academic research.

"I'm glad to hear you're finally taking some pride in your work," Chisek observed.

"So what brings you here? I didn't know you were working on anything right now."

"Oh, I always have something in the works," his attempt to be casual failed and Sam knew he was definitely up to something.

"Mind telling me a bit about it? I'm always interested to learn the views of a more experienced scholar," Sam figured he probably wouldn't go for the bait to his ego, but at the very least it might run him off.

"I really don't have time right now," Chisek quickly replied and glanced at his watch.

"How about if I catch up with you at your office tomorrow then?" Sam offered.

"You'll have to arrange that with my secretary," he lied, "I've got all kinds of meetings going on this week and I couldn't tell you when I'll be free."

"What a shame. I really wanted to hear about your theories on the missing artifacts," Sam threw that comment out as casually as if he was remarking on the weather, but he watched Chisek closely for any signs that he might know what Sam was talking about.

"Missing artifacts?" If Chisek wasn't truly puzzled, he was doing a good impersonation of it.

"Nothing major, just a couple of pieces that were discovered on the same site as these," Sam gestured to the tray pulled out in front of Chisek.

"Some museums just aren't well organized," he snorted contemptuously, falling back into his usual self-important demeanor. "They probably just misplaced them."

"Probably," Sam agreed.

Chisek excused himself before Sam could ask him any further questions. He was glad to see him go and wished he had never let the museum know where he'd be today. Chisek surely harassed them until they told him where to find Sam.

But Sam was perplexed as to why he would go to all the trouble of driving to Philadelphia to spy on him, and how he managed to be right where Sam was doing his research.

He shrugged and tried to brush it off as overzealous micromanaging on Chisek's part and too much paranoia on his. But as he began to examine the axe and other items found near it, he couldn't shake the feeling that there was one more thing going on that he knew nothing about.

He pulled the whole tray out and carried it to the nearest table. After gently setting it down, he pulled out his cell phone and called George, mentally cringing at the cost of an overseas call.

"Hello?" Anna's sleepy voice answered the phone.

"Anna, it's Sam. Sorry to wake you, but I need to speak to George."

"Hang on a minute. I think he's out in the living room with Peter. I swear he hasn't gone to bed in two days."

Sam waited while Anna walked the phone out to George.

"Did Emily find something already?" George asked when he came on the line.

"No, but I need Peter's special skills to find out something for me."

George chuckled heartily, "I'm sure he can manage something. Did you check on the records at the museum yet?"

"I'm there right now. Same story. A Dr. Adama signed out the artifacts and never returned them. He said he was with Yale this time."

"Damn the man," George grumbled. "Here's Peter."

"Hi, Sam," Peter greeted him, "What can I do for you?"

"I need a little background investigation on someone. His name is Dr. Robert Chisek and he's a department head at Thompson State University in New Jersey."

"Turned you down for a raise, did he?" Peter joked.

"Years ago," Sam admitted, "but that's not why I need your help. He's been hanging over my shoulder ever since I got back home and I think it might have something to do with our find in China. Is there any way to check on his activities and see if he's affiliated with any organizations or companies that would be willing to pay for what we found?"

"And just how am I supposed to do that," Peter feigned surprise at Sam's suggestion.

Sam took the hint that Peter didn't want anyone to overhear a discussion of his hacking activities. "I'm sure you have a few connections that may help you out."

The small house had only one floodlight at the front door which Lundgren had no problem avoiding on his way around to the backyard. The quiet street was sheltered by enough trees that he could probably have walked straight up to the front door and picked it open without anyone noticing. But Harry's previous experiences in the field of breaking and entering had trained him to be exceptionally cautious.

The back of the house had a small deck off of a pair of French doors. Harry smiled to himself, knowing he'd be inside in a matter of seconds. French doors were some of the easiest to get open. And he knew there was no security system to be concerned about. A quick check on the homeowner's credit history had shown no contracts with security firms.

Less than a minute later, he was walking slowly through the dining room of Sam Hunt's house, looking for his office. He carried a penlight that kept enough light focused in one small spot to keep from tripping over the furniture in the dim light.

He found the spare room that Sam used as his office and got to work searching for the papers he had come to acquire. He knew he could easily take Emily's disk whenever it was convenient, but it would be better to get the originals sooner rather than later. Hunt was already on his guard from the previous attacks and Harry hoped that made him wary enough to not carry the original information with him. After fifteen minutes of searching through disorganized stacks of papers, books and floppy disks, he decided to move on to other rooms. There was plenty of time for a thorough search because Harry had checked with the security desk at the museum and found out that Sam was working late that evening and had said he would be there until at least midnight.

He went to the kitchen first, thinking he may have hid the documents in the refrigerator, a favorite hiding place for valuables by people who don't realize that it's one of the first places that burglars check.

Harry's nose was assaulted by odors the likes of which he had never before experienced when he opened the refrigerator. It was obvious that Sam had not cleaned out the fridge before he had left for China, and hadn't bothered to take care of it since he had gotten home either. Harry quickly closed the door and decided to look in the living room first.

He had just stepped into the front hall when the door swung open in front of him. He made a dash for the kitchen, but was spotted before he got there.

"Hey! Stop!" Sam yelled, not knowing who was in his home. He chased after the intruder without stopping to consider whether they were carrying any weapon.

The burglar was reaching for the handle on the French doors when Sam tackled him.

They rolled around the floor in a tangle of arms and legs until Sam got the upper hand and pinned the man to the floor. But a moment later, Sam found himself struggling to get free of the choke hold the other had on him. He was a few inches taller than Sam and a lot heavier. He used his weight as a weapon and crushed Sam's ribs as he shoved him against the wall.

A swift kick to the groin loosened the man's grip long enough for Sam to break free and he ducked under the arms of the intruder and threw an elbow into his kidney. A grunt acknowledged Sam's accuracy as the big man turned for his next attack.

Sam didn't know if he could take another round. His shoulder was still sore from the accident in China and now his chest felt like he had been hit with a sledgehammer. The light from outside was to the intruder's back so Sam could see his outline clearly. Sam hoped the other man couldn't make him out as well and tried ducking under the breakfast bar that ran between the kitchen and dining room. Apparently, he could see Sam just fine because Sam ducked directly into a large fist that knocked him unconscious.

Sam awakened groggily a few minutes after his attacker made his escape and found himself alone, lying on the kitchen floor.

Not again! was his first thought. His next thought was for his copy of the inscriptions. He rushed back his safe where he had put them earlier and found them still in place. Why would his attacker not have searched for it after he had been knocked unconscious? Unless it was just a run-of-the-mill thief and not one of their attackers from Greece.

But Sam doubted that. It would be too much of a coincidence. Not knowing who was behind the attack worried him and he decided he had better warn Emily.

"Hello," Emily's voice was sleepy on the other end of the line.

"Em, it's Sam."

"I don't have all the symbols deciphered yet. I need some sleep first."

"I know. I just wanted to make sure you were taking some extra precautions."

"Like what?"

"Like keeping your door locked at all times and making sure someone knows where you are every second of the day."

"Aren't you being a little obsessive? This is a luxury hotel. No one's going to break into my room."

"Are you sure about that? Someone just broke into my house and gave me a couple more bruises to add to my collection."

Sam heard a gasp and what sounded like the phone being dropped.

"Emily! Are you there?"

"Yes. I was just a little startled. Do you know who it was?"

"No. But I don't think it was the same man that attacked us in Greece. He didn't seem to care what he had to do to get the disk and destroy all evidence. This guy took off as soon as he had the chance."

"What's on this disk that everyone wants?"

"That's what I'm hoping you'll find out. Those inscriptions may give us a clue."

"I'm doing as much as I can, but I'm putting in some pretty long days at MorGen."

"I know. That's why I'm going to get a room at your hotel tomorrow. I can work with George as he deciphers the text and I can make sure there aren't anymore incidents."

"Trying to protect me again, Sam?" Emily remembered Sam's tendency to be overprotective, another thing that got on her nerves when they were dating.

"No, Em. I know you can take care of yourself. I'm more worried about the copies of the inscriptions being stolen."

"I don't know whether to say thank you or be offended."

"Good," Sam gave a short laugh, "Ouch! I think I've got a few more bruised ribs."

"Well go tape them up and let me get back to sleep. I have to be up in a few hours."

"I see you still get cranky when you're tired," Sam restrained himself from laughing this time. "I'll be back in Harrisburg sometime tomorrow."

"I should be done at work by eight. I'll find out what room you're in and call you when I get back to the hotel."

"Goodnight, Emily."

"Goodnight, Sam."

Emily hung up the phone and burrowed back under the covers. Why did everything Sam got involved in have to be so complicated? He could never start a simple project in college either. It was always something involving visits to museums and libraries all over the tri-state area and multiple late night debates over what would be the best way to approach the subject matter.

She closed her eyes and found herself smiling, remembering that one of those late night debates ended in their first kiss. They had both been shocked to find themselves in each others' arms, but it seemed to work and they began seeing each other on a more personal level and not just as lab partners.

She drifted off to sleep, her thoughts wandering over their years together, not imagining that right then Sam was doing the same thing.

11

"He showed up before I could find anything," Lundgren voice came from the speakerphone on Morgan's desk.

Morgan closed his eyes for a moment and leaned back in his chair.

"That's not what I wanted to hear, Harry."

"I didn't think it would be wise for him to discover who was ransacking his house."

Morgan listened to the tone of Harry's voice and tried to judge his feelings on the matter. He didn't seem very apologetic nor did he seem embarrassed by failing to get the disks. He had known Harry a long time, but was still never able to sense his moods.

"You may be right," he conceded. "And we do have another way to get the information for now. We'll just make other plans to get Hunt's copy."

"Do you want me to get Ms. Forrester's disk?"

"Not just yet. I don't want her getting too suspicious. I still need her to complete her work in the lab. That's just as important."

Morgan thought Harry might not share his opinion, but as usual, he couldn't tell for sure. He took his lack of objection as agreement though.

"Anything else you need me for tonight, Louis?"

"No, Harry. Go home and get some rest."

Morgan wasn't sure where Harry called home. He never shared personal information and Morgan didn't care enough to ask. It was an odd relationship he had with Lundgren. Strictly business, no personal involvement. They never went out for cocktails after work or to football games. Morgan didn't even know if Harry liked football. Not that it mattered. He did what was necessary to make MorGen the fastest growing pharmaceutical company in the world and that's all Morgan wanted.

Unfortunately that sometimes meant dealing with people he would rather not have anything to do with. He turned to his computer to wonder over the information they had gleaned from Emily's computer when the phone rang.

Robert Chisek strode down the corridor of the university's administration building, looking like he had every right to be there at one in the morning.

Now and then he did work late, but tonight he had stayed even later than the janitorial staff so he would have complete privacy. The clandestine nature of his current project was somewhat dangerous, but the rewards were well worth the risks.

His life had always revolved around his work. Even though he never spoke to anyone about it now, he never let go of his original idea of an ancient civilization that existed before modern man. He had tried a few times to share his theories with women he had dated, but they thought he was a crackpot and stopped talking to him. After that happened he gave up completely on relationships and just focused on his work.

He stepped into his office with a smile on his face and seated himself behind the massive cherry desk he had specially made to intimidate anyone sitting opposite him. He had come so far since the early days of his career, days which could have also been his last.

Reflecting on what a fool he had been to think he could change the status quo, he chuckled softly to himself. He had learned from those mistakes and found he could continue his work only if he kept quiet about it. It had been a long, hard road, but now he had nearly arrived at his destination.

After deciding just how much information to share, he picked up the phone on his desk and dialed a number. After a couple of rings, a voice answered.

"What is it?"

Chisek had come to expect that kind of greeting from this particular business associate. He always got straight to the point, never stopping for pleasantries.

"I found something you might be interested in," Chisek said.

"Make it quick."

"Another disk has been found."

"Where?"

"China, but the disk isn't there anymore."

There was silence at the other end of the line.

Chisek had expected an immediate response telling him to acquire it.

"I'll need some help to find it," he volunteered.

"That won't be necessary."

"Won't be necessary? But-"

"I believe I can handle that. Was the disk discovered by Dr. Samuel Hunt?"

Chisek nearly gasped in surprise, "Yes."

"I wasn't aware that it was from one of your sites though."

"It is. But how did you find out so quickly?"

"A little bit of luck I must admit," the voice chuckled. "We have copies of the inscriptions, but we're still looking into the location of the disk. I don't think it will take too long to acquire that as well."

"What inscriptions?"

"I'll have copies sent to you tomorrow. Maybe you could translate some of the text. It's like nothing you've ever seen before. But then again, maybe you have, a very long time ago."

"I can't believe it."

Chisek was getting so excited he stood up and nearly knocked the phone off of the desk.

"Settle down, Bob. You'll see it tomorrow. It's quite amazing really. It might just be what we've both been looking for."

Chisek sat back down and made himself relax.

"I don't understand."

"I'll explain it to you later. Just see what you can make of it and let me know as soon as possible."

"Right."

He hung up the phone, still amazed that he was finally going to have more of the ancient writing in his hands. Or at least a copy of it. As his mind began to clear from the rush of excitement, he began to wonder just how they had come across Hunt's discovery.

He had been trying for years to locate and have sole access to any artifact connect to "Eternal Ones", as he had designated the civilization he believed to have existed long before Homo sapiens. There had been several disks in museum collections around the world that he had seen and studied, compiling information on their similarities and making conjectures as to their use. And he was more than a little disturbed, after his visit to the museum in Philadelphia, as to why all of them had recently started disappearing.

His boyhood friend and fellow explorer, Jonathan Waltman, was the initial reason Chisek had begun working on the Alpha culture. It was a blow from which he had never fully recovered when Jonathan's team went missing on an expedition to locate one of the mysterious sites.

Thinking about that tragedy and his failed attempt to locate his friend brought to mind something he had forgotten long ago. He had examined Jonathan's research papers after he was presumed dead and had found nothing pertaining to his discovery of the location of the city. He had wondered if there weren't more records somewhere of which he was unaware.

Maybe now was the time to look into it further.

Sam was sitting in the small lounge area of Harrisburg International Airport waiting for George to arrive. It was early in the morning and the other people around him looked as sleepy as he felt. He had been up a good portion of the night working with Emily on their theory of what had happened from the information found on the disks. It sounded crazy, but all the pieces were starting to fit together.

Then George had called at four am from Newark saying he would be on a flight to Harrisburg within the hour and could Sam meet him at the airport.

"What?" Sam tried to shake the cobwebs out of his head and understand what George was saying.

"I need you to pick me up at the airport."

"You're coming here?"

"Yes, I'll be there in a couple of hours,"

"Care to tell me why I have to get out of bed at this ungodly hour and pick you up?"

"Because I have some information that you need to see immediately," George sounded more serious than Sam had ever heard him.

"Okay, I'll see you there then." Sam had hung up the phone fully awake, wondering what George had discovered that was big enough to make him fly all the way to the States.

So here Sam was, waiting as patiently as he could for George's flight to arrive. The initial excitement had worn off and his exhaustion began to creep up on him again. He had already had three cups of coffee and that was hardly enough to keep him awake in the subdued atmosphere of the airport. The designer had gone so far in his quest to make the airport relaxing they had even placed rocking chairs on the balcony overlooking the glass walled entrance.

After another twenty minutes, Sam heard the announcement that George's plane had arrived and would be at Gate 7A momentarily. Sam pried himself out of his chair and headed toward baggage claim.

George was beaming when he came down the escalator. Sam thought he looked like a man who had just won big at the racetrack.

"You must have found something good on those disks," Sam noted.

"Better than good, it's amazing!"

"You can tell me about it over breakfast at the hotel. Emily's waiting for us."

"So you're staying there now?"

Here he goes again, Sam thought,

"In separate rooms, George."

"I'll keep praying for you, Sam."

Sam didn't dignify George's comment with a response and continued to the baggage claim area.

"I hope you have the disks on you and didn't put them in your luggage," Sam said.

"Sam, I can't believe you think I would do such a dim-witted thing."

"Well, you're certainly off the mark in other areas," he referred to George's comments about Emily.

"Whatever you say, Sam. But I think it's obvious that you still care about her."

"Just because I still care for her doesn't mean I want to get back into a relationship with her," Sam didn't feel the words as forcefully as he said them.

"I struck a nerve there, didn't I?"

Once again Sam didn't reply. He just watched the baggage carousel make its never-ending loop out of one door and back into another, like the women in Sam's life.

"All right, I'll drop it," George promised.

"Good. Did Peter find anything on Chisek or Morgan?"

"He did indeed. I'm thinking of recruiting him and starting my own spy network," George joked.

"He found a lot then?"

"And it's good stuff too," George lowered his voice, "Your Chisek is a dirty old man."

"I don't know if I want to hear this," Sam rolled his eyes.

They arrived back at the hotel and, after checking George into his room, went up to Emily's suite for breakfast.

"George!" Emily gave him a hug. "You don't look a day older than the last time I saw you."

"It's all due to clean living, Emily."

"Right, George. And in your world I suppose clean living means taking a shower every day."

George nearly roared with laughter, "You haven't changed a bit!"

"So what was so amazing that you had to come all the way to Pennsylvania to tell us?" Emily asked as she directed them over to the table laden with a variety of breakfast fare. Heaps of fried potatoes, sausage, and eggs mingled aromas with hotcakes and fresh fruits.

"It really is amazing, but I came mostly because I didn't think it would be safe to tell you the news any other way but in person. And an old man like me doesn't get many chances for adventure in his life," he chuckled.

A thought struck Sam at that moment that he didn't like at all.

"George," he began, "If you think someone was monitoring our phone calls and emails, what makes you think they haven't bugged our rooms?"

"Good point, Sam," he raised his eyebrows. "That is exactly why I brought this."

He held up a smooth, silver rectangular object the size of a PDA with a single knob, LED readout and a short antenna on one end.

"What is it?" Emily took it from George and examined it more closely.

"It's a bug detector. It picks up high frequency transmitters as well as any other wireless bugs. You just turn that switch on and it emits an alarm tone when it finds one. I really wanted one that could also pick up the actual transmission the bug was making, but they're difficult to make and expensive to buy."

"Where do you come up with all of this stuff?" Sam asked.

"Blame it on watching too many spy movies," George grinned. "Now let's see if it really works," and he began walking around the room, waving the gadget near all the furniture, light fixtures, television and phone.

"Maybe we're getting too paranoid," Sam said.

But just then there was a high pitched squeal as George passed the receiver by the bedside lamp.

Emily jumped from the ear piercing noise as George quickly turned off the device.

He lifted the lamp off of the nightstand and turned it over.

"Bingo," he said and pulled a device out of the base that looked like a fat poker chip with a tail.

"I- I can't believe it!" Emily stammered. "Morgan is insane."

"This wasn't necessarily put here by anyone at MorGen," George told her.

"But who else would do such a thing?"

"Let's finishing checking the room and then I'll tell you."

He continued scanning the room and found another bug in the phone, and one in the smoke detector.

"All right, George. Now that we've concluded watching spy movies can be educational, will you tell us who you think put these here?"

"Certainly," he sat at the table and began piling sausage and eggs onto a plate. "When Peter was doing his research into your two suspects, he happened across an interesting tidbit about a legendary treasure that sounded like the same story you came across in China. It was in connection to Chisek that he found it."

"Let me guess, he had published a paper on it," Sam interjected.

"Right. Back when he was just a lowly professor in the late1970's, he pieced together a theory from artifacts found at sites around the world that pointed to a common origin."

"Kind of like Von Daniken?"

"Very similar, except Von Daniken thought it was from spacemen, Chisek just attributed it to an earlier race, so ancient that it has been wiped from our memory in all but myth. That's a common enough theory now among 'alternative archeology' as they like to dub it, but back then he was made a laughingstock in academic circles."

"That would explain a few things about his pleasant personality," Emily noted with sarcasm.

"I was smart enough to keep my mouth shut about my theories until I had established myself academically," George said, giving Sam a sly grin.

"Something you somehow managed to get through my thick skull before I totally ruined my career," Sam laughed.

"Anyway, in Chisek's research, he had come across an obscure reference to a group that was supposedly the original inhabitants of the planet, direct descendants of the gods, and they lived in an underground fortress beneath a great mountain. He followed up on that by speaking to tribal elders about their myths only to find that anyone he spoke to wouldn't go so far as to say where their fortress was. He received plenty of warnings not to continue his quest or else he might end up in the arms of his ancestors."

"An interesting threat. But what has that got to do with our spies?" Emily asked.

"I'm getting to that," George told her and then turned to Sam, "I see what you mean about no patience."

"Men," Emily groaned and rolled her eyes.

George chuckled and continued his story, "Would you believe he spoke to tribes in Ecuador, South Africa, Alaska and Egypt and got the same story from all of them?"

"I see why they laughed at him," Sam actually felt some pity for Chisek. No one would take that kind of story seriously, especially from a newly hired college professor.

"And he was told to drop that line of research or the university he worked for would not consider him for tenure."

"Ouch," Sam cringed, thinking that could have been him if he hadn't listened to George. "So now he's a bitter old man who delights in making my life a living hell."

"So you say. But the point of this is that he started a line of research that someone else picked up on, or he may have even worked with Chisek. That person got as far as bribing the location of the fabled fortress from a weak willed villager. He left on an expedition and never returned." George stuffed a forkful of scrambled eggs into his mouth.

"I feel like I should have a marshmallow on the end of a stick in my hand," Sam remarked.

"It's no ghost story, Sam. I knew Jonathan Waltman well. He worked with me at the museum before I went to the States to teach. In fact he was the one who helped me get the job there. I had no idea where he had gotten his information, but I talked to him before he left and he seemed convinced that it was based on a real civilization that once existed, and he was determined to find some trace of it."

"Did anyone ever find out what happened to him?" Emily asked. She was starting to become engrossed in George's strange story.

"A search party was sent out and found some traces of a camp, but no one in the expedition was ever found. After Chisek heard about it, he quit his job and disappeared for a year."

"Disappeared?" Sam asked.

"We couldn't find any trace of him working anywhere that year and no one documented seeing him during that time. We couldn't find anything and we looked everywhere. After that he showed up at Thompson State and has been working there ever since."

"Maybe he went to make a search of his own," Emily suggested.

"That's what Peter and I thought as well, but to mount a search like that, he would have had to get special equipment and take a team of rescue experts with him. There would have been some record of his journey."

"As interesting as all of this is, George, I'd still like to know what this has to do with our present circumstances."

"Haven't you been listening, Sam? You found the proof that Chisek was looking for. Those disks, that room you found, they're both remnants of that ancient civilization."

"So is Morgan connected to all this?" Sam asked impatiently.

"That's where things get interesting," George began refilling his plate. "The reason why we couldn't find Chisek for that year is because he *was* on an expedition to find his lost friend."

George smiled at the confused looks on Sam and Emily's faces.

"We never found any record of Chisek organizing an expedition because he wasn't the organizer."

"You mean Morgan sponsored the expedition?" Emily asked incredulously.

"Indeed he did. We checked with travel organizations on expeditions they led around that time and found an expedition paid for under Morgan's name right before Chisek left. Chisek was on the list of travelers."

"So how do those two know each other?"

"As far as we could tell, Chisek went to him to ask for the funds. I'm not sure why though. Peter checked their backgrounds looking for a match in time and place and only found that they both lived in Jersey City when they were children and in neighborhoods far removed from one another."

"Maybe they're related," Emily ventured. "They certainly have similar personalities."

"I don't think Chisek has a family. I always thought he'd crawled out from under a rock," Sam added. "So if Chisek got his money from Morgan, he most likely told him all about the expedition."

"Then Chisek would have told Morgan about the disks you found as well," Emily pointed out.

"But Chisek couldn't have known about the disks. I didn't report finding them to anyone at the university."

"Someone on your expedition probably mentioned it to him."

"Dammit, you're right!" Sam jumped up and began pacing around the room. "I'm such an idiot! Of course Chisek would interrogate all of the students who were on the trip. He probably wanted to find some way of making me look bad."

"You do a good enough job of that on your own," Emily reached for the coffeepot and poured herself a cup.

Sam stopped pacing, "Very funny."

"Sit down, Sam," she poured him a cup as well. "We have to figure out what Morgan's planning to do with this information."

"Like I said earlier, Emily," George wiped the corners of his mouth with his napkin, "Who says it was Morgan who bugged your room?"

"Enough with the mystery, George!" Sam was growing exasperated. "You obviously have a theory. Out with it."

Sam leaned back in his chair and crossed his arms. Emily sipped her coffee and looked at George expectantly.

"If I had students like you two now, I'd never teach again," George growled good-naturedly.

They made no comment.

"Alright, here it is. Morgan could have done all of this except for one thing. He had no way of knowing about the disk and getting someone to Greece fast enough to attack us. The students didn't get back to the university until a few hours before that happened."

"Make that two things, George." Sam interrupted. "He also couldn't have caused the explosions at the dig site."

"Unless he was a part of the same group who have been destroying or stealing evidence of the lost civilization around the world."

"So you're saying there's some kind of conspiracy behind all of this?" Emily sounded as though she was holding back laughter. "I think it's more likely that it's coincidence. He's not really interested in Sam's find. Chisek's the one who would care about this 'lost civilization'."

"I wouldn't call it a conspiracy," George frowned at her, "I would consider it more of a defense initiative."

"So you think it's some kind of government project?" Sam sat heavily back into his chair.

"I really don't know. But it seems to fit the evidence." George reached into his briefcase and pulled out a stack of papers.

"I've made some small breakthroughs with the translation, but I haven't even scratched the surface yet. Peter found billions of bits of info and it will take years to decipher it all even with his program. What I've got so far is only small pieces of a few passages."

He handed the papers to Sam who began reading immediately.

"I think the disks we've discovered may have been a record of some kind of scientific research," George explained to Emily,

"Genetics?"

Her question made Sam look up, "The inscriptions look like they referred to genetics as well."

"Well, George?"

"It looks pretty technical to me. There are some sections I've been having trouble with that I thought may have more to do with the treatment of some genetic disease. There's reference to some kind of apparatus they used to create the treatment, but I'm not familiar enough with microbiology to figure out what they mean."

"Can you show me what you've got so far?" Emily asked.

"Sure," George pushed aside the remains of his breakfast and set his laptop on the table.

He booted it up and opened his translation program.

"See this part here," he pointed to a section in the middle of the screen that was a jumble of strange looking characters mixed with a few words of English. "There's nothing comparable in the dictionary the computer has available to translate this."

Emily started reading the paragraph before the untranslated one.

"They're talking about using test subjects right before that, so it may explain the technique used."

"That's what I thought as well, but I have no idea what they would have done."

Sitting back in her chair with a frown, Emily concentrated on the problem for a moment.

"If there really was a civilization that existed a million years ago- and I'm *still* having a tough time swallowing that one - they could have used a technique that we haven't thought of or are not even capable of duplicating."

"If that's the case, we don't have to worry about MorGen," Sam said and went back to his reading.

"Sam, Morgan is obsessed with finding a cure for cancer. If he believes this information is the key, do you really think he's going to give up that easily?"

She paused while Sam and George absorbed that possibility.

"And if this civilization created those disks that have survived this long, who's to say some of their other technology didn't survive?"

Sam knew some of it had survived in the form of the room he had found in China. But he hadn't had the chance to see what else it may have contained besides disks.

12

"Has anyone heard from Harry yet?" Morgan was getting more than a little concerned by the time Elliot came by with his midday report at lunchtime.

"Nothing yet. But I wouldn't worry too much. He'll turn up eventually," he answered him.

"He's never missed a day of work before."

"There's a first time for everything."

Elliot's lack of interest concerned Morgan. He was usually meek and eager to please, but now he seemed rather cavalier about Harry's disappearance. Morgan sat in silence for a moment.

"I suppose so," Morgan agreed guardedly and quickly recovered his composure. "But Harry's whereabouts aren't what you're here to discuss. How is the vector coming along?"

"We're still having some issues with stability. The latest tests show a breakdown after twenty-four hours."

Elliot almost seemed to be robotic in his responses, like he had something else on his mind.

"Well, keep at it. I'm sure you'll figure it out." Morgan couldn't account for the change in Elliot's behavior. It worried him to see his normally eager underling acting as though he could care less about his work. He decided he needed to give Elliot a jolt. "And if you don't, I've got a project in the works that may solve our problems."

"I wasn't aware that you were working on the vector. I mean," Elliot explained hastily, "I didn't realize you had the time to work on it with all of your other responsibilities."

Morgan smiled coldly as he noted Elliot's sudden interest and apprehension, "When something this important is on the line, I take a personal interest in it."

"Of course."

Elliot finished his report and left the office more subdued than when he arrived. But that did little to improve Morgan's mood. He could sense Elliot was up to something.

Damn it, Harry! Where are you? Morgan grumbled to himself. He needed Harry to keep an eye on Elliot now in addition to Emily. There were too many things to be done and not enough time to do them in.

He had expected Harry to be back that morning at eight am. When he didn't arrive, Morgan waited an hour and then tried calling his cell phone. He also left a text message. But there had been no response.

Morgan just hoped that Harry hadn't decided to take matters into his own hands and try to get the file and disk from Sam Hunt again. It made him more than a little angry to think Harry would go against his direct orders.

But perhaps Harry was just sleeping in for once. He did have a rough night.

Since Lundgren wasn't there to report on Dr. Forester's activities, Morgan had accessed the security files himself and was happy to see she had new data on her computer. It looked like she had received more information from Dr. Hunt, but it didn't make much sense. Perhaps some files were garbled in the transmission, he thought, looking at the combination of strange symbols and what appeared to be a section of a genetics textbook. After studying the images for several minutes he still couldn't make sense of it and shut his computer off in disgust.

If he could just find out where Harry had gotten to everything would be under control. He decided to go down and talk to the security staff in person to see if they knew anything. It was better than sitting around waiting to find out what happened.

The agitated look on Morgan's face as he passed Emily in the hall made her think twice about asking him if she could leave early that day. Something had obviously gone wrong for him and she didn't want to stick around to find out first hand just how wrong.

Leaving the office area, she headed back down to the lab resigned to staying until at least six, the standard end of the MorGen workday. She was definitely not staying late tonight because she had to meet Sam to update him on her progress with the disks.

She punched in her code to get back into the lab and returned to her workstation. Something seemed odd as she turned on her computer and she looked around the lab.

No one was there and it was well past lunchtime. Was there a meeting she was supposed to be at and forgot about? She didn't think so. She couldn't figure out where everyone had gone. She saw the workstation that Elliot's assistants had been at that morning and noticed it was completely cleaned off with all equipment returned to its places on the shelves. It was standard procedure to clean your work area before going to lunch, but usually people would leave out any equipment they were still using. It was unusual to see a completely bare desktop.

She had an unnerving feeling that something major had happened and no one told her about it. She got up from her chair and walked down the hall to Elliot's office.

There were no noises coming from inside, but that didn't mean he wasn't in.

She knocked on the door. No answer. She tried the handle and was surprised when it opened the door.

That was definitely weird. No self respecting scientist would ever leave his private lab unlocked. There were too many things that could happen if someone who didn't know what you were working on touched anything.

"Elliot, are you here?" she called out and received no reply.

She walked around to look behind the shelves of equipment and was surprised to see stairs leading upwards to another level.

"Elliot?" she yelled up the stairs, "I'm coming up."

Emily heard nothing but her own footsteps as she mounted the stairs.

The desk at the top of the stairs was cluttered with computer printouts in contrast to the orderly work area on the first floor. Bookshelves were crammed with binders all around the walls and she could just make out a small refrigerator buried under a stack of files.

But Elliot was not there.

She was tempted to take a closer look at the work he was doing. What harm could a little peek do? She glanced at the papers lying on his desk and saw they were test results from some animal trials.

Without touching anything she took a closer look. She couldn't tell much by the results other than the vector had failed miserably. Unless they were trying to kill all of the mice. She shuddered thinking of that possibility.

A feeling of guilt began to intrude on her conscience and she decided to get out of there before Elliot came back and she was caught snooping.

She made her way back down the stairs and out of his office before she heard him returning with his assistants.

"I know it's not much to go on, but he wants to see some results fast," Elliot was saying.

They came around the corner and Emily acted like she was just about to knock on his door.

"Oh, there you are! I was just looking for you," she said casually, but her heart was pounding knowing how close she had been to being caught.

"Go ahead and prepare the first samples," Elliot instructed his assistants and then turned to Emily. "What did you need?"

"Oh, I just wanted to let you know I wouldn't be staying late tonight. I'm not feeling well," she lied.

"You do look a little flushed. Leave early if you like."

She was surprised at his lack of emotion about it. She thought he would act a little more concerned. Maybe I'm just flattering myself, she thought.

"Thanks," she said as he entered his office and closed the door in her face.

He was definitely not acting like his usual self. Or maybe this was his usual self and the last few days were all an act. Either way it certainly made her more suspicious about what was going on behind closed doors.

Sam knocked on the door to Emily's room and stood nervously in the hall. He wasn't nervous about meeting Emily in her room, but because he thought he had been followed to the hotel.

He had spotted the same car behind him at several stoplights and again in the parking lot of the hotel. And walking through the corridors he could have sworn he heard footsteps behind him. But when he turned to look, there was no one there.

He was looking back down the hall when Emily opened the door.

"Hi, Sam."

"Hi," he greeted her and stepped quickly into the room, shutting the door behind himself.

"Please, come in," Emily stood leaning against the dresser where Sam had shoved her when he entered.

"Sorry, I thought someone might be following me."

"It wouldn't surprise me after what I found on the disk George brought," she walked over to the table where her computer sat.

"So what is it? He refused to tell me, saying I wouldn't understand it anyway," he grumbled.

"Some of it is a map to the human genome," she sat, motioning Sam to pull up the other chair next to her.

"Like the Human Genome Project?"

"More complete than that. This map has detailed information on what each gene does and what other genes it works with. At least I think that's what it means, George doesn't have it all translated yet."

"That's incredible. What else was there?"

"The rest of it's more like a genetic recipe. It looks like someone's plans for a germ line gene therapy program."

"That's when the altered genes are passed on to the following generations, right?"

"Right. And it's a highly regulated field. It's illegal to test on humans in most countries including the US."

"Is it dangerous?"

"Only because we don't know enough about how different genes are dependent on one another. What we know so far shows us that most of the time more than one gene is responsible for a certain trait. And each gene can be responsible for more than one job. If we mess with one, we mess with others. Throw in recessive traits and pure chance in reproduction and who knows what could happen to the next generation. The altered genes may be rejected completely or they could result in a chain reaction that would cause multiple birth defects."

"And I thought doing my taxes was complicated," Sam joked.

"Which is why I'm concerned about where this disk really came from. If someone has taken this research as far as this shows, there could be widespread mutations in the human gene pool."

"I don't think that'll be a problem, Em," Sam slipped back into the abbreviated form of Emily's name he used to use when they were dating. "The person who did this work is long gone. So are a few thousand generations after him."

"According to you and George," she said, looking over the top of her glasses dubiously.

"Just tell me what you found and we'll argue over my harebrained theories later," Sam felt a pang of discomfort as he was reminded of their stormy relationship once again.

Emily turned to the computer and pulled up the section of the disk she had been analyzing before she had called Sam.

A chain of DNA appeared on the screen, rotating slowly. But it wasn't the usual double helix Sam had seen before in biology textbooks. It looked like someone had taken several strands of DNA and woven them together to form an intricate spiral.

"This is the part I don't get. I think it's a theoretical model they're using to demonstrate future possibilities in genetic engineering. But I don't see why anyone would want to pack more information into the genome. It wouldn't necessarily improve things."

"Why overcomplicate an already complex system?"

"Exactly. And I didn't understand it until I looked at the information on the next section Peter and George accessed. It shows the development of a viral vector that can successfully alter the genetic code without the body rejecting it before its job is done."

"And what does that mean to those of us who don't have a degree in microbiology?"

"It looks like they were using a viral vector where the virus itself had been altered, beyond what we would normally do to render it harmless, before the genetic material was injected into it."

"That sounds risky."

"It is. Especially since they used genes from microbes that were adapted to oligotrophic environments."

"You mean environments with low available nutrients? Like a cave?"

"Yes. The microbes' ability to stick tightly to a surface makes them ideal for anti-cancer treatments. Unfortunately the way they used them made the vector nearly indestructible. It would continue to express the genetic material indefinitely within the cells."

"And if the vector had found a way to reproduce itself?"

"It would spread as rapidly as a flu epidemic and be even harder to stop. That wouldn't be a problem if the vector remained unchanged, but coming into contact with a virus could lead to unforeseen mutations."

"What kind of 'unforeseen mutations' were shown on the disk?"

"I still have a lot to look at before I can determine the effects of the vector."

"Can you tell what it was targeting?"

"Not without knowing what this text at the bottom of the screen means. George needs to finish his translation," her voice took on a note of steel, "Which is why I think you need to tell me where you got these disks."

"It's nothing to worry about, Em. Nothing's going to happen," Sam reassured her.

"Sam! Aren't you listening to me? Someone has created a new biological weapon! This could be a terrorist campaign! Now tell me where you got this information!"

"As far as I know you're the first person who's seen this in a million years. George is the expert on these disks, but I know the flowstone I found mine in was at least 250,000 years old."

"Seriously, Sam."

"Do you want to see the pictures of it *in situ*? Do you want to interview the students who were there when we found it?" Sam couldn't help raising his voice as he grew angrier at Emily's disbelief.

"It's not possible!"

"But it's true."

There was a tense moment of silence as they weighed each other's opinions. It reminded Emily of the times they'd get into a heated debate over various theories of modern anthropology. Sam invariably tried to shoot down accepted theory as a popularity contest with little hard evidence to back it up, while Emily defended the presumptions as proved beyond all practical doubts. Frustration stemming from those arguments was a part of what made her switch her major from anthro to microbiology.

But the memory of what would usually happen after the battle of wits brought a blush to her cheeks as she looked across the table at Sam. The arguments used to excite more than their brains. She hoped he couldn't tell what she was thinking about.

Emily looked as though she might have something else to say, but a curious expression came over her face and she sat dumbfounded for a moment. "Okay, I know you're the cave expert, but is George positive the disks are that old? I mean, isn't it generally accepted that our ancestors were only making crude stone tools at that time?"

"Yes. But that doesn't mean it's true." Sam was surprised and pleased that Emily's temper had mellowed over the years. And he also felt somewhat ashamed that he had raised his voice.

"Hang on a minute," she stood and began pacing the room. "If the disks actually are that old--" she stopped and looked him in the eye with a dubious expression, "and I'm still not saying I believe that- then maybe the vector was used already."

"What do you mean?"

She sat back at the computer again, "Look at this," she hit a few keys, "Only part of it was readable, but from what I can tell, these chromosomes making up the additional strands in the more complex chain *are* from a human species. Actually, it seems as though they're Homo sapiens version two-point-oh."

Sam looked at the screen and could only tell that the chromosomes weren't the same as the human ones Emily had just shown him.

"I have no clue what you're trying to say, Em."

"I don't believe it, Sam Hunt admitting he doesn't know something."

Sam feigned anger he didn't feel, "Just explain it to the dumb ape."

"It's been awhile since I studied this particular DNA sequence, but it looks very similar to ones I've seen in autistic children."

"Autistic? They were trying to create autism?"

"No," Emily shook her head and searched for the right words. "It's not as simple as that. I'm saying someone was experimenting with gene sampling, trying to mine the best aspects of what would be considered a genetic defect and inserting it into a relatively normal genome. There are other sequences here for other genetic anomalies as well. And before you ask, I have no idea why someone would do this and what effect it would have."

"I don't believe it, Emily Forester admitting she doesn't know something!"

They glared at each other and then suddenly burst out laughing.

Emily caught her breath and shook her head, smiling. "I missed you, Sam."

"You just missed arguing with me."

"But you were the only man on campus who would actually argue. The rest of them just agreed with me to get on my good side."

"Something I was never very skilled at."

"You had enough other skills to make up for it," Emily cringed inwardly. *I can't believe I just said that!*

An awkward silence ensued until there was a knock at the door and they heard George's voice in the hall, "Room service!"

"What did you find out today?" George asked Emily as he walked through the door carrying bags of takeout Chinese food.

"Something strange is going on at the lab," she returned to her computer after taking one of the bags from George, "Morgan is all worked up for some reason and I didn't see that bully of his around all day. And then there's the way the lab supervisor is acting."

"And how is he acting?" Sam took a seat next to Emily and began rummaging through a bag, pulling out white cardboard containers and setting them on the table.

"He's been avoiding me ever since Morgan started him on a new project the other day."

"Isn't he the one you said has been hanging over your shoulder nonstop?"

"Yes. Don't get me wrong, I'm glad he's not bothering me now, but it just doesn't seem normal."

"Don't scientists always tend to be secretive?" Sam poked fun at their professions.

Emily smiled and shook her head, "I guess I'm getting as paranoid as you."

"Now what I really wanted to know about was if you made any progress on the disk," George said between mouthfuls of lo mein.

"Not really. Without knowing what all those symbols mean at the bottom of the screen, I can only guess at what the pictures represent."

"I'm working on it," George reached for the fried rice.

"Sam," Emily set her food down and looked him straight in the eyes, "Did you ever think that if someone really is trying to take this information away from you, it's because it's dangerous."

"Yes, I have thought of that. But who's to say they aren't planning to use it for something even more dangerous. They obviously have little regard for the safety and well-being of other people."

"You may be right," she admitted, "I'd feel better knowing what was on those disks myself. But you have a point, too," she agreed.

"And I must admit I'm not ready to give up on this project just yet. It's too intriguing."

"That it is," Sam smiled.

Emily wasn't sure by the way he said it that he was referring to the project of the disks or some other project he had going.

"Here's another problem," Emily began typing some commands into her computer. "Some of my programs aren't responding the way they should. I think the information from the disk messed up my system somehow."

"What exactly is going wrong?"

"The whole system is a little sluggish and some of the files won't open right away when I want to access them."

"When did you first notice it happening?"

Emily thought for a moment, "It started the day I came to Harrisburg."

"Maybe something happened to it in transit."

"I had it on the front car seat next to me the whole time. And I called the system manufacturer and they weren't able to figure out what the problem was either."

"Well, it's about time for me to check in with Peter. I'll ask him if he knows what the problem might be."

Sam pulled his phone out of his jacket and dialed.

"I still haven't made much progress, Sam." Peter answered on the first ring. If I can figure out the operating system, so to speak, it would be much easier."

"Is there a chance it could compromise a different system?"

"How do you mean?"

"I'll put you on speakerphone and Emily can explain."

"Hello, Peter," she greeted him.

"Hello, Emily. I've heard a lot about you from George."

"Don't believe a word of it," she joked. "I'm having some problems with my system and Sam thought you might be able to help."

"That's my specialty. What's the trouble?"

Emily explained the situation to him.

"Why don't we link up and I can get a better look at what you've got on your hard drive," Peter suggested and asked for her IP address.

They quickly linked the two systems so Peter could perform a diagnostic.

"It doesn't look like your hard drive is overloaded," Emily could hear him rapidly typing. "But what's this?"

"Did you find something?" she asked.

"There's a program here trying to hide itself. It's very small and seems to be running in tandem with your wireless driver. I'll see if I can isolate it." He continued typing.

George and Sam watched her computer screen jump from one window to the next as Peter searched.

"Here it is," Peter announced. "That's odd. Did you install any PC monitoring software?"

"What is that?"

"Mostly people use it to keep an eye on what their children or spouses are viewing on the internet. It records snapshots of the screen at intervals, lists websites visited and captures incoming and outgoing emails."

"I never installed anything like that. I'm the only person that uses this computer."

"No one else has had access to it?"

"Not with my permission anyway."

"Hang on a minute, I'm going to run a check of installed hardware. I've got a suspicious feeling about this."

"This does not sound good," George's brow creased, "If someone has been monitoring your computer, they'll know about the disks."

"Emily, we've got a problem," Peter interrupted, "Someone has been monitoring everything you've done on that computer. Probably since you first noticed the problems."

"That was when I came to my new job."

"I think your employer may be a little overzealous in protecting their interests. Right now I'm looking for the IP address it's been routing to and then we'll know for sure who's been doing it."

"If MorGen has been watching everything I do outside of work, I am definitely going to press charges. This is a total invasion of privacy," Emily fumed.

"I don't think that'll do any good, Em. They're a huge multibillion dollar corporation and unfortunately in this country, more money means more freedoms. Whatever charges you bring up against them will get thrown out by whatever judge they gave the most campaign funding to," a crafty look spread across Sam's face,

"Besides, if they don't know that you know, this might be a good opportunity to spread some misinformation."

Emily mulled it over, her anger fighting her common sense. It would be better for them to take advantage of the situation and throw MorGen off the track. It frightened Emily to think what Louis Morgan would do with information like this.

"I've got the number," Peter interrupted her thoughts, "But it has a firewall thicker than a whale omelet. Do you want me to go further?"

"Go ahead, Peter. We won't tell." Sam reassured him.

"This won't take long."

"The address is registered under the name of "AE Security' in Harrisburg, Pennsylvania." Peter announced.

"AE Security?" Emily reflected for a moment. "Is there any way you can find out who owns it?"

"Hang on a minute," the clack of computer keys could be heard in the background. A moment later, "This is really buried. I've gone through three fake names already. Ah, here it is. Harold T. Lundgren."

"That's Morgan's security chief," Emily fumed.

"Makes sense." George noted. "So what should we do about it?"

"I can alter the programming so it only transmits what you want them to see," Peter volunteered.

"Do that," Emily agreed. "And then we'll send Morgan some info that should put a stop to his spying and hopefully make him not want to use any of the material he stole from my computer."

"Do you think he would do that?" George asked, more than a little worried.

"He wouldn't hesitate if he thought he could make a buck off of it."

"I wonder if he was behind the break-in at my house as well," Sam mused aloud. "I think we need to find out what else MorGen is into besides genetic research and pharmaceuticals. Whether Morgan is on the board of trustees for any museums or universities and just how many corporations are affiliated with them."

"I can look into that," Emily offered, "A few questions around the office will just make it seem like I'm interested in becoming a permanent employee."

Sam thanked Peter for his help after he had reconfigured the monitoring program and bid him farewell.

"We're making some good progress. And now that we know who's behind at least some of our problems, we can fight back." Sam rubbed his hands together in anticipation.

A thought struck Emily at that moment that she did not like at all.

What if Elliot's new project had to do with the genetic experiments shown on the disks? If Morgan had already passed on the information, there was more than enough there for a genius like Elliot to work with and possibly even succeed. Any misinformation they fed to him would probably be ignored.

"We might be too late, Sam."

"What makes you think that?" Sam felt his throat tighten as he waited for the answer he didn't want to hear.

"The lab director has been working on a new project behind closed doors. I tried to find out what was going on, but I didn't have enough time."

"We can't let them fool around with this. There's no way of knowing what could happen," George said anxiously.

"So we all agree that something has to be done to stop them?" Sam looked at Emily and George, who nodded in agreement. "We have to get in there somehow and destroy any data they have."

"I think we should go to the NIH first and report what we've found," Emily said.

"Do you really think they'd believe you?" George asked her.

"I'd hope so, but I'm not sure they would to begin with."

"And if they take the amount of time the federal government usually takes to investigate a crime, Morgan will have the vector finished and in production by then!"

Emily knew he was right, but was very uncomfortable with the idea of sneaking into the labs after hours. If Morgan was doing something illegal, it didn't give her the right to do the same to stop him. But she didn't think anyone who could legally stop him could do it in time.

And part of it was just being afraid of getting caught. She had never done anything illegal in her life. At least that she had been caught doing. Underage drinking was an unfortunately accepted way of life at college and she had gone to more than a few keg parties. But other than that she had never even gotten a speeding ticket.

She reluctantly agreed that this was a case where she had no choice. If she didn't do something about it now, it might be too late for someone else to take care of it later.

"You're right, Sam. What should we do?" She felt better having made her decision to help.

"What kind of security do they have around the building where you work?"

"There's a main gate with a camera and a lock that my passkey opens. And they've got cameras at all the entrances, on both sides of the doors. The main door and the lab door both need the passkey to open."

"That's pretty simple," George observed.

"Do you know how many security guards there are?"

"At least ten that I've seen. The security chief, Lundgren, wasn't in today. Rumor has it he's got a drinking problem and may have gone on a week long binge. "

"I wonder if it isn't because he was fired for not getting the disk from me."

Emily looked at him in shock, "Do you think that's who attacked you?"

"It wouldn't surprise me. At that point they may have known about the disk."

"This is insane," she shook her head.

"Which is why we've got to do this as soon as possible," Sam urged. "Do the security guards make rounds outside the building at night?"

"I never noticed any."

"We'll check on that before we go in. Where would the least used entrance be?"

"Around the right side of the building. No one uses it except the janitors, but my key should work there as well."

"Sounds good."

Sam watched Emily yawn and decided to call an end to their all-day conference.

"You have to be to work early," he said to her, "Why don't you get some sleep. George and I will work out the rest of the details in my room."

"Okay. How soon are we going to do this?"

"I was thinking tomorrow night,"

Emily let that sink in and managed a smile, "Then I'd better sleep now since I won't get any tomorrow."

After their goodnights, Emily was alone in her room again. She got ready for bed, turning over all the things in her mind that she had learned that day.

The possibilities of the situation she was in were almost too much for her to grasp. A viral vector that could alter the entire human genome, unchecked, until humankind turned into a completely different species. It sounded like something out of a science-fiction movie.

But this was a reality. Her reality and she had to deal with it. Morgan was the one man in the world who would use a vector like this for his own gain and she had all but presented it to him gift wrapped. She found herself feeling immense guilt.

No, there was no way I could have known he would bug my computer and my whole room as well, she reassured herself.

A resolve she didn't know she possessed welled up in her. She would stop Morgan no matter what. If this vector could actually do what she though it might, the consequences of his actions would be catastrophic for the entire planet.

She didn't know how things would turn out at the end of the next night, but she prayed fervently that Morgan would be out of a job and on his way to jail.

13

"I don't care how you find him, just find him!" Morgan yelled at the cringing secretary.

She grabbed the phone and rolodex and tried reaching Elliot at his home for the fifth time that day.

Morgan paced the floor nervously and tried to think of every place he might have gone. Elliot didn't show up for work that day and Harry was still missing as well. He had no idea what was going on, but when he figured it out, whoever was responsible would pay dearly.

All of the office staff had been attempting to avoid Morgan since he had discovered that Elliot was nowhere to be found. He should have known there was going to be trouble when Elliot had come to his office without being called there.

There had been a tentative knock on Morgan's door yesterday afternoon as he sat going through the year to date earnings report.

"Come in!"

Elliot poked his head around the corner, "May I speak with you for a few minutes?"

It wasn't late enough for Elliot to be leaving for the day, so Morgan knew this wasn't his daily report.

"Certainly, Elliot. I always have time for you," Morgan put on his best fatherly tone and pushed aside the stack of papers. "What's on your mind?"

"I have some concerns about this vector design," Elliot fidgeted and continued standing.

"Have a seat and tell me about it," Morgan's tone was pleasant, but inside he was mentally grinding his teeth.

Elliot sat across from him, cleared his throat and composed himself as if he were preparing to give a speech.

"I don't think MorGen should be pursuing this line of research," he said firmly.

"You don't?" Morgan almost laughed at Elliot's haughtiness. "It's not your job to decide what MorGen should and should not do. It's mine. But I am curious as to why you feel this way. If you're concerned about this negating Emily's research, I can assure you we'll be keeping her on as long as we can."

Morgan was trying to get Elliot to lose his focus on his arguments and he knew of his attraction to his new coworker.

"This has nothing to do with Emily," Elliot blushed slightly, "This is germline therapy way beyond the small tests we've run before."

"That's why it's so important. This is the vector that will succeed."

"From what I can tell on the disk you gave me, it will succeed," Elliot acceded the point, "But it will succeed at the cost of thousands of lives."

"Now, Elliot, I think you're exaggerating a little."

"I think I underestimated, actually. It could be as high as millions."

"Now you're getting just plain ridiculous. If you don't have any real reasons to objecting to the vector, then please leave my office and get back to work."

Morgan began to sort through his papers again.

Elliot stood, put his hands on the desk and leaned towards Morgan.

"I'm not leaving until you hear me out," he said quietly but with much force.

For one second, Morgan thought Elliot was going to reach across the desk and choke him. The look in his eyes was almost murderous.

"This is too dangerous, Louis! The vector will mutate in the following generations and cause worse genetic defects than the ones we're trying to fix."

Elliot was actually showing some strength as he faced Morgan across his desk. Morgan was surprised to see the anger on his face, but it didn't frighten him in the least. There was nothing he could do to stop MorGen's march toward its place in the history books.

"Elliot, if this was dangerous, I wouldn't ask you to do it," Morgan said in his most soothing tone. "The probability of something going wrong with this vector-"

"-Is way too high to risk it in trials!" Elliot interrupted him. "We shouldn't even be trying to create it. Germline therapies are still illegal!"

"But not for long, Elliot." Morgan refused to lose his temper with Elliot because he needed him to head this project. He had to find a way to pacify him. "The NIH is already being pressured to alter their views on germline research and I'm sure they'll pass a new resolution within the year. By the time we have the vector ready for the market, it will be perfectly legal."

"That doesn't justify what we're doing right now."

Elliot had curbed his anger somewhat and merely stood in the center of the room with his fists clenched at his sides.

"Even if does become legal, do you really think it's okay to take risks with human lives?" Elliot asked.

"If we didn't take risks, we'd never accomplish anything. And anyone who volunteers for a trial knows there are dangers, but they're willing to try. For their own survival and the survival of others who may be cured by the treatment."

Morgan glared at Elliot and sat back in his chair.

"No one really understands the true risks of what we're doing," Elliot said quietly, looking at Morgan as if daring him to contradict him. "There's no way to predict what could happen to artificially altered genes several generations from now. We just don't know enough to continue with this line of research."

"I'm well aware of the risks, Elliot," he spoke as if explaining something to a child, "But the advantages far outweigh them."

"According to whom?"

"According to the man who signs your paycheck. Now get back to work Elliot before I do something I regret later,"

Elliot stood for a moment, his eyes locked with Morgan's. Then he lifted his chin and the corners of his mouth turned upward slightly.

Morgan wasn't sure if Elliot was smiling or about to cry. But he only had a quick glance at his expression before Elliot turned on his heel and hurriedly left the room.

The slamming of the door echoed in Morgan's ears as he shook his head and smiled. It was almost like having a son again. He remembered his son challenging him over who was the better baseball player, Babe Ruth or Joe DiMaggio, and storming out of the room in much the same manner when they came to no agreement. Thinking about it made him wish Joshua was alive, even if it was just to argue.

But wishing wouldn't accomplish anything, so he shoved his personal feelings aside and focused on the problem he was having with Elliot.

If Elliot felt that strongly about the risks, he might do something rash and endanger the success of the project. Morgan needed his genius to complete his project. There were other microbiologists who would jump at the chance to work for MorGen, but none were quite at Elliot's level. He had an instinct for the work that Morgan imagined Einstein must have had for physics.

He fervently hoped that Harry would soon return. He needed him to monitor Elliot's every move. Morgan would do it himself, but there were so many other details he had to attend to. He decided to entrust the job to one of Harry's hand-picked security men. They could be trusted to be discreet about their surveillance and to report everything that Elliot did in detail.

The problem of Harry's disappearance was gnawing at Morgan's insides. He hated to go to the police because of the reason he sent Harry out of town. If they were to look into it, they may become suspicious about MorGen's activities. Not that that would cause any major problems, Morgan knew enough high placed officials to put them off the track, but it was an inconvenience he didn't have time for.

Harry would just have to fend for himself. Morgan wasn't being callous by thinking this because Harry had certainly gotten himself out of enough tough situations before. He just had to prioritize his troubles. And right now, making sure that Elliot wasn't going to back out of his contract with MorGen was foremost.

He hit the intercom button on his phone, "Lois, get my attorney on the phone."

A little threat of legal action usually made employees reconsider leaving before their allotted contracts were up. The clauses his attorney had written stipulated that they had to repay MorGen for the remaining time on their contract, to "buy" themselves freedom. In Elliot's case, he had five more years with the company and the cost to him upon leaving early would most likely bankrupt him.

But now, Elliot hadn't shown up for work and no one could reach him. Morgan started off just making curt demands that someone find him, but by lunch time he had turned to shouting at anyone who walked by.

"There's still no answer, sir, "the secretary bravely interrupted his thoughts and braced herself for the inevitable screaming.

But Morgan didn't yell at her this time. He merely threw her a look that would make an alligator run home to its mother and stormed into his office, slamming the door behind him.

Besides his anger clouding his thoughts, Morgan was feeling slightly adrift without the steady support of Harry Lundgren. He had always been the one to get things done for him, no matter what. And the more time that went by, the less likely it seemed that Harry would be coming back.

He was sure Elliot had turned traitor and abandoned the research. He just hoped that he hadn't gone to the authorities. The procedures they were planning on using would normally be fine for a private corporation under the current NIH restrictions, but MorGen got a large amount of its money from government sources. They had military contracts for various vaccines, and several research grants in their pharmaceuticals division. And because of that, they were not permitted to engage in any germ line gene therapy research.

But those same government contracts were what supplied MorGen with enough income to support the genetic research operations. Morgan had always been careful to conceal any evidence of unsanctioned research, but if Elliot had gone to the NIH with his allegations, there would surely be an investigation.

And now was not a good time for government officials to be examining MorGen's operations. They were so close to reaching Morgan's goal and he would not be stopped by anyone.

At least he still had Emily. He would find some way of getting her to stay and finish Elliot's work even if he had to lock her in the lab.

The MorGen complex looked more like a military compound than a park at night. The tall halogen lights that were scattered around the buildings seemed to highlight the hard angles of the structures and brought into sharp relief the razor wire topped fence. Sam and Emily sat in her car parked one block down the street in a shadowed spot next to a neighboring building.

"Morgan may still be there," Emily peered through the windshield, trying to see if she could spot Morgan's BMW parked at the main building.

"But it's after midnight," Sam was checking out the front gate for any guards or cameras.

"That doesn't matter to him. This place is his whole life I sometimes thinks he lives here."

"So besides the security guards and Morgan, is there anyone else who might be here?" Sam turned to her with a raised eyebrow.

"I don't know. What does it matter anyway? We're going to have to be careful no matter who's in there."

"I just want to know how many people I'll have to fight off if they find us."

Sam's sarcastic tone was one way in which he was dealing with a situation he felt was beyond his abilities. Sneaking into a well-guarded scientific facility was not something in which he had any experience. The closest thing he'd ever done to this was playing paintball with his older brothers when he was in high school. That memory gave him no comfort as his Army trained siblings would always gang up on him and he would go home humiliated and covered in red and blue paint.

He didn't plan on using his Glock for anything other than waving it threateningly at anyone who tried to stop them, but decided he had better load the clip just in case. He had also brought along a pair of night vision binoculars that he had purchased that day at a local gun shop, which he now used to get a better look at the front gate.

"I don't see any guards," he told Emily.

"They probably rely on the gate to keep anyone out that isn't authorized. And they can see who's coming in from the cameras above it."

Sam weighed their options and decided on the direct approach.

"Okay, I'm going to hide in the back while you go in through the gate. If they ask why you're coming in so late, tell them you couldn't sleep and decided you may as well get some work done."

"That'll work. Morgan loves anyone who's crazy enough to be at work this late."

Sam smiled at her as he climbed over the seat, "I think I've seen you coming out of the lab at the university in the small hours of the morning before."

"You must have been working late yourself then," Emily retorted as Sam slipped down to the floorboards before she could reach him to punch him in the arm.

She took a deep breath and started the car. She was at the front gate in a few seconds and pulled up to the security box where she inserted her passkey into the slot provided.

A moment later, a voice came out of the speaker beneath the camera.

"Good evening, Dr. Forrester. What brings you here so late at night?"

She recognized the voice as that of Lundgren's assistant security chief.

"I couldn't sleep so I thought I may as well come in and get some work done," she hoped she didn't sound too stilted.

There was no immediate reply and Emily began to get nervous.

"Sorry about that Dr. Forrester," the security officer's voice came back on a minute later, "I had to change the camera tapes. Come on in and join the rest of the night owls."

She breathed a sigh of relief as the gate went up in front of her and she pulled through to the parking lot.

"Find a spot away from any cameras," Sam said, still lying on the floor behind her.

It wasn't difficult to locate a parking space out of view of the security cameras since they were only located near the gate and the front door of the building. She turned off the car.

"Okay, now what?"

"Now we quietly get out of the car and you lead the way to that side entrance you mentioned last night."

"There are cameras there, too," she warned him.

"I thought there might be, so I planned a little diversion for the security team."

"Sam, what did you do?" She turned around in her seat and looked at him anxiously.

"It was George's idea," he grinned in such a way to make Emily even more nervous. "Just get out of the car and we'll go in."

"Not until you tell me what you two did." She crossed her arms.

"I don't have time to explain now. We only have a short time to get in," he opened his door.

Emily gritted her teeth and made a small growl as she, too, got out of the car.

"It's this way," she whispered to Sam as he looked around the parking lot.

They made their way along a narrow sidewalk at the side of the building. About halfway down its length was a doorway with a small floodlight focused on it.

Sam stayed back out of the light and hit the illuminator button on his watch, aiming the glow towards the trees on the other side of the fence.

"Any minute," he spoke to her quietly.

"What--"

Sam put his finger to his lips and pointed at the door.

She peeked around the corner and glanced at the camera. It went from its usual behavior of panning back and forth across the small vestibule to pointing straight up to the ceiling.

She looked at Sam questioningly, but he just urged her forward. She took her passkey that she had been holding at the ready and slid it through the slot. They moved quickly inside and beyond the view of the camera inside the door which was also pointed upwards.

Emily didn't comprehend what was going on with the security system, but she had sense enough to keep them moving until they were in a safe part of the building, away from any cameras or work areas.

"Now will you please tell me what is going on," she spoke in a hushed but angry voice.

"George had Peter break into their security system. It's all run through their main computer so he had no problem creating a temporary glitch in the cameras. I signaled George to let Peter know we were in position."

"George is out there in the trees? Honestly, you two are like a couple of little boys playing spy games." Emily wanted to stay mad at Sam for not telling her what was going on, but she had to admire the way in which he handled what could have been a risky situation. Now, if she could just get her heart to stop pounding.

"By now, all the cameras should be back to normal," he continued. "That's why we had to time it just right."

"When all this is over, I want to go to Greece and meet Peter."

"Sorry, Em. He's married," Sam teased.

Emily ignored his comment. "The lab is down one level and at the other end of the building. There are a lot of unused rooms in that wing because it's newer, so if we hear anyone coming we should be able to hide in one of them."

"Good. How many cameras?"

"That I know of, just around the lab entrance."

"We'll take care of that when we get there. You're sure the information from the disk is in Dr. Burdette's lab?"

"I know he was working on something big for Morgan up until yesterday. I can't think of anyone else he'd trust to work with them."

"Alright then. Let's go."

Emily led the way to the elevator down the hall.

Sam grabbed her hand before she pressed the button to call the elevator, "Are there any stairs?"

She walked to a door down the hall to their right with Sam close behind her, glancing nervously about.

Their steps echoed hollowly in the stairwell as they descended to the next level. Upon reaching the door, Emily looked cautiously through the glass pane in the center of it to make sure there was no one around.

"It looks deserted," she told Sam who was standing off to one side.

"How far is it to the lab?"

"About fifty yards down this hall and then we make a left and go another twenty or so. There's the locker room first, and then the main labs. Elliot's office is in a hall at the back of that."

"Are you ready?" Sam put his hand on her shoulder and squeezed it reassuringly.

Emily nodded in reply and opened the door.

Walking as softly as they could in case someone was in one of the adjacent rooms, they made their way down the hall. There was a door every twenty feet, some marked with signs indicating their use, and some without. They passed rooms labeled Sequencing, Genotyping, and Bioinformatics and were almost halfway down the hall when they heard the unmistakable ping of the elevator arriving on their floor.

They glanced at each other's startled expression and quickly darted into the nearest room, which turned out to be one of the smallest they could have possibly chosen.

Sam nearly fell over a mop and bucket as Emily closed the door behind them. They could make out two voices approaching their location.

"That was weird with the cameras," one of them said.

"They seem fine now, though," the other replied.

"Think this place is haunted?" the first one actually sounded a little worried.

The second snorted, "Get off it! It was just a computer glitch. That kind of thing happens all the time when you depend on technology too much."

"Yeah, you're right. The more complex the system, the more things that can go wrong," he said it like he was repeating a quote he had heard.

"Exactly. That's why I prefer to keep it nice and simple. Give me a walkie-talkie and a gun and I can take care of any building."

Squeezed into the janitor's closet, Emily and Sam could barely move. And they dared not while Morgan's security guards were hanging around outside. If they accidentally knocked over a bucket or mop, they would be easily found.

Emily's body was pressed against Sam's as they stood as quietly as possible in the dark closet. She tried to slow her breathing from their quick dash to cover. She could feel the firmness of Sam's muscular frame and the strength of his arm wrapped around her shoulder in an awkward embrace, and found herself getting distracted from the danger at hand.

"I think they're gone, now," Sam's breath was warm against her cheek as he whispered to her. "I don't hear anything."

Emily focused her attention back to their mission, "Can you take a look?"

Sam opened the door an inch and looked down the hall. There was no sign of the guards. He pulled the door closed again. The closet was as good a place as any to plan their next move.

"Which way is the lab again?" Sam asked.

"Keep going the same direction we were and take the first left," she explained. "There's a security camera at the door, though. As soon as we get within five feet of it the guards will know I didn't come alone."

"That's why you're going into the lab by yourself. You know your way around down there better than I do."

"But there's a camera outside of Elliot's office, too. It'll look pretty suspicious if I'm seen trying to break into it."

"I'll take care of that."

"What are you going to do?"

"I'm going to go back to the stairwell and try to call Peter. He and I can make a few adjustments to their system that'll really make them think they have a ghost. Give me ten minutes before you try to get into his office."

"You'd better know what you're doing, Sam."

The expression on her face told Sam the same thing as the quaver in her voice. She still cared. Without hesitating, Sam pulled her close to him and kissed her. Not a quick peck or a passionate embrace, but somewhere in between. A questioning kiss, asking for her to respond.

And she did respond.

Emily completely forgot where they were and lost herself in their embrace. All the old passion of their past relationship flared anew and threatened to overtake her senses completely, when she remembered where they were and quickly separated herself from Sam, nearly falling over the bucket again in the process.

She thought could hear his heart pounding, and then realized it was her own. She began to ask him if he was ready to go, but he just laid a finger over her lips and nodded with a smile.

Reaching for the knob, Sam listened carefully again for any sign of the guards. He heard nothing and slowly turned the knob, easing the door open an inch.

He saw no one in the hall and risked opening the door further. It looked clear.

He turned to Emily and held up both hands, fingers spread wide.

Ten minutes, he mouthed silently.

She nodded in reply and stepped out into the hall. She watched Sam dash in the other direction and around the corner, praying he would make it back alright.

Now that she was moving on her own, it didn't matter if someone saw her. She had every right to be there and moved confidently towards the labs.

Sam moved quickly to get back to the stairwell, glancing over his shoulder a few times to make sure no one had seen him.

He made it through the door and listened for the sounds of footsteps. Hearing none, he started upwards, intending to go back to the first level. He doubted his signal strength would be able to penetrate the thick concrete of the building unless he was close to an exit.

He stopped at the head of the stairs and still heard nothing, so he ventured a peek through the window.

He quickly stepped back. There was a security guard coming directly for the stairwell. Sam didn't think he had seen him, but he had to find somewhere to hide before the guard came through the door. That gave him about thirty seconds.

He looked wildly around the confined space and saw a door in the wall behind him. It was labeled *Maintenance Personnel Only.*

Sam had no idea what was beyond the door, but he had nowhere else to go.

He silently thanked whoever had failed to properly latch the door as he yanked it open and stepped inside the dark space. He closed the door behind him and kept still while he waited for the guard to pass.

Feeling a little silly from jumping in and out of closets kept him from becoming nervous as he heard the guard enter the stairwell. His footsteps echoed off of the concrete as he descended and Sam heard him open the door to the next level.

Suddenly a light switched on and Sam heard a voice behind him.

"Care to tell me what you're doing in here?"

He spun around and saw an overweight man in what looked like a janitor's outfit holding a foot long piece of steel pipe in his hand.

"Just wanted to see how the other half lives," he said lightly and turned to leave.

But the janitor snagged the back of his shirt collar and put him in a choke hold.

"I don't think so. I don't recognize you and you're not dressed like one of those snobby scientists."

"That's because I'm not," Sam gasped.

"You're a corporate spy or something like it, I'll bet!" He seemed pleased with himself for figuring it out so quickly. "I'm calling security."

Sam had to break free of the meaty arm that was wrapped around his neck. He stomped on the inside of the janitor's foot and was rewarded with a loud expletive and the grip loosened.

Grabbing hold of the janitor's wrist, Sam twisted and stepped behind him, dropping the man to his knees. But before he could find a way to knock the janitor out, the security guard he had seen approaching the stairs tore open the door with his gun drawn and aimed directly at Sam's head.

"Let him go!" the guard roared.

Sam released his grip and stepped away with his hands up. The janitor struggled to his feet.

"Turn around and put your hands on the wall."

Sam never reached the wall because the enraged janitor chose that moment to punch him in the stomach. He fell to the floor gasping for air. Every ounce of the man's weight had been behind the blow.

"Stand back, Johnson," the guard ordered him. "I'm taking care of this."

Johnson kicked Sam in the ribs as a parting blow and then stepped aside for the security guard to take him into custody.

After searching Sam for weapons and removing his gun, the guard picked him up roughly from the floor and shoved him into the stairwell.

"Down the stairs. Get moving!"

Sam stumbled on the first few steps and had to clutch the railing for support. He tried to think of some way out of the situation he was in, but the pain made it difficult to concentrate. His body had taken more abuse in the past two weeks than it had his entire life and the strain was beginning to wear him down.

The guard half shoved, half carried him to the security office. Sam was thankful when they finally reached it and he was thrown into a chair. His ribs were on fire and his stomach felt like he had been hit with a sledgehammer.

Another guard came in from an attached room.

"What've we got here, Davis?"

"Found him attacking one of the janitors."

"Probably one of those wacko protesters. You shouldn't have roughed him up so much."

"Wasn't me. Johnson was a little pissed, I guess."

The other guard chuckled, "Serves him right. As soon as he can talk, find out his name and all the particulars and then we'll turn him over to the cops."

He left Sam alone with Davis who pushed him back in his chair until he was sitting upright.

"Care to tell me who you are and what you're doing here?"

Sam acted like he was more out of it than he really was to avoid answering.

"Don't feel like talking, huh? I'll give you five minutes to pull yourself together, then you'll tell *me* who you are or you can tell the police."

Davis sat back in his chair and looked at his watch. Sam thought the man was probably used to this ploy working on teenagers in his days of working in retail security. They'd break in less than a minute.

But Sam said nothing. He actually wanted them to call the police rather than find out who he was themselves. They surely would connect him with Emily and then she would be in danger as well.

Five minutes passed.

"Time's up. What's your name?"

Sam didn't answer.

"Still not ready to talk?" Davis raised his voice so his partner could hear him. "Better call the police, he's not talking!"

"Actually, I think we'll keep him here," a new voice came from behind Sam.

He turned to see who it was.

A middle aged man with a smile like a snake stood in the doorway.

"Of course, Dr. Morgan. Whatever you want," Davis rose and stood at attention.

Morgan looked at Sam. "Hello, Dr. Hunt. I wish we could have met under more pleasant circumstances."

"I wish we hadn't met at all," Sam took an instant dislike to Morgan's smug attitude.

He leaned back in his chair and casually felt his ribs. They hadn't healed fully from before and they were tender enough that a deep breath sent shooting pains through his side.

Morgan smiled, unperturbed by Sam's hostility.

"I would expect a little more courtesy from someone in your position. But then again, you aren't known for your tact."

Sam knew he was hinting at the fact that he had researched his background and played up his shock to keep Morgan confident he had Sam under his complete control.

"I see you underestimate my intelligence, Dr. Hunt. I know everything about you. Including your- how shall I say it… liaison with Dr. Forrester."

"I'm flattered you take such an interest in my love life," Sam snapped back. "Care to go on a date sometime?"

Morgan's smile faded at Sam's joke. He motioned for the two guards to pick Sam up out of the chair.

"You won't find me so amusing for much longer. Why don't we go visit Dr. Forrester and see if she has a sense of humor as well."

Emily glanced at her watch for the fifth time in the last minute. It had been fifteen minutes since she had entered the lab on top of the ten minutes she had waited like Sam had asked.

She wondered what was taking him so long to get back to the lab. Did he get lost? She didn't think so. It was pretty easy to find.

Trying not to think about it, she continued searching Elliot's office for any traces of an experiment with the viral vector.

She was surprised to see the door standing wide open when she entered the labs. At first she though maybe, Elliot had returned to continue his work. But the lab was deserted.

The computer showed no record of his work and the samples in his mini-fridge weren't labeled. There was nothing indicating what he had been working on at all for the last few weeks. It was more than a little strange. She had been in his office only a few days ago and had seen all kinds of paperwork and test results lying around. Now there was nothing. He couldn't have taken it all with him. Morgan would never allow it.

She was wondering where Sam was again when she heard footsteps approaching. But it wasn't a single person. It sounded like three or four. She ducked down behind Elliot's desk.

"Emily!"

She heard Morgan's voice calling her.

"The guards told me you were here so I thought I'd drop by to see how things were going."

His voice sounded calm and friendly, but Emily knew he was up to something and remained hidden.

"I ran into a friend of yours on the way here and brought him along."

Sam! She didn't know whether she should stay under the desk or come out. Deciding they would find her eventually, she stood up and called to them.

"I'm up here."

A moment later Morgan walked into the room. Behind him, Sam was being held between two security guards. He looked a little roughed up but he still managed to wink at Emily.

"Ah, there you are! Come down and join us, Emily," his pleasantness picked up a sharper edge, "We have a lot to discuss."

She walked slowly down the stairs, her mind racing. They were pretty much trapped at this point. She'd have to go along with whatever he wanted until there was an opportunity for her and Sam to escape. And she really wanted that opportunity to present itself soon.

"Hello, *Louis*," she greeted him coldly.

"No need to be unpleasant, Emily. If anyone should be angry here, it's me. But as you see, I am perfectly capable of dealing with this in a civilized manner."

"You're not going to call the police?"

"Why should I bring them into what is a completely private matter? I think we can come to a suitable arrangement."

Emily didn't want to hear what he was thinking but she had to ask anyway.

"What kind of arrangement?"

"You can continue the work that Elliot began – you're obviously interested in it or you wouldn't be snooping around his office – and I'll refrain from putting Dr. Hunt out of his misery."

He announced his plans as casually as if he were asking for a small favor from a dear friend.

Emily could only stare at the arrogant smile on Morgan's lips. He knew she had no choice but to agree to the bargain.

She glanced over his shoulder at Sam whose eyes were grave, but a smile played around the corners of his mouth.

Emily found her voice, "Do you realize what this vector is capable of?"

"Why else do you think I want to see it succeed?"

Emily shook her head. "Then you don't have a clue."

"You sound like Elliot. He tried to tell me it was dangerous as well. But I saw it for myself. It's perfect."

"It's flawed! It causes unpredictable mutations! Don't just look at the vector, look at the projections!" Emily was pleading now.

"I did. The odds are enormous against something going wrong. It will never happen."

"It already did!"

"Now you're just talking nonsense. I'll send down a copy of the information I gave Elliot – he seems to have made off with the one I gave him. I expect you to be hard at work when I come back in a few hours. Right now I've got to see to Dr. Hunt's accommodations."

He turned and left the lab along with one of the guards and Sam. The other guard, Davis, stayed behind to keep an eye on Emily.

"Better get started, Dr. Forrester," Davis suggested with a grin, "Dr. Morgan hates slackers."

Emily walked numbly over to the refrigerator for samples. She couldn't believe how quickly things had turned against them. She only hoped Sam had been able to get in touch with George before he was caught.

14

The paragraph still didn't make a lot of sense to George, but he supposed it would to a geneticist. He had bought a book at the local bookstore on the basics of microbiology. Some of it he could comprehend, but on the whole it was beyond him. He wished Emily was there to help. It was like translating a language within a language.

But he had deciphered a few interesting passages. He believed one of them gave the name of the people who had created the disk. Translated into its English counterpart, he thought it would mean "Eternal Ones", but he couldn't come up with any kind of phonetics for a language he still didn't understand. There was something distinctly odd about the structure of the phonetics. Something familiar he couldn't quite place.

The program Peter had designed was amazing, but it could only work with the linguistic rules it had been programmed with. Rules that fit modern and known ancient languages. Which, when compared to the language George was attempting to decipher, were not ancient at all. It wasn't even known how to correctly pronounce ancient Egyptian and here he was trying to speak a tongue that was thousands of years older.

The description of the location of one of their underground installations intrigued him the most. Their main lab had been built in a place that George roughly translated as the "bottom of the earth". He assumed they used those terms because it was underground. Along with this description he found what looked like a map. The image was somewhat distorted, but it was definitely a continental coastline. He couldn't tell exactly which coastline by the shape of it alone, he wasn't that good with his geography. Not to mention that this map would be of the coastline before any current maps he could compare it to had been made. But it did look vaguely familiar. If only it showed a larger portion of the continent he could possibly figure it out.

Another problem to send to Peter, he thought and emailed him an encrypted message with the map attached.

It was well past five a.m. when he realized Sam should have contacted him over an hour ago. He had left them at MorGen after he passed on Sam's signal to Peter that they were about to go in. He hoped that they just forgot to call him when they had completed their mission, but he doubted that was the case.

George's next thought was to go to MorGen to look for them. But someone wandering around at five am would look more than a little suspicious. George didn't have any way to get inside either unless he could come up with a legitimate excuse to be there.

He picked up the phone and dialed Peter's number.

"Hello?"

"Peter, how's the weather?"

"Clear skies, George," Peter answered in the code George had insisted he use to let him know the line was secure. "What's up?"

"How good are you at making fake IDs?"

George explained his plan to Peter and though he expressed his doubts, Peter agreed to help. With any luck, George would be inside MorGen's laboratories by that afternoon and he could find out what happened to his friends.

Emily found it difficult to concentrate with an armed security guard hovering over her. And it didn't help that every test she ran came back on the computer as gibberish. It made no sense.

She was exhausted as well. Morgan hadn't let her get any rest since her capture the previous night and she had been working on the vector for the last ten hours with no break. Any time she made a request to go to the bathroom or get coffee, she was escorted into the restroom while a guard waited outside the stall and then she was taken directly back to the lab where a cup of coffee would be waiting for her.

As yet another test failed, she dropped her head into her hands and felt like bursting into tears. She was full of conflicting emotions. She didn't want to complete the vector because of all of the suffering it would bring to mankind, but if she didn't do as she was told, Sam would be killed. And they'd still probably find some other way to force her to finish it.

She clenched her teeth and pulled herself together. She was doing her best and it wasn't enough. Maybe there wasn't enough information on the disks to build the vector after all. Or perhaps it was that their technology wasn't sufficiently advanced to recreate it. That could be why the results were coming out as nonsense.

Or was it the technology? She realized *someone* and not something was foiling her attempts to complete the vector.

But who could it be? Were George and Peter at it again? But how could they know what was going on? Sam surely hadn't been able to contact him since they locked him in the storeroom.

The alternative was one she had a hard time believing. But considering her current situation, she didn't care who was responsible, as long as it kept the vector from being finished.

Her positive outlook was knocked down a peg when Morgan entered the lab. He didn't say a word, but went to the nearest computer and pulled up the test results. His usual dour expression changed to one of outright anger.

"Why do you insist on toying with me, Emily? I know you're stalling for some reason."

He approached her, his anger faded, but still lurked beneath his crocodilian grin.

"Do you think someone is coming to rescue you?"

Emily refused to back away from him as he stopped inches from her face. His breath smelled of tobacco and she could see every line framing his hard grey eyes.

He turned away from her quickly and walked back over to the computer. Whether from annoyance that his attempt to frighten her failed, or from some fear of his own she couldn't tell.

"I'm doing my best," Emily thought her voice sounded a little shaky. She took a deep breath. "I don't know why it's not working."

Morgan turned to face her again.

"Well you'd better figure out why and fix it quickly. Dr. Hunt won't last forever, locked in a room with no food or water."

With that horrible threat, Morgan left the lab, resealing the doors behind him.

Emily still stood by her workstation, trying not to think of how Sam's life was in her hands. The hope she had felt growing only a few minutes ago was crushed under the weight of her task.

Sam wasn't sure what time it was. It seemed like he had been locked in the storage room for days, but he knew it was probably closer to one day since he had awakened in the dimly lit room. He didn't remember being knocked unconscious, but knew he must have been by the lump on the back of his head.

He had been trying unsuccessfully to free himself of his bonds, but the rubber tubing just seemed to get tighter as he struggled. Just my luck to get caught by a security guard who got his scout badge in knot tying, he grumbled.

Looking around the room for the hundredth time, he still saw nothing within his reach that he could possibly use to free himself. The only thing in the room that might work was a sharp piece of metal that was sticking out of a shelf five feet away and three feet off the floor from him.

But being tied to a pipe running along the floor prevented him from going anywhere. He kicked at a nearby stack of boxes in frustration, sending them tumbling to the floor. One of the boxes split open at its seams and its contents spilled out across the white tile.

Sam looked at the mess he had made and would have pinched himself to make sure he wasn't dreaming if it were possible. The boxes had been filled with office supplies including scissors, a pair of which now lay on the floor only a few feet away from him.

He stretched his foot out as far as he could and just touched the scissors with his shoe, but he couldn't quite pull them towards him. He used his other foot to slide off his shoe and tried again.

This time he got his big toe over the handles and dragged them across the floor towards him. When it was close enough, he turned his body as far as he could, parallel to the wall. He couldn't quite reach it with his hands yet.

Repositioning himself, he almost laughed, picturing the method he was using to scoot the scissors closer to his hands. It was always a good thing to find another use for the *gluteus maximus* other than sitting on it.

Once he had the scissors in hand, he carefully positioned the blades and cut the rubber tubing. In a matter of seconds he was finally free.

Sam hadn't realized just how much the circulation in his hands had been restricted until he attempted to push himself off the floor and nearly fell on his face. It was a wonder he had been able to cut through his bonds.

He shook his hands out until they felt a little closer to normal, while he surveyed the room for possible weapons. He dismissed the scissors, they might be good to cut through rubber tubing, but they wouldn't be much use against a man armed with a gun.

He opened some of the other boxes and found more office supplies and some contained old files, but nothing that would help him defend himself if he came up against the security guards again.

Cursing at himself for even getting caught in the first place, he spotted something he hadn't seen the like of in years. An old electric typewriter sat on a desk in the corner, covered with dust and looking like an overgrown computer keyboard. The size of it was what drew Sam's attention. It had to weigh at least thirty pounds and if he could find some way to heft it over the door and onto the head of the guard outside, he could knock him out or at least give him one hell of a headache.

Sam moved a chair behind the door before carrying the typewriter over.

"Hey!" he shouted as loud as he could.

"Shut up in there!" the guard shouted back.

"I need to use the bathroom," Sam knew it was a lame excuse, but keeping it simple sometimes worked better.

"Too bad," the guard wasn't being very sympathetic.

"Yeah, it'll be too bad if Morgan makes you clean it up!"

Sam didn't hear any reply and was about to try a different approach when he heard the keys going into the lock.

He lifted the typewriter over his head.

The guard opened the door and stepped in, not concerned about any danger because he thought Sam was still tied up.

"Don't even try to escape because-"

The guard hit the ground a split second after the typewriter landed on his head.

Sam jumped down off of the chair and quickly disarmed him. The guard didn't move a muscle and a large bump was already forming on the top of his head. But he was still breathing regularly so Sam knew he hadn't hurt the man severely.

"And I thought typewriters were obsolete," he commented as he pulled the guard the rest of the way inside the room and quickly closed the door.

It would probably be some time until he woke up, but just to be safe Sam used some twine he found in one of the boxes to tie up the guard. He took his wireless radio as well so he couldn't call for help.

Now he just had to find his way back to the lab.

It was hard to believe that Jonathan had been gone over thirty years. To Chisek it seemed like yesterday they were discussing plans to mount an expedition into whatever unknown land contained the remains of the lost culture. A lot had changed since then and Chisek felt now he had everything he needed to complete that mission.

As he searched through the boxes of papers left behind from his research, he wondered if Jonathan really had found the location of the Eternal's lost library. If he had, it was possible, however improbable, that he was still there. Now he would get a second chance to find him.

And this time he would succeed because Morgan would be very motivated to find the library. Thirty years ago, Chisek had to call upon past favors to get the money to finance his search and rescue operation. Now Morgan would want to go himself to see if anything remained of their technology and Chisek could tag along to complete his own mission. It was all coming together nicely.

Morgan had explained the content of the disks as being a design for a treatment that could be the ultimate cure for disease of any kind including cancer. Chisek didn't think that was actually possible, though he did recognize the animations of the double helix of DNA. He wasn't sure what they were illustrating, but he knew beyond a shadow of a doubt that the collection of symbols across the bottom of the screen was the written language of the Eternals and that was enough for him.

He and Jonathan had first discovered writing exactly like it carved on the underside of a stone placed at the center of an Incan temple. That was during their graduate work in Peru. They told no one about it, knowing it would only be dismissed as a ritual incantation of some kind and forgotten by the days' end.

They had spent years trying to decipher the glyphs, but with only one small tablet containing fifty or so symbols, it was nearly impossible. And they had never found any more examples of that type of writing.

But now Chisek had more than enough to work out a translation. Having a copy of George Baltazidis' partially completed work and the pictures along with the text only made it easier. With the resources he had at his disposal, he figured it might take him a year at the most to have a complete phonetic alphabet and basic dictionary of the language completed.

He was searching through Jonathan's old papers from the months before his disappearance, trying to find some clue as to where he intended to search for the lost civilization. At that point in time, he was working in Greece for the National Archeological Museum. Chisek had envied him, but he could admit to himself that of the two of them, Jonathan was by far the brighter one. He could see so much more in a Stone Age tool than just its construction. He could picture the owner using it in his daily chores and the whole village around him.

Chisek envied his ability to create a world from one artifact. It was one of the reasons he found himself behind a desk instead of in the midst of an excavation. Jonathan had always told him he was better at organizing things and that was his contribution to their professional partnership.

He smiled as he looked at the unindexed boxes of miscellaneous papers that had been crammed into a storage room at the university. They had only been uncovered recently, when more space was needed for the artifact preservation department. No one had even attempted to find order in Jonathan's papers; it would have been a daunting task. But Chisek was thankful for that. If someone had gone through his files, they may have discovered the journal that he now found himself holding.

He opened the tattered leather-bound volume and began to read Jonathan's scrawling handwritten notes.

May 25, 1974
I found it! Finally, the last clue to the hidden city of the Eternal Ones! I can't believe it took me so long to figure it out, it was just about staring me in the face...

Chisek could almost hear Jonathan's voice. He skimmed over the rest of the page, his excitement building. But there was no mention of the city again until several weeks later.

June 28, 1974
I'm going to do it! I'm gathering together the best of my staff for an expedition to Eternity Base, as I will call it until I discover its true name...

He went on to name everyone who would accompany him, all of whom disappeared with him as well. But there was no more than that.

Chisek continued to skim ahead through the journal, stopping at each mention of the expedition.

Finally, in an entry on the next to last page, he found it.

September 16, 1974
Tomorrow we leave for Johannesburg and from there we will set out for the Eternity Base...

George was genuinely impressed with the size of the MorGen facilities when he drove in through the front gate. The fake press pass that Peter had created got him inside with no problem.

He sat on a leather sofa in the luxuriously appointed reception area while he waited for his tour guide to greet him.

It was a crazy thing to do, George admitted to himself, but he had to know what was going on. If Sam and Emily were in danger he couldn't sit idly by and just hope for the best.

A woman in a dark grey suit came out of one of the back offices and approached George with a practiced smile.

"Mr. Papadopoulos, welcome to MorGen," she said pleasantly.

George rose and shook her outstretched hand.

"I'm Flora McGovern, MorGen's Public Relations Director," the way she said it made the capitalization of her title very clear.

"I was told the flora of Pennsylvania was beautiful," George put his natural charm to work, "I can't wait to see the fauna."

The required girlish laugh was performed by Ms. McGovern and she began to lead him back through the offices.

"Thank you for seeing me on such short notice. It was kind of a last minute idea by my editor," George said.

"We usually require more notice for a private tour, but I must admit I was eager to show off MorGen's facilities to someone with your credentials."

Her tone was neutral, but George was concerned that she may be suspicious.

"What part of Greece are you from?" she asked

"I grew up in the Dodecanese Islands, but I work out of Athens," he replied cautiously.

"I've always wanted to visit the Greek Isles," she paused in front of a set of double doors. "This tour is only through a portion of the labs. Obviously, some areas are restricted due to the type of work being performed there."

"Of course. You can't have any visitors contracting strange diseases, can you?"

She smiled condescendingly, "No we can't. Exactly why is the Athens press interested in MorGen?"

"Well, genetics is such a rapidly expanding field and MorGen is a leader in research. It's only natural that an up and coming nation like our own would be interested. We have a few companies in this line of work, but they're small. They appreciate a little help from the press demonstrating how a little government grant money could help them be as successful as MorGen."

"And the newspaper sells a lot of copies because it's such a hot topic?" she ventured as they walked down a concrete hallway to another set of double doors.

"Exactly."

On the other side of the doors was a locker room with white cotton jumpsuits hanging on pegs. A box of slip-on shoe covers and another box of disposable rubber gloves hung on the wall next to them.

"This is more for the protection of the facility than you," Ms. McGovern explained as she stepped into a jumpsuit.

"I hope you have one large enough for me," George joked as he looked down the row of pegs to find the right size.

Once they were both suited up, she handed George a plastic cap to put over his hair.

He laughed as he put it on, "Paging Dr. Papadopoulos."

Again the condescending smile.

They left the locker room and entered another concrete hallway that looked exactly like the first. Ms. McGovern led the way through another set of double doors marked with the sign *Authorized Personnel Only*.

"This of one of the original labs from when MorGen was simply Morgan Pharmaceuticals," she turned on her tour guide voice. "It is still used occasionally by Dr. Morgan himself when he misses the old days."

She paused for George to laugh.

"Through here," they entered the next room, "is one of our many sequencing labs. Since we focus on so many aspects of the human genome, we have found it more economical to keep our own database instead of relying on the Human Genome Project."

She continued showing him through various rooms, some where scientists were working, others deserted. The whole time he kept thinking about how much money it would take to run a facility like this and how that much money could buy you almost anything.

Like a man's soul, he thought. Maybe that's the hold he had over Chisek.

"As you can imagine, running a facility like this one is very expensive," Ms. McGovern echoed his thoughts, "but Mr. Morgan still manages to donate millions of dollars every year to various charities."

"He sounds like an amazing man," George put on his best fake grin and received one in return.

George's thoughts refocused themselves on finding Sam and Emily. Throughout the tour, he kept his eyes open for any sign of them.

As Ms. McGovern led him through yet another lab, he spotted a watch lying on a desk. It was unmistakably Sam's. No one else had a custom made watch with a trowel and brush for hands and a progression of evolution around the dial. George had given that to Sam for completing his master's degree.

The fact that the crystal was cracked did not make George feel any better about finding it.

The tour started to wind down about half an hour later. George had appeared to be paying close attention to her every word and occasionally jotting down a line or two in the notepad he had brought along as they walked through the facility. In actuality he had been making a crude map of the doors they had not been allowed to go past. One in particular looked like it led to the heart of the operation.

"Excuse me, Ms. McGovern," George interrupted her closing speech on how hard work and perseverance made MorGen the leader in pharmaceuticals.

"Yes? Did you have a question on something you've seen?"

"Um, actually," he looked a little sheepish, "I was wondering where the nearest restrooms might be."

"Oh," she looked disappointed that he didn't have a tough question for her. "Just down the hall here."

She led him around the corner and pointed to restroom sign sticking out of the wall.

"The doors at the end of the hall lead back to the locker room. You can take off your jumpsuit there and meet me back in the office. Then I'll give you our press packet as well."

George smiled. She couldn't have been more obliging.

"Thank you. I'll see you there shortly."

George watched her walk away before he entered the bathroom. He waited a moment to be sure she wasn't coming back and then quickly exited the bathroom and headed back the way they had come.

The images on the computer screen taunted him. No matter how often he looked at the structure of the vector, he couldn't fathom its complexity.

Morgan leaned back in his chair and sighed heavily. He had been working on the vector since Emily claimed she couldn't make it. Though he acted as if he didn't believe her, he was troubled by the feeling that there was something unique about the vector design that would be difficult to reproduce.

He leaned forward again to examine the diagram. All of the symbols were of no use to them without a translation and Chisek hadn't been able to come up with one yet. So they had to go by the atomic structure of the pictured vector. It looked simple enough, but somehow all of their attempts to recreate it failed.

He pulled up the data on Emily's first tests again, and compared them to the information on the disks for the tenth time.

The only difference he could see between the two vectors was the original virus used to deliver the genetic material. It appeared as though the virus itself had been genetically altered before being used in the creation of the vector. But he couldn't tell from the diagram exactly how it had been changed.

Feeling like he was starting to get a grip on the problem, he reviewed the rest of the information on the disk, looking for some reference to the virus. After two hours of careful examination, he found nothing.

He growled in frustration and jumped out of his chair to angrily pace the room. They were so close, but something in the vector's production was beyond their capabilities.

But he wouldn't give up, he never did. Even when all the doctors told him his son wouldn't live another week, he kept trying to find a way to keep him alive. And finding the key to this vector was just as important to him as his son was.

He returned to his desk and stared at the screen until his eyes began to water from the strain.

"Dr. Morgan," his secretary's voice on the intercom interrupted his trance.

"What is it," he snapped back.

"Dr. Chisek is here to see you."

He directed her to send him in.

Morgan noted Chisek's rough appearance. It looked as though he had slept in his clothes or not slept at all. He realized he probably looked the same.

"I found it," Chisek stated simply.

"Found what?"

"I know where the Eternity Base is."

Morgan sat up quickly.

"What?"

"It's right here in this journal," Chisek handed him a tattered leather book.

He took it eagerly and began leafing through the pages.

"I marked the pertinent passages," Chisek explained and took a seat opposite him.

Morgan couldn't believe his eyes. The journal that lay open before him read more like a H. Rider Haggard novel than the notes of a real life adventurer and scientist.

"Are you sure about this?"

"Jonathan was sure enough about it that he used all of his money and resources to get there," Chisek replied.

Morgan eyed him suspiciously, "Why didn't you use this journal when you went to track him down?"

"I didn't know it existed then. I just found it last night."

"It just seems too easy. Why would he have disappeared? What could have happened?"

"There are a lot of things that could have gone wrong. South Africa wasn't exactly a safe place in the seventies. Even now it can be a dangerous place for an inexperienced traveler."

"And what do you think we'll find when we get there? This Alpha Base of yours is supposedly over a half-million years old. What could survive that amount of time?"

"We know the disks can. There may be more of them there. If I have enough, it will make a translation much easier."

Morgan thought this over for a moment. Chisek was right. They may even find a disk that contained the information on the virus. And if these people could make one substance that could withstand the passage of eons, why couldn't they make others.

"Alright, Bob. We'll go. Why don't you join me while I tell Emily the good news?"

Sam couldn't imagine how his nerves could be strung any tighter. Every little noise made him jump as he inched his way down the corridors, trying to find his way to the labs. So far he hadn't seen anything that looked familiar.

He decided they must have moved him somewhere far from the work areas after he had gone down two hallways and hadn't seen a single person. He could be anywhere is the vast MorGen complex for all he knew. He just prayed he was still in the same building as Emily and that he would eventually find her.

Distant footsteps brought Sam to a halt, and he strained to tell from what direction they were coming. Peering around a corner, he saw a stairwell and thought perhaps someone was coming down. Maybe to relieve the guard he had knocked out.

He made a quick decision to stand his ground and use the gun he had taken from the guard if it was necessary. He was tired of running and hiding and was determined to take control of his situation.

The footsteps drew nearer and stopped on the other side of the door. For a long moment there was no sound and Sam feared that the person was aware he was concealed around the corner.

He heard the door open slowly. A single footstep followed.

Sam slipped the safety off of the pistol and readied himself for the confrontation.

A few more stealthy footsteps echoed down the corridor. Sam figured they were no more than five feet around the corner and he made his move.

He stepped into the adjoining hallway and leveled the gun at the approaching figure. And just as quickly dropped it to his side with a great wave of relief washing over his body.

"George," Sam gasped in surprise, "what are you doing here?"

"Sam! You scared me half to death," George clutched at his shirtfront, his eyes wide. "I came here to find you and Emily."

"How did you get in?"

George pulled out his press pass and showed it to Sam.

"Peter does good work," Sam noted. "Too bad it can't get us out of here."

"Where's Emily?"

"She's probably still in the labs, but I really don't know for sure. I spent most of the time locked in a storage room back that way. And I'm not really sure how to get to the labs from here."

George consulted his notebook, "I can get us back to the main level if you know how to get to the lab from there."

"Great, let's get moving," Sam started towards the stairwell.

"I was supposed to be back from the bathroom by now so they're probably looking for me. We'll have to move slowly."

Sam turned to face him, "We don't have time, George. If they find out I've escaped before we get to Emily, I don't know what they'll do. They're forcing her to finish the vector by threatening to kill me if she doesn't. If I'm gone, they may hurt her."

George's normally jovial expression suddenly hardened, "Let's go."

They almost ran up the stairs to the next level, quickly checking that everything was clear before each landing. Oddly enough, they ran into no one until reaching the main level.

Waiting inside the stairwell for a security guard to pass, George motioned to Sam that they were to go right upon exiting. The guard turned at the end of the hall and they sprinted out of the door and in the opposite direction.

George led them around another corner and Sam finally saw something that he recognized. It was the stairwell where he had been apprehended the night before.

"George," he hissed and motioned for him to follow.

The maintenance door at the top of the stairs was fully closed this time, Sam noticed before he started down towards the lab level.

They moved as fast as possible without making too much noise and soon reached the floor at which Sam had left Emily.

Sam walked boldly through the door at the bottom of the stairs and headed in the direction of the lab. George followed closely behind him.

As they neared the last intersection before they would arrive at the locker rooms next to the lab, they heard raised voices. They stopped where they were and listened.

"Keep looking. He's probably still in the building," Louis Morgan growled.

The one sided conversation led Sam to believe he was on the phone, probably to his security chief.

Sam started to move, but George grabbed his arm and held him.

Emily, he mouthed and Sam understood that he wanted to make sure Emily was there before they went in.

"Well, Ms. Forester, it seems your hero has escaped for the time being. But no matter, he'll soon be recaptured and punished properly this time."

"He's probably miles from here by now," Emily's voice was strong, but a hint of exhaustion lay over her words.

"What? And leave his lady in the clutches of the evil doctor?" Morgan laughed at his own joke.

"You're hardly evil. Misguided is more like it."

"Don't!" a new voice joined the exchange.

It was a very familiar voice to Sam. One he had heard berate him a thousand times. But what was Chisek doing here?

"Or what?" Morgan's voice had a smug note to it. He chuckled softly. "Alright, Bob, I'll leave her alone. You can even take her along for company if you'd like."

"I'd sooner stay locked up in here," Emily retorted.

"As much as I would love to oblige you, I think it would be best if you came with us."

"Where are we going?"

"As much as I hate to admit it, the technology needed to produce this vector is beyond us. So we're going straight to the source."

"And that would be where?"

"Don't play dumb, Emily. I know you've been working with Dr. Hunt and his Greek friend. We're going to visit the creators of the vector. At least what's left of them. I think we'll find what we need there. Davis, start making arrangements for our trip to Johannesburg and make sure you bring reinforcements. I'm not sure Dr. Hunt will give up so easily."

George turned to Sam and motioned for him to follow him back to the stairwell where they could speak without being overheard.

"Whatever you're going to say had better be good. We need to get back there and get Emily before they drag her off to South Africa," Sam whispered

"That's exactly why we can't go back and free her."

Sam couldn't believe what he was hearing and started towards the door.

"Sam, listen to me," George spoke as loudly as he dared, "Unless you want to go in there and kill Chisek and Morgan in cold blood you're not going to be able to rescue her anyway."

Sam knew he couldn't do that, but he also couldn't let them kidnap Emily.

"We can't just sit here and do nothing," Sam countered.

"No, we can't. We're going to get out of here before we're caught and then we're going to follow Morgan wherever he goes. He can't hide from us. Peter can track him on the computer, and we can tail him in person"

Sam was torn. They were so close to Emily but they couldn't even let her know they were there. He didn't want to leave without her.

"Come on, Sam. We've got to get moving," George started up the stairs, "They know you've escaped and they're looking for you."

Sam took one last painful look down the hall towards the lab and then quickly followed George up the stairs.

15

Emily sat at her desk and toyed with the sandwich the guard had brought her from the lunchroom vending machine. She was hungry, but was distracted by too many concerns racing around in her head.

One thing she wasn't too concerned about was Sam. She had been elated to hear that he had escaped and knew he wouldn't leave her a prisoner for long. Emily had overheard Morgan loudly berating his guards when he discovered Sam had escaped the entire compound with the help of an unknown Greek reporter who could be none other than George.

But she wasn't just going to sit there and wait to be rescued either. She had been making friends with the security guards as each one came on duty and hoped she could use that to her advantage later. She was also collecting small items from the lab that she could easily conceal on her person and that could be used as a weapon.

She hoped she would be able to escape before she was taken to wherever they were going. She had heard Morgan and Chisek making some of their plans and knew they would be flying somewhere the next day, but she hadn't been able to catch the name of the airport as they walked away.

It seemed like it was years since Sam had sent her that first email about meeting her to show her the disk. So much had happened in such a short time. She tried to sort it all out in her mind and was getting a headache for her efforts.

First of all, she still wasn't sure who had bugged her room. It made sense to think it was Morgan because she was positive he was the one who had bugged her computer. But George made a convincing argument for his government conspiracy. It could be anybody. For all she knew, a perverted hotel employee did it.

And then there were the disappearing artifacts. All signed out under the same name by a nondescript male. Emily was pretty sure it hadn't been Chisek or Morgan behind it because they didn't seem to know any more about the disks than she did.

The physical attacks on Sam and George seemed to be the work of two different groups. On Patmos, the house was ransacked and the attacker didn't seem to care if he killed someone to get the disk. But at Sam's house, the attacker fled as soon as he was able to get away from Sam and didn't even find the disk.

She finally gave up trying to figure it out and took a bite of her sandwich. The ham and cheese tasted more like cardboard, but she ate it anyway to keep up her strength. If and when she had an opportunity to escape, she needed all the energy she could muster.

"She's safe here, Bob. My men are keeping an eye on her."

Morgan was in his office signing a few papers that needed his attention before he left while he spoke to Chisek on the speakerphone.

"That had better be all they're keeping on her," Chisek sounded anxious

"You just worry about getting to the airport on time and make up that list of supplies we'll need once we get to Johannesburg."

"Of course. And I'll find a guide once we get there."

"Excellent. I'll see you at two o' clock."

Morgan ended the call before Chisek could say anything else. He was starting to get on his nerves. He'd love to leave Chisek behind, but they needed his knowledge of the so-called "Eternal Ones" culture to find the location of their lab. But what they would actually find when the got there not even Chisek knew. Morgan hoped it was more explicit instructions on creating the vector or even the remains of the equipment originally used to create it. Even if there wasn't a lot left, they could probably construct a replica.

He still had his doubts about whether the lab would still exist; he didn't completely trust Chisek's theories. But he knew there was no way the vector could be completed with their current technology. It would be years, or perhaps even decades, until they would be sufficiently advanced to accurately recreate it.

It's worth a shot, he decided. And expense certainly wasn't an issue. He would spend his entire fortune to reach his goal if necessary.

After their unsuccessful interrogation of Emily, Chisek had explained to him in depth all of the work he had done on the subject of the Eternals in the last twenty years. It was an interesting subject, and would be invaluable if the legends proved to be true. The disk that Hunt had found was proof that something had occurred in the distant past that wasn't currently known.

Morgan signed the last paper, neatly returned it to the stack lying to his right and got up to leave the office.

Before he took two steps, his intercom buzzed and his secretary informed him that a Sgt. Ramsey was there to speak with him about the break-in.

"Send him in," Morgan sighed and sat back down.

It was tedious to have to speak to the police on the matter, but he wanted to make sure they would pursue the case actively and make Sam Hunt a fugitive from justice. He would have a difficult time following Morgan to South Africa in a foolish attempt to rescue Emily if he was a wanted man. After his security men had searched the grounds for several hours with no sign of Hunt, they gave up. And the mysterious disappearance of a Greek reporter during a tour made it obvious that he had help in his escape.

Half an hour later, Morgan had finished his statement and dismissed the officer. He hadn't bothered to mention the fact that one of his employees was missing.

No one knew what had happened to Elliot and that didn't bother Morgan at all. He assumed he had quit with no notice and left it up to his lawyer to track him down and serve him the papers for breaking his contract.

Yes, everything is working out for the best, he thought. He didn't need Elliot anyway. Or Emily for that matter. There were only two reasons he even bothered to keep her; to make sure Hunt left them alone and to keep Chisek on his side until they had found his Eternity Base.

He had only known him for a few years and wasn't sure how far he could trust him yet. Introduced to him by Harry, Chisek was a useful resource for acquiring any new research at the university laboratories. But Morgan had found over the years that people who will sell to the highest bidder don't think twice about stabbing someone else in the back if it suits their needs at the time. It was one of the reasons Morgan liked him, but he would no longer be necessary after the vector was complete.

Morgan left his office and headed to the parking lot. He decided along the way that this would be the last time he and Chisek worked together.

He met Harry's assistant security chief at his car.

"Davis," he greeted him.

"Hello, Dr. Morgan," Davis opened the door for him. "Mr. Lundgren is already loading the equipment onto your private jet."

Morgan had been quite shocked that morning when he walked into his office to find Harry sitting behind his desk. He had apologized profusely, explaining that he had been called away on a family emergency and hadn't Morgan gotten the message he left with the secretary.

He was going to fire that secretary when he returned from their trip.

Sitting quietly in the backseat until Davis had pulled the Mercedes out of the parking lot and into the street, he smiled to himself thinking about how pleasurable it would be to fire her.

"Were you able to contact your friends?" Morgan asked as they turned onto the highway.

"Yes, sir. They'll meet us at the airport as we discussed."

"And they're aware of the risks?"

"They live for it, sir."

Morgan could see Davis grinning broadly in the rearview mirror. He was an ex-Marine and had several friends who had also left the service with less than distinguished records and now found themselves working as "freelance security guards", as they preferred to be called.

"And the salary is to their liking?"

"Without a doubt. But it did make them wonder how dangerous this trip was going to be. I told them that you're just a generous man."

Morgan chuckled, "Very good, Davis. You'll be seeing a bonus on your next check."

"Thank you, sir," Davis grinned even more broadly.

"I'm coming with you and that's final," Anna stood with her arms crossed and a determined look on her face.

They had been arguing about Anna accompanying them on their trip since they had arrived on the island that morning.

"Anna, it's going to be too dangerous-"

"Which is exactly why I should go with you. You'll need someone with medical training along in case anyone gets hurt. I know the mountains of South Africa better than you do and there will be more dangerous things out there than a mad scientist."

Sam figured Anna had a good point. It would be better to have someone along to handle injuries and she did know the terrain well from her days as a nurse in the Peace Corps. Not to mention she spoke Afrikaans and a good bit of Zulu as well. But Sam was only half listening to their argument. His mind was more focused on how they would rescue Emily once they caught up with Morgan. They knew he was headed to South Africa, but beyond that they'd have to follow him. Peter had arranged their flight to Johannesburg so they would arrive two hours before Morgan and his entourage after finding record of their flight plans on the airport's database.

George continued to argue with his wife as he selected the equipment he wanted to bring along. Sam had agreed with him that they should fly back to Patmos first so they could rendezvous with Peter and collect certain pieces of equipment that would make tracking Morgan easier.

And since communications aren't always reliable in the middle of nowhere, they had decided it would be better for Peter to run his end of their operations from somewhere closer than Patmos. He would stay in a hotel in Johannesburg and track Morgan from there.

They were moving as quickly as possible since their escape from the MorGen labs the previous night. Luckily for Sam, George had brought along several of his spy gadgets for picking locks and bypassing security systems while Peter befuddled the cameras once again, and they were out of the building before any guards caught up with them. He was still unhappy about leaving Emily behind, but at least they had a plan to free her and stop Morgan's plans for recreating the vector.

"Alright, you win," George threw his hands into the air, "Pack up some things quickly, our flight leaves Izmir in five hours."

Anna smiled triumphantly as she headed to her room to pack.

"She always gets her way, doesn't she?" Sam asked George.

"Always," George shook his head. "Why don't you go see if Peter's ready yet. We'll have to leave in about an hour to make sure we get to Izmir in time."

"Good idea."

"I just hope Eleni doesn't have any crazy notions of coming along as well."

George's foreboding proved to be correct. When Sam arrived at the Korais residence, he found Peter and Eleni arguing in much the same way as George and Anna had been only moments ago.

"You are *not* going with us and that's final."

Peter had two suitcases packed and sitting next to the door. Eleni stood nearby holding a third. She set it down heavily next to the other two.

"I *am* going with you-" Eleni jumped as she noticed Sam standing there.

"Hi, Sam," Peter greeted him. "Come in, I'm just about ready to go," he turned to Eleni with a commanding stare, "by myself."

He picked up the suitcase that Eleni had just set down and began to carry it back to the bedroom. She leaped after him and pulled the suitcase out of his hands.

"I don't see why she can't go along," Sam interrupted the beginnings of a new fight, "Anna's going."

"You're joking," Peter stopped fighting Eleni for the suitcase.

"No, George agreed her skills could be useful to us."

"I may not have a lot of skills," Eleni glared at her husband, "but I have connections."

Sam didn't really care who came along at that point, he just wanted to get going. Every minute that Emily was held hostage by Morgan and Chisek made him feel more frustrated, and he longed to get on the plane and hunt them down.

Peter looked thoughtful. "Hmm…you do, don't you?"

Eleni beamed as she saw Peter was changing his mind.

"But you have to promise me you'll do whatever I tell you when we get to Johannesburg," Peter took her by the shoulders.

"So it'll seem just like being at home," she joked.

"I'm serious, Eleni. If something goes wrong, I need you to do what I ask immediately with no argument."

"Anything you say, Peter," she went up on her tiptoes to kiss him.

Sam was somewhat embarrassed being present at such a tender moment. They seemed to have forgotten he was there.

He cleared his throat, "Well I'm glad that's settled."

They quickly separated and managed to look sheepish.

"George wants to leave as soon as possible so we don't miss our flight."

"We're ready. I have a lead on where they'll be headed and I think there are one or two things I can do to slow them down as well."

That was the best news Sam had heard all day. "Maybe we can get there ahead of them then."

"Since we know they're going to Johannesburg, I compared the map from the disk to the coastline of South Africa. Granted, things have changed a bit over a few hundred millennia, but I could still get a general idea of what part of the country the site is located in."

He pulled out a map and pointed at a location on the northeastern section of the country.

"The Drakensberg Mountains seems like the most likely place to find our cave if it still exists. Though there's been enough seismic activity in the area over the years to have possibly destroyed it."

"I think it would have been well protected. But we can hope there's nothing left."

Peter looked at him questioningly.

"As much as I'd like to find the remains of an unheard of ancient culture, I'd rather Morgan didn't."

The hotel that Morgan and his group had taken over was situated in the heart of the Johannesburg and the night sky was lit up with the activity of its inhabitants. The view from the balcony of Emily's room was spectacular and she only wished she could enjoy it more.

But being confined to her room while Morgan and Chisek sat at a table in the courtyard restaurant put a damper on her enthusiasm. That and the fact that she was still a prisoner who had been brought there against her will.

She never had the chance to escape before their flight because they had slipped a tranquilizer into her coffee the previous morning. She was asleep during the entire flight and was just starting to come around as they left the airport. She remembered being in a wheelchair and imagined they told the flight crew she was an invalid.

During the ride to the hotel, she slowly regained her senses and became aware of the gun jabbing her in the ribs. The beefy man sitting beside her gave her a menacing glance as she shifted uncomfortably.

She looked at the rest of the passengers in the van and saw Morgan and Chisek towards the front. All the rest of the men were as big as the one sitting next to her. She recognized only one of them as being a security guard at MorGen and wondered who the rest were.

Their arrival at the hotel had apparently been prearranged. They were met at the side entrance and given the keys to their rooms in relative silence. The bags were unloaded from the back of the van and taken directly upstairs along with Emily.

After being unceremoniously shoved into her room, Morgan came in.

"Hello, Emily," he smiled. "I hope you're not suffering from any after effects of the tranquilizers."

She didn't answer him.

"Or maybe they haven't completely worn off yet. I'm sorry we had to do that, but it was the easiest way."

"And it would be a little difficult to take me on board the plane at gunpoint," Emily retorted.

Morgan's smile widened like an alligator preparing to devour its prey.

"Yes it would. But now that we're here, it's not so difficult. There will be guards across the hall from you at all times. The hotel management is under the impression that you're some kind of celebrity and those are your body guards."

"I wonder how they got that idea."

He walked over to the phone and unplugged it, wrapping the cord neatly around the receiver and then tucking it under his arm.

"And I don't think you'll need this. One of the guards will bring you your meals."

And he left without any further explanation of what was going on.

Now she sat on the balcony watching the two men at the table sipping on their drinks. They seemed to be arguing about something. But that was nothing new. She couldn't imagine that they could be friends because they seemed to disagree on almost everything. Chisek got up and went inside to the restaurant lounge.

If she only had some way to contact Sam and let him know where she was. She had thoroughly searched the gaudily decorated room after Morgan left and found no other phone or even stationary to possibly drop a note somewhere. And there certainly weren't any items that would be useful if she had an opportunity to escape.

She looked down at the courtyard again. It was about thirty feet from her balcony to the ground, with another balcony ten feet under her. If they didn't put a guard outside that night, she would put her rock climbing skills to good use and try to descend that way under cover of darkness. And it helped that she was dressed for action as well. Morgan had sent one of his goons to buy her some clothing appropriate for trekking through the Bushveld and amazingly enough he came back with the right sizes and good quality materials. The boots were a little snug, but they would loosen up once she started walking in them. The thick cotton khakis and shirt fit well enough, but they reminded her of a military uniform with extra pockets everywhere.

Emily hated that there was so little she could do about her situation. She felt the anxiety and despair trying to force their way back to the forefront of her emotions. But she took a deep breath and focused on the fact that she had a plan and she would not give up trying to escape. And though she wouldn't admit it to anyone, not even herself, she also had faith that Sam would come to help her.

After two hours of staring at the breathtaking view that she couldn't really enjoy, the security guard, Davis, came to bring her some supper.

"It's about time," she snapped at him, "I thought you were going to let me starve to death."

She wasn't really hungry, but she felt the need to be strong in front of her captors so they knew she wasn't intimidated. And if they were going to tell people she was a movie star she might as well act like one.

Davis just smiled.

"Did you bring me anything to drink with that?" She continued in a hostile tone.

He held out a peculiar looking bottle of a local brand of soda pop.

"I'm not going to drink that. Get me some wine."

Davis' grin widened, "Of course, your majesty."

He turned to leave the room.

"And don't bring me any cheap shit," she yelled after him. "I want the good stuff."

He left, closing the door quietly behind him.

Emily knew she was pushing her luck. They really had no reason to keep her alive. For a man with Morgan's money, explaining away a corpse was a relatively simple matter. Or they could even dump her body in the mountains and no one would ever find it. But she had a feeling that Chisek was most of the reason why she was still alive, thought she hardly felt grateful for that.

She started eating her dinner, a spicy mix of beef and vegetables though she didn't really taste anything as she chewed. Her mind was on her escape plans which she would act upon in only a few hours.

After managing to eat most of her dinner, with the plastic cup of surprisingly delicious wine that Davis had turned up with, she decided she had better get some rest. The wine made her feel a bit drowsy, but she didn't think she'd sleep very long, if at all, and would get up in a few hours.

Stretching out on the bed, she reached for the bedside lamp and shut it off. As she lay in the darkness, she found herself thinking of Sam and wondering if he even knew where she was.

"That's impossible. Run it through again," Morgan growled at the woman behind the counter.

"I'm sorry, sir. But it has been declined. Do you have another card?" She looked as though she wished she could hide under the counter.

"Of course," he reached in his wallet, "try this one."

It made no sense for any of his credit cards to be declined. He had no set spending limits, and he certainly didn't have any problems with late payments. He was one of the richest men in America.

"There must be something wrong with our system, Mr. Morgan. This card won't go through either."

The woman was obviously trying to placate him by lying about the equipment malfunction. But Morgan had a suspicious feeling that his cards wouldn't work anywhere. His anger began to simmer.

"Never mind," he stalked off, infuriated by this new obstacle.

Back at the hotel, he tried every credit and debit card he had with him in the ATM in the lobby. All of them were declined and one of them was even held by the machine. Something was definitely wrong and he had an idea who was responsible.

He returned to his room and went online to access his bank accounts. He wasn't surprised to find them "temporarily unavailable".

There was a knock at the door.

"What," he shouted.

Davis stepped into the room. "We have all of the equipment ready, sir. Should we take it to the helipad tonight or tomorrow morning?"

"There's been a change of plans. We'll be driving instead." Morgan was angrier than he let show, but he would not allow himself to appear to be weak in front of his employees. "Find Chisek and tell him to get up here now."

Chisek arrived a few minutes later. "You wanted to see me?"

"How much do you know about George Baltazidis?"

"I know a little about his career and personal life. He's pretty well known in my business. Specializes in Neolithic cultures and ancient languages."

"And I understand he's a bit of a techno wizard."

"I guess so," Chisek shrugged. "I worked with him a few times and he always had the latest electronic gadgets. He even built a few of his own."

"Would you say he was also a hacker?"

"He could be. I don't really know," Chisek sat down in an armchair nearby. "Has something happened?"

Morgan explained what had happened at the airport and with the ATM.

"I don't think a regular hacker could do that. It sounds more like a government operation," Chisek suggested.

"But why would the government freeze my accounts? I haven't broken any laws."

Morgan was aware of the fact that kidnapping was a felony, but if no one knew he had done it, he didn't consider it illegal. The only person that knew he had brought Emily to South Africa against her will was Sam Hunt. And he was probably in jail right now, hardly a reliable witness to a kidnapping. He was almost positive that Sam or one of his friends had to be behind it, and it made him wonder if someone was just tracking him electronically or if he had actually been followed. If he had been followed, he would need to know before they left Johannesburg so they could take steps.

"We're going to have to drive," he continued. "How much cash do you have with you?"

"A few hundred in American."

"Good. We'll need it to rent some jeeps."

It would take an extra day to drive and then hike to the site instead of taking the helicopters, but Morgan consoled himself with the fact that one more day wasn't much more to wait for the culmination of his life's work.

A knock on the door heralded the return of Davis.

"The last of the equipment will be delivered to the hotel tomorrow morning and we have a truck to transport everything. We just need to find a guide to take us to the cave."

"Is that a problem?"

"It shouldn't be. You usually have your pick of twenty or so natives who are willing to take you."

"Not this time," Chisek spoke up.

"What do you mean by that," Morgan snapped.

"It's on private property and the locals don't appreciate trespassers. We'll need permission first"

"I'm impressed, Bob," Morgan smirked, "you actually do know something useful."

Chisek glared at him.

"You wouldn't be here at all if it weren't for me."

"I wouldn't say that. We could have eventually figured out the information on the disk. But it would have likely taken us years to perfect it. Doing things your way was just more cost effective."

Davis snickered at Chisek's discomfort.

"Is our guest settled in?" Morgan asked Davis.

"I just took supper up to her room," the grin was back. "She's quite a feisty lady. Demanded that I bring her some wine."

"Good. Maybe she'll get drunk and pass out so we won't have to listen to her."

"Is there anything else you needed me for?" Chisek interrupted their little joke.

"No, Bob. You can go ahead," Morgan waved him away. He didn't want Chisek to know what he planned to do next. He was too squeamish when it came to taking physical action.

"Davis, I have a little job for you," Morgan smiled to himself, feeling in control of his world once again.

16

Sam could only see half of the balcony to Emily's room and she had moved out of his view. He was sitting at a sidewalk cafe next to the hotel where Morgan and his men were staying, trying to be inconspicuous while looking through binoculars every five minutes.

Their flight had been delayed so they arrived in Johannesburg after Morgan's group left their smaller private airport. But it didn't take long for George and Peter to find out what hotel they had checked into. As much as Morgan was paying the hotel to be secretive, it couldn't overcome the natural tendencies of people to gossip about unusual happenings. The supposed appearance of a movie star was quickly known by all the locals who spread the word to any tourist with some extra cash.

Sam called the hotel immediately to inquire about recent arrivals and the rumors about a celebrity guest were denied - until he described Emily in detail and told the front desk manager he was a personal friend and promised that he would get him an autograph. The man even gave Sam her room number, but attempts to call resulted in endless ringing and no answer. Then he realized that they probably wouldn't have left the phone in her room.

After George had bought a map to the city, they located the hotel and began some basic reconnaissance. They watched the front entrance for two hours and saw nothing, so they went down an alley next to the building and found a cafe with a good view of the hotel courtyard.

They had a late lunch there, watching Morgan and Chisek lounging at a table. Sam fought the urge to leap over the short wall and hedges separating them and strangle Morgan. George was snapping an occasional photo of the scene with his digital camera and was the first to spot Emily sitting out on her balcony.

Sam leapt out of his chair and began waving his arms to get her attention. George pulled him back down into his seat.

"Stop it, Morgan might see you."

"But she's right there."

"Maybe she'll look in our direction and spot us for herself."

Sam agreed and waited with hopeful impatience for Emily to look his way. But she just watched Morgan and occasionally looked down the side of the balcony.

It was nerve wracking having to wait for Morgan to leave the courtyard. Chisek left at one point and Sam hoped Morgan would follow, but he continued to sit there, with various large men coming up to speak with him every now and then. George carefully got a picture of each one for future reference.

"Sam, do you know who any of those men are?" George asked after the third one had left.

"I suppose they're his hired help."

"I wonder what they're telling him."

"What? You didn't bring a directional mike with you?" Sam joked.

George had brought one suitcase entirely filled with electronic gadgets, telling airport security he was a ghost hunter. He said they would come in handy, but Sam didn't know how he could find a use for all of it.

"No," George replied glumly. "I forgot it."

They continued watching Emily and Morgan for another hour when George suggested they follow one of the men who was reporting in to Morgan.

"Why?"

"We might be able to find out more about what they're up to."

"Can't Peter do that? I'd rather stay here and keep an eye on things."

"Peter can only track them if they leave an electronic trail. If they're using cash, there won't be any way to trace them."

"You could plant one of your bugs in their equipment."

"I plan on it if I can get close enough."

George's cell phone rang.

"Yes... really? ... Okay, I'll be there shortly."

"What is it?"

"Peter has more of the disk deciphered. He thinks he knows where they're headed."

Sam wanted to go, but he wanted to stay and watch the hotel more.

"Let me know what you find out. I'll be here."

George nodded and left.

After he had gone, Sam noticed that Morgan had left as well.

So here he sat, not knowing exactly why he felt the need to continue watching Emily. He glanced up at the balcony again, willing her to look his way. She stood up and his heart jumped. But she just went inside and pulled the curtains halfway across the sliding glass door. Now he could only see her if she walked to one side of the room. She seemed to be pacing.

His thoughts were meandering through the past they had shared as he watched her pace in and out of view. She used to walk up and down the floor the entire time they were having any kind of argument or academic debate, as if she thought better on her feet. He could only imagine what she was thinking about now.

She suddenly turned as if someone had entered the room. She sat down on the edge of the bed, but Sam couldn't tell if she was talking to anyone or just sitting there. A moment later she got up and sat at a table in front the window that was to the left of the balcony. Someone had brought her supper and she began to eat.

Another memory came to Sam's mind as he watched her. The fabulous meals she used to cook for him in the apartment they shared. The kitchen was hardly big enough to turn around in and Sam wasn't allowed to set foot in it while she was cooking.

"You'll just be in the way," she would say whenever he offered to help.

The bittersweet pain he often felt when he thought about her washed over him again. He could admit to himself now that he had pushed her away with his overzealous behavior. He had always been a loner and channeled his emotions into his work instead of their relationship.

Now he would give anything to be close to her again. To be in the same room with her, sitting across the table from her. Telling her everything he had been too immature and too foolish to say before.

She got up and walked over to the bed and stretched out. Then she rolled over and shut off the bedside lamp.

Sam closed his eyes and imagined he was lying next to her the way he did for five years' worth of nights. He used to lay behind her, his body enclosing her curves, one leg thrown over hers in a protective embrace. The heat of her body, the smell of her hair, the silkiness of her skin, all the sensations came back to him as he let himself remember.

"Sir," a voice interrupted his fantasy.

He opened his eyes and sat up. A waiter was standing next to the table with a pot of coffee.

Sam declined the coffee and asked for the check. He took a deep breath and one last look at the darkened windows of Emily's room and made a silent vow that wouldn't leave South Africa without her.

It was nearly midnight when Sam returned to the small but luxurious hotel where Eleni had found rooms for them. It was usually reserved for visiting dignitaries but, since there were none visiting, the rooms were available to someone with a UN identification card. Though the accommodations were much more lavish than they needed, they were able to get them at a cheaper rate than most of the other hotels because of Eleni's connections.

In his room he found a note that George slid under his door telling him they were all going to meet in Peter's room.

"It's about time," George was sitting next to Peter when Sam walked in.

They were hunched over a desk on the far side of the room as they worked on more of the disk translation. Eleni and Anna were sitting in the dining area sipping on coffee and having a late night snack.

"Sorry," Sam stretched out wearily on a velvet covered sofa. "What have you got?"

"We know exactly where they're headed," Peter said

Sam sat upright so quickly he nearly fell off the sofa, "What?"

"Come here and take a look," George waved him over.

On the computer screen was a map of South Africa detailing the natural wonders and tourist attractions. Sam could hardly focus on the image as he waited impatiently for their explanation.

"I found a reference to an ancient city whose name, roughly translated, meant 'bottom of the earth'" George explained, "I wasn't sure exactly where it was located. But then Peter deciphered a portion of the text that I was having problems with."

Peter pulled up another image on the screen.

"This," he pointed to a highlighted passage, "is a more precise description of the location. George was having trouble with it because it includes three dimensional coordinates. Something similar to our latitude and longitude, but with a depth as well. So besides finding the numerical equivalent in modern terms, we also had to discover from what point they began their mapping."

George interrupted him at this point, "Not to mention that the geography has changed somewhat over the years. The continents were basically the same as they are now, but the mountains were still growing at that time. A lot of the volcanoes in the region had just been born."

"If there was all this upheaval, wouldn't it be highly unlikely that any underground installation would have remained intact?" Sam asked.

"Yes," George admitted, "if this was built like Los Angeles. But we're not dealing with modern man here. We know they developed technologies that go far beyond anything we have today, just look at the disks. Who's to say they didn't have some kind of mechanism to stabilize the rock?"

Sam thought it over and admitted it was possible. He had certainly seen enough amazing things already to make believing in the impossible easier.

"I take it you figured out the coordinates."

"Just a few minutes ago," Peter answered and typed something into the computer.

The tourist map was overlaid first with standard latitude and longitude markers, then with a second grid marked with the spidery script he had seen on the disks.

"This is the surface only with just the first two coordinates highlighted here in red," George pointed out a spot in the middle of the Drakensberg Mountains near the Great Escarpment. Peter typed in some more commands and the map rotated into a three dimensional view, showing the elevations of the various mountains.

"And this is with the additional third coordinate."

A spot hovered in the space below the surface.

"Is there a way to get down there?" Sam asked as he studied the map.

"It's located in the Free State. It's something of a tourist spot for people who want a more adventuresome vacation," Peter handed him a travel brochure on rock climbing.

"I'Tshe lika Ntunjambili" as it is called by the Zulu people of the region. "The rock with two openings" is at the center of a legend that says two Zulu maidens were swallowed up in the caves when they were going to get water. Also known as Modimo Lle in the northern Sotho communities, they believe it is inhabited by ancestral spirits. But today, the mountain is sought out by mountain climbers from around the world. This is located on private property, so please get permission before entering.

"If we can get to the site before Morgan and his men, we could set up an ambush or maybe strike a deal with him to let Emily go in exchange for the information we have," Sam suggested.

"You're forgetting what Morgan is planning to do with that information," George turned to him. "I'm sure Emily wouldn't want you to resort to that to free her."

Sam knew he was right. Emily was the rare type of person who actually stood by her principles no matter what the consequences. She wouldn't back down and would expect Sam to do the same.

"There was something else I discovered about the writing on the disc," Peter interrupted Sam's thoughts.

"I felt like there was something familiar about it when I was working on it before," George noted.

"It should seem familiar since it's made up of several existing languages. It's more of a code than a language."

"Are you sure it's just not the root for modern languages?" George questioned him.

"I'm sure. My program was designed to search for commonalities between this language and existing ones. The reason it was only finding partial matches is because there were so many similarities between multiple languages. It couldn't decide which was right."

"That would have to be an extremely complex code," George shook his head, "it doesn't make sense."

"You're right," Sam agreed, "How can this be thousands of years old if it's using languages that exist now?" He struggled with his thoughts. "I found it buried under fossilized flowstone!"

"Does it really matter how old it is or where it came from?" Anna interrupted, "We know the information on it could be dangerous in the wrong hands, and the wrong hands are reaching for it right now."

George grinned at his wife, "I couldn't have said it better myself." He turned to Sam, "We'll figure out some way to stop him. Right now we should probably try to get some sleep. We have to get up early to arrange our transportation."

"How long will it take to get there?" Sam asked.

"I estimate about four hours to reach the village where we can get a guide and then we'll have to stay overnight before we can get permission to go to the cave the next morning," Peter replied.

Sam groaned at the amount of time it would take them. "I'm sure Morgan won't be so polite. But I guess there's nothing we can do about that."

"Of course there is," Anna spoke up from across the room.

The men all turned and waited expectantly for her to elaborate.

She took one more sip of her coffee before beginning. "I think I know someone who can help us," she smiled demurely, "*And* he owes me a favor."

Emily opened her eyes as the sun streamed in past the open curtains. A moment of panic ensued as she sleepily got her bearings. But once she recalled where she was, the anger and despair returned.

She had first woken up a little after midnight the night before and was chagrined to find one of Morgan's men sitting at a table in the courtyard smoking a cigarette. She had waited for an hour, hoping he was just suffering from insomnia, but when he was relieved by another guard, she went back to bed knowing there would be no escape that night.

She heard a lot of noise in the hall and looked through the security peephole. The men were packing up their equipment and getting ready to leave. One of them approached her door and knocked.

The door opened as she jumped out of the way.

"Don't you people have any manners?" she growled at him.

"I knocked," he replied innocently. "We're leaving in thirty minutes. Do whatever you need to and be ready by then."

He turned and shut the door behind him.

Morgan had yet to tell Emily exactly where they were going. She had guessed they were heading into the mountains by the type of clothing they provided for her. She tried to recall anything he or

Chisek might have said about their destination, but couldn't remember it ever being mentioned in her presence.

Realizing this might be her last chance for a hot shower for who knew how long, she climbed into the tub and cranked the water up as hot as she could stand it. The steam became so thick she couldn't even see the towel rack when she was finished with her shower. She stepped out of the tub dripping water along the floor as she fumbled for a towel.

Back in front of the vanity, she wiped the moisture off of the mirror and examined her reflection. The strain of the last few days was making itself evident on her face. Dark circles were forming under her eyes and she swore she saw a few new wrinkles.

The steam quickly fogged up the mirror again and as she began to wipe it clear, an idea began to form in her mind. She turned the shower back on and cranked the hot water up as far as it would go and threw on her clothes, shoving what few possessions she had with her into the pockets. Then she moved back out into the bedroom leaving the bathroom door open, shut the drapes and turned off the bedside lamp. Crouching behind the small table next to the door she waited, watching the dim light leaking from around the edges of the drapes illuminate the roils of steam pouring into the room.

A hard knock on the door made her jump and her heart pounded. The knock came again, louder and more insistent. Suddenly the door was flung open and one of Morgan's men stepped into the room. He glanced immediately at the bathroom door, "Ms. Forester?"

Not getting an answer, he entered and headed toward the bathroom where Emily had left on a single vanity light.

Moving slowly out of her hiding place, Emily peered into the hallway. She didn't see anyone and darted out of the room, making for the stairwell at the end off the hall at a sprint. She reached the door and pushed it open, only to be grabbed from behind by Morgan himself.

Two of his henchmen stood behind him.

"I'm glad you're so eager to get going, Emily. But we're parked out back," he smirked, enjoying his own wittiness.

Five minutes later she was being escorted to a jeep parked at the rear of the hotel, the hotel staff peering curiously out of windows and through doorways trying to catch a glimpse of the entourage. No one set foot outside though. Emily figured they had been warned not to or face the consequences.

As they pulled away from the hotel, Emily noticed two other jeeps that had been parked on the side of the building begin to follow them. Though she couldn't see their faces, she could tell by the size of the men inside that they were a part of Morgan's entourage. And she also noticed that their party seemed to be a few men short. There had been eight men other than Chisek and Morgan in the shuttle from the airport, and there were only two each in the jeeps behind them. That left three of them unaccounted for. They had probably been sent ahead to find accommodations, but for some reason their absence seemed more sinister than that to Emily.

She sat in the back seat with the guard she had seen outside the night before having a cigarette in the courtyard. He carried no visible weapon, but Emily didn't think he'd need one since he was approximately the size of a house and barely fit in the seat. On her left was Chisek. She tried her best not to touch him, but the rough condition of the roads kept throwing her into him. Morgan sat in front of her, absorbed in what appeared to be a tattered guidebook.

She was shocked to see Lundgren sitting behind the wheel. She knew he had been missing for a few days and Morgan had been frantic at his disappearance.

Lundgren caught her staring in the rear view mirror, the smile on his lips not matching the threatening look in his eyes.

The buildings were a blur as they wound their way through the streets and they were soon on a generic highway winding its way through the vast suburbs of the city.

"Where are we going," she finally ventured to ask.

No one answered her.

She raised her voice and did her best imitation of her mother, "Am I not speaking English?"

Morgan turned around in his seat and gave her an annoyed look. He nodded tersely at Chisek, signaling him to explain, and then went back to his book.

Chisek nervously cleared his throat as he turned to Emily.

"Well, first we're going to the town of Memel to find a guide. Then we'll be moving on to a ranch where we'll set up a base camp before-"

"I didn't ask for an itinerary," Emily snapped, "I want to know exactly where our final destination is, and why we're going there."

"You're being rather demanding for someone in your position," Morgan had turned around again. "It will make no difference if you know where we're going or not. You'll still be under guard and escape will be impossible."

He chuckled, "But if by some miracle you managed to escape, you'd never find your way out of the mountains alive. Wild animals, hidden crevasses and caves, and the Zulu can still be violent if they feel you're endangering their way of life. So I would suggest you stick close to us once we reach Memel. I would hate for something to happen to you."

It was clear by the menace in his voice that he could care less what happened to Emily. He probably planned to abandon her in the mountains, leaving her to die in one of the ways he previously mentioned.

"Being eaten by a lion would be an improvement over having to be in the same vehicle with the lot of you."

Morgan's sneer made it obvious he found her comment amusing, but still saw straight through her bravado.

She kept her gaze locked defiantly with his anyway, just to reassure herself she wasn't going to give in to his intimidation. If she let him gain the upper hand in their mental sparring match, she knew she would lose respect for herself as well as possibly lose the will to continue fighting. That was one thing she had learned from her mother who still kept the family ranch running on her own even though she would be sixty-five next spring. Emily hoped she'd be there to celebrate that birthday with her.

The mountains soon crowded the road on either side of them as the miles passed by. Occasionally they saw a team of men working to keep the road clear of the regular rockfall. There were also small groups of huts or more modern stucco cottages hidden here and there amongst the scrubby trees. Villages of no more than four or five houses down a dirt lane were caught only in glimpses as they sped by.

Emily tried to fix in her mind the locations of some of the settlements, hoping she may have need of them if she managed to escape.

But hours later they were still traveling the same road and she saw fewer signs of civilization as they penetrated the depths of the mountains. The Great Escarpment stretched for over three thousand miles from eastern Angola to Zimbabwe. Native villages were scattered throughout and most were only accessible by poorly maintained dirt roads. The area they were headed for was in the territory of the Zulu tribes. Emily recalled discussing them in one of her cultural anthropology classes in her freshman year of college. The very class where she had first met Sam. It was a long time ago, but the lecture stuck in her mind because of the legendary warrior chief Shaka, who battled and defeated any other ethnic group he could find for ten years straight. The Zulu were no longer such a warlike tribe, but Emily hoped they still had some fight left in them. She knew Morgan would use them as he was using her, as a means to an end.

17

Sam knew that Anna had worked for many years in the Peace Corps as a nurse and probably spent a lot of time in remote villages and poor suburbs of developing nations, but the part of town she directed them to the next morning certainly didn't fit Sam's idea of places she would have visited. Of course, Sam hadn't known her before she married George. Before the end of apartheid, many neighborhoods were inhabited by mostly white lower middle class families in small homes and high rise apartment buildings. But in the last decade, the influx of black families with higher incomes had increased the population beyond the capacity of the available homes. The result was ten or fifteen persons crammed in a small house, sometimes with an extra room or building tacked on to the outside. This also meant a lot of the residents' time was spent outside where there was a little more room, and most of them were closely watching the progress of Sam's entourage.

Peter and Eleni had stayed back at the hotel to finish preparing all of the gear that the others would need on their trek through the mountains. They would not be accompanying Sam, George and Anna, but would run a sort of command center from the hotel, relaying information and tracking their progress as well as that of Morgan and his men.

Anna strode purposefully towards the door of a one-story concrete block building that appeared to be a bicycle repair shop by the looks of the various bicycle parts lying on the sidewalk and leaning up against the building in front of it. After stepping nimbly over the debris, Anna knocked on the door.

A moment later, the hinges protesting loudly, the door was opened an inch and an eye peered at them through the crack. At first it looked sleepy, then puzzled, then opened wide in surprise, followed by the door being quickly flung aside.

"Anna!" the owner of the eye was a short black man of San descent. His head was shaved so no grey hairs belied his age, but a smile as wide as his face showed his many laugh lines and his crooked but very white teeth.

Sam couldn't follow the conversation at all when they began speaking in one of the unusual San dialects. But the man appeared to be thrilled to see Anna. He looked at George at one point in the conversation, apparently Anna had explained this was her husband, and the man grabbed his hand and shook it vigorously.

"Ndawbe is congratulating you on making such a wise choice," Anna smiled.

"Tell him it was the smartest decision I ever made," George replied laughing at the man's choice of words.

Sam was surprised Anna knew the San language. It was considered a difficult one to learn because of the unique clicking and popping sounds made with the tongue and lips that made up some of their consonants.

Anna spoke to him for another minute and then translated his reply for Sam and George's benefit.

"He says his uncle passed away last year…"

Sam held his breath.

"…but his other uncle is now chief elder of the tribe. He owes him a favor, too."

Ndawbe led them down the street to his house. Along the way, Sam noticed the previously curious residents were now going about their business, talking in small groups, children running between them and women sweeping off their porches.

Sam asked Anna about their behavior.

"I thought they'd be used to seeing tourists," he commented.

"They are. Just not in their neighborhood. This isn't exactly the trendy arts and crafts district and old fears take a long time to die."

"So he knows how to get to the cave?"

"His people are only few miles away from the site. Morgan will most likely take the tourist's route and go straight to the property owner. But we're going to the original owners of the land who know it better than any rancher."

Sam recalled the cultural anthropology class he took his freshman year of college and the chapter on the San tribes. There were several different tribes, each with their own dialect, but with similar ways of life. Recent studies in genetics concluded that they were of the oldest racial stock on the planet and their rock art, some dated as far back as 25,000 years, was found all over southern and eastern Africa. That was about all he remembered because most of his time in that class was spent trying to get the attention of Emily who also shared that class.

Ahead of them, Ndawbe stopped in front of a large two-story house that stood out from its neighbors not only by its size, but by the obviously new coat of paint. That and the fact that all its windows were sparkling clean and the front door was made of carved mahogany gave the impression that a person wealthier than most lived here.

That impression was validated when a butler opened the door seconds before they reached it. They exchanged a few words and Ndawbe led the group into the front hall.

Sam began to wonder how Ndawbe's family could afford such luxurious accommodations. The hall reminded him of the type you would see in an English manor house with marble floors, a grand staircase leading to the second story balcony, and various pieces of statuary on pedestals around the room. But the large mural along one wall made it clear the owner was still proud of his tribal heritage. It stretched for nearly ten feet and was an excellent reproduction of the San rock paintings Sam had written a paper on in college. Sam's next thought was why in the world that someone who owned a house like this would choose to keep it in such an impoverished neighborhood.

His musings were interrupted by the arrival of a man who Sam thought could not possibly be a relation of Ndawbe. Wearing a camel Armani suit and an ingratiating smile, he came down the staircase with a greeting for Ndawbe that ended in an enormous hug.

They spoke to one another for a few moments and then Ndawbe started to make introductions.

"There's no need for that, father," his son spoke in the Queen's own English, "I can introduce myself." He turned to the group and bowed slightly, his greeting directed mainly at Anna, "James Elton Ndawbe at your service."

James certainly wasn't of full San blood as he was over six feet tall and most of the San were closer to five. He looked more like he had just walked off of the cover of a romance novel with biceps and pecs rippling under his tight shirt. His lustrous black hair was intricately braided and reached down to his shoulders, his coffee colored eyes were the type that women would stare into for hours, and the goatee he wore accentuated the whiteness of his teeth. Sam felt inadequate merely standing in the same room with him.

The tension Sam had seen in George's face when the man continued to eye his wife relaxed soon enough when James flattered him as well, "And you must be an amazing man to have captured the heart of such a beautiful woman."

"I like to think so," George smiled. "George Baltazidis," he held out his hand. "And this is my wife Anna."

He shook George's hand and kissed Anna's.

"And you are?" he looked at Sam as if he really couldn't care who he was.

It took all of his manners to not come back with a sarcastic reply, "Sam Hunt." Sam knew he needed to be polite because, even though this was the type of successful, handsome, almost perfect man that set his teeth on edge, he could also help them find Emily.

The formalities gotten over with, Ndawbe led them through the back of the hall into a courtyard. More opulence was present here in the elaborate fountain in the center of the space and the glass and wrought iron table with cushioned chairs nearby. They seated themselves while another servant brought out a tray of refreshments. Sam knew these social niceties were expected before getting down to business, but he was impatient nonetheless.

"My father tells me you wish to see Ntumjambili," James settled back into his chair with a glass of fruit juice.

"Yes, we want to go to as soon as possible," Sam explained and wondered why the son was doing the questioning.

"Ah," James sipped his drink. "What is there that you need to attend to so urgently?"

Sam didn't know how much to tell him since they had just met, so he decided to keep the information to a minimum.

"A friend of ours needs help," he said simply.

"They are not in some kind of trouble with the police are they?" James smiled and took a sip of his drink.

"No. Nothing like that."

"That is good. Is there some danger to this friend?"

Sam was soon going to lose his patience entirely and reach across the table to strangle James

"Some."

"I apologize, Mr. Hunt," he held up a hand to stay Sam's anger. "I ask these questions only to determine what I must do to be prepared.

If there is some risk in helping your friend, it would be kind of you to make me aware of it."

"I understand and I apologize as well."

Sam felt some relief that James seemed willing to help them as long as the danger did not involve anything illegal.

He explained their situation as far as Emily being kidnapped, but left out any reference to the disks or lost cities. And he only partially described Morgan's plans. He feared if he went into too much detail, James would find it hard to believe and suspect they were lying.

James seemed to be genuinely outraged. "I will be honored to help you rescue her." An icy calm settled over his features. "And if I happen to meet this Morgan, I will personally chastise him for his actions."

Sam was pleased they had a new ally, but he was a little worried that his enthusiasm for chastisement would land them in trouble. He also wondered how James had obtained an Oxford education and owned such an opulent home if his father was from an isolated San village.

James obviously noticed the suspicious look on Sam's face. "You would like to know why I am so willing to help you?" he asked.

"Sorry," Sam apologized somewhat facetiously, "I'm just not used to magnanimous gestures."

"It was through such a kindness that I have all you see before you. My father's work with a noted anthropologist gained him many influential friends. One of them was generous enough to send me to England for schooling and also helped me set up my own business. When he passed away, he left us both substantial sums which, after making ourselves comfortable, we have used to raise the fortunes of the neighborhood where we live and the village where I was born."

Sam found himself having to readjust the narrow-minded opinions he had been forming about James. He was ashamed of himself but granted that some of his attitude stemmed from being anxious about Emily.

"Don't stop now," Peter moaned.

"You big baby," Eleni laughed as she stopped massaging his shoulders. "I want to go get some lunch."

"I suppose that's alright, if you bring me something, too."

“I’ll be back in a few minutes,” she grabbed her purse and went out the door.

“And I’ll be here, slaving away on the computer, with no one to rub my back.”

He did his best to sound persecuted and was rewarded with more laughter from his wife as she closed the door.

Peter really didn’t mind being behind the scenes, coordinating their plans. He loved working with computers almost as much as he loved his wife’s massages.

While Anna took Sam and George to see her friend with the connections, Peter kept an eye on Morgan’s movements and outfitted their equipment for the trek through the mountains once they reached the village. Eleni didn’t have as much to do and Peter could tell she was feeling left out, so he sent her shopping that morning for last minute supplies.

It was one of the more mundane things any of them had done in the past few weeks. Ever since George handed him the disks, Peter’s world hadn’t seemed as stable as he thought it was. He knew Eleni was enjoying their adventure, she watched too many spy movies not to enjoy it. But he was nervous. There were so many things that could go wrong. Morgan was not a sane man by Sam’s description and he would stop at nothing to attain his goal. Assault and kidnapping were probably just the beginning.

If Morgan found that he was being followed, Peter didn’t doubt that their lives would be in danger. That was why he was being more careful than usual about covering his tracks. He normally took precautions during his ventures into cyberspace so his activities couldn’t be traced. He had every anti-spy program available loaded into his laptop. But for every measure he took, he knew there was a countermeasure. He didn’t think Morgan had anyone capable of tracking him, but it was better to err on the side of caution. He even went so far as to change their names in the hotel computer after they registered.

Fortunately, the part he and Eleni were to play in their operation was out of the direct line of fire. When the others went into the mountains in pursuit of Morgan, they would remain behind in the relative safety of the hotel.

To make their stay in the hotel even safer, Peter began working on patching into the closed circuit security cameras he had noticed throughout the building. It was a hardwired system, but he could easily intercept the frequencies using some of the equipment George had brought along. He was adjusting the television set to receive the signals when Eleni returned.

"I bought some things in the market and thought I'd trying whipping up something myself," she said as she set two bags of groceries on the table. "Since we have a microwave and fridge in our rooms we won't have to go out for meals all of the time."

Peter was only half listening to her as he fiddled with the TV. "Sounds great," he mumbled to her.

She shook her head and began putting the fruits and vegetables she had bought into the refrigerator.

At first he couldn't tell why the picture wasn't coming in clearly and then realized it had a simple encryption he had forgotten to disable. He turned back to the computer and corrected the problem in a matter of seconds. The image on the screen sharpened dramatically and he had a view of the main lobby.

Eleni closed the refrigerator, "What show is that?"

"It's not a show. I patched into the hotel security cameras," he announced proudly.

"Well if it was a TV show, I'd say those were the bad guys," she pointed at the screen.

The instant Peter laid eyes on them he knew her joke wasn't far from the truth. They were the same men that George had taken photos of at Morgan's hotel.

"We've got to get out of here fast," Peter jumped up and grabbed her by the arm.

"What?"

"Those are Morgan's men. I don't know how they found us, but they're certainly not here for lunch."

After grabbing his pocket PC, he dragged Eleni into the hall and towards the staircase.

"Where will we go?" she asked nervously.

"To find the others and warn them. But first we need to get out of the hotel."

He cautiously opened the door to the stairs and, not hearing any noise, started down with Eleni glued to his side. They reached the ground floor without incident.

"We'll have to go out the back way, they're probably watching the lobby," Peter said and guided her through the corridors used only by hotel employees. Luckily, the exits were signed clearly and they found their way outside easily.

"Let's get a little further away from the hotel before we call George," Peter suggested.

They kept looking over their shoulders for the next three blocks until they were sure they hadn't been followed and then stopped in a small café.

Peter immediately called George, while Eleni ordered some food.

"George, where are you?"

"We're on our way back to the hotel to pick up our gear."

"Don't. Meet me at the café three blocks down from the hotel."

"What's going on?"

"I'll tell you when you get here."

"Alright. We'll be there in a few minutes."

Peter put his phone back in its holster and reached for his pocket PC when he realized his hands were shaking.

"I wasn't meant for a life of espionage and intrigue."

"What was that, dear," Eleni asked as she calmly perused the menu.

"Nothing."

She never ceased to amaze him. He shook his head and went back to making a connection with his laptop. If he could access his computer, he might be able to continue monitoring Morgan's men. He also needed to quickly transfer the files from the disks to his pocket PC before they were discovered. There hadn't been enough time to secure the system before they left and if Morgan's thugs got into the room, they would have all of the information that Peter and George had deciphered.

By the time a waiter brought their bowls of spicy bean soup the others had arrived and pulled up chairs.

"So why can't we go back to the hotel?" Sam asked.

"Take a look," Peter handed the PC to Sam. "This is live feed from the hotel security cameras. Wait for the view of the hallway outside our rooms."

The look on Sam's face made it clear to Peter that he saw Morgan's men.

"It looks like they're trying to break into the room."

George looked over his shoulder, "I'm sure they are. Are the disks still in the hotel safe?"

He nodded. "And I just downloaded all of our translation and wiped the files on the laptop."

"Good. At least the bastards won't get that."

"Did you arrange everything with your friend?" Eleni asked Anna.

"Yes, we were going to leave this afternoon."

"I hope you still can," Peter replied. "We'll have to get the equipment out of the hotel without them seeing us somehow. They'll probably leave someone behind to watch the place."

"We may not have any equipment left," George interrupted and showed them the PC screen.

The men were no longer in the hall.

"Maybe they left," Eleni suggested.

"I doubt it. They-" Peter froze as the connection was lost. He tried in vain to reestablish it, but it was to no avail.

He laid the PC on the table dejectedly. He only hoped that all of his equipment hadn't been demolished.

The sun was still high overhead in the late afternoon hours, but the steep walls of the canyon they were driving through blocked out most of the sunlight. Emily was amazed that there was a road here at all. It looked as though the rock face could collapse at any time and they would be trapped. She had never really traveled much, any vacation time she had was usually spent back in New York with her mother, so South Africa seemed unbelievably vast to her. But since they had entered the mountains she felt as if the walls were closing in on her. The fact that she was sitting in a cramped vehicle against her will with the two people she despised most in the world didn't help much either. Fortunately Chisek had given up trying to talk with her after the first hundred miles and now was leaning against the window dozing. Emily wished she could do the same but she couldn't stop thinking about what would happen to her once Morgan found the information he was looking for. For the first time in her life she felt helpless and she didn't care for it at all.

When the town of Memel finally came into view, Emily let herself be distracted by the sights and sounds. Children ran alongside the jeep as it reached the outskirts, shouting and laughing. Some adults who were walking along the streets even waved. Maybe there was some hope of getting help here, she thought and let muscles relax that she hadn't even known were tensed.

Morgan's grating voice brought a quick end to her moment of relaxation.

"Head straight for the ranch. I want to set up base camp before nightfall," he ordered Lundgren.

"I don't think they'll just welcome us with open arms," Chisek had awakened from his nap.

"We'll tell them we're anthropologists here to study the old legends."

"I'm sure they'll find it hard to believe when the see the equipment we're carrying."

"Then there are other ways."

Morgan neglected to elaborate, but Emily was relatively certain those other ways would involve violence.

When they pulled up in front of the ranch Morgan immediately put on a humble expression and began his attempts to deceive the elderly rancher who came out to greet them.

Emily could see Chisek's distaste for what Morgan was asking him to translate to the old Afrikaner. Emily thought she would have choked on the words they were so obviously false. And it was apparent the old man could tell that as well. His greeting smile slowly turned into a frown as he was told what Morgan was asking of them.

The man shook his balding head and began speaking rapidly and loudly enough in the Germanic dialect that a crowd of ranch hands, some of whom were obviously of Zulu descent, began to gather around the jeeps.

"What did you say to him," Morgan demanded of Chisek.

"I told him exactly what you said," he raised his arms in a shrug. "I guess they could tell it was a pack of lies. Telling someone you're a cultural anthropologist when you're carrying thousands of dollars worth of excavation and electronic equipment doesn't make much sense."

Chisek folded his arms while Morgan glared at him. Emily found that she might actually have some respect for Chisek after all.

"That's what you're here for, Bob," Morgan said quietly through clenched teeth. "Tell him something that would make sense to him then."

The old man had finished his tirade and now stood staring at Morgan with contempt. He barked out a few words to Chisek.

"He wants to know why you're really here. He thinks you're from a mining company and you want to take his land," Chisek translated.

"Assure him that is not true and the equipment is to explore the caves as we research the old legends. Tell him we're looking for rock carvings."

Morgan looked rather pleased with himself for coming up with this new lie. Emily wished she could kick him, but she was being held beside the jeep by one of Morgan's men.

The new explanation was accepted and they were grudgingly invited inside the house. Apparently the rancher was getting tired of all the tourists. They sat at the kitchen table with Morgan explaining exactly where they wanted to go when the rancher's wife came into the kitchen to make coffee. Emily thought at first that the beautifully graceful Zulu woman was a housekeeper or maid, but the warm greeting and kiss she received from the master of the house soon dispelled that impression. Emily found herself being ashamed of her automatic presumption that a black woman would be a servant to a white man. Granted, that was usually the case in South Africa, but she still felt ashamed of her reaction as well as being pleased to see that not all Afrikaners had issues with skin color.

Emily sat in the chair next to Morgan and smiled at the man, trying to get him to notice her. He seemed to be an intelligent man and maybe he would realize she wasn't a willing member of the party. But he just smiled back and nodded his head toward her in greeting.

"He says we can go in a day or two. His grandson usually leads people to the caves, but he's not here right now."

Morgan looked as though he wanted to strangle Chisek. "Tell him we're on a tight schedule and we have to set up camp tonight and be in the caves by tomorrow morning."

Chisek told him and the man just shook his head. Even Emily could tell that he meant the request was impossible. The old man obviously knew something wasn't right with this picture.

But Morgan wouldn't give up, "Then tell him it would be worth the trouble for him to find another way to get us there."

Chisek gave Morgan an "I warned you" look and told the rancher what he had said.

The man's reaction startled even Emily. He yelled something that sounded to Emily like a war cry and all of the Zulu men on the ranch who had merely been standing by idly watching or doing chores, approached rapidly, most of them now carrying rifles.

Morgan ignored the old man's anger and signaled to Lundgren and the other guards who were standing behind Emily. Simultaneously, they pulled out automatic weapons that they had concealed under their jackets and aimed them at the rancher.

His face went blank as he sat back in his chair. There was some commotion outside, and Emily glanced over her shoulder out the window to see that the rest of the guards had drawn their weapons as well and covered the crowd that had formed. A few more men approached brandishing rifles which were no match for the weaponry Morgan had at his disposal.

"Now tell the old man that he will bring us a guide who will not lead us astray and we will leave the ranch in one hour," Morgan's voice was cold and malicious.

Emily looked from the old man to Chisek. They were both sitting with a dazed look on their faces.

"Tell him!" Morgan prodded Chisek.

Chisek did as he was told and the rancher stammered a quiet reply.

"He wants to know what will happen if they do not help you."

"There will be a large accident resulting in the untimely deaths of everyone on this ranch," he made his threat as if he were delivering the daily weather report.

Emily felt herself shudder involuntarily as she realized without a doubt that Morgan had slipped out of the realms of sanity making his megalomania complete.

The room was silent for a moment after Morgan announced his ultimatum. The old rancher finally spoke up, looking Morgan directly in the eyes.

"I will do as you say. But be warned, the spirits of our ancestors will protect the innocent and a terrible fate will fall upon you if you harm them," Chisek's voice carried the same weight as the old man's as he translated his exact words.

Morgan chuckled. "A fancy way of saying 'you'll get yours'."

He rose from his seat and started towards the door, "You have one hour to bring me a guide."

Emily was shoved back towards the jeep, Morgan's men surrounding her, and acting as if they owned the place. The Zulu men and other ranch hands cleared a path as they went by, but they didn't completely retreat. Looks of hatred and disgust were on every face surrounding them.

She wanted to scream out "I'm not one of them!" and make a run for it, but she knew any attempt to escape would be impossible here. Even if she managed to break free of the guards, they would probably fire randomly into the crowd to try to stop her, killing indiscriminately. She didn't want to be responsible for anyone's death so she meekly followed Morgan and tried to ignore the helpless feeling that was again taking over.

Morgan ordered his men to prepare the climbing equipment while Chisek handed Emily a sandwich and a drink from the cooler in the back of the jeep. She felt there was something different in Chisek's demeanor and was surprised to note the angry look on his face as he watched Morgan order his men around.

"Why are you doing this?" she suddenly asked him.

He seemed startled by her question. "Doing what?" he replied defensively.

"Working for that bastard," she nodded in Morgan's direction. "What hold does he have over you?"

Chisek looked at her curiously, seeming to judge whether he could trust her or not. "I'm not working for him. He's just the means to an end." He walked around to the other side of the jeep and got in, going over some notes he took from his briefcase.

Emily didn't know what to make of that and ate the rest of her sandwich in silence.

Forty minutes later, the old man showed up with a guide.

"This is my grandson, Moses," Chisek interpreted his words, "he can be trusted to guide you without error."

The old man looked beaten down and defeated as he introduced his grandson, but Emily saw something that looked like a mischievous twinkle in his eye as he backed away. She hoped she wasn't imagining things and felt that he wasn't going down without a fight.

After their rooms had been broken into and Peter feared his equipment was destroyed, George called the front desk at the hotel and told them they needed to check out immediately and could someone please bring their belongings in the hotel safe to the café. The hotel manager was reluctant to do something so unheard of, but the promise of a large tip changed his mind.

When the hotel porter walked through the door ten minutes later with the disks in hand, Sam thought George was going to kiss him, he was so excited that they hadn't been stolen.

"Who's going to get the rest of our stuff out of the hotel," Eleni interrupted George's celebration.

"That's a good question," Sam added. "I'm sure they know what we all look like and Peter's probably right about them leaving someone behind to watch."

"I could go in disguised," George suggested.

"George, it would be hard for you to conceal your size," Eleni put a kind hand on his arm. "You tend to stand out in a crowd. Sam could-"

"Sam is no less conspicuous," he protested.

"As I was going to say," she continued with a raised eyebrow, "Sam could go, but he's too pale to pass off as a native. I'll go."

Sam had to admit her Mediterranean tan could be dark enough to fool someone not watching for an African woman. But it would still be dangerous.

Of course, Peter protested immediately, but Eleni got her way and was soon buying a new outfit in the flea market around the corner. She reappeared from the restaurant bathroom after getting changed.

"How do I look?" She twirled around in the colorful caftan.

"Absolutely gorgeous," Peter said, "But they can still recognize you."

"Not with this," she plopped a huge floppy straw hat on her head that nearly covered her entire face.

They waited nervously for Eleni to return. Sam thought Peter was going to break the handle off of his coffee cup he was gripping it so tightly. He knew how Peter felt. It was all he could do to not think of Emily every second of the day. Sam became so preoccupied with his thoughts that he didn't realize George was speaking to him.

"Neither one of you is listening to me," he said.

"I'm sorry, George. What were you saying?" Sam pushed his concern for Emily back to his subconscious.

George waved a hand in front of Peter's face to get his attention, too. "Don't worry, she'll be alright. But I don't know what to do with you two after we get our gear from the hotel."

"Our cover's blown now, they know we're here. If we just switch to another hotel they'll find us eventually," Peter said in a determined voice. "Is there room in the truck for two more?"

George had objected, fearing for their safety. Sam thought Peter may have felt a little insulted at George's lack of confidence in their survival skills.

"I may have been a monk and a computer geek, but I'm not helpless, George. And Eleni, amazingly enough, seems better at this sort of thing than I am."

George was outnumbered when Sam and Anna agreed that they should come along, and he grudgingly admitted it would probably be for the best.

"Or I'd be worrying about you the whole time. This way I'll know where you are at least."

Eleni returned half an hour later carrying a small suitcase. Peter wordlessly stood and took her in his arms.

"Peter, you're suffocating me," came the muffled voice from his embrace.

He let her go so she could sit down, but pulled his chair closer to hers and rested his arm on the back of the seat.

"How bad was it," George asked.

"The electronic equipment was mostly destroyed. What I could salvage is in this suitcase," she handed it to Peter. "The rest of the gear seems to be okay. I packed up everything and the hotel will bring it to us wherever we choose."

"Eleni, you're a marvel," Peter finally spoke.

"Thank you, dear," she beamed.

After George called the hotel with the location of their rendezvous, they left the café and went to meet Ndawbe and James.

Sam thought James had a warped sense of humor when he showed them the truck they would be using. Sam had expected a large, brand new SUV or even a Hummer. The truck before him was at least fifty years old and looked as though it would fall apart if you leaned against it.

James saw Sam's look of consternation and smiled at him, "Looks can be very deceiving my friend."

And deceived Sam had been. The interior of the vehicle was sparkling clean and outfitted with various pieces of electronic equipment, some of which Sam suspected were military issue. The cargo area had a small table and chairs bolted to floor next to a bank of surveillance equipment.

George leaned over Sam's shoulder, "It seems Anna had better connections than I suspected."

Sam almost laughed at George's fatuous looks of envy at the array of equipment.

"My father was a tracker in the Angolan civil war," James' voice came over Sam's shoulder. "I've just taken it a step further."

"What exactly do you do for a living?"

Anna laughed, "They're private investigators."

"Usually private," James nodded, "Now and then we do something for the government."

Which would explain the quality of equipment, Sam thought.

They loaded their few bags into the back of the truck and climbed in.

"Once we reach the village and introduce you to the elders, we can start for the caves," James explained. "It is not an easy climb to reach the two mouths. This Morgan will probably not be able to find it without a guide."

"I'm sure he'll find a way. Money speaks louder than words," Sam added acerbically.

"How long will it take to reach your village?" George asked as he wedged himself into one of the small chairs.

"About two hours on the highway and another two off road."

"I have the feeling this is going to be an uncomfortable ride," George grimaced.

18

As the terrain grew more uneven, Morgan's convoy was forced to stop over two miles from the base of the mountain and hike the rest of the way in. Though Emily would rather not be in the company of Morgan and his men, she found herself becoming exhilarated with the hike and fresh air. Scraggly bushes and trees dotted the landscape between boulders the size of elephants, which then gave way to a small forest with sparse shrubs for undergrowth. The entire time, Emily could see the peak they were heading for, towering over the Tugela Valley.

Once they reached the mountain itself, problems soon arose. Moses and Emily as well as most of the guards would have no problem negotiating the steep sides and crevasses, but Morgan and Chisek were another matter. After some discussion it was decided that Moses and two of the guards would run lines down from the top and Morgan would go up in a harness. Chisek declined the harness, but used the ropes frequently to aid his ascent. Emily managed just fine freeclimbing and actually found herself forgetting the danger she was in as she lost herself in the minutiae of balance and leverage needed to execute the climb.

Once she found herself at the top, however, Lundgren was waiting for her with the same conceited smirk on his face that she had seen at their first meeting. The guard coming up behind her unceremoniously shoved her out of his way as he got his feet under him and she fell directly into Lundgren's arms.

"I didn't know you cared," he sneered and pushed her along the narrow trail on which they now found themselves.

Another thirty minutes of stumbling over loose rock and occasionally slipping dangerously close to the edge, brought them to a small amphitheatre-like platform on the side of the mountain. It almost looked as if it had been carved out deliberately for a staging area.

Moses spoke up for the first time, “The cave entrance is just on the other side of those rocks.” He pointed to a jumbled mass of boulders at the far end of the plateau. Morgan sent one of the guards to check it out while he and Lundgren had a private discussion some yards away from the rest of the group. Emily couldn’t hear what they were saying, but she could see Morgan first shaking his head negatively, and, after listening to Lundgren some more, nodding in agreement. Then the guard came back and reported there were two openings about ten feet apart, each leading in a different direction.

“So which do we take?” Morgan asked of Moses.

“The second one,” he replied shortly.

“And how do you know that?”

“The legends.”

Morgan turned to Chisek, “Well what do you think? You’re the scholar here.”

“The legend states that the two maidens were swallowed up upon entering the second cave. Perhaps they fell prey to some kind of booby trap.”

“Then there must be something worth protecting in there,” he remarked. “Or there may be a bottomless pit. Harry,” he turned to Lundgren, “take two men and look into it. Don’t be gone more than an hour though. I just want a general description of the two caves.”

“I’ll go with them,” Chisek volunteered.

Morgan seemed surprised and just about to contradict him, but instead acquiesced, “Good idea. If there are any markings or signs of civilization you’ll be able to spot them better than anyone.”

Lundgren didn’t look very pleased with the addition to his party, but gathered up what gear they would need and headed to the caves.

The rest of the group began setting up tents and equipment while Morgan kept an eye on Emily.

“You’re not going to get away with this,” Emily baited him.

“Why do people always say that?” he asked, clearly amused. “I constantly get away with it. Whether you like it or not, Emily, I am going to be the one receiving the Nobel Prize for curing cancer, not you.”

“I don’t give a damn about the Nobel Prize! What you’re doing is going to destroy the human race.”

“I’m getting bored with that line, Emily.”

"Really? Well what do you think happened to the people that invented the vector in the first place?"

"I don't know. It could have been anything. War, famine, pestilence, even a meteor like the one that wiped out the dinosaurs."

"Do you really think a civilization that advanced would fall to any of those things?"

"I seriously doubt they were much more advanced that we are now. And as far as we've come, we still deal with all of those threats."

Emily gave up trying to get him to see reason and was soon confined to a tent with a guard stationed outside. They had left her only with a little bit of food and water and a sleeping bag on the ground. With nothing to distract her thoughts, she began to worry about Sam. She knew he had escaped from the labs, but whether or not he had escaped from the police and federal authorities she didn't know. She had a feeling that he had, there was nothing to back up this hunch, but for some reason she felt he was on Morgan's trail.

Lundgren and Chisek returned after being in the caves for an hour. Emily unzipped her tent a little to watch.

"It's definitely the second one," Chisek pronounced confidently.

"How do you know?" Morgan demanded.

"There were rock paintings at first, showing the horned serpent and the two maidens. Then a little further on there were remains of an inscription in the Eternal's language."

"Do you know what it said?"

"There wasn't much left of it, but it looked like the ones that were found in China."

Morgan looked to Lundgren for confirmation. He nodded once.

"Alright. Let's get underway."

The rest of the men, including the one who had been guarding her tent, hurriedly gathered up halogen lamps, more nylon rope and climbing gear, and a few instruments that Emily didn't recognize. As she watched the preparations, Chisek came up to her tent.

"Emily," he whispered.

"What do you want?"

"I want to help."

"Really? What brought this on? Trying to get on my good side again? It won't do you any good."

"No, Emily. I mean it. Once we find the lab, I'm going to get you out of here."

"Once you find the lab, the world is going to come to an end."

"Not if I can help it."

And he strode away, leaving Emily very puzzled. This was not the Chisek she knew and his behavior just added to the confusion and sense of unbalance she was feeling. It was only a short time ago that she was blissfully spending her days doing research in her lab at the university, contented and enthusiastic about her future. Now she wasn't sure she had a future. She wasn't sure if the human race had a future if Morgan couldn't be stopped. She was more scared than she had ever been in her life. And now, as she finally admitted this to herself, she let go of the tears that had been building ever since she had discovered the dangerous possibilities of the vector. Or was it since she discovered that Sam's life was in danger? She was horrified at the thought of the vector being loosed upon the world, but she felt a gut-wrenching pain at the thought of Sam being gone from her life forever. He had always been there, in the background, even if she did her best to ignore him.

Enough of the schoolgirl gushiness! Emily chided herself, wiping away the tears. *If you don't do something, Morgan will kill Sam and everyone else on the planet if he gets his hands on the vector.*

She went back to watching the activity outside her tent, hoping she could find a way to stop Morgan before it was too late.

"Any idea what we're going to do when we find them?" George asked Sam as they were thrown repeatedly against their seat belts as the truck bounced over the rough terrain.

"None whatsoever." Sam answered tersely.

It was true he didn't have a specific plan in mind, but whatever they did, he planned on making sure Morgan was either behind bars or dead when it was over.

"Village" was probably not the word Sam would have chosen to describe the dozen or so San living in a cave in the Great Escarpment. But then the San usually didn't settle anywhere for long, and their family groups remained small so as not to strain their resources. He had always been amazed that a hunter gatherer society still existed in modern times, and now that he was seeing it in person he found himself wishing his life was more like theirs.

The cave was dry and warm from the fire they had built near the entrance. Animal skins hung on the walls along with some more modern looking blankets to make partitions for sleeping areas. Off to one side a woman was preparing some roots to be baked along with the rabbit than another woman was skinning nearby.

It almost looked like a diorama from the muscum. It would have looked more like it if there wasn't a portable solar generator on wheels sitting outside with wires trailing inside the cave to the electric lights and small shortwave radio. The two women appeared to be enjoying the discussion on the program as they laughed uproariously at what were presumably the commentator's jokes.

"You'd think they'd have a microwave, too." Sam said to no one in particular.

"But it would be too heavy to carry very far," James smiled. "They only like what can be easily moved. If there were service available here, I would get them a cell phone."

Sam was about to suggest a satellite phone, but decided James was joking since he probably knew they existed. His family probably didn't want one.

James spoke to a grey haired man, apparently his uncle, at some length, while Sam and the others made themselves comfortable on various rocks outside the cave. They were almost at their final destination and Sam felt a new resolve take hold of him as he looked at his friends. George was seated on an egg-shaped rock a few feet away, his considerable bulk taking up the entire space so Anna was forced to sit in his lap to be near him. Peter and Eleni were sitting close to one another on a rock to the right of George. They all shared the same serious expression, but when George caught Sam's eye, he winked and grinned boyishly. Getting George to go along with his idea would be difficult. He was having too much fun.

James approached their little group after speaking with his uncle. "He'll show us the way right after lunch."

Sam started to protest, but George stepped in, "Great! When do we eat?"

They all sat around the fire and ate the rabbit stew the women had cooked up while discussing their options.

"I don't relish the idea of climbing up a mountain if Morgan's already at the top of it," Sam said, polishing off the last of his stew.

"We can reconnoiter once we get there," James suggested. "If they've already gone up, my uncle knows a back way."

"How difficult is this back way?" George asked.

James chuckled, eyeing George's paunch, "It may be a tight squeeze in some places. But it's actually less steep than the usual route."

"Sounds good," Sam approved. "Once your uncle and I get up there, we'll find Emily and get her away from Morgan."

"Hold on a minute," George interrupted, "You're not going without me."

"Yes I am. You're all staying here. If we all go trouping up the mountain we'll be a lot more noticeable than just the two of us."

"You can't take on Morgan and all of his goons by yourself," Anna protested.

"I'm not going to take them on. I'm going to be sneaky."

"But-" George started in again.

"George," Anna laid a hand on his arm, "he's right. He has a better chance to sneak up on them by himself. We couldn't really do much anyway. We're not soldiers."

And that was the truth, Sam thought. No matter what they had done or been through up to this point, they were still just a group of civilians trapped in a web of intrigue. Sam was amazed they hadn't been killed already. Emily was already in danger and he didn't want his friends put in any more jeopardy. He wondered if his father would be proud him or if he would say he was still being a lone wolf. Whatever he would have thought, Sam realized that it no longer mattered to him. What mattered now was saving Emily.

19

Morgan was getting a little winded from their trek through the mountain. At first it had been an easy descent down a long sloping corridor, but it rapidly became steeper until they were forced to use the climbing gear and lower themselves down. Morgan was in excellent physical condition for his age, but he nevertheless felt the strain as they went deeper into the mountain. He also had to admit to himself that the sense of thousands of tons of rock over his head was making him a little nervous. The walls of the passageway seemed to become narrower as they went further along. The heavy coveralls and boots they wore seemed to weigh a ton and the helmet with its halogen lamp and battery pack was making his head itch. He seemed to be uncomfortable inside and out.

"Stop!" the guard in the lead ordered them.

"What is it?" Morgan asked and cursed himself silently for sounding so afraid.

"A shaft of some kind."

"Well don't just stand there, check it out!" Morgan barked at him.

He was growing frustrated because they had been slowly descending in the cave for over an hour and had not seen anything else to indicate the presence of any advanced civilization other than the inscription Chisek had found near the opening. There had been a few rock paintings and piece of primitive pottery, but that was all. And the descent was becoming more difficult by the minute.

Watching the lead man lower himself into the pit ahead of them, Morgan leaned over the edge just enough to see that his headlamp couldn't penetrate the depths of the shaft. He shuddered involuntarily and stepped back against the wall. Out of the corner of his eye, he saw Lundgren grinning at him and chose to ignore him.

"There's another opening about twenty feet down in the wall," the guard called up. "It looks like it goes back quite a ways."

Morgan looked across the shaft at the blank wall ahead of them and knew this was the only way to go. He looked at the smirk on Lundgren's face and steeled himself for the descent.

"Alright, hold the line steady and we'll come down one at a time."

He readjusted his harness and attached himself to the line. He brushed off Lundgren's offer of assistance and managed to let himself down to the opening under his own strength. The waiting guard pulled him into the passageway and turned to help the next man in. Morgan sagged against the wall behind him, flooded with relief.

Once they were all down, they continued on. Morgan noticed Chisek was staying close to Emily and allowed himself a private moment of amusement over Chisek's repeated attempts to kiss up to her. Surprisingly, Emily now seemed to be responding to his attempts. Who could ever anticipate the desires of a woman?

The walls of this passageway seemed smoother than the ones above them. Almost as if someone had constructed the tunnel instead of it being a natural formation. It was probably the remains of a mine, he thought to himself, gold and diamonds abound in this region. If it was a mine, that means someone had been here before them. He hoped they hadn't discovered the true wealth buried inside this mountain. If Chisek was right, Morgan would be the most powerful man in the world when he came back out of the cave.

Morgan waited for Chisek to catch up, "Do you have any idea of what we may come across?"

"Well," Chisek thought about it for a moment. "The other sites had a metal door sealing the chamber."

"Anything else?" Morgan was disgusted with the paltry information Chisek was providing.

"Probably more inscriptions."

"Remind me again why I brought you," Morgan's patience was wearing thin.

"Look, I may not know everything about this culture, but I damn sure know more about it than you do! You wouldn't be here at all if it weren't for me."

Something was not right. Chisek never stood up to anyone, let alone Morgan. Was he feeling cocky because Emily was paying attention to him? Or was something else going on. Morgan decided to be cautious.

"You're right, Bob," he smiled in a conciliatory manner, "you have been a great help to me and I'll see to it you get exactly what you deserve."

The thinly veiled threat was enough to make Chisek's confident look waver and disappear altogether as Morgan continued to glare at him with his crocodilian smile.

Chisek managed to muster up a shred of his tattered ego, "Thank you, Louis. It's nice to be appreciated," he said quickly and retreated back to Emily's side.

Feeling once more in control, Morgan led the way. The tunnel continued to slope downwards and twisted and turned back on itself as it descended. Lundgren estimated they were a thousand feet below the surface when they stopped for a break a half an hour later. They had seen no more signs of artifacts and Morgan's frustration was once again bubbling its way to the surface. The fact that his legs were aching didn't help matters any.

He trudged along with Lundgren now in front of him with two other men. At one point they stopped so suddenly that Morgan almost ran into them. They moved apart and let him pass.

It was breathtaking. He couldn't believe a room so large could exist underground. It was too large for their lamps to penetrate, but he estimated it was at least the size of Yankee Stadium.

"Turn off your lamps," Lundgren said quietly and clicked his off.

Morgan was puzzled, but followed suit as did the others. He expected to be plunged into total darkness, but was surprised to see a faint greenish light around them. The whole place had a subtle glow to it.

"What is it?" Morgan asked in a hushed voice.

"Bioluminescent microbes," Emily answered just as quietly. "The chemical reactions involved in their digestion produce light."

"What are they digesting?"

"Other microbes probably. Maybe chemicals in the rocks or air."

Lundgren's light went on and he checked the air quality, "All levels normal."

Morgan turned his light back on, "This is all very fascinating, but it's not why we came here. Let's get moving."

The floor of the cavern was slippery from the microbes and groundwater that seeped through cracks here and there. Morgan almost lost his footing and fell in the muck, but caught himself at the last second against an enormous stalagmite. It almost seemed to be a trick of the light at first, but once he turned his lamp down to a lower intensity he could see more clearly the vague shapes beneath the milky stone.

He stumbled backwards and fell into Chisek. Morgan heard the sharp intake of breath as Chisek noticed the forms inside the rock as well.

Morgan stepped forward and looked more closely. The stone was translucent enough to see the shapes, but still too cloudy to see any details. "Chisel away some of this rock. I want a better look."

"I don't think that will be necessary," Lundgren tapped Morgan on the shoulder and pointed around the side of the stalagmite.

Morgan stepped around Lundgren for a better look.

At first his headlamp only revealed more lumpy outcroppings of milky calcite, glistening with water droplets. Then a familiar shape appeared through the side of the formation. A human skull. Or rather, humanoid. It didn't seem to be Homo sapiens.

Morgan took a few steps back and realized that this was merely the tip of a vast mound of bones. Skulls, femurs, ribs, scapula-everything tossed together in a heap that wound its way across the cavern into the darkness.

"Thousands-" Chisek choked on the word, "There must be thousands of them here."

"There don't seem to be any teeth marks on them," Lundgren commented, looking more closely at the remains.

Morgan was startled by his remark. He hadn't thought of there being any predators in the cave.

"Would you expect there to be?" he asked.

"Just being cautious. We don't really know what to expect." Lundgren continued smirking in the fashion that was now annoying to Morgan.

"I'm not sure how they died," Chisek continued to examine the bones, "but there is definitely more than one species represented here. I can't say for sure under these conditions. There may even be some species here that we've never seen before."

"This is all very interesting, but not what we came here to find," Morgan found his impatience growing along with the pain in his legs.

"You don't think this has something to do with what you're looking for?" Chisek snapped, waving his arm over the massive catacomb. "How do you think these got here? They didn't just walk in and throw themselves in a heap."

Morgan almost growled and clenched his fists. "I don't care how they got here. Unless one of them is holding the vector in their bony hand, we're moving on." He spun around and marched off as best he could with the pain shooting through his legs.

"They were probably test subjects," Emily spoke up.

That stopped Morgan in his tracks, "Is that possible?"

"I think it's highly probable. There's no opening here for them to have been dropped in from the surface as a sacrifice and I don't think they could have been washed in either. It actually reminds me of the mass burials during the plague outbreaks in medieval Europe."

Emily had remained silent until now, but felt this may be her chance to convince Morgan that his quest was a dangerous one. The sight of so many hominid remains thrown haphazardly away like garbage made her almost physically ill.

Morgan looked thoughtful for a moment. "You may be right. They probably would have used primitives like lab rats."

The fact that he sounded as if he admired their ingenuity frightened Emily.

"So they obviously didn't care what kind of suffering they caused in their research," she tried to sound ominous, but it came off more like pleading. "You don't really know what this vector might do."

"I know it's our best chance to advance medicine beyond its current boundaries."

"You're insane!" Emily finally let her rage break through. "You have no idea at all! All you can see is your own greedy desire to be rich and powerful. You don't want to save the world, you want to control it. Well, you can't turn back the clock and you can't cheat death! You're an old man, Morgan, and you'll die just like the rest of us!"

Morgan felt like slapping her, but decided he'd wait until after they found the vector and could take his time teaching her what a smart-mouthed woman deserved.

"But some will die sooner than others. I think we'll leave Dr. Forester here," Morgan turned to her, "This may be dangerous and I wouldn't want her to get hurt. At least not yet."

He stormed off with Lundgren and ordered one of the men to stay behind and guard her.

Sam entered the far end of the vast chamber as Emily finished shouting at Morgan. He had been following a safe distance behind since a few minutes after they entered the cave. Sound carried for a long distance in the enclosed space, so he moved carefully, being sure not to make any noise that could be heard over the ruckus the group in front of him was making. He also kept his headlamp off and used only a small flashlight to keep from stumbling over rough surfaces. He could see enough by the lights of Morgan's team to prepare himself for what lay ahead.

He couldn't believe his luck when Emily was left behind with a single guard to keep an eye on her. He was confident he could handle him even if he was almost twice Sam's size. The element of surprise would work in Sam's favor and, if he was careful enough, he could sneak up behind the guard and knock the man out before he knew what was happening. He watched as Emily continued to examine the mass grave they had discovered. The guard merely stood behind her, his face impassive except for his eyes which were traveling all over the curves of Emily's body.

A flush of anger, or was it jealousy, nearly made Sam come out from his hiding place and attack the guard head on. But he got himself under control and began to slowly make his way across the room, hiding behind stalagmites and pillars. Emily was now facing the guard and speaking to him. Sam could only catch bits and pieces of the conversation as he moved through the maze of rock. Apparently, Emily was trying to get friendly with the guard. Sam smiled to himself as he understood what she was up to. If the guard didn't have lightning fast reflexes, he would soon be on the floor writhing in pain. Sam had seen Emily do the same thing to any man who dared corner her at a bar or party.

In less than two minutes she was standing inches away from the guard, smiling her most winsome smile and he was returning it with a lascivious grin. The inevitable happened as her knee suddenly connected with his groin and she took off running as the guard fell to the floor. She was about ten feet past Sam when he took off after her. He caught up as they reached the first bend in the ascending passage.

He made the mistake of grabbing her without speaking first and nearly had his eyes gouged out before she recognized him.

"Sam!" she gasped and hugged him fiercely.

He wished they had more time for their embrace, but he dragged her on through the passageway. The guard wouldn't be on the floor for long and then he would either come after them himself or call the others for backup. They had to get out and down the mountain before Morgan caught up with them.

They had reached the point where they needed to make the twenty foot rope climb up to the next corridor when Emily stopped short.

"Come on," Sam urged her. "It's not that hard, I'll help you."

"No, Sam. It's not that. We can't let him find the vector formula. We have to go back."

She gave him a resolute stare and turned back the way they came.

He grabbed her arm and spun her around. "No, Emily. *I'll* go back. You have to get out and get to George and the others."

"Like hell I do!"

"This is not a good time for an argument," he lowered his voice and looked nervously down the tunnel looking for any sign of light.

Emily's eyes flashed "How do you propose to stop Morgan when he's surrounded by armed guards," she whispered hotly.

"I don't have to stop him, just delay him," Sam replied, exasperated. "That is if you'll get up there and find George. They'll be bringing the authorities."

She stood her ground for one minute longer until she finally gave in. "Alright. But be careful," she whispered forcefully and planted a quick kiss on his lips. She was up the rope in an instant, climbing as fast as a cat up a tree.

Sam wondered at his own sanity for an instant, going back to face Morgan and his henchmen alone. But there wasn't time to wait for help. They might find the vector and get back out of the cave before George could convince someone this was urgent. And once they escaped South Africa, Morgan would be even harder to catch.

20

"She ran back up the passageway. I heard her talking to someone," the guard's voice echoed off the walls as he ran towards Morgan's group.

"I'm sending a couple more men back with you. Find whoever's helping her and stop them!" Morgan growled. To say he was angry about Emily's escape would be an understatement.

"I think we should just forget about her," Lundgren suggested.

Surprised that his second-in-command would make such a suggestion, Morgan was at a loss for words.

"I agree," Chisek, of all people, added. "We've almost reached our goal and there's nothing she or her friends can do to stop us."

Lundgren looked as shocked as Morgan felt, that he would be agreeing with Chisek on anything.

"You're probably right," Morgan relaxed and smiled, letting his emotions give way to his reason. "To hell with her. Hopefully she'll fall in a pit somewhere." He ordered the guard to stay with them.

Lundgren laughed though Chisek looked a little concerned. Morgan knew their reasons for letting Emily go were different, but he had to agree it wasn't worth the effort to recapture her.

The tunnel they had entered after discovering the hominid remains was definitely not naturally formed.

They continued on for another five hundred feet with a vertical descent of one hundred feet, when they came to a chasm directly in their path. A gaping hole twenty feet across where an ancient earthquake had split the tunnel open lay before them. Without a word, Lundgren's men took off their backpacks and began pulling out pieces of titanium pipe, quickly assembling them into a ladder which they laid across the gap. After pounding several stakes into the rock to secure the ladder, one of the men tied a rope to two upright poles on the end of the construction and started across. Once across, he tied the ropes to two more poles he attached to the ladder on that end.

"After you," Lundgren gracious stepped aside for Morgan to cross.

With a self-satisfied but slightly timid step, Morgan crossed the bridge with the other men following one at a time behind him. He was starting to feel invincible once again. With Lundgren on his team there seemed to be nothing they couldn't accomplish. He almost laughed aloud with the rush of power he felt as they continued on their journey to destiny.

Emily finally saw a glimmer of light ahead and knew she was nearing the cave's exit. She paused to catch her breath and felt the unmistakable vibrations of a helicopter coming in for a landing. She crept cautiously toward the exit and was nearly knocked over by a small group of people darting in.

"Emily!" George nearly crushed her in a bear hug and lifted her off of her feet.

Emily was momentarily befuddled by the unexpected appearance of her friends. Anna, Peter and Eleni all surrounded her.

"Where's Sam?" Anna interrupted the reunion.

"He stayed behind to try to stop Morgan. We have to find help." Emily started for the entrance.

"There's no one out there to help us," George grabbed her arm. "I don't know who they are, but they don't look like any government agency."

Emily shook off George's hand and peered around the corner to see what was going on. Several helicopters were in the process of landing, the first had already landed and men in black combat gear and others in blue hazmat suits were rapidly unloading equipment.

"How are we going to get past them?" Emily started to panic.

"Don't worry, we sent James back to rally the troops," George reassured her.

"What troops?"

"Any troops he can find."

Emily didn't feel any more confident after that statement, but there was no time to worry about it.

"Come on," she urged the others, "we have to get back to help Sam."

It didn't take Sam long to catch up to Morgan again since they had stopped to argue about Emily and then had to build a bridge. They made so much noise that he didn't have to tiptoe either. They were louder than a tour group of school kids in Luray caverns and Sam hoped that the cave was stable enough to take the vibrations. He sat crouched along the wall for another fifteen minutes with his light shut off, waiting for them to clear the bridge and get out of sight again.

As soon as their light was no longer visible, Sam risked turning his light back on and started after them. He crossed their bridge and followed as slowly as possible in case someone turned around and saw his dim light. It was hard to move so slowly when all he wanted to do was catch Morgan and strangle him. But apparently Morgan was the reason they were moving at a snail's pace. He caught occasional snippets of the rear guards low conversation, complaining that the "old man" was holding up the operation.

They referred to Morgan as though he wasn't necessary to reach their goal, like he was an underling rather than the boss. Sam began to wonder who was really in charge of this expedition. *Chisek?* Sam had to keep himself from laughing at that thought. Chisek didn't have the nerve to pull off something like this. *Maybe Lundgren?* He struck Sam as someone who would have no qualms about getting rid of anyone who got in his way.

Sam shook his head and re-focused his attention on the group ahead of him. The echoes seemed to be overlapping as it sounded like there were footsteps coming up behind him. He stopped for a moment and listened more closely. They weren't echoes, there were distinct sounds coming from behind him. He quickly crouched along the wall of the tunnel.

His heart jumped as he thought that Morgan had kept some men back somewhere, but remembered he hadn't seen anyone at the campsite before he entered the cave. It had better not be Emily coming back, he thought. He remained where he was, concealed by the darkness as he saw lights approaching and heard the soft whispers of whoever it was. One voice was louder than the others and sounded familiar.

Sam stood up and turned his light on the approaching group. "George, what are you doing here?"

His large Greek friend started guiltily as the light hit him.

"Well, we decided James could just as easily go for help so we came along to see if you could use a few extra hands. Though I may need a few extra hands getting back up that rope."

Sam could see George was sweating profusely even in the coolness of the cave.

"There's something going on up there," Emily interrupted.

"What now?" Sam groaned.

"Helicopters are bringing in men and equipment. Lots of equipment," George explained "And the men are wearing blue hazmat suits."

"Any idea whose side they're on?"

"The only thing I could make out before we ducked into the cave was some kind of crest on the side of one of the helicopters. My eyes aren't what they used to be."

Sam had no idea what that could mean, but he was sure it meant the new arrivals were not a government agency. They didn't usually advertise their presence.

"Did it look like they were coming into the cave?"

"Not right away at least. They were just starting to unload their gear when we slipped inside. They had plenty of firepower, too."

"We'd better get moving then. Morgan's only a few hundred yards ahead so we'll have to keep the noise to a minimum. And they may be keeping a watch on their rear now that Emily has gotten away from them."

"Sam, I think this could be worse than we imagined," George looked more serious than Sam had ever seen. "I saw that mountain of hominid remains. Whoever dumped them there was working with something more dangerous than the plague."

"Then we'd better get moving."

"Any idea how much further it is to whatever it is we're looking for?" Peter asked as they started to move out.

"I don't think it will be too much further. It will probably be a room like I found in China."

Sam's estimate proved to be correct as they rounded a bend and saw Morgan's group standing in front of a metal door. Chisek was attempting to decipher the inscription covering most of its center portion.

Morgan was standing in front of the door in awe. He reached out and ran his hand over the surface, tracing the inscription with his fingertips. It was almost ten feet wide and just as tall.

"This is it," he whispered reverently, "Everything I've ever dreamed of and more. I'm right aren't I?" he spoke over his shoulder to Chisek.

Chisek shook himself out of his reverie and leaned forward to examine the writing. He pointed to the first group of symbols.

"This is the language I've seen before, but l-look down here," Chisek stuttered in his excitement. "It's Cyrillic," he pointed to another section of writing, "And this is Japanese!"

"What? Is this some kind of secret military base?" Morgan was confused.

"This doesn't make any sense!" Chisek's eyes grew wide as he dropped to his knees and hurriedly brushed away some dirt from the lower portion of the door. "It can't be!" He sat back in stunned silence.

"What is it, you fool?"

Chisek looked up at him. "It's in English."

Morgan crouched down next to him to see for himself. "So you were wrong."

Now Chisek looked even more confused.

Morgan laughed and stood back up. "This isn't some ancient race after all, just some old military installation, probably from the 50's. I suspected they were doing all kinds of illegal human experiments then, no matter how they tried to cover it up."

"It has to be older than that," Chisek protested. "All of the evidence of these sites has been accurately dated to hundreds of thousands of years ago."

"You archaeologists are always getting things wrong."

Chisek looked more closely at the writing. "I think you should read this."

Morgan shook his head, but bent back down to read the inscription.

"*WARNING! Toxic chemical and biological storage unit. DO NOT ENTER!*"

"Harry, what do your scanners say?"

Lundgren pulled out a biohazard scanner and checked the door. "Nothing. If there's anything in there, it's totally contained."

"Let's find a way in here," he ordered the men.

Sam knew it was now or never. "Everyone, shine your lights in their faces," he whispered to his companions as they inched their way closer to the group.

He raised his voice, "I don't think so, Morgan."

The whole group spun around at the same time and they were blinded by six halogen lamps and one flashlight at full power.

"Dr. Hunt," Morgan shielded his eyes from the glare. "I just can't seem to get rid of you."

"And this time I brought a few friends."

"You'll need an entire army to stop me."

"That can be arranged."

"This is all very amusing, gentlemen," Lundgren interrupted, "but this discussion is a waste of time. Dr. Hunt, you can either surrender what meager weapons you have now and stand aside while we continue our work, or we can be less civilized about the whole thing and I can almost guarantee someone getting hurt."

"Nicely put, Harry," Morgan smiled at his right hand man.

"Which will it be?" The click of multiple safeties unlocking followed his words.

"My mother used to say I was a little savage," Sam dove forward and took Lundgren's legs out from under him, causing him to fall onto two of his men. He knew they had to keep a close-quarters fight or Lundgren's men would resort to their guns. Though Sam didn't take his eyes off his quarry, he knew George and Peter had joined the fray. He hoped the others had enough sense to stay out of it, but he doubted they would. Out of the corner of his eye he saw Eleni duck under the arms of one of the men and land a sucker punch to his diaphragm then took a knee to his chin as he doubled over.

His attention was fully drawn back to Lundgren as he got his feet back under him. The scuffle continued around them as Sam prepared for another attack. Lundgren smiled suddenly and relaxed from his fighting stance. Without looking, Sam knew what that meant.

"Just in time, boys," Lundgren greeted his backup as they covered Sam and his friends with their automatic weapons.

Sam took a step back as the others were roughly shoved towards him.

"Like I said, this has all been a waste of time," Lundgren continued, brushing some dirt off his coveralls.

"Harry," Morgan beamed, "You are definitely getting a raise when we get home. And a bonus. And how about a new car?"

"Thank you, Louis," Lundgren replied indifferently.

"How did you do it? All my assets were frozen and we had no way to transport the equipment," Morgan was clearly astounded.

"You forget I have connections, Louis."

"Of course. Sometimes I think you must know God himself." He rubbed his hands together gleefully, "Shall we get started?"

Emily didn't know what else they could do. As it stood, they would be lucky to get out alive. Not that it would matter much. If Morgan succeeded, mankind as it was now would cease to exist. And they would be the first to go. A thousand thoughts raced through her mind as she struggled to come up with another option. There had to be some way to convince Morgan to stop before it was too late. She watched in trepidation as the workers created an airtight seal around the metal door and set up a portable air scrubber. Others ran thousands of feet of ductwork back to the surface. The halogen lights on their tripods brightened the entire area as if they were outside on a sunny afternoon.

Looking at the faces of her friends didn't help her state of mind much. Various levels of dejection and hopelessness colored their expressions. Except Sam. He looked as though he would jump forward at any moment and strangle Morgan with his bare hands. That made her feel better almost instantly. They wouldn't give up, no matter what. She forced herself to think straight and come up with some angle that would work with Morgan. What weaknesses did he have? She pondered this while Sam continued to fume by her side.

He certainly had an immense ego and felt that nothing could stop him. Unfortunately, at the present time, it seemed that way to Emily as well. The only other vulnerable spot she knew of was his sensitivity to the loss of his son and brother. Elliot had told her about that during her orientation as part of the story of MorGen's beginnings. But how could she use that to convince him to give up his dangerous quest?

Then it came to her- Lundgren. He was the weak link in Morgan's chain. Not that Lundgren himself was weak. Far from it. But Emily had sensed that things weren't quite as they seemed in his relationship with Morgan. On the surface, it appeared he was completely at the beck and call of Morgan's whims and gladly served him in any way he could. But something didn't ring true about that assumption. And how did Lundgren manage to get all these helicopters and equipment and people here. Emily didn't recognize any of the personnel in the hazmat suits as having been employed at MorGen. Of course there were other facilities around the world, but these people didn't seem like regular laboratory scientists.

She didn't know much about how Lundgren got started at MorGen, but she knew he had his own private security company as well. He must be under contract, but that didn't seem to fit Morgan's character to have a free agent in his company. Something was floating just out of reach in her subconscious and it was about to drive her crazy.

She leaned over to Sam, "The crest on the helicopters that George mentioned," she whispered loud enough for him to hear her over the racket of the air scrubber which had just been started, "It looked familiar to me but I can't place it."

"What did it look like?"

"It was a typical shield design overall, but in the center was a serpent coiled into a circle."

"Ouroboros. That's the same symbol we found on the inscriptions and on the disk case."

Emily's eyes widened as the pieces clicked together.

"Wouldn't it be quite a coincidence if Lundgren was really working for someone other than Morgan? We know someone had been stealing all of the artifacts. Chisek didn't have a clue who was doing it and Morgan doesn't give a damn about anything but the vector and finding a cure for cancer."

"But what's the purpose behind it? If he is a part of some group obsessed with this ancient civilization, what's their goal?"

"I don't know. But I think Chisek could probably tell us."

"That moron?" Sam scoffed.

"I don't think he's as big a moron as he lets on. He's been hinting at something to me since we got here."

"Really? Other than the fact that he'd like to take you to bed?"

"Sam, knock it off! This isn't a joking matter," she responded hotly.

"Sorry, call it a defense mechanism to high stress situations. So what's he hinting at?"

"I think he might be a government agent."

"CIA?" Sam looked astonished.

"One of those initial groups. I think he's been monitoring the situation the whole time."

"I find that hard to believe. He went out of his way to demolish my career. Why would the CIA want to do that?"

"Who knows? Maybe they wanted you in a position to be right where you are now."

Sam was definitely startled by that statement.

"Okay, even if that was true, and I don't see why it would be," he haltingly conceded, "how is knowing this going to help us now?"

"Just watch," she said and stepped forward toward the guards.

"Get back over there," he barked at her.

"No. I need to speak with Dr. Morgan," she spoke loudly, hoping Morgan would hear her.

"Well he doesn't need to speak with you," the man shoved her back.

Morgan had heard her and approached. "No reason not to be civil,'" he told the guard and then turned to Emily. "If this is another attempt to make me change my mind, you can save you breath."

"No. I know nothing can stop you," she paused dramatically and looked him straight in the eyes. "At least that you know about."

"Threats?" he chuckled.

"No. I just have some information you might want. It could keep you from losing what you've been working so hard to gain."

Morgan stood defensively in front of her with his arms crossed, facing away from the door of the chamber. The guard was watching over the conversation in case he was needed to slap anyone around and failed to notice George get up and creep closer to the bustling workers. She hoped he wasn't going to do anything dangerous.

"What could possibly keep me from getting the vector?" Morgan scoffed.

"Someone who wants it more."

"And who might that be?" she could tell Morgan was becoming annoyed with her.

"Your pal Lundgren."

Morgan looked at her as if she had gone mad. He laughed then. "Harry would never do that. We've known each other since we were children. He's been there by my side as I built my empire."

"Is that so? Are you sure *he* wasn't building your empire? Using you as a tool to get what he wanted?"

Only a second's doubt passed over his features. "Hah! Harry's just the brawn of this outfit. I'm the brains. Are you quite finished with this gibberish?" He looked back over his shoulder. "As you can see, we're just about to enter the chamber. Consider yourselves privileged. You and your friends will be witnesses to the greatest discovery in the history of mankind. My discovery."

Then he noticed George standing next to Chisek who was examining the inscription on the door and making notes. "And get him away from there," he ordered another of the guards

She watched Morgan stride away full of arrogance as she returned to Sam's side.

"No dice, huh?" Sam asked.

She shook her head. Suddenly it hit her all at once. This was it. Morgan was going to open that door and unleash an unknown plague onto mankind. She clenched her teeth and balled up her fists as tears welled up in her eyes. *NO!* She cried deep inside herself. *I will NOT give up hope! There's always a way.*

She felt Sam's arm go around her shoulder and drew from his strength.

"We'll stop him, Em," he whispered to her.

George and the others got up off of the floor of the cave where they had been resting and stood by Sam and Emily. Morgan was slipping into a suit in the outer airlock. The clear acrylic of the airlock only slightly warped his features, but it was enough to make his triumphant smile look like the evil grin of a demon. After he had donned his suit and hooked himself up to his respirator, he gave Lundgren a thumbs-up and turned to face the metal door.

"I don't see any kind of buttons or keypads," Morgan's voice sounded muffled over the speaker situated outside the airlock.

"Look on the left side of the door," Lundgren suggested.

Morgan turned to his left and examined the rock. "I see something. It looks like three indentations."

He reached out and touched the spots. The sound was muffled from outside, but a slight rumble preceded the door slowly sliding open. Morgan stood on the threshold for a moment taking it all in.

Over his shoulder they could see the light from his helmet reflecting off of shining metal surfaces.

"Sam," George leaned over and whispered. "Why do you think they bothered with the airlock and all of these safety measures?"

Emily knew by the tone of his voice he already had an answer.

"I read the rest of the inscription. Chisek was right. It is a warning. This isn't just an information storage site. The actual virus was sealed in here."

"But how old is it? I mean, if the inscription is in English it can't be as old as we thought. Could it?"

"I'm not sure, Sam. But you can't deny the age of the disk or inscriptions you found or the thousands of hominid remains out there."

"Emily," Sam turned to her, "is it possible that their experiments caused normal Homo sapiens to genetically regress to an earlier species?"

"I don't know," she answered truthfully and not a little horrified. "I suppose it's possible. We just don't have enough information."

"I don't think we had the technology for this in the 1950s either," George added. "We've barely scratched the surface of genetic science today."

"So how did all this advanced technology get buried 400,000 years ago and yet have a warning translated into English on the door?" Anna asked to no one in particular.

"That is what you would call a leading question," George commented and hugged his wife protectively. "I have a feeling that we'll all be very surprised by the answer."

Sam was starting to get an idea himself, but dismissed it as impossible. He continued watching Morgan.

"How long can a virus survive in these conditions?" Peter interrupted their discussion.

"Some viruses can remain dormant for eons," Emily explained. "Or if it found a food source it could have kept on reproducing."

"Let's hope this one died of starvation," Sam gazed through the open doorway, his face a mask of consternation.

Morgan hadn't moved beyond his first step into the room. He stood transfixed by the enormity of the room and how modern it looked. He motioned for the lamps to be turned down to reduce the reflections and began examining the walls. On the far wall there seemed to be row upon row of small doors like a safe deposit vault in a bank, presumably some kind of storage lockers. To the left of the door was a control panel or workspace of some kind and areas of its smooth surfaces seemed to change color in the light as if it were absorbing the energy. But Morgan was focused on the storage area. He was hardly visible at the angle Sam's group was standing from the airlock. Emily could just make out the blur of his blue suit through the plastic gateway. It looked as though he was opening the lockers one by one. She couldn't see by what mechanism, but they slid out like filing cabinet drawers as Morgan made his search.

"There are thousands of disks in here," his voice was subdued in awe. "This must be the repository for all their research." He became more business-like then, "Bob, you'd better come in too and help me find-"

He stopped mid-sentence as he opened the next drawer.

"This is it!"

Everyone edged closer to the airlock as Morgan reached into the drawer and pulled out a metal canister, bullet-shaped and about six inches in length. He held the object, turning and examining it from all sides for some moments. No one spoke.

Slowly shaking himself out of his reverie, Morgan approached the airlock. "Bob, take a look at his and tell me if it's what I think it is."

He held it up along the side of the plastic and Chisek stepped forward to study it. He squinted through the barrier and looked at the markings on the side of the canister.

"They're the same warnings that were on the door," he paused and looked at Morgan who was still absorbed in his fascination with the object in his hands.

Surprising them all, Morgan began to search for a means to open the container.

"Are you crazy?!" Chisek exclaimed and stepped back even though he was safely separated from Morgan by the airlock. "Don't open it!"

But it was too late. The canister popped open at one end and a clear tube encased in a metal framework rose out of it. The tube appeared to be empty.

Morgan looked at more closely, apparently puzzled by the lack of contents.

"Oh," he said finally, "I think I see a crack here."

He started to say something else when he suddenly dropped the canister, clutching his helmet. A small groan escaped his lips as he doubled over in pain. He fell to the floor, writhing in pain as his groans grew louder and turned into agonized screams.

Emily wasn't sure what she was seeing at first with the distortion of the airlock, but she soon wished she hadn't looked. Mottled patches of purple began appearing on Morgan's face as he tore at his suit. His skin continued to grow darker until it was nearly black. Inside the suit, his body seemed to deflate and his features disappeared. As a final gurgling scream escaped his lips, the form of Morgan collapsed completely. Black ooze seeped out of the pinhole on the front of the empty blue suit and began puddling on the floor.

21

The echoes of Morgan's screams faded away into the further reaches of the cave, leaving them in silence once more. No one moved in the brief moment it took for Morgan's body to be reduced to a slimy, misshapen mass on the floor.

Their astonishment was interrupted by a soft chuckle behind them.

"Louis was always so careless with safety precautions. If only he had checked his suit first," Lundgren commented.

Sam looked over his shoulder at Morgan's former right hand man and was surprised to see a happy grin on his face.

"Why am I so happy? Is that what you're wondering?" Lundgren voiced Sam's unspoken question. "How could I be so callous about the demise of my dearest friend?"

Lundgren stepped towards the airlock and took a closer look at Morgan's remains like he was viewing an exhibit at the zoo.

"I've always said his obsession would be his undoing," he laughed again. "Though I didn't foresee it happening so literally. But he was not a friend. He was merely a tool to help me complete my mission. And you," he turned to Sam, "have been helpful as well."

Sam finally found his voice, "What mission? Who are you really working for?"

"I am working for myself and my family," Lundgren straightened up to his full height and spoke proudly. "And you have been privileged to witness the culmination of over a hundred years' worth of planning and effort." Lundgren sighed wistfully, "If only Grandpapa were here to see it."

"Are you insane?" Emily spoke up. "What we just witnessed could be the death of the entire human race."

Lundgren smiled again, "Yes, it could be."

He motioned to the remaining guards who took Sam and Emily by the arms with guns drawn.

"And it will be if our demands are not met," he continued. "And it's not too much to ask really. Our family already has a great influence on the decisions of the world's governments. Only now we'll be taking a more direct hand."

Echoing footsteps sounded in the passageway as another group of Lundgren's men approached along with three people dressed in blue hazmat suits.

Sam had forgotten Chisek was even there until he posed a question that seemed ludicrous after the frightening declaration made by Lundgren.

"What about the other artifacts?"

It just made Lundgren smile even more. "You've never changed in all the years I've known you, Bob. I do admire your single-mindedness in pursuing your goal. But it's insignificant in comparison with the decades of hard work and sacrifice my family has endured to make this happen."

"But I did most of the work to find this place!" Chisek argued.

"And you will be compensated handsomely. But you will never publish any papers on this or any similar finds."

"And if I do?" Chisek uncharacteristically challenged Lundgren.

"No one will believe you without proof, will they?"

Chisek sputtered in reply as he realized Lundgren meant to destroy all evidence of the base. This made Sam seriously doubt Emily's CIA theory.

He cleared his throat nervously, "Are you going to kill us as well?"

"Why should I?" Lundgren shrugged, "There's nothing you can do to stop me. Nobody will believe anything you say. But I may kill you," he pointed at Chisek, "just because you are so annoying."

He didn't need to elaborate any further. Sam knew he was right. Without any evidence who would believe there were secret bases buried all over the world containing deadly viruses and now an international crime family was planning to control the entire world? Maybe some of the more off-the-wall conspiracy theorists would believe it, but Sam was sure no one who had the power to do something about it would. As unlikely as it seemed, Sam knew he and his friends were the only ones who could stop Lundgren and his demented family.

Sam watched as Lundgren's men attached a filter unit and began to clean the air in the lab. It looked like a portable design of one of the air scrubbers he had seen at MorGen, running the air through HEPA filters and then superheating it before it made its way outside along the conduits snaking through the cave.

Lundgren mistook Sam's expression of deep thought for one of fear.

"I assure you Dr. Hunt, none of the virus will escape. At least until it suits my purposes."

Sam merely glared at him in return and the guards who still held them began to lead them out of the cave.

"This won't take long, and then I'll drop you and your friends off in Johannesburg."

Lundgren's smug confidence was starting to get on Sam's nerves. *Unfortunately*, Sam thought, *he has every reason to be cocky. He's outwitted all of us and there is no way we can escape with so many heavily armed guards.*

Cursing himself for giving in to the defeatist attitude he had so recently conquered- no matter how justified it may seem- he knew he could not sit idly by while Lundgren carried out his unspecified, but most likely insane, plan.

After marching them back through the caves, the guards unceremoniously shoved Sam and his friends into one of the cargo carriers that had contained the filtering equipment. It was a five by seven foot steel box, unbroken by any windows or doors. The six of them stood in stunned silence as the door clanged shut behind them followed by the tiny beeps of the electronic lock being engaged

"Sam," Emily's voice came firm but quiet in the darkness, "What is Lundgren going to do?"

"I wish I knew." Sam leaned against the wall and soon felt Emily's head resting on his shoulder. "You could probably figure it out better than I could. Just what would that virus do if it were released into the general population?"

He felt Emily shiver as she contemplated the answer to his question.

Before she could answer, Sam was startled by the sudden appearance of a light next to him. He turned and found George's hairy mug leering at him.

"Had it hidden in my shoe," he grinned, referring to the small penlight he now held.

Sam found himself somewhat comforted by the light and the fact that the rest of his friends still seemed to be in good spirits despite their situation. He looked around at the others in the dim light and found nothing but resolve and determination in their expressions.

"What it did to Morgan was extraordinary," Emily began. "From what I was able to figure out from the disk, it looked like the original virus altered the DNA enough to result in a new species. But this.....Well, it seemed as though his molecules were destabilized at such a rapid rate he just came apart."

"But what could cause something like that?" Anna's pallor was an obvious sign she was shaken by the events she had just witnessed, but her medical background kept her from breaking down.

"I'm not sure. A mutation of the original virus certainly. If it formed a symbiotic relationship with a host that wouldn't destroy it, it could easily survive thousands of years down here."

"But the only life down here is bacterial."

"Exactly. And considering that most microbes living that deep in a cave system are also chemo-autotrophs, leeching their nutrients from the rocks themselves, a combination of that ability along with the virus' capacity for triggering genetic reversals might explain Morgan's...um...dissolution," Emily concluded.

Sam couldn't see any change in her expression, but her voice lost some of its control as she groped for a word to describe Morgan's demise. He found himself shuddering when he thought back to that moment.

"But how could it happen so quickly?" George asked.

"In a nutrient rich environment, a combination of the microbe and virus could possibly reproduce at an alarming rate."

By 'a nutrient rich environment', Sam assumed she meant Morgan's body.

"Okay, we know this virus is dangerous, to say the least," Sam agreed, "But we can't do anything about it while we're locked in here."

"I think George and I could come up with something," Peter volunteered and began pulling assorted pieces of electronics and small tools from various hiding places on his person.

Sam found himself starting to believe that they just might have chance.

"We've found it," Lundgren leaned back in the plush leather seat in the back of the helicopter. His 'flying office' as he called it, aboard a renovated Chinook helicopter was designed to carry him alone. The interior had been lined with soundproofing materials to diminish the roar of the rotors and it was furnished with the usual office equipment, though bolted down to prevent mishaps during abrupt maneuvers.

"You're positive?" the heavily accented voice that came from the speakers was only slightly out of synch with image on Lundgren's screen. The gray-haired man sat in an oak paneled library somewhere in eastern Europe.

"I've seen it with my own eyes," Lundgren smiled coldly, "It's even more lethal than we expected."

A soft chuckle filled the room. "I can hardly believe it after all this time. How long will it take you to complete the extraction?" the man leaned forward eagerly.

"Maybe an hour or two. We weren't able to bring in as much equipment or men as we had hoped due to the location, but it hasn't been too difficult."

"No other problems then?"

"I'd hardly call it a problem, but we did have a few unwanted guests to deal with."

"Oh? I take it you have politely asked them to leave."

"Yes, we'll be escorting them as far as Johannesburg."

"And what about our friend Morgan? How is he taking all of this?"

"I'm afraid it was too much for him. He went to pieces when he found the virus."

"Really?"

"Yes. The virus disassembled him down to the floor."

The laughter of the two men filled the cabin.

"Excellent work, my son," the foreign man replied, "We will anxiously await your arrival and then we can begin the next stage."

Lundgren turned off his computer and leaned back in his chair. Things couldn't be any better. All the years of hard work and putting up with the incompetence of small-minded lackeys was finally paying off.

The empire his great-grandfather had begun in the 1860's was finally in a position to gain control of the world economy. Though he would never have imagined just how immense that would be when his descendants seized power.

A knock on the door interrupted his musings. He pressed a button on his desk and was annoyed to find Chisek standing outside.

"What is it now?" Lundgren snapped.

"You can't do this to me."

"You don't seem to realize I can do whatever I want."

"But I've spent my entire life searching for this kind of evidence!" Chisek stepped inside the cabin.

"And my family has been working on this for generations," Lundgren replied.

Chisek looked dumfounded by that statement.

"Would you care to hear a little of my family's history? Perhaps that would make you realize just how insignificant your claim to this find is." Lundgren motioned for him to have a seat.

Chisek wordlessly seated himself.

"My great grandfather was a miner in the Neander Valley in Germany. You recognize the name of course."

Chisek nodded.

"He was there when the first Neanderthal skullcap was found. He became fascinated by the idea that a race existed before modern man and returned often to Feldhofer Grotto to search for more fossils. He had quite an extensive private collection and made good money selling some of the pieces to various universities for study. But the more interesting pieces he kept for himself. One of these fossils was a complete skull that had been carefully sealed in a small chamber, probably by the Neanderthals themselves. Most likely they revered it as a god, but I'll not speculate as to their religious beliefs."

Lundgren stopped his narrative and turned to the safe behind his desk smiling to himself as he imagined Chisek's reaction to what he was about to show him. He opened the safe and removed a metal case. He turned back to Chisek and invited him to open it.

Chisek gasped as the skull was revealed.

"Impressive isn't it?" Lundgren smiled.

"I- it's incredible!" His eyes quickly took in the features. It was definitely Homo sapiens, but there was one difference. The entire skull cap had been covered by the same material as the disks. There were no scratches or tarnish to indicate its age, but it had obviously been attached to the ancient skull while the person was still alive.

"He knew he had found something unique and continued searching the cave and others like it until his death in 1890. He found over 50 unusual metal fragments he believed to be from the same period as well as this."

Lundgren laid a fragment of a disk in front of Chisek. He almost laughed as Chisek's eyes nearly jumped out of his skull.

"The very first fragment found by modern man. It was this that convinced my great grandfather to set up a modest organization to do further research on this species. At first it was only he and his two brothers, but as the family grew, so did the organization. Their goal was to find every vestige of this ancient race and discover how they created such an incredible material. Of course they didn't know what the disk was really for at the time, but as technology advanced we discovered more and more about them. And we recently discovered the most interesting thing about them is that they were not an ancient race at all."

"The warning in English…"

"Yes. And not from the 1950s either as our friend Morgan thought. If it weren't for advances in modern physics, we would never have dreamed it possible that the Eternals were from our future."

Chisek remained silent. Lundgren assumed he was in shock and continued.

"And now that we have a complete library along with the virus, we'll find a way into that future."

Chisek seemed to recover his senses a little, "It's quite a coincidence you came up with the same name that Jonathan did."

"Not really," Lundgren was really enjoying dropping these little bombshells, "since he was a member of our family. At first we used 'Eternals' to designate what we thought was the first civilization on the planet. After we learned more, it just became shorthand we used to describe the personnel who worked in the labs. The real name given to these installations was the Ǽternitas Project. Jonathan took advantage of your eagerness and, I must admit, insightful theories to advance our cause. It was unfortunate that he was lost though. He was one of my best men. We would have found this place long ago if things had gone better."

"But you can't be serious about using this virus!"

"I'll do whatever is necessary to complete my great-grandfather's task. You see, he was not only interested in the Eternals, but was at the forefront of the industrial revolution in Germany. He made sound investments with his savings and quietly bought up interests in iron, coal and railroads. The family's power grew enough that even Otto von Bismarck looked to us for support. And we remain a silent political power today. Not just in Germany, but around the world. Our holdings are worth not billions, but *trillions*."

"If you really have such power, why do you need to threaten mankind with extinction?"

"Because, my dimwitted friend, the world is changing. There will no longer be individual countries, but a world government. No more presidents, chancellors or queens. No cabinets, congresses or parliaments. Just a single governing body working for the good of the world."

"You don't seem to be very concerned with the well-being of mankind."

"The end justifies the means. Revolution is never a peaceful affair."

"And I suppose you're electing yourself to head this new government?"

"Hardly. That would be my father's job. I will continue to be his chief aide though. Now if you'll excuse me, I have things to attend to. It's been nice talking to you though." Lundgren smirked and waved Chisek out of the room.

"There may be guards outside the door, so we'll have to be quick," Sam instructed his friends.

They were all huddled around Peter who had broken into the back of the electronic lock and was finishing overriding the code.

"Okay, I think I've got it," Peter said.

Sam looked to each of his companions and they nodded in readiness. "Go ahead, Peter."

Grasping two wires in his hands, Peter made the final connection and the faint click of the lock unlatching could be heard. All as one, they shoved open the doors, prepared to overwhelm and disarm any guards who might be outside.

Instead they only found a very startled Robert Chisek gaping at them. George immediately moved forward and restrained him by twisting both of his arms behind his back.

"Wait! I'm here to help you," Chisek said between clenched teeth.

"Let him go, George," Emily instructed him.

George shrugged and released him.

"How are *you* going to help *us*?" Sam asked. "I think we were doing fine without you."

"You won't get out of here alive if you don't come with me now," Chisek explained and abruptly began walking off.

"Threats," Sam laughed, "from you?"

Chisek stopped and turned around, "It's not a threat, it's a warning. Now come on!"

"Sam," Emily laid a hand on his arm, "I think we'd better go with him."

He didn't want to agree with Emily, but she was right. He nodded and they quickly followed Chisek through a maze of equipment and transport containers to a concealed grotto. He darted behind a large rock and motioned for them to follow.

Sam was surprised to see a satellite transceiver unit which Chisek quickly put to use.

"We've got sixty minutes."

Sam couldn't hear the reply, but plainly heard Chisek's reaction.

"Shit!"

Chisek hung up the phone.

"Care to tell us what's going on here?" Sam asked, not even trying to keep the anger out of his voice. He was starting to feel very manipulated.

"I'm sorry you got involved in this. We tried to stop you from coming here, but you're rather persistent."

"I had a good reason," Sam glanced at Emily and was surprised to see her blush.

Chisek waved his hand, "It doesn't matter anyway. We have to get you out of here before this place goes up in flames."

"Hold on a minute," George interrupted. "Who's 'we'?"

"A concerned government agency," Chisek replied tersely.

"Which government?"

"Which do you think? It doesn't matter! Look, there is going to be an assault team arriving in about two hours and this place is going to be leveled, alright. So get moving," Chisek ordered them.

"Two hours?" Sam asked. "I thought you were just telling your people they had sixty minutes."

"It's going to be close. We'd prefer to finish the operation here where it's relatively isolated, but we'll follow them if it's necessary. I'll just try to delay them."

"Can we help?" Sam couldn't believe those words had just come out of his mouth.

Apparently Chisek couldn't either because he was looking at Sam like he was insane.

"We've done alright so far," George added.

Chisek turned his expression on George and shook his head. "You've all done enough already."

"If you try to delay them, they may get suspicious," Emily warned. "They already know that I don't want them to succeed. Let me talk to Lundgren."

Chisek started to protest, but changed his mind. "Alright. But I want to warn you that he can be unpredictable. If he gets tired of listening to you, he may decide to silence you permanently."

"I have to do something. I can't just run away."

Emily's words echoed Sam's feelings exactly.

"Okay," Chisek relented. "You and Sam come with me. The rest of you stay here or start back down the trail. The guards will come back soon and realize you're gone."

"Where'd they go?" George asked.

"I gave them a six-pack and told them to take a break," Chisek actually smiled.

There was definitely a lot more to Chisek than Sam could ever guess.

Chisek decided the best way for them to get to Lundgren's helicopter would be to put on a bold front. Emily didn't care for the restraints he had put on her wrists, nor the fact that he was prodding her with a very nasty looking pistol, but it certainly convinced the guards to let them through. Once they reached the helicopter, Chisek quickly slashed their bonds, but instructed them to keep their hands behind their backs and be as submissive and imploring as possible.

"You just don't give up do you, Bob?" Lundgren smiled with just a trace of annoyance.

"Not when the stakes are this high. Please, just hear us out. Dr. Forester knows a lot about this virus."

"I'm sure she does, but why do you assume I don't? We were looking for it before you ever knew it existed."

"If you really knew anything about it, you would destroy it," Emily couldn't help but be angry.

"And if you knew what I did, you would want to join me."

"I find that hard to believe," she scoffed. But a part of her feared what he would say next. She didn't really know that much about the virus, other than it was the deadliest virus she had ever seen and it would probably kill billions if it was released into any major cities.

"But don't you want to end disease and suffering as well?" he spread his hands and leaned back in the chair.

"Not by killing the patient." She didn't look at him, but she could feel Chisek radiating a warning to her to stop pushing Lundgren.

Lundgren merely smiled. "You are really quite beautiful when you're angry, Dr. Forrester. It's no wonder you have these two fighting over you."

Emily knew he thought he had read them like a book and was trying to play them against one another. But they all retained control of their tempers which did not go unnoticed by Lundgren.

"Very good," he raised an eyebrow, "This may not be quite as boring as I anticipated." He turned his computer screen around to face them. "Let me show you something," he tapped on a few keys and an image of the virus as it was shown on the disk came onto the screen. "This is what they ended up with. But obviously it had unforeseen consequences. Do you know what they were trying to accomplish?"

"I assume they were trying to create a viral vector to treat terminal diseases," Emily answered.

"Wrong," Lundgren paused obviously enjoying his audience's reactions. "They were trying to treat terminality."

It took a moment for Emily to realize what he meant. "You mean they were looking for immortality?"

"Mankind's oldest quest has never ended. But where they failed, we will succeed."

"What makes you so sure?" Sam finally found his voice.

"Because, Dr. Hunt, we will stop at nothing. They may have given up, but we will not."

"And then you'll create an immortal ruler with an immortal army to back him up?" Chisek guessed.

"How insightful of you, Bob. I didn't know--"

Lundgren's gloating was interrupted by the sound of automatic weapons fire. He jumped out of his chair and ran into the cockpit.

Sam leaned over to Chisek and whispered, "I thought you said your guys wouldn't be here for two hours?"

"I don't know what's going on out there, but if it were my men, it would be a lot noisier than this."

Intermittent blasts of gunfire were heard coming from all directions. But among the automatic weapons, the clear shots of rifles and the blast of shotguns could be heard. To Sam it sounded like two televisions on in the same room, one tuned to a western and the other to a war film.

"You're behind this!" Lundgren came back out of the cockpit headed towards Sam.

"Me?" Sam feigned astonishment.

Chisek pulled out his pistol and aimed it at Lundgren's forehead, but Lundgren quickly stepped to the side and knocked his hand away, sending the gun across the desk and onto the floor. Lundgren darted to the door and was out before they could catch him.

The gunfire was deafening now that the door was open and Sam was getting a taste of what life had been like for his father and brothers. They ducked down and ran towards the nearest cover, a stack of steel footlockers, as shot rang out all around them.

"Sam! Over here!"

Emily couldn't believe it. George was waving at them from behind a boulder and a tall black man with long braids was covering him with a rifle. They dashed over to George's hiding place.

"What the hell do you think you're doing?" Sam shouted at George over the crack of his partner's rifle.

"Saving the day," George replied with an enthusiastic grin.

Emily looked around and saw several of the Zulu tribesmen from the ranch Morgan had taken over, all armed with rifles and continuing their barrage against Lundgren's men. But there were also some shorter men whom she had not seen before, dressed in less modern clothing but still brandishing modern weapons.

The man who had covered their escape stopped firing to reload.

"Emily," George began, "this is James. We would never have gotten here in time if it weren't for him."

Emily felt it was an awkward time for introductions, but managed to find some manners. "Pleased to meet you."

"Likewise," James replied and kissed her hand before going back to shooting.

"He brought along some of his family," George motioned to the shorter men, "and a few friends from a nearby ranch."

"This is insane," Sam broke in, "they can't hold off men with automatic weapons."

"It looks like they're doing all right to me." Chisek noted.

Emily watched as one of the guards made a dash for a helicopter and went down from a shot to the knee.

"I just hope a stray shot doesn't damage whatever container they use to transport the virus," Emily added nervously.

"I told them to make sure they just shoot people, not things." George said sagely.

Emily couldn't believe he actually said that.

"Besides," he continued, "we just need to delay them for an hour or so until the real troops arrive."

"Oh, that's all we have to do?" Sam countered.

Emily ignored their banter as she saw Lundgren making a run for the cave.

"Sam!" she tried to get his attention.

"These are not professional soldiers, George."

"What does that have to do with anything?"

"Sam!" she tried to draw him away from George again. "Lundgren's heading back to the cave."

Finally he looked around just as Lundgren reached the entrance and darted inside.

Sam took one look at George, who tossed him a flashlight and handgun, "Good luck!" he shouted as Sam raced after Lundgren dodging bullets along the way.

22

After reaching the safety of the cave, Sam wondered what the hell he thought *he* was doing. Lundgren was no fool and wouldn't have gone into the cave if he didn't have a plan to get back out. Not to mention there were still an unknown number of Lundgren's men inside. Sam decided to stop wondering and just keep moving. He knew Lundgren was going after the virus and would do anything to escape with it and Sam would have to do everything he could to stop him.

The echoes of gunfire faded away as Sam hurried deeper into the cave. The electric lights Lundgren's men had strung up along the way made it much easier going than the first time he had been there and he was able to keep up a steady jogging pace. When he reached the rope, he considered just cutting it loose to prevent Lundgren's escape, but his caving instincts told him there must be another way out.

Lowering himself to the next level, he realized he already knew where the alternate exit was. In the cave in China there had been an access in the ceiling which had fallen and crushed its unfortunate discoverer. Most likely, all of the Alpha sites had the same features and that was how Lundgren was planning his escape. Sam quickened his pace and nearly ran directly into the arms of three guards waiting inside the entrance of the large chamber.

Luckily they were too involved in examining the towering pile of hominid remains to be immediately aware of his presence. Sam ducked back around the corner and willed his heart to stop hammering against his ribs while trying to think of a plan to get past them.

It was so simple Sam almost laughed. He simply picked up a loose rock and pitched it over the guards' heads to distract them. Unfortunately for Sam it didn't work quite as well as it did in the movies. Only two of the guards went to investigate and the third one maintained his position. But this would be his only chance before the other two returned and Sam was outnumbered.

The guard pulled out a pack of cigarettes and a lighter as Sam made his move.

"Got a light?" Sam asked as he approached.

Startled, the guard looked up and began to reply, "Sure—hey!" But he never finished as Sam's fist connected with his jaw.

Sam was off and running before the guard hit the ground. He was about halfway across the chamber when a distant rumble caused the ground beneath his feet to vibrate and he skidded to a halt. His eyes darted over the ceiling, looking for any cracks or unstable areas. A stalactite or two were shivering, but no imminent danger was apparent. The rumble ceased as suddenly as it started and he continued making for the tunnel on the opposite side.

There was a small commotion behind him as the other guards found their fallen comrade, and Sam prepared himself to be chased. But to his surprise, the guards decided it would be more prudent to make a hasty retreat. No doubt they assumed the unconscious man had been struck by falling rock. They picked him up and headed for the surface, never knowing Sam had been there.

Before Sam could enjoy his good luck, a second rumble dislodged some pieces of stone and he had to pick up the pace to avoid them. Slipping several times on the gooey mat of bacteria, his heart pounded with every step. He reached the tunnel just as an enormous stalactite crashed to the ground behind him and sent him sprawling.

He lay on the cold rock, afraid to move, covering his head with his hands. But there was silence in the cave again. Cautiously rising to his feet, he looked back into the cavern and saw that several other stalactites had fallen as well, burying the mound of bones like a makeshift cairn. He shuddered to think what would be left of him if he had been struck. But the artificial tunnel appeared to be stable. Taking a deep breath, Sam made his way down the passage, hoping he could catch up with Lundgren in time.

"We've got to get out of here!" Chisek yelled over the roar of six unmarked HueyCobra helicopters maneuvering around the peak, their vulturesque forms silhouetted against the setting sun. One of them was attempting to land near the smoking remains of Lundgren's private copter that it had destroyed only minutes before. The other helicopters continued to fire on what was left of Lundgren's men and equipment and several small blazes were quickly spreading to the nearby bush.

"I'm not leaving without Sam!" Emily could barely hear herself over the chaos surrounding them.

She felt George put his hands around her waist as he prepared to lift her up and carry her away.

"No! I won't leave!" She tried to break away, but George held her firmly.

"Sam would kill me if I let you get hurt," he declared simply and tossed her over his shoulder.

"Besides, we can't get in this way now," Chisek pointed out the rock fall that had sealed the entrance to the caves.

They retreated as quickly as possible to the edge of the clearing and made their way around to the helicopter which had now landed. Chisek jumped aboard and motioned for George and Emily to do the same. James and the other men had left as soon as Chisek's unidentified forces arrived and were already approaching the base of the mountain. They rose into the air amidst a few shots from the remaining resistance and headed for the old rancher's house where Anna and Eleni had stayed during the fighting.

But Emily's thoughts were still back on the peak praying that Sam found a way out before it was too late.

The tremors were coming more frequently now and Sam realized that Chisek's troops must have arrived and were possibly shelling Lundgren's encampment. He just hoped they held off with the rocket launchers until he was safely outside the caves. He knew he didn't have much time in any case, and started across the bridge without even checking to see if it was damaged. He was halfway across when it became apparent that one of the bolts fastening it to the other side had come loose. The tremors had created a wide crack in the floor. Every step he took loosened it further and one side of the bridge began to sag. Five more feet, one step at a time and he would be on solid ground. How long it would remain solid was something he didn't want to worry about just yet.

One step and the bridge groaned as most of Sam's weight was being supported by a single bolt. He took a second step and the metal began to bend under the strain. Quickly deciding it was now or never, he jumped the final three feet. The bridge gave way as his feet touched rock and it crashed into the pit. Sam hastily moved away from the edge where the floor continued to crumble away.

He had no real plan of action as he came around the final bend and approached the airlock. He crouched behind the air scrubber and looked around. No one was outside, but within the chamber were four people in full protective gear minus, surprisingly, their helmets. Lundgren was one of them.

Sam hoped they had isolated or neutralized the virus somehow. If he entered the room and found that they had been inoculated against it, he would be dead in seconds. But he considered that unlikely since Lundgren hadn't had access to the virus to make a vaccine and even its creators hadn't succeeded in killing it. His questions were answered as he saw two of the men placing a small metal box inside a larger one as Lundgren supervised.

The fourth man was poking the ceiling with a long rod. As Sam watched, the man located the concealed hatch in the ceiling and opened it. He disappeared from view for a moment and returned carrying an aluminum ladder which he then used to climb through the opening. The two other assistants followed him a moment later while Lundgren loaded the metal box into a carrying case and prepared to leave as well.

Another tremor, stronger than any before it, knocked Lundgren to his knees. If Sam hadn't already been down he would have fallen as well. Lundgren quickly got to his feet, picked up the ladder from the floor and set it back into the hatch. While his back was turned, Sam took the opportunity to make his way through the airlock and into the chamber. Lundgren was halfway up the ladder when Sam got a hold of his boot and yanked him down.

Lundgren fell heavily on top of Sam and knocked the wind out of both of them. The box containing the virus was knocked from Lundgren's shoulder and went sliding across the floor. Sam shoved Lundgren off of him and struggled to regain his senses. But Lundgren recovered more quickly and pulled a pistol out of an ankle holster.

"Dr. Hunt," Lundgren put the barrel to Sam's head. "You just won't quit will you?"

Sam's answer was lost in the roar of a massive blast that tore through the cave. Both men were thrown to the ground as the walls around them trembled and chunks of rock and twisted metal rained down. The groan of thousands of tons of rock echoed through the passageways as the entire peak shuddered. The sharp report of stone breaking apart filled the chamber and brought Sam to his senses.

He found his legs pinned under a large sheet of metal and chunks of rock and struggled to free himself. It didn't take a genius to realize the entire peak was going to collapse under the barrage of missiles-- there was already a gaping hole in the floor not five feet away from him. He had worked one leg out from under the debris when through the clouds of choking dust, he noticed Lundgren crawling towards him. Or rather, he was crawling toward the metal box that was within Sam's grasp. Lundgren's eyes were locked on the case containing the virus. His face scored with bloody gashes, his coveralls shredded and one arm obviously broken. But he continued making his way towards the box, going around or over the debris.

Sam took one look at the maniacal gleam in Lundgren's eyes and knew what to do. As Lundgren got closer, Sam reached for the box. Lundgren picked up his pace and stumbled over the last few feet towards him. At the last possible second before Lundgren reached out for the case, Sam shoved it as hard as he could across the floor and into the pit.

And Lundgren dove after it.

Sam cringed as he heard Lundgren's terror-filled scream when he went over the edge. It trailed off into the abyss and ended abruptly as his body struck the bottom somewhere below.

Using the adrenalin coursing through his veins, Sam shoved the rest of the debris off of his legs and managed to stagger over to the ladder and set it upright again. As he started climbing, he was thankful that the metal from the ceiling had fallen over him before the rock struck. It most likely prevented his legs from being broken. At the top of the ladder, he fumbled through his pockets and was relieved to find his pocket flashlight was still working. He found himself inside another artificial tunnel, smaller than the first with only enough room for a single person to pass through. There was no sign of Lundgren's men and Sam assumed they decided to wait for their employer outside.

He jogged along the tunnel, ignoring the aches and pains that seemed to be everywhere. The continuing sounds of distress emanating from the mountain kept him moving as quickly as possible. Not knowing if it was merely wishful thinking or real, he followed a faint breeze that seemed to carry the perfume of sunshine and warm earth to his nostrils. After a few hundred feet he knew he wasn't imagining things. There was definitely an opening to the outside somewhere ahead. He picked up his pace and noticed the tunnel was gradually sloping upwards. Exhaustion was slowly creeping up on him, but the scent of fresh air grew stronger and he soon saw a faint ruddy glow in the distance.

Almost running, Sam arrived at an opening in the mountainside. Nearly blinded by the light of the setting sun, he looked at his surroundings and figured he was on the opposite side of the mountain from the trail they had used to ascend. He lowered himself onto a flat rock to catch his breath, feeling he was in a relatively safe location. He looked up at a familiar sound and saw several black helicopters hovering near what remained of the peak, possibly admiring their handiwork.

Now that he had made it out alive, he wondered about the rest of his motley crew. Especially Emily. Had Chisek kept his word and gotten them all to safety? Only one way to find out, he told himself and slowly got to his feet and headed in the general direction of where he thought they had met James' family.

EPILOGUE

Sam's body was numb all over. He couldn't remember the last time he had been so relaxed. The heat radiating off of the terracotta tile warmed his back while the sun toasted his front. He had no future plans to get up off of the lounge chair on which he was sprawled in George's courtyard. Nope, he was going to stay there forever. Or at least until the sun went down.

After trudging several miles through the bushveld, Sam had finally found James' family. Though it was probably closer to the truth to say they had found him. He barely remembered the drive over to the ranch where the rest of his friends were safely ensconced. About the only thing he remembered before collapsing into a bed, was Emily's reaction when he walked through the door. Every hint of defensiveness was gone as she held him in a fierce embrace like she would never let go.

And she had found some way to be near him almost every moment since then. Though at the moment she was inside helping Anna whip up some more drinks. Sam still couldn't believe they had done it. Granted they had a lot of help, but the odds against them were enormous. When he woke up at the ranch hours later, Chisek informed him that the last of Lundgren's men had been rounded up and what had once been a majestic peak rising above the valley floor was now a plateau.

"That'll take a little explaining to the South African government," Sam remarked.

"They're fully aware of the situation and we've already begun negotiations for reparation."

"And what about Lundgren's family? He's gone, but I don't think that would slow them down for long."

"We're taking care of it."

"What does 'taking care of it' supposed to mean?"

"It's being handled. Their family won't be a threat any more."

"So tell me," Sam asked, sure he wasn't going to get a truthful answer. "Are you really an archaeologist or was that just a cover?"

"I really am. And that's how I got involved in this project. I met Jonathan Waltman and was shortly thereafter contacted by the CIA and questioned about my relationship with him. They decided I might make a good agent and the rest is history."

"Ah," Sam thought he'd finally figured it out. "So, you work for the CIA."

"I used to."

Clearly, Chisek didn't plan to elaborate. Sam and George had argued about who he was affiliated with the whole way back to Patmos. George was convinced he was part of an unknown world security council while Sam was sure he was still CIA.

"What does it matter?" Emily had interrupted their latest debate on the charter boat back to the island. "We'll never see him again and nobody will believe any of this happened even if we did tell them."

And she was right. It was just too farfetched. The whole thing wrapped up like an ending to a sci-fi show. They had a vague idea of what had happened and who was behind it, but there was absolutely no proof. As far as they knew, all of the hidden chambers had been destroyed. And whatever artifacts Lundgren's family had in their possession were probably being confiscated and transported to a warehouse in the middle of nowhere, heavily guarded and surrounded with barbed wire and attack dogs.

What really ticked Sam off though, was the fact that they had also taken the evidence that he and his friends had found. The disk and fragments had been removed from James' truck and all of their computers were wiped clean.

Sam's exasperation was interrupted by some of those friends emerging from George's kitchen.

"But how can people from the future be their own creators?" Eleni was still arguing with Peter over the mind-boggling implications of what had occurred.

"Do I look like Stephen Hawking? I don't get it either."

"Well, there are several theories," George proceeded to lecture for several minutes on the latest advances in physics.

Oh well, Sam thought, at least I'm on a sunny Greek island with my friends, alive and healthy.

The patio doors to his left slid open and Emily came out carrying a tray of George's famous brew.

"Are you going to sleep the entire week?" she laughed as she set the tray on a side table next to him.

"I'm considering it," he smiled back and sat up to reach for a drink.

He couldn't help admiring her long tanned legs as she stretched out in the lounge next to him. The short sarong she wore over her swimsuit didn't hide her figure as much as it accentuated her curves.

She raised her eyebrows, "Enjoying the view?" A tiny smile played around the corners of her mouth.

"Indeed."

"Care for a closer look?"

She held her arms out to him and he slid over next to her. After a few preliminary kisses she whispered in his ear, "Sam Hunt, I love you."

"Really?" he did his best to act offended, "after I save the world, *then* you love me."

They shared a laugh and Sam reached for his drink, knocking George's journal from the table. George had been furiously writing down everything he could remember about their adventure since all of the evidence had been confiscated.

"Just in case," he had said. "I might come across something in the future that has a connection to this and I don't want to forget any details."

Sam lazily rolled over to pick up the journal as a breeze ruffled the pages of the open book, flipping them to a sketch of the ouroboros symbol George had tried to recreate from the outside of the metal case they had found. He held the drawing up to Emily.

"Is that the design you saw on Lundgren's helicopter?"

"Yes, that was it."

Sam looked at it again, frowning. Had Lundgren's family adopted the design from artifacts they had found? Or had the artifacts been made with the family's crest……..